Settle in with this expertly crafted tale of murder, intrigue, and savage blood rites in gas-lit Philadelphia by **FRANCIS JOHN THORNTON**.

Critical acclaim for **THE SNAKE HARVEST** by Francis John Thornton: "Ranks with the classics!"
—*Daily Press*

"Thrilling escapist reading!"
—*The Birmingham News*

"Wow! What an enjoyable book!"
—Philadelphia *Sunday Bulletin*

"Outstanding . . . brilliantly done!"
—*Buffalo News*

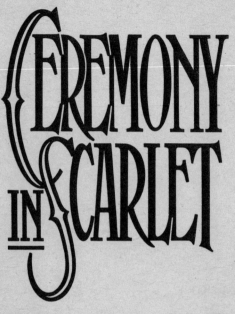

CEREMONY IN SCARLET

FRANCIS JOHN THORNTON

LEISURE BOOKS   NEW YORK CITY

To Mary Margaret,
for everything.

A LEISURE BOOK

January 1991

Published by

Dorchester Publishing Co., Inc.
276 Fifth Avenue
New York, NY 10001

Printed in the United States of America.

Chapter One

"**G**ive me the creature. Now!"

She heard the gamekeeper, a gnarled, surly old man, mutter under his breath.

"And stop swearing at me in that ugly tongue of yours."

He smiled through sparse brown teeth and held up the cage.

"No, not the cage, you moron. Take him out and hand him to me."

He had a gaze that never quite met hers, an unctuous squint. It was that above all that infuriated her about him. He glanced with uncertainty at the cage. He and the falcon were not on the best of terms. She, of course, knew that.

He put the cage on a bench, opened the little door, and stealthily placed his hand inside.

"Be careful with his blindfold," she snapped.

As the falcon perched arrogantly on her leather sleeve and the gamekeeper wiped nervous sweat from his brow, she appraised it for a moment, made some tiny kissing sounds—the kind of affectionate little noises uttered to a baby—then ordered her horse to proceed.

"I shall require you when I return and I do not wish to be kept waiting. I shan't be more than an hour."

That was all right by Stashu Kalinka. He wanted his breakfast. Always Big Boss Lady was making him miss his breakfast.

He watched her riding off at a slow, steady, patrician trot that soon became a canter, dark hair dancing on her shoulders as the big stallion sprayed mud across the horizon. She rode like everything else she did—haughtily but gracefully, as if the rest of the world were comprised of bumbling, foul-smelling oafs. Over a hillock, down a slope, past a thicket, over another rise, she disappeared into the darkness of the woods.

He grasped his crotch and spat into the crusted mud, then looked around to be sure no one had seen him.

Small, diehard snow patches, imposing drifts not long ago, dotted the shaded hillsides, but spring foliage was sprouting along the way. There was fog in the lowlands where streams meandered through pastures and fed the lake. The air was brisk, and she felt her cheeks turning color as her whole body came to life. Wading through the streams was chilly enough to make the stallion grunt long, low messages of displeasure, but they soon passed. On both sides of his great sorrel head steamy breath flowed through his nostrils like volcanic vapors, and she knew he was feeling the same surge of joy that she was because on such mornings she and the horse and the falcon were one.

They found a trail leading uphill through white birch and linden and climbed a mountain that overlooked the valley and the lake. The scene was gothic in a way—nether regions shrouded in fog, slate gray cumulonimbus clouds drifting through and over the knobby hills, the sun flickering on and off in tantalizing brilliance, the naked trees beckoning skyward like primitive suppliant maidens.

She wanted to strip off her clothing and join them, strip off everything and race Modock through the mountain trails and down through the fog as she had done on so many past mornings. She wanted to feel the sensation of sun bathing her body where it was seldom felt before, of rain prickling her skin like so many little needles awakening all her senses, of cold air puckering her nipples and flowing through the warm, damp foliage of her own body.

She wanted all of that very much and promised herself that it would soon happen again, but this time there was a task to perform. She and the horse and the falcon dawdled awhile anyway, savoring the moment.

Down the slope 100 yards or so they came to a small flat where they usually stopped to set the falcon free. She touched him gently on the down high on his crest, made some more little affectionate noises, pecked him lightly atop his beak and removed the blind. The gesture always annoyed Modock, who neighed resentment until she patted his mane.

She had christened the falcon Iago, fitting because of his cold, unswerving method of destroying his prey, his raw malevolence.

He looked around with quick, jerky head movements, adjusting his vision to the daylight.

She waited until the blinking stopped, and when the breeze was appropriate she loosened his ties. He fluttered over the valley, caught an updraft off the lake and floated in and out of the drifting clouds.

The sky overhead was brightening gradually. She shielded her eyes and watched him as he did lazy figure-eights for awhile, each time creating a wider air space. He passed before her then soared almost out of sight, becoming barely more than a black dot in the sky. Then as she blinked into the sun he became one among a field of black dots. This was customary with Iago, who needed to flex his muscles and test his skills after a period of confinement. And from that vantage point he could look down not only on the land but on any other creature that had the temerity or mere misfortune to wander into his world. Then he would dive and snatch his victim from the earth, out of the water, out of the trees or the air, and carry it wounded, squirming, often frightened to death in those long, ironlike talons, as doomed as if it were in the jaws of a crocodile, and bring it to her as an offering. It was overwhelmingly primal. It caused her heart to race and something to come to life between her legs. Sharing the hunt often drained her, left her clothing soaked, her hands trembling, her breath short.

She followed his progress as best she could until the dot disappeared behind a hill, flying in tighter circles now, descending gradually, scanning the ground. She could see him in her mind, hovering, focusing, moving in for the kill.

She closed her eyes and tried to see it all through his.

For a moment there was silence, only the soft rushing of the morning breeze through the hills and some starlings chattering in the distance.

Then Modock stirred and snorted. Somewhere beyond her hearing, but audible to him, a victim had cried out. Iago had struck. She felt perspiration running down her ribs and the familiar tingling between her legs.

When he returned, Iago had something in his grasp, a rabbit or a squirrel. She could not be sure because its body was tangled in the claws. It was dead, though; she was certain of that. Death disturbed Modock. He stirred again and pawed the ground until she calmed him down again.

None of it disturbed her—the blood, the pain, the terror. It was stimulating and rejuvenating, like an aberrant but wholly pleasing celebration of life. There had been times when the prey was alive, twisting frantically in the falcon's grasp, and she had coaxed it from him and wrung its neck.

She felt a little cheated this time.

Francis John Thornton

It was a young, female rabbit, fully grown. Iago deposited it in her open palm.

Its blood ran down her forearms as she held it toward the sun and recited a short prayer.

Chapter Two

"He isn't budging an inch."

"So I've noticed."

"Not an inch."

"I believe we've been over that."

"It's your fault, you know. Your fault."

"Is it?"

"You know very well it is."

Blakeley chuckled. "I'd have been rather surprised if you had not said that."

"Would you?" Chidsey insisted, "Would you really?"

Not the least of Uriah Chidsey's annoying habits was that of repeating himself anxiously.

"I would. It's a comment worthy of your style and reputation."

Their dialogue was under the breath and hurried as the Hon. Algernon Magwood mumbled something to the clerk of courts. On the stand, looking dapper and confident, Christopher Beecham smiled at his attorney who smiled back smugly.

Chidsey tilted his head at a matronly woman in layers of silk and lace who was wiggling her fat little fingers daintily at young Beecham.

"She'll have me on a spit for this."

Cybel Ashbaugh, at least 20 years the defendant's senior, had been his eager patroness and constant companion for the past six months. She was not without influence at City Hall, and more than once she had cast furious glances at the prosecution, each time striking greater fear into the faint, bureaucratic heart of Uriah Chidsey.

"And what's so amusing about that?" he asked.

"I've just been trying to picture you with an apple in your mouth."

The image was apt—small eyes, pug nose, porcine jowls. Blakeley laughed aloud, and Judge Magwood peered at them over his eye glasses.

"It's easy for you to scoff," Chidsey protested. "You can go back to your wretched little test tubes and I'll be, I'll be . . ."

Blakeley's patience had worn thin. He completed the thought for him.

"Back to pettifogging, where you belong, old boy."

Chidsey huffed and turned away.

Blakeley sat back and looked around at the faces in the courtroom, first at the members of the Beecham family who had come down from

8

New York in surprisingly large numbers. They looked understandably ill-at-ease, now and then solemn, now and then feigning transparent good humor, and no doubt wishing at this moment that Blakeley were in Timbuktu. He had to admire their stiff upper lip.

There was the usual sprinkling of idlers and the morbidly curious, including an old woman with a long, lugubrious face known to all as Madame Defarge because she sat inscrutibly knitting and never missed a murder trial. Rumor had it she was Judge Magwood's sister. There was a distinct resemblance.

Behind the crone, winking flirtatiously when he caught her eye, was perhaps his only ally in the room, Sophia Blakeley, beautiful as ever. He winked back. She gasped, pretended to be shocked, then smiled again.

Clustered in the front of the room were members of the press, mostly youngish, well-dressed and overly eager, now brasher than ever after all but creating that damned silly war with Spain. They were buzzing about the trial, the defendant, the wobbly case for the prosecution and, of course, about him. He did not really hate the press, though it was hard not to nowadays.

Chidsey noticed him looking at them.

"I still think you're a cheap headline grabber," he said quickly, then hid in a pile of official looking documents.

"Eh?"

It really was, as Uriah Chidsey had whined so frequently during the past week, all his fault. It was, moreover, none of his business. But something about the haughty young man on the stand had bothered him from the start, something strong enough to make him follow his instincts.

It was more than Christopher Beecham's disagreeable demeanor, as Chidsey now accused, though that alone could have done it. There was his disdainful tone, the supercilious smile, the way he waved a linen handkerchief as he spoke, like a Restoration-period dandy shooing flies that were presumably attracted by others around him.

To begin with, there was this preposterous tale, which everyone had been much too quick to believe, that Lydia Beecham had fallen out of a canoe and had simply sunk when the canoe capsized—like some anemic, uncoordinated dolt—because her clothing had become immediately saturated, weighing her down and making it impossible to stay afloat. Then, after sinking to the lake bed 15 feet below, she had become caught in the timbers of a sunken raft—more specifically, skirt and petticoats on a nail—and had been thus unable to unsnag herself before the lake water rushed into her lungs. As the tale was told, her devoted son, Christopher, had dived repeatedly into the depths of the lake, even sustaining a rather serious injury when his middle finger was caught in something —an iron hinge, he thought—and had been severed at the first knuckle as he struggled to extricate himself and his mother.

No one had seriously questioned the cause of

death, the actual cause, that is. The coroner was satisfied when he found a concentration of sodium chloride on the left side of the heart and bloodstained fluid in the pleural cavities that her death was caused by drowning. And the tests had been conducted at the insistence of young Mister Beecham, lest the disposition of his mother's estate arouse any suspicion.

All very up and up.

"Twaddle," Blakeley had said. "Simplistic twaddle."

"Of the worst kind," Sophia had said.

Lydia Beecham was a woman whose life, in particular the eight years of her widowhood, defied the simplicity of that tale.

Every spring since the passing of Silas Beecham, who had been using morphine to control his insomnia and, evidently, had miscalculated his last dose, she would leave her New York townhouse and stay at her summer home not far from Blakeley's Philadelphia estate.

And every morning before breakfast Lydia Beecham would swim around her private lake —the lake whose waters took her life—four times, which was approximately two and a half miles.

Looking at Christopher Beecham as he sat cross-legged on the stand and fussed with his frilly cuffs, Blakeley was reminded of the victim —same aquiline nose and sandy hair, square jaw with dimpled chin, even the slightly high cheekbones that Lydia once explained were traceable to a French-Canadian trapper in the family line.

He could be a weaker version of his mother. Blakeley had guessed his age at 30, but the court records had him two years younger than that. This morning he was attired in deep brown velveteen with a black string tie over a silken ruffled collar. He might have been the painter Whistler or perhaps poor Oscar Wilde, and the press would no doubt observe the same thing.

"Why do you think your mother was unable to extricate herself, Mr. Beecham?" the coroner had asked him then. The coroner was a kindly man, much too kindly for the job, and he drank to excess. "Her clothing was of a kind of fabric that could easily tear away."

Beecham had shrugged and looked at the floor, tears welling in his eyes. Cybel Ashbaugh sat next to him as usual, putting a fat little hand on his shoulder, oozing sympathy.

To ask further questions would have seemed importunate at best, cruel at worst. A heavy bandage was wrapped around his finger, and it was obvious the bleeding had not been stopped. When an assistant had started to repeat the question the coroner had signalled him, and the question had died in midsentence.

"Perhaps she was in too much pain," young Beecham had volunteered when the time was right, his red eyes pleading for an answer. "Drowning is probably a terrible way to go. Or perhaps she was gripped by fear and . . . and simply lost her composure."

"Of course, of course . . ."

And then he had fallen apart as he offered one last possibility.

"Perhaps . . . perhaps she chose death rather than to go naked in her son's eyes."

"Of course. Thank you, Mr. Beecham. Terribly sorry to have to trouble you."

"Quite all right, gentlemen."

And that was apparently that.

Blakeley and he both knew that Lydia Beecham could not only swim 15 feet to the surface and safety, no matter how heavy her clothing, but she could never have sunk like a dead weight without someone seeing to it. And as for the clothing, they realized, she had been known to shed it for much more frivolous reasons. Under those circumstances she would have eased out of it even if the shore were crowded with archbishops.

She was a person of unapologetic appetites, one of those George Bernard Shaw called the New Woman. She was too modern for Blakeley's taste. To discuss her sexual liaisons would be both ungentlemanly and redundant. No doubt she could have lived in Paris without ever blushing.

He thought about the bleeding finger for awhile, wondering how Christopher Beecham would be able to write the poetry that Miss Ashbaugh was convinced would render him immortal. But Sophia said that poetry was only a sideline with Beecham. His first love and the field in which he hoped to make his mark was as a scholar in the Classics—Greek tragedy, to be exact.

"Eh?"

"Yes, darling. Didn't you know? He's been

eagerly translating the works of Aeschylus for years."

"You don't say . . ."

And that was when Blakeley had obtained the court order to have the body of Lydia Beecham exhumed.

Judge Magwood peered over his glasses at Uriah Chidsey. His tone was inhospitable.

"Mr. Chidsey?"

"Yes, Your Honor." Chidsey fussed with his papers, stalling. "One moment, please."

Blakeley shook his head in disgust. The deputy district attorney was about to bumble the next step just as he had so many other parts of the case.

For example, when the victim's body was exhumed, Blakeley had found what he had expected to find—arsenic traces in the hair and nails. This, of course, did not sit well with the coroner, who then realized he should have been more thorough. He became nervous. He was also Judge Magwood's brother-in-law. One night, as they played chess and drank too much bourbon he had let it be known that he considered Dr. Ian Blakeley an interloper. "Thass what he is, Al. He's an in, in . . . innerloper." "Your move, Charley." "Well, actually, Algernon ole friend, ole chum, there's something I wanna talk to you about."

So it should have come as no surprise when Judge Magwood decided to suppress the evidence of poisoning.

"Too much time elapsed between the death and exhumation."

"Oh," Chidsey had said, "I didn't realize that."

"That's hogwash," Blakeley had said.

"Do not interrupt, Dr. Blakeley. The court sees no reason why this evidence can be considered scientifically conclusive."

"Yes, Your Honor," Chidsey had said.

"This is patently ridiculous."

"I'm warning you, Dr. Blakeley."

"Your Honor, arsenic remains in the hair and nails long after death. It—"

"You are in contempt, Dr. Blakeley. This court is fining you two hundred fifty dollars."

A rap of the gavel and the bailiff stepped forward. Blakeley had shrugged him off.

"Dammit! Do something, Chidsey!"

"Sit down, Mr. Chidsey."

"Yes, Your Honor."

Blakeley spent the next 72 hours in jail rather than giving Judge Magwood the satisfaction of a fine, and ever since then the deputy district attorney had been on the run.

"Very well, Dr. Blakeley, if you honestly think you can do a better job of it, you are certainly welcome to try."

Blakeley looked up from his notes, thought for a moment, then looked Chidsey in the eye.

"Are you serious?"

"I seldom josh, sir."

True, he was too dull for a sense of humor.

"You'd like me to take over, would you?"

"Your meddling got us into it. It seems appropriate that you get your hands dirty, doesn't it?"

"True."

"That is, if you don't think you'd lose your nerve?"

"I dare say, Chidsey, I couldn't make a greater mess of it than you have," Blakeley chuckled.

"Then, dammit, go ahead."

"This is no time for a chat, gentlemen," said Judge Magwood.

"Your Honor," Chidsey stood up, "may I have a word with you in private?"

"Good Lord, Mr. Chidsey, this trial has already taken more time than it deserves. Can we not get on with it?"

"Yes, Your Honor."

"Go ahead, Chidsey, tell him what's on your mind."

"Be quiet, Blakeley."

"Mr. Chidsey, will you *please* proceed with your cross examination?"

"Yes, Your—"

"Your Honor, may Mr. Chidsey approach the bench?"

As soon as he said that, he realized he must have sounded like a nervy schoolboy asking if his slow friend may go potty. Chidsey might have sensed that, too, because he blushed vividly.

"Mr. Chidsey," said the judge, "is there something wrong? Have you lost your voice?"

"There's your excuse, Chidsey."

"Oh, dear Gawd . . ."

Chidsey stepped forward hesitantly and conferred with Judge Magwood in whispers.

Blakeley turned and winked at Sophia again, but Mme. Defarge looked up from her knitting

16

just then and intercepted it. She did not appreciate his familiarity. When Sophia covered her mouth to stifle a giggle, he looked away quickly.

On the bench, the whispers grew louder. Magwood was shaking his head while Chidsey held out his hands in mock innocence.

It was a pretty morning. Gone were the gunpowder skies of winter. The early April sun spilled through tall windows, bathing the room in rich colors. The shadows were dark, the walls mahogany. Blakeley was reminded, quite vaguely, of something once observed in an art gallery. He let the impressions take him away for a time.

Most of the onlookers could have peopled a Breughel print—motley, mostly bulbous, some gaunt and gothic, like gatherers at a rustic feast. They seemed to think they were witnessing a trial of some importance. Blakeley failed to see how Christopher Beecham could match the status of a Lizzie Borden, but the press had been hard at work. The war news had fallen off lately.

Granted, young Beecham was a bit eccentric, but he was not all that colorful. In fact, he seemed to grow more eccentric and colorful with the notoriety, as if something in him that had been starved for attention was finally being fulfilled. The Beechams were prominent—good crime copy—but not *that* prominent. Certainly they were not in a sphere with the Astors, Mellons or Biddles.

"Dr. Blakeley, approach the bench."

The voice sounded weary, but it startled him. "Your Honor?"

17

"How difficult is it to understand? Get up and approach the bench, Dr. Blakeley."

The courtroom was abruptly silent as he stepped forward.

"What makes you think you can cross-examine?"

"What seems to be the trouble?"

"As I understand it, you're a scientist of some sort, surely not a lawyer."

"Well, actually, I am, sir, though I don't speak of it much."

"I beg your pardon?" Judge Magwood snarled.

"I beg your pardon?" Chidsey echoed.

"What I mean, sir, is that it rarely comes up. I'm a forensic pathologist and criminologist with degrees in Law and Medicine."

"Right out of a dime novel," Chidsey explained.

The judge paused, thinking. He sucked air through his teeth and chewed on a particle of something dating back to breakfast. Chidsey toyed nervously with his tiny mustache. Blakeley shifted his attention from one to the other and eventually to a pigeon that had roosted on the ledge outside.

When the judge finally nodded assent it was with a scowl and a grunt.

Chidsey rolled his eyes and groaned.

D. T. Sewell, the New York defense attorney hired by the Beecham family, had been doodling on a pad, and he now decided a comment was expected of him.

"This is highly irregular," he said, yawning.

"I know," the judge answered, "but it's legal. And if it gets this business over with, I'm all for it."

Sewell sat back in his chair and returned to his doodling. So far the case offered nothing to worry about, and his fee depended in part on the length of the trial.

"Thank you, Your Honor," Blakeley said.

Judge Magwood grunted again and ordered the bailiff to deputize him. Chidsey returned to his seat, head bowed. The gentlemen of the press leaned forward in their reserved rows.

The look on Christopher Beecham's face as Blakeley approached was hostile. In the corner of his eye, Blakeley noticed Cybel Ashbaugh looking at him with suspicion and equal hostility.

He glanced at his notes briefly and began.

"Mr. Beecham, you told the court you were seated behind your mother in the canoe when it overturned."

"Correct."

"The weather was calm."

"Correct."

"No winds, no waves?"

"Correct."

"Then as you recall it, there was no good reason why she should have fallen out of the canoe."

"I told you, it tipped over."

"Well, *why* did it tip over?"

"Canoes tip over, Dr. Blakeley. It . . . well,

there was a sudden awkward moment and it just capsized."

Blakeley turned to face the spectators and looked very confused.

"Well, did you stand up or something?"

"Of course not."

"I see. Then did your mother stand up?"

There was some twittering in the courtroom. Magwood rapped his gavel once and scowled. It subsided quickly.

"This isn't vaudeville, Dr. Blakeley."

"I assure you, Your Honor, there was no humor intended."

"Then kindly control your glibness."

"Your Honor, we have yet to hear a satisfactory answer to how the canoe overturned. I think that is central to this case."

Sewell objected. "Your Honor, my client has had to relive the pain of that moment often enough."

"And each time his story gets cloudier," Blakeley countered, turning to face the jury. "We are being asked to believe that some malevolent force reached down, snatched Lydia Beecham out of the canoe and held her under water."

"She was overly animated," said Christopher Beecham.

Sewell shook his head, trying to stop him from volunteering information. Beecham's love of attention had been cause for his lawyer to worry throughout the trial.

"Mr. Beecham, please . . ."

"Do go on, Mr. Beecham," Blakeley said.

"She . . . she'd been drinking."

Beecham did a good job of displaying his discomfort for the spectators. As if on cue, Miss Ashbaugh sobbed aloud.

"Drinking? Your mother rarely imbibed."

"That's what the world thought, Dr. Blakeley."

Blakeley paused and stroked his beard. When murmuring was heard in the press rows, Judge Magwood rapped his gavel again.

"Rather early for that, wasn't it? Nine-thirty, according to your statement."

"I know." Beecham was barely audible.

"Did she often drink in the morning?"

"Occasionally."

"For any particular reason?"

"You knew my mother, Dr. Blakeley. A blithe spirit."

"She must have had quite a bit that morning to become so careless."

"Enough," Beecham said, almost in a whisper.

Blakeley crossed to the table, opened a valise and took out some papers. He studied them as he spoke.

"Would you say, more than one drink?"

"I didn't count."

"More than two drinks?"

"I said—"

"What sort of drink was it? Whiskey?"

Beecham blushed.

"Was it whiskey, Mr. Beecham? Brandy? Gin?"

21

"Gin."

"A rather strong drink, gin."

"Yes, it . . . Mother favored gin because, as you know, it is not easily detected on the breath."

There were nods of recognition among the spectators.

For the most part, though, the jurors remained stony-faced. As Chidsey had stood by, always a step behind, the New York attorney had stacked the deck for the defense. The jurors who had little sympathy for blithe spirits had been given an overdose of Lydia Beecham's scandalous history, and Blakeley thought it appropriate that all 12 wore black and varying shades of gray.

"What brand of gin was it?"

"Plymouth, I think. Maybe Boodles. She kept it in a flask."

"The sort one carries?"

"Yes, in her purse."

"And she drank a substantial amount of it, evidently."

"Yes, she did."

"That's odd," Blakeley said, looking up at Judge Magwood. "There was no mention of alcohol in the victim's bloodstream in the coroner's report."

Magwood grunted. Obviously, his brother-in-law had slipped again. Blakeley thought he actually signaled the defense attorney to object to something, but D. T. Sewell apparently saw no reason.

"Was she carrying the flask while you were canoeing?" Blakeley proceeded.

"I don't . . ."

"Of course not. How silly of me. She wasn't carrying a purse in which to hide it if she was occupied with rowing."

"I . . ."

"You were each using an oar, she in front of you rowing on the left, and you rowing on the right."

He thought he saw beads of perspiration forming on Christopher Beecham's brow.

"Correct."

"Then she had left the flask in the house. Correct?"

"Correct."

"Good. Then in the absence of a thorough coroner's report," he reminded the judge, "we ought to be able to determine roughly how much she'd drunk when we enter the flask into evidence."

Sewell, who had been sensing the judge's eyes on him, stood up. He had a patronizing tone.

"Don't you think we've overdone this a bit, Dr. Blakeley? My client has admitted, to his embarrassment, that his mother had, among other things, a drinking problem. All this line of questioning will do is besmirch her reputation that much more."

"True, Blakeley," said the judge. "The press doesn't need any more gossip about the deceased."

"If anyone is creating gossip about her, Your

Honor, it's her son. I find it hard to believe that anyone could be so ruthless that he'd actually lie about something like this, but he did."

"Can you prove that, Dr. Blakeley?" Sewell asked icily.

"I can call her family physician as a witness. He ought to be able to tell us whether or not she drank to excess."

"A very competent man whose testimony can be believed." Sewell smiled. "Only he happens to be in Europe at the moment, attending a conference on psychosomatic illnesses."

"And," Judge Magwood added, "this court will not prolong the trial by bringing him back from Europe to confirm or deny something that is at best tangential to the case."

Sewell bowed and returned to his seat.

At the prosecution table Chidsey smiled with bratty spite. When Blakeley turned and made eye contact, he looked away.

Blakeley cleared his throat and went on.

"You say you dived repeatedly into the lake to rescue her."

Christopher Beecham seemed to have regained his composure.

"Yes. You know that."

"Are you a good swimmer, Beecham?"

"I'm an adequate swimmer."

"Your mother, however, was an excellent swimmer."

"Objection!"

"Why the devil are you objecting? May I not compliment the deceased?"

"Innuendo."

Blakeley looked up at the bench for help. "Sustained."

He was visibly angry now, but only to Sophia who knew his quirks. He had a tonelessness in his voice as he spoke to Beecham, and at times a redness in the cheeks, a hoodedness in the eyes, and a slight tic in the right corner of his mouth. If all four were present at the same time he would undoubtedly explode.

There were other means of getting to Christopher Beecham, but he had hoped the judge would let him avoid them because they bordered on brutality. However, it was clear that Magwood, whose vacation was to begin as soon as the trial was over, was anxious to cripple anything that might prolong it. No wonder D. T. Sewell could sit back, doodle, and probably even daydream.

Judge Magwood was also visibly annoyed. He had expected to have the trial wrapped up by noon. The jury could deliver a verdict right after lunch. Chidsey was a fool, but he was at least experienced in court. Letting Blakeley take over was intended as a signal to Sewell that it was time to wrap it up. Only Sewell was playing it cute, and Blakeley, the interloper, a supposed amateur, was surprisingly, damnably, stubborn.

He plodded on.

"The raft," he said, "did its presence there surprise you?"

"I'm not following."

"The sunken raft, Mr. Beecham. Located immediately below your overturned canoe."

"Why are you asking me that?"

"Yes, why are you?" Sewell echoed.

Blakeley looked at the jury as he answered. They were less mannequinlike, perhaps giving grounds for optimism.

"Because it is simply, well, possibly, too convenient that she fell overboard precisely where her clothing was so likely to get entangled."

"In that case," Sewell said, "I object."

"On what grounds, sir?"

"Because—"

Magwood intervened.

"Because you're still on that confounded business of a canoe capsizing—and I warn you, Dr. Blakeley, that you're almost in contempt of court again."

Blakeley exploded. "If I have to spend another seventy-two hours in jail for doing this job as it ought to be done, so be it. But it is still, I insist, important to note that Christopher Beecham himself sank that raft in exactly that spot when he was a younster. On that raft, nailed to the deck like something crucified, was a man-size dummy dressed in his father's clothing!"

Beecham screamed at his attorney to interrupt, which he did.

"Objection. This is irrelevant!"

"Sustained."

"I do not consider it irrelevant that his mother died *in fact* on the same spot where he had killed his father symbolically. To me it suggests something pathological."

"Suppose," Sewell said, "this little fable of yours had relevance. What proof do you have of it?"

"I'm so glad you asked that, Mr. Sewell."

Blakeley opened his valise and removed a small, black, cloth-bound book which he waved before the jury.

"You can find it recorded in his diary, dated June the Twelfth, 1885. He was quite proud of it. He even went into detail about how his father—and I think it really *was* his father in his mind—had suffered as he was nailed to the timbers."

Beecham sank into his chair, his face ashen and sweaty.

The mumbling in the press rows grew livelier as notes were being scribbled hastily.

The jury was no longer a collection of stiff, bloodless bodies. Looks were being exchanged, color appearing amid the tones of gray.

Magwood was livid.

"Order! Order!"

"This should be Exhibit C for the prosecution," Blakeley said.

Magwood rapped his gavel several times.

"The jury will please disregard the comments just uttered by Dr. Blakeley regarding motive. This is a Philadelphia courtroom, not a Viennese mental hospital."

But the seed had been planted, and everyone, especially those in Christopher Beecham's corner, knew that. Several members of the Beecham family left the room as quietly as they could, looking pale and resigned. Blakeley felt for them, but he took it as a good sign for his case.

"Where did you get that?" Chidsey snapped as Blakeley jotted "Exhibit C" on a piece of paper and handed it to the clerk, ignoring Chidsey who huffed and recrossed his legs.

Judge Magwood's tone was theatrically menacing.

"*Dr. Blakeley.*"

"Yes, Your Honor?"

"One might think you actually enjoyed your stay in jail."

"Well, Your Honor, the cuisine lacked surprise, but . . ."

"You are on the verge of sampling it again, sir."

Blakeley stood before the bench, considering his few options and angry with Magwood for forcing what had to come next. He looked up and smiled cryptically.

"I suppose, in that case, I have no more questions for the time being."

"The defendant may step down," Magwood announced with a sudden trace of a smile.

Beecham looked up, rose cautiously and moved on rubbery legs. He exchanged soulful looks with Miss Ashbaugh then glanced at the few Beechams who remained. They looked strangely relieved.

As he passed, Blakeley said something to him under his breath that made him stop and stare as if he were seeing the Headless Horseman.

Only he and Blakeley understood because the words, enunciated very deliberately, were in Greek.

"*I believe, my father, had I face to face questioned him if I must my mother slay, would have earnestly pleaded with me never to thrust a sword through my mother's heart."*

Neither Magwood nor Sewell, consulting their notes, heard or saw the exchange. When he got to his chair, Christopher Beecham virtually collapsed into it.

Blakeley checked his pocket watch. 10:45. Time was his ally now. Beecham was cracking, and the jurors seemed almost eager to see what would happen next.

Several rows back, immediately behind Mme. Defarge, who was blowing her nose loudly, Sophia nodded approval.

"If it please the court, the prosecution now calls Detective Sergeant Nathan McBride to the stand."

It did not please the court, but Judge Magwood did not swear or groan. His horsy face just drooped as he let out his characteristic grunt. If he missed the 5:30 train for New York, he would most assuredly miss his poker game with the boys at the Algonquin. He had had it all so well figured—a steak and some good Scotch on the train, a nap, poker until dawn, then in the morning the boat for Europe and the wine, the painted ladies, the anonymity. So much for careful planning.

D. T. Sewell eyed the detective as he entered from the anteroom where he had been waiting in case he was needed. An impressive young man, he was close to six feet and slender, and Sewell thought he was dressed pretty well for a cop. Must be on the take in an affluent neighborhood. He noticed that Christopher Beecham seemed to hate him on sight; his nose flared and his jaw jutted, but he said nothing as McBride passed by and stepped onto the witness stand.

Sewell looked around for information. A law student who was sitting close by, hoping to be of any use to D. T. Sewell of Willoughby, Harcourt, Sewell, Lipsitz and Greene, leaned over the railing and whispered a hasty profile. He had eaten onions that morning.

Nathan Patrick McBride was familiar to almost everyone else in the room as a friend and respected colleague of Blakeley's, enlisted whenever the latter found himself in a particularly challenging situation. The arrangement relied on the cooperation and good will of the Eleventh Precinct, but Blakeley had a much better relationship with the rank and file than he did with the denizens of City Hall. Lieutenant Hudson of that precinct knew he could call on Blakeley for highly educated guesses and forensic fine points whenever needed.

The McBride connection had started a few years before when the city threw up its hands and dropped a problem with a serial murderer into Blakeley's lap. At the same time he was working on a book, not coincidentally, on serial murderers and planning a lecture tour, so as a concession for interrupting him the city gave him McBride for the duration. It was limited generosity. McBride was raw, just up from the patrolman ranks, and viewed with some suspicion because of his background, his taste in poetry and Wagner, and because of a shyness that usually made him seem rather aloof.

That was long past him now. Handsome, athletic, articulate, he was easy to dislike if one were a Christopher Beecham, or a fat, bespectacled, smarmy type like the young man now whispering. Nathan McBride was a mystery—a degree in philosophy, a youth spent mostly in an orphanage, and a very tough street cop. Whatever was known about him, and especially about his childhood, was reserved for the department's personnel files and entrusted to a very privileged few. His name had initially inspired speculation about his origins, but if there were jokes told about a Jewish traveling salesman and an Irish scrubwoman, they were told in cautious whispers.

Blakeley liked him—in a way even loved him. They could trust each other in situations where trust was imperative.

D. T. Sewell was not made aware of all of that, only that "the cop," as the law student put it, "does Blakeley's dirty work." It was a churlish remark uttered in latent falsetto and should have been recognized as such.

"Thank you, Mr. . . ."

"Suckling." He spelled it out in one breath. "Richard P. Suckling, but they call me—"

"Thank you, Mr. Suckling."

"If there's anything else you need to know . . ."

But by that time Sewell had turned away, and young Mr. Suckling was left to dream of a future when he too could defend the world's well-heeled maggots.

McBride was sworn in and took his seat.

"Sergeant McBride," Blakeley asked, "how did you come to discover the book just entered into evidence?"

"I saw a few things outside that made me curious enough to want to look around inside the house, so I got a search warrant and rummaged around in the defendant's room. I found the book under a false bottom in a dresser drawer."

"A secret compartment, in other words."

"Yes."

"And what else did you find in that compartment?"

"Mostly just childhood memorabilia—marbles, an Indian feather, sulphur diamonds, and the like. I also came across a small medicine box labeled 'Seidlitz powders' but which later tested out as arsenic."

Sewell was on his feet. "Objection!"

"I know, I know," Blakeley chimed in. "Inadmissible evidence."

"Sustained."

And as Judge Magwood went on to instruct the jury to disregard McBride's mention of poison, Blakeley smiled and lip-synced his words. There were more twitters in the audience and one of the ladies on the jury cupped her hand over her mouth to hide a smile. Magwood realized that something was amiss but was more interested in getting on with it.

"Very well then, Sergeant McBride," Blakeley

resumed, "besides the . . . you-know-what . . . was there anything else of interest in the compartment?"

McBride paused and chose his words, mostly for the benefit of the female jurors.

"There were pictures of a very intimate nature."

"You mean . . . like French postcards, to use the vernacular?"

"No, sir, I mean drawings, rather primitive drawings that might have been done by a child. They were, as I've said, of an intimate nature."

"Of a sexual nature."

"Yes."

"Objection!"

"Your Honor," Blakeley interrupted, "if the court will permit me to pursue this for only a moment, I believe I can prove its relevance."

Magwood, about to say "Sustained," stopped after the first syllable, shook his head and sighed.

"Very well, but it had better *be* relevant. Overruled."

"Your Honor—"

"Mr. Sewell, I said overruled." Magwood had a headache.

"Go on, please, Sergeant McBride."

"My first impulse was to ignore them. They seemed more personal than criminal. Then I realized they'd been stuffed into a copy of Lamb's *Tales from Shakespeare* at precisely the moment when Hamlet assails his mother for remarrying. Admittedly, the late Mrs. Beecham had not remarried, but the combination of the drawings and the scene of Hamlet's so-called sexual betrayal changed my mind. The figures in the drawing suggested evidence of a sort. The female figure was tall, an adult with honey blonde hair and brown eyes like Mrs. Beecham's. Those features had been colored in, along with the . . . nipples on the, well, rather prodigious breasts and, of course, the . . . hirsute pudendum.''

There were puzzled looks in the court. They became silly smiles and blushes as wiser heads turned and other words for ''hirsute pudendum'' were whispered. Some of the prim female mouths on the jury fell open, some faces turned terribly red.

McBride continued. ''The rest of the features in the drawings were just pen and ink, no color. The male figure was that of a little boy who was engaged in various forms of coitus, uh, sexual intercourse with the female adult. It was rather grotesque—a little boy with a . . .'' He cleared his throat. ''A male organ that was grossly out of proportion with his little body.''

As McBride was giving his testimony, Blakeley again opened the valise, this time to remove an envelope that contained the drawings.

''You never told me about any of this evidence,'' Uriah Chidsey hissed.

Judge Magwood tried to appear blasé as he scanned the drawings, some of which showed remarkable imagination in a boy of, say, 11. It was hard to gauge, and if the exact age had to be determined, Magwood knew he'd have to call in a specialist of some sort, which would take more time and . . . oh God! will this damn trial never end? He looked at the Lydia Beecham figure in one particularly provocative pose and struggled to put the European painted ladies out of his mind. In another she was wielding a whip.

As Christopher Beecham tried to sink into his chair and avoid eye contact with everyone in the court, some more members of his family stole out of the room and his attorney got up to look at what was now called "Exhibit D for the prosecution."

"All this tells us," Sewell suggested, "is that my client went through a troubled period as a child. I don't want to burst your Victorian bubble, Dr. Blakeley, but lots of kids do—*if* in fact they're his drawings at all. You've no proof of that either."

Magwood, recalling some awkward moments from his own adolescence, snapped out of it abruptly.

"You may bring that up in your summation, Mr. Sewell."

"I intend to."

"Are you through with your witness, Dr. Blakeley?"

"I believe so, Your Honor."

"Then I'd like to question him," Sewell said.

"All yours, old chap."

Blakeley returned to his seat and smiled at Chidsey who again recrossed his legs huffily.

"Sergeant McBride, why were you poking around the Beecham estate after the police department itself was satisfied no crime had been committed?"

"I was checking the raft. I'm a reasonably good swimmer, you see. Dr. Blakeley knows that, so he asked me to dive into the lake and investigate the scene of the alleged crime. He was of the opinion that the nail on which Mrs. Beecham was supposedly caught was not of a shape and angle to do so accidentally."

"Were you satisfied that it was?"

McBride sat up, looking more relaxed now that the previous testimony was over and he could speak of less delicate matters. Even from a distance, Sophia had noticed that he too was blushing. She might have also, except Blakeley had warned her of what was coming.

"Actually, I couldn't find anything of value to our case. The nail, if she had indeed been snagged on it deliberately, was so twisted and pulled that it was useless as evidence. After my third dive, I was about to go back with the bad news."

"And?"

"And I saw something that made me wonder if I'd been underwater too long. Sometimes holding the breath induces a kind of brief drunkenness."

"I know," said D. T. Sewell, his intelligence insulted. Sewell was a neat, trim man, unimposing in contrast to the rounder, heartier Blakeley.

Blakeley was himself a fashionable gentleman, quite traditionally British, favoring tweed until the heat of the Philadelphia summers made its wear impossible, and then he would switch to light-colored worsted wool. He sported a closely cropped black beard under a rather full mustache and wore a monocle which he liked to hold in his fingers as he gestured to stress a point. D. T. Sewell was already dressed in light-weight wool, fawn-colored, the latest New York chic, tailored as neatly as his little red mustache. Like Blakeley's monocle, he had a trademark prop, a cane that was said to date back to a college sports injury but which he now used for effect.

"What was the apparition or whatever it was that you say you saw, Sergeant McBride?" he insinuated.

"Funny you should say that, apparition, because it's exactly what I thought I saw. I remember shaking the water off my face and blinking a few times. Across the lake, standing on the dock, was Mrs. Beecham."

The courtroom stirred, Magwood rapped his gavel, Sewell smirked, and McBride quickly explained.

"That is, I *thought* it was Mrs. Beecham. Slender shape, Parisian fashions, honey blonde hair—all the basics."

"Really, Sergeant McBride . . ."

"So I went under again and swam a little closer. She was still there on the dock, lifting her skirt and dancing alone. I thought I heard her humming something like the 'Skater's Waltz' so I got closer as quietly as possible."

"And then what happened? Don't tell me. She went *poof*! and disappeared into thin air."

There were more twitters, mostly among the newspapermen, to whom D. T. Sewell had played during most of the trial.

"No. He stayed there for awhile. Long enough for me to get a good look."

"*He?*"

Blakeley stood up, waving a folder.

"This is Exhibit E for the prosecution, Your Honor. We want to enter it at this time."

McBride nodded toward the folder as Judge Magwood opened it and studied its contents with a look that bordered on shock. He studied each of them carefully, even suspiciously.

"I returned the next day with a camera. Fortunately, the sky was clear and I was able to get a number of good shots from pretty close range. The pictures being entered into evidence are of your client."

"What the hell are you talking about?"

Blakeley stood up and requested that Sewell look at the photographs. Magwood handed them down, his face showing skepticism. He and D. T. Sewell soon made it obvious that they shared each other's reservations.

"Really, Dr. Blakeley," the defense attorney said, making a sweeping gesture toward the jury, "I'm amazed that you'd have such little regard for the intelligence of these men and women that you and your hireling would try to pull a stunt like this."

McBride bristled slightly. Though predictable, he did not like Sewell's tone.

"What seems to be the discrepancy?" Blakeley asked.

"Well, it's obvious, isn't it? Those are pictures taken of Mrs. Lydia Beecham not long before her death."

"Look at them again, please."

Magwood's headache grew worse.

"Dr. Blakeley, if this is your idea of how to conduct a trial, then I suggest you return to your cadavers and never darken my courtroom again."

Everyone in the press rows took pains to get that quote word-for-word.

"And I suggest, in all due respect, that you take another look also, Your Honor."

Magwood turned livid. He was thinking of just how well he could phrase it when he once again sentenced Blakeley for contempt of court. Blakeley stared back at him, thinking in passing that Magwood had eyes like a basset hound.

"Look at the finger, Your Honor," McBride spoke up. "Look at the photograph marked '5-E' and note the hand holding the parasol."

Magwood glanced briefly at McBride then stared for another few seconds at Blakeley. When he turned to Sewell, the defense attorney was pale and his lips were muttering barely audible obscenities.

"Give them to me," the judge demanded.

Sewell reached up and dropped them under Magwood's eyes, then walked away. The hand that gripped the trademark cane was slightly palsied. He wondered if he would have to speak again and hoped not to, because anger and embarrassment had clotted his voice.

Magwood pushed his eyeglasses back from the tip of his nose.

"Do you see it now, Your Honor?" Blakeley asked after another few seconds. "The finger that had been bitten off, or if you prefer to believe him, lost in the struggle to save his mother?"

Christopher Beecham jumped up and screamed, "You bastard!"

Then he started, not for Blakeley, but for McBride.

"Order! Order!"

A constable who outweighed Beecham by 100 pounds intercepted him, but in his rage he showed surprising strength and agility, the kind of power a madman can call on when cornered. He grasped the constable by the lapels and shoved him over the railing like a big sack of potatoes. The constable hit his head on one of the chairs vacated by the Beecham family, and by the time he was back on his feet Judge Magwood and D. T. Sewell were hiding behind the judge's bench, Cybel Ashbaugh had fainted, and Beecham and McBride were grappling on the witness stand. And McBride, too, was having a hard time.

Finally, McBride landed a clean right cross, Blakeley and two more constables jumped into it, and Christopher Beecham was dragged screaming from the courtroom.

When he returned a quarter of an hour later he was sedated and wrapped in a strait jacket, and his attorney looked as if he were in a condition to share it.

Gone was the wig that had covered Beecham's shorn head. Gone were the rest of the Beecham family as well as half of the reporters, anxious to get the story told first. Those who remained were there to write sidebars and to see if they could squeeze an interview out of the principals. It was front page stuff.

They noticed that Blakeley and Christopher Beecham had a brief exchange in a language that none of them understood. It took place shortly after Beecham had been brought back to the courtroom.

They did, however, understand an exchange between Blakeley and the attorney from New York.

"Blakeley, you set me up, you sonofabitch!"

"My dear Sewell, life, they say, is an endless rude awakening."

"Go to hell!"

Blakeley clucked his tongue. "What a terrible thing to say."

He also enjoyed the look on Judge Magwood's face when he told him he would make his poker game and the boat to Europe after all. A good attorney studies his judges closely.

He left the rest of the case to Uriah Chidsey. The jury was charged by 11:30 and the verdict returned by noon. And now there was talk of exhuming the late Silas Beecham.

Outside the courthouse, as the April sun made Blakeley shield his eyes, the reporters congregated on the landing and blocked his way to the street. Sophia, who had been walking between him and Nathan McBride, took McBride's arm and the two stepped away discretely.

They laughed aloud when they happened

upon Uriah Chidsey, who was speaking to a small crowd of reporters.

"I know it must have seemed, well, rather devil-may-care of me, but I decided the introduction of Dr. Blakeley would unsettle him, so I took the calculated risk. I think Blakeley handled it well for a rank amateur, but I was there directing him every step of the way."

Seeing Sophia and Sergeant McBride and hearing them laugh, he never even blinked. Chidsey, they decided, will go far.

But most of the reporters were well-aware that Chidsey was a pompous imbecile, so most of them had intercepted Blakeley, and Sophia knew that her husband, despite his protests, enjoyed the celebrity, which was why she and McBride had drifted off.

"What happens now, Doc? The hangman?"

"I hope not. Beecham's a rotter, to be sure, but he's worth much more to medical science alive than dead."

"You think Judge Magwood will see it that way?"

Blakeley just shook his head and shrugged. There was no telling Magwood's mind, but it was not known for its depth. They understood.

"What was that line you gave Beecham when he came back, Doc?"

"It was something spoken by Orestes that I thought he'd recognize."

"By who, and how do you spell that?"

"It's from a Greek tragedy. Translated, it says, 'I slew her. That is not to be denied. With sword edge pressed against her throat'."

He had to repeat that several times which became annoying.

"Okay, then what'd Beecham say to you?"

"I can't quote it, gentlemen. The ancients also had their unprintable expressions."

After some laughter, his irritability softened.

"So, uh, what does that line mean? The one from the Greek guy."

"Orestes, you see, murdered his mother. He felt he had to because she'd betrayed and murdered his father. But matricide is a terrible crime in any society, and in his grief he bit off his own finger. As you can see, so did Beecham. And as you've also seen, both shaved their heads. Among the Greeks that, too, was a sign of remorse."

"But Beecham isn't a Greek."

"I know, but he's a Greek scholar. I gambled on how he would handle his own remorse, and certainly enough, he turned out to be a rather good case of the Orestes complex though not a classic case, for such individuals usually kill more violently, rarely with poison. But something about Beecham, an oily unmanliness, I suppose, made me look for him anyway. Arsenic, you see, is colorless, odorless and tasteless, and, better yet, has a delayed reaction period. So he could take her boating, wait for her to pass out, and see to it she looked like a drowning. Having possibly disposed of his father because he wanted his mother to himself, he was sick enough to convince himself that his mother had actually murdered Silas Beecham. Then, instead of giving him her exclusive affection, she betrayed him by enjoying a rather . . ." He glanced at Sophia and lowered his voice. "A rather indiscriminate romantic life."

"What's that about romantic life?"

"Can you speak up, Doc?"

"One at a time, gentlemen."

"Are you an expert on cuckoos, Dr. Blakeley?"

"I beg your pardon?"

"Well, how come this kind of cuckoo dresses in his mother's clothing?"

"I'm not certain. Possibly, this kind of cuckoo, as you put it, thinks he can take on the more admirable qualities, the mental strength, most likely, of the victim by donning her clothing."

"That's pretty disgusting."

"Yes, it is. Now if you'll excuse me, I have a golf game I'd like to get to."

There was a clamor so he gave them another minute.

"Just one thing Dr. Blakeley," someone asked. "How come he went after Sergeant McBride instead of you? You were the one who really nailed him."

Blakeley chuckled.

"Gentlemen, look at Sergeant McBride and look at me. At the risk of sounding humble, I'm a chap of some girth, middle-aged and quite happily married. Sergeant McBride is, obviously, the sort of young man Lydia Beecham favored. He must have triggered a lot of unhappy memories in Christopher Beecham by his handsome appearance."

There was general agreement among the reporters. Though a flush of embarrassment crossed over Nathan McBride's face, Sophia was amused.

And then one of the reporters, a voice he had not heard before, spoke up.

"You sure you aren't being just a little *too* humble, Dr. Blakeley?"

"No, not really."

The face was also unfamiliar. Like the voice, it possessed an inherent sneer. Blakeley had learned to suffer the local guttersnipes gracefully, but there was something about this one that reminded him of eating raw liver.

They read each other carefully.

"My name is Bernard Spector, Doc, but you may call me Bernie. I work for a little sheet up the road called the *Morning Star*. Know it?"

"My name is Ian Blakeley, Bernie, but you may call me Dr. Blakeley. I am aware of your rag."

"So, what about your humility? Whatsamatter? You only wanna answer the easy question?"

"Meaning?"

"Meaning what about the rumors about you and the late Lydia Beecham?"

"What rumors?"

"Ah, c'mon, Doc—*tor* Blakeley. You went after that kid with a vengeance. And I mean *vengeance*. As in 'sayeth the Lord'."

Well now, that might explain a few things that had troubled him of late though not enough to cause insomnia, but there had been mysteries—

like the careful choice of words he'd noticed in casual conversations, and the casual conversations that had ceased abruptly when he entered a room. It was appropriate pig slop for a tabloid like the *Morning Star*, and this kind of case attracted such flies.

"As I said, I've a golf appointment . . ."

"Gimme a break, Doc. You're news now. They say she had very exotic tastes."

Blakeley stopped and eyed Spector as if he were something deposited on the lawn by a stray.

"You, sir, are toxic. Should you ever, God forbid, procreate, the result would be a mutation."

"Hey, c'mon, Doc. Just a few minutes . . ."

And then Sophia stepped in, smiling sweetly and taking Blakeley's arm. He wondered if she had heard the same rumors.

"Mr. Spector, *Bernie*, are you suggesting there was an illicit liaison between my husband and the late Mrs. Beecham?"

Spector did not reply for a moment. He looked her up and down and tried to formulate a thumbnail description in his mind—petite, great shape like a ballerina, cultured voice, authoritative and sultry at the same time, a real sharp tootsie.

"That would mean cheating. Am I right, *Bernie*?"

"Yeah," Spector replied, "it sure would."

She had a very devastating giggle. If she wished to, Sophia could make one feel as if his pants were down in church during the Easter

Sunday services and the Bishop had just turned and noticed.

"Cheating? On *me*?" She giggled and grasped Blakeley's arm a little tighter.

"Really, Mr. Spector, *Bernie*, it must be true what they say about you newspaper chaps. You do drink too much."

Chapter Three

It was warm for early April, a day when shirts cling and collars chafe. The wool in his well-worn trousers itched, and the deadpan faces of the other passengers told him that the rose water he had doused himself with was not enough. The sister had said, in so many gentle but unmistakable words, to get cleaned up, but some things are beyond salvation, sister.

Tony stepped down from the trolley and glanced around uneasily, blinking into the late afternoon sun which hurt his eyes.

The car grunted forward, turned around with a loud screech and rumbled back toward the city, and when it was a little distance away he heard the soft cry of wild doves and spotted a pair of male cardinals squabbling over control of an apple bough. The air smelled faintly of honeysuckle and the breezes conjured little twisters along the road that eddied upward through white birch and linden. That road, he guessed, led to the estate. He was anxious to see it and get on with the deal.

When his eyes adjusted, the sky was achingly blue, the landscape plucked right out of a fairy tale.

No one greeted him. Nobody even looked at him. He felt very awkward there, like an unfunny, off-color joke at a polite gathering. The other riders on the last half-mile of the journey, a frumpish woman and a portly girl of 18 or so, whom he took to be servants at some nearby manor house, and a tubercular-looking man who could have been anything from a poet to a bookkeeper, had gone their separate ways, the ladies westward on foot over a small stone bridge that spanned a swollen brook. The rains in the spring of 1898 had been heavy, turning the Philadelphia slum alleys he knew so intimately into a network of soggy garbage and rancid mud. But out here in the country, where the winds blew unimpeded and the sun had no ugly brick skeletons to fight, the footpaths and access roads had already become dusty brown causeways.

The plump girl paused in the middle of the stone bridge, braced her sunbonnet with one hand, and lobbed a stone into the stream with the other. It plopped into a deep bankside pool, scattering a cluster of dragonflies. The frump turned and snarled, showing two prominent canines. The girl giggled, tossed two more stones just to make a point, then skipped along the westward path, passing her companion.

Maybe he was early. Without a watch it was hard to tell. But the sister had said that someone would meet him right there at the end of the line at five o'clock exactly, and if you can't trust a sister then who the hell can you trust?

The tubercular-looking man had a coughing spell that interrupted his thoughts. It was quite a seizure—wheezing, gagging, near convulsions, a deeper shade of gray. He caught his breath after about a full minute, then cleared his throat and spat into the dust. He looked uphill impatiently, mumbled something to himself, and settled down on his haunches like a debased holy man. Tony had seen that look before—sallow skin, sunken eyes, bluish fingers. Down in the Sink it was a common look that they called The Hick.

Someone was late for him, too, but there was no need to discuss it. If anyone had wanted to talk to Tony it would have happened during the long ride from Front Street, but everyone had seemed intent on pretending he was not there. If you can't see him, you can tell yourself the body odor assailing your nostrils is actually coming from some inanimate source, like a bit of something inadvertently carried aboard on the sole of someone's shoe. He made it easier for them by avoiding eye contact and saying nothing. If you can't see him or hear him and you pretend you can't smell him, then you'll never have to touch him. The feeling was a very familiar one, which was why he had not ventured out of the Sink for two years.

The tubercular-looking traveler was blowing his nose with a honking vengeance and cursing a fly that was determined to land on his face.

Tony reached into his trousers and felt around for the stubby cigar butt he had found on the sidewalk near the trolley stop, picked some lint from the soggy end, and struck a blue tip match with his thumbnail. He lit it carefully to avoid singeing his mustache and looked around for a private place to relieve himself now that the ladies were gone. Trolley rides were hell on the kidneys, especially after half a fifth of musky. He spied a lilac bush in full flower and stepped behind it.

The hillside was green, but most of the trees had not blossomed. On the cloudless horizon they seemed almost ghostly. He hated open spaces. They gave him the chills.

Once, in his army days—must have been 20 years ago—he and the 15th West Virginia were chasing Chiracahuas along the border from Nogales to Sassabi Flat and back, and the lieutenant had sent him out on a scouting mission—not for Apaches, however. The lieutenant had promised the colonel's wife that he would bring back a wild turkey to surprise the colonel at Sunday dinner. It was the lieutenant's favorite means of sucking around. Tony had gone off into the desert telling himself that at least this time it was only a goddamned turkey; last time the lieutenant had promised venison. Then, about five miles north of Oro Blanco, it had dawned on him that he was behind Apache lines—the goddamnedest meanest Apaches in the whole worthless territory. Eyeless, bloated bodies were rubbed with berry juice and tied down over anthills, or blackened to the waist after hanging headfirst from tree limbs over smoldering bonfires, or stared stupidly while squatting over spears that entered through the rectum and protruded through the open mouth. He had seen such hellish things which had unnerved him, and when he found his way back to the troop he was put in irons after doing his best to strangle the lieutenant. Two years and 11 months later he was released from the guard house and given his dishonorable discharge, and when he left the fort he turned, gripped his crotch, and shouted an obscene good-bye to the lieutenant who was now a captain. And Tony was a bum.

There was dust rising in the distance and a wagon was making its way downhill. The tubercular-looking man either heard it or sensed it and got up with a grunt. As the wagon approached he gave Tony a reptilian smile that meant the ride was his, not Tony's.

Tony leaned against a tree trunk, took the cigar out of his mouth and glared as the man walked away. If this were the Sink instead of some God-forsaken countryside where he was a stranger, he'd have taken the sickly little punk into an alley and squeezed him like a pimple on the ass for a look like that. Tony was still glaring when the man turned around and spoke after a brief, whispered conversation with the driver.

"You with the cigar, you the dishwasher?"

"Who deserves to know?"

"I asked you a question."

"He's the dishwasher, you moron," the driver determined. "He fits the description. Get in, mister."

Nobody spoke for the first mile as they climbed the hill and entered the woods. Tony felt in his pocket to be sure he had his knife. He didn't like either of them; the driver was just as surly as his partner and took up too much space. The other one stared straight ahead, sniffing now and then to let it be known that he found Tony offensive. One more sniff and the knife was coming out.

"Where'd they dig you up," the driver asked as they bounded over a deep rut.

"Probably the same kind a place they get all their help."

The tubercular one reacted quickly. Now that the driver was with him, he was like a coiled rattlesnake waiting for an irritant.

"You callin' us a couple a Sink scum?"

"Shut up, Pluto," the driver said. "Me and the gent are havin' a nice conversation."

Pluto started to say something but another coughing spell got in his way. This time it was one of those deep bronchial convulsions that leave the lips blue and the eyes red and runny.

The driver was unsympathetic.

"Listen, Pluto, if you're gonna throw up, you

better let me know right now." Pluto could not reply; he was too busy wheezing. The driver shook his head in disgust. "Some guys I know are makin' book on when he's finally gonna croak. One a these days he's gonna make them pukin' noises 'n spook the horse, and I'm gonna wind up wid a broken neck! What a waste youse are, Pluto."

They were silent again. Leaves that had fallen over scores of past autumns scattered as the coach picked up speed on a flat stretch. Then the woods grew darker as the leafless trees gave way to acres of evergreens.

Tony decided to answer. He liked the way the driver had humbled Pluto. Besides, after so many nights in the crowded, noisy beer shops, silence made him uneasy.

"I was hired at the mission."

"Whazzat?"

"The Edwards Street Mission. It's a flop house."

"Oh yeah, yeah, I guess I heard a that one."

He thought he detected a brief smirk exchanged between Pluto and the driver. He was about to say something about their mothers' sexual habits when the coach hit another rut. They tilted forward for a few seconds, cursed, then sat back abruptly.

"Gettin' the butterflies yet?" Pluto asked, spitting out the window.

"For what?"

"Y'know . . . sun, heat, bumpy road, no booze in your gut."

"You ask a lotta questions, asshole."

"I'm concerned about yer health . . . ass-hole."

"I'll let you know so you can watch."

The driver leaned over and guffawed at Pluto.

"A physical wreck like you has a lotta nerve askin' somebody about his health!"

And nothing more was said. Pluto sulked while the driver continued to laugh. They flew downhill over a smoother roadway, then quickly up and out of the woods, and the estate came up suddenly, massively, majestically, as intimidating as it was elegant, a monster of unfamiliar beauty.

Now they were on a drive leading into the house, and there were indeed butterflies in his stomach.

Somewhere he had once heard the words "baronial splendor" but had never come close to seeing anything like it. He was confused, vaguely angry, but mostly frightened and awed by it all.

The driver noticed.

"Never seen nothin' like this before, did you, sport?"

"Who owns it?"

The driver smiled, and Pluto coughed again. Ever since they slowed down, the wagon had been shrouded in thick yellowish dust.

He decided it was not worth pursuing. A job's a job, and this one was his first in two years. The sister had said there was room and board, hot water, self-respect. Self-respect had a nice sound, like "baronial splendor." Maybe he'd find out what it tasted like. Probably like some

56

kind a rich man's booze. He had no idea. Maybe in time he'd save up for new duds, some fancy cologne to splash on, a box of good Havanas. Maybe he'd even find a woman. Maybe tell these two to kiss his ass.

They passed a row of cherry trees in pink bloom and the driver decided to speak up.

"I'll tell ya this much, sport. They're filthy rich, the people who own this."

"Fer Chrissake, Grover, even he can see that!"

As usual, the driver ignored Pluto, who was muttering to himself.

"Coal mines upstate," Grover went on, "steel mills in Pittsburgh, banks in New York, land out in California. The kind a just plain folks we're killin' down in Cuba for. You been in the army?"

He thought for awhile, then lied.

"No, I ain't."

"Took some shrapnel in the thigh myself, down in Oklahoma territory fightin' Indians."

Pluto snickered. "Indians don't have no artillery."

"These ones did. Shut the hell up, Pluto."

When Grover turned to speak he showed a mouthful of plug tobacco and thin brown creases in the corners of his mouth where the juice flowed freely. His face reddened. He stared angrily at Pluto for a full 15 seconds until he was satisfied that Pluto was nervous. They were like two punks in a schoolyard, Tony thought. The more time he spent with them, the more he decided they weren't much of a threat.

"Anyways," Grover continued, "I'd a thought the Salvation Army lady would a told you who

was tryin' to rescue you from hellfire 'n brimstone. If she didn't, then it ain't me or Pluto's
place to."

"I don't remember no Salvation Army lady."

They passed under a tall archway and approached a circle which surrounded the house.
The roadway was cobbled as they turned left
toward the servants' quarters. The wheels made
a deafening sound.

"It wasn't a Sally. It was a sister."

"Huh?"

"A nun."

Grover kept his eyes on the road, smirking.
Pluto emitted a hissing laugh.

They pulled up in a shaded area behind the
back entrance to the scullery. The horse let out a
grateful little shiver and swatted a fly with its
tail.

"What's so funny about the nun?"

Pluto shrugged his shoulders.

"I dunno, wino. I guess one do-gooder's the
same as another. Right, Grover?"

Grover pointed toward the doorway.

"Better get movin', sport. You got lots a dishes
to wash."

Chapter Four

His name was Jack Brown and Hudson couldn't get him out of his thoughts—the straw-like, unkempt hair, the greasy collar, the chin stubble, the irksome, breezy way he had draped his arm over the back of his chair as they awaited the magistrate, and most of all, the sneer. It had started to appear as the decision became inevitable, and as the decision was announced it had been aimed right between Hudson's eyes. Better luck next time, Lieutenant; go study your law books. More than eight hours had passed, and instead of cooling off he was seething even more than he was when he left the magistrate's office. He wanted Jack Brown on a slab in the city morgue so badly that it soured his sarsaparilla.

He slammed his fist on the top of his desk, and Officer Fatzinger, seated across the empty squad room, jumped out of his chair.

"Jesus, Lootenant, you could scare da wits out of a person."

Wilmer P. "Bones" Fatzinger had come down from somewhere in the hay country with one of those giddy, sort-of-German accents. It went annoyingly well with his billy goat voice. Hudson had always regarded Fatzinger's assignment to his precinct as an exceptionally cruel form of revenge exacted by some bitter enemy in City Hall, and to make matters worse, the war and other acts of madmen had placed Bones only a rung below detective's rank. Hudson had spent many a troubled night contemplating the horror of such an eventuality. Fatzinger was probably the worst cop in Philadelphia, but he had once endeared himself to the commissioner's wife by capturing, quite by accident, a halfwit who had exposed himself to her bridge club one Sunday afternoon. It had all seemed very funny at the time. Now it was a matter of putting Bones wherever he was likely to do the least harm.

"I presume I didn't ruin your appetite, Bones?"

"Vell, I don't tink so."

"What a relief."

"Huh?"

"Never mind."

Fatzinger was eating his third lunch, a limburger and onion on pumpernickel, which was another good reason to keep him busy and at a distance.

"You finish those files yet?"

"Dis mornin'. You been shleepin' or what?"

"In alphabetical order?"

"Vell, I tink so."

"What about the inventory?"

"What about da what?"

"The inventory. The things in the supply room."

"Huh?"

"Count them and make a list."

"Schidt."

Fatzinger stuffed the rest of his sandwich and half of a garlic pickle into his mouth and trudged off in that gangly walk of his.

Hudson's thoughts returned to Jack Brown. That was not his real name, of course; the real name had been clouded by so many aliases that the most recent was simply the most convenient. He had drifted into the neighborhood just like the other flotsam and jetsam; the Eleventh Precinct seemed to contain an amalgam of things attractive to riffraff. Unfortunately, Brown had been there for 18 months before Hudson had taken notice.

The phone rang in the outer office, empty now but for Fatzinger, until Hudson made the evening assignments. At the moment the desk sergeant was helping a patrolman restrain a mean drunk in the lockup at the rear of the station. It rang again, an abrasive clanking like the sound made by chains being jerked through a tin pipe.

"It's da squire, Lootenant," Fatzinger shouted. "Are you in or out?"

He groaned and got up, noting as he approached the telephone that Fatzinger had again pinned something strange on his tunic.

"What the hell's that?"

"An eck, Lootenant. I got it up home in Ebenezersville. Dey bet me I couldn't shtuff six piggled ecks in my moudt. I showed dem! It ain't real, y'know, chust fer nice."

Hudson shook his head.

"Sorry about this morning, Larry," the magistrate's voice squawked on the other end. "You took off before I had a chance to say I was as unhappy as you were to let him go."

"I doubt that very much."

"I don't know how you can doubt it. I have two little girls myself."

"I'm not the only one who thinks he did it. Dr. Blakeley studied the evidence and agrees with me. He thinks Brown's a classic psychopath."

"But I'll bet Blakeley didn't advise you to try to hold him on that evidence."

"I didn't ask."

"I didn't think so."

"Look, we traced him all the way back to San Francisco and they said he left town under similar circumstances. The same thing happened in St. Louis. If we could have held him, they had a few questions to ask, too."

"We couldn't hold him and you know it. It's all too goddamn circumstantial. His lawyer could turn us into village idiots."

"I'll find the bodies. You can bet your ass on that."

"I hope so, Larry, because I'll bet my ass he won't stick around Philly very long after this morning."

They hung up. Hudson picked up a paper-weight and threw it across the room. It hit the wall with the sound of a shotgun blast.

Chapter Five

The kitchen was so hot that he felt at times he would pass out and fall into the expensive bone china, or maybe get so dizzy that he would mishandle some of the Waterford. It did not help that he had been assigned a vest and jacket to be worn over a stiff shirt and a heavy apron to be worn over all of that.

Maids, busboys and kitchen help, chattering busily, now and then bickering over who had spilled what, flew by as if on skates. No one seemed to notice him. He, however, had spied the two women from the trolley, both now dressed primly in black and white, looking laundered by God but swearing like a pair of dock foremen.

If they had walked westward along the path and he had gone northeast over the hill with Grover and Pluto, and they had been at the estate when he got there, what the hell kind of a game, he wondered, was somebody playing with him? Grover and Pluto had been twisting his dick ever since he met them, and he did not like it. Probably took him on the long, bumpy ride just to see if he would get sick. There would come a time, soon, when he would have to straighten them out.

He felt his pants leg for the contours of his knife and felt a little more secure when he touched it.

He put the last of the dessert plates on the stack and bent backwards with a grunt, stretching and realizing that there were many parts of his body that had not been in use for some time. There had been little time to relax. Someone— he seemed to recall Grover—had told him that help would arrive when the dishes from the main course were brought in, but there had been no one.

But the pickings were good, and he had not had to share them. First had come the bowls of politely unfinished turtle soup, cold by that time but reeking of cooking sherry, then the small dishes of veal salad with artichoke hearts—his first ever—then the large plates of roast goose in orange sauce with gobs of trimmings, then untouched caviar—again, his first ever—and here and there a tiny glass containing wines that must have come from France. Life at this grand estate seemed to Tony an eternal Christmas dinner.

The pace had definitely slowed; there had been no trays delivered for the past five minutes.

Dessert that evening was chocolate cake and vanilla ice cream with some kind of syrupy sauce on top. He scooped up a generous serving of each and looked for a quiet place to finish his dinner.

The frump entered, gave him a no-nonsense glare as she passed and sat in a corner under an open window. In another minute she was snoring, feet propped up on a nearby crate. The voices that had been drifting in from the dining room soon faded, and the scullery was peaceful.

He settled into a chair near the icebox and scooped up huge portions of dessert with a tablespoon, looking around to be sure that no one saw him licking the brandy sauce from his plate. He took off his apron and the sweat-soaked jacket, lit up a stogie, and sipped a jelly jar full of wine that he had been collecting over the evening. No matter if the wines had been red, white, pink, dry or fruity, the collected dregs were better than anything he had sipped in his life.

Somewhere nearby, a couple of young girls, their chores finished, giggled and chatted privately. The small orchestra, a piano, two violins and a clarinet, was playing a delicate Strauss medly somewhere farther away. In the shrubs behind the open window there were crickets and other night sounds.

"Hey! Who the hell sez you could smoke in the kitchen?"

Pluto's pallid face was staring through the door which opened into the hallway, keeping the kitchen a respectful distance from the dining room. When he was not speaking, Pluto breathed through an open mouth and did his best to look like a threat.

"If you really want me to put it out, you might not like where I'll put it."

"Where you gonna put it, wino, huh?"

Tony jumped up, his hand close to the pocket that contained the knife.

"Let's go outside, just you 'n me, and I'll show ya."

Pluto laughed.

"I'm really scared a you, wino, no shit."

"Let's go," Tony repeated.

Pluto smiled a weasel's smile, but refused to take a step. He was holding a bundle of something and Tony wondered whether it was a weapon.

"Anyways," Pluto said, the smile fading, "they sent me to tell ya your big break is about to happen. One a the waiters got sick. Musta snuck too much booze."

"So what?"

"So? Put these on and get to work, ya dumb wino!"

Pluto tossed him a black tie and jacket. They hit him in the face before he could catch them.

"I . . . I don't wanna do that."

He had visions of himself spilling something gooey and expensive on somebody important. What if he threw up out of panic and somebody told the sister?

"The sister said I was a dishwasher," he protested.

"Y'know, I don't think you're happy here."

"Can't you find anybody else? I don't know

nothin' about bein' a waiter," he pleaded, his voice slightly above a whisper.

He looked at the tie and jacket. Even the uniform made him nervous. He thought about quitting.

Pluto felt a little braver now and took a step and a half closer.

"Maybe I'm jist gonna go up there and tell them the wino ain't happy. Whattaya think?"

The tray was laden with after-dinner liqueurs that he hoped to sample before the evening was over. Might as well make the best of it. The tray was not very heavy fortunately, because he was feeling a touch of the palsy that always came on when he started to dry out. For him it had been an abstemious period. And then there were the butterflies, now bigger and more fluttery than ever.

His route was up the wide marble stairway over a red carpet to the second level. He passed naked statuary, medieval tapestries and knights in hollow armor. The lighting was dim, cast off by lamps hidden in deep alcoves.

His destination was a room in the east wing. He knocked and Grover, now dressed in a butler's tie and tails, opened the door. Tony was surprised to see that it was not just a supper party; it was more like a costume ball.

"Took ya long enough, wino."

"But I didn't spill nothin', right?"

"I dunno. Didja?"

"You got goose grease on yer shirt."

"Jist serve the guests, wino."

"Sure thing."

Meandering through the crowd and distributing drinks, he noticed that the costumes were a little unusual. There were no clowns, Napoleons or Indian chiefs, not even a witch. There were only religious figures—monks, prelates and nuns in various kinds of habits of brown, gray, black and white. He counted three monsignors, two bishops, a cardinal, and a pair of mother superiors. Not being a churchgoing man himself, their presence did not help his nerves.

A bishop, or maybe it was an archbishop— hard to tell—took the last glass of cognac. Tony thought his eyes looked strange but the cleric turned his back before he had a good look.

He filled his tray with empty glasses and started to leave, feeling much less uneasy with his new surroundings and his future place in them. The first trip had to be the worst one.

"The door's locked, Grover."

"I know. I locked it."

"Well, open it, all right?"

"No. I don't think so, wino."

"Anybody ever tell you you got a stupid sense a humor?"

But Grover was not smiling.

"Uh-uh. They usually compliment me on my sharp wit."

"I gotta get more drinks for the guests. Open the door."

"They don't need no more drinks. Whattaya think this is, the Sink?"

Grover stood his ground, blocking the doorway with his large body.

The room was silent which he had not realized until now. He turned and saw the guests staring at him. Their eyes, too, looked strange—cowled monks and nuns with piercing, manic eyes.

He spun around. Grover put a large hand on his chest and he backed up.

A chant that he could not quite make out was swelling gradually in the back of the gathering. It sounded vaguely like Latin, but Tony had never been much of a scholar, and the only time he had ever heard it was in the nightly ranting of a mad, defrocked priest on one of the many cell blocks he'd called home.

"What the hell is this, Grover?"

"Didn't Pluto tell ya this was your big break? You're the center of attention, wino—the honored guest."

Te Diabolem laudamus. Lucifer, dominus moscarum, in honore tuum nunc bibimus . . .

The guests raised their glasses and emptied them.

"I don't need no break."

"Sure ya do, wino. What the hell, you ain't exactly settin' the world on fire."

He heard Pluto's little hyena laugh from somewhere nearby, but Grover did not crack a smile. His face was blockish brutality itself.

Muscarias tuas consumamus . . .

"Get outa my way, you!"

He slammed his tray against Grover's ample stomach and glass shattered all around them. When Grover cursed and lunged for his throat, he slipped by and tried to open the door. The knob would not turn. His palms were sweaty, and his mouth tasted like alum. He yanked the doorknob with all his strength, but he was seized by a pair of monks and wrestled away from it.

In honore tuum peccatores sumus . . .

Grover and the monks dragged him across the room. The crowd parted, a curtain opened, and he saw what seemed to be a mound of stones in the center of a small space. In the shadows was a cloaked figure, its back turned.

Lucifer, the cloaked figure entoned in a piercing voice, *Ecce agnum tuum . . .*

Tony managed to pull out his knife and dig it deeply into Grover's shoulder. He had aimed for the throat, but Grover had ducked and the blade had glanced off his cheek and landed just below the collarbone. Grover howled in pain as the monks wrested the knife away from Tony. He cursed and pleaded at the top of his voice, but the chant was now loud enough to drown out his words.

In honore tuum, O Lucifer, peccamus . . .

A bishop in a tall black headdress stepped forward and bowed solemnly toward the cloaked figure. The figure turned. The eyes were those of a cat whose prey was cornered and crippled and could only hope that death would not be stubborn. She smiled when she saw him, a cold smile of indescribable cruelty.

"Sister?"

The bishop assisted her, chanting as she raised her arms and her black cloak parted.

In honore tuum, O Lucifer, corpores nostros denudamus!

The crowd repeated that as the figure was

revealed in stark torchlight, astounding in her nakedness.

"Sister? Is it you?"

She was by far the most magnificent woman he had ever seen. Once in prison someone had smuggled in a picture torn out of a book, a picture of a naked statue. Someone who could read had said it was a goddess named Venus, and he had dwelled on her magnificence for long torturous nights. With the cloak covering her arms just below the shoulders he could swear right now that she had stepped out of that picture. The skin was ivory. It seemed to glow in the firelight. The breasts were large and brazen, swaying gently as she drifted toward him. She seemed to move without touching the ground.

The monks forced him onto the stony altar. He gagged as he breathed the heavy, acrid incense.

In honore tuum mali sumus, enim interficiantes . . .

They held him down and tore away his clothing. Above their eerie chanting he could hear Grover cursing the pain in his shoulders and swearing that he would kill any monk who tried to keep him from Tony's throat. He felt the stones on his back, cold and hard.

The naked figure approached and hovered over him for a moment. She was humming something unintelligible in that high, piercing voice. Her nipples were puckered in excitement, her lush black bush only inches from his eyes. His terror left him briefly as he wondered, hoped, begged aloud that this was only some kind of sex ritual the idle rich had invented for tonight's amusement. He would do anything, of course. He knew all the tricks. You don't spend all that time in prison without learning the ins and outs. Maybe he'd even show them a new thing or two. Anything that comes to mind, Sister. She was beautiful, a goddess, the most desirable woman in . . .

The bishop handed her a dagger. Tony gasped. "What're ya gonna do, Sister? No, please . . ."

He heard Pluto's laugh again. He felt Grover's huge hands on his throat, and his head snapped back. The naked figure raised the dagger overhead in both hands and chanted in a strange, frightening pitch.

Lucifer! Sanguinem iuius cani offerimus . . .

The dagger plunged downward. His body convulsed. He heard himself screaming.

Te Diabolem laudamus . . .

The dagger plunged again and again and again.

Chapter Six

There was a downpour that morning, and Lieutenant Hudson had been caught in it. Soaking wet he resembled an aging terrier. He took a clean towel from a neat pile on a medicine cabinet and rubbed his sparse hair vigorously.

And that also afforded him an excuse to look away from the sight on the table.

He had seen worse during his 20 or so years on the force, but this morning his stomach was unprepared for it. Blakeley was still poking around, explaining something to Sergeant McBride. They could go on like that for hours. Blakeley loved an audience.

Hudson was anxious to get back to the station and try again to deal with a very aggravating burglar. It annoyed him that the department had dumped another dead bum in his lap. The Eleventh abounded in dead bums, and he could only hope that maybe one day Jack Brown would be among them, but these dead bums had some odd things in common. And even if they came from nowhere and everywhere, it just happened that most of them had turned up in his precinct, six in the last four months. Then there was the burglar, the one the papers were calling Kid Slippery, hitting every big taxpayer in the neighborhood, getting City Hall on his back, threatening his equilibrium, helping Jack Brown to stir up the gastric juices that lived in uneasy peace with his ulcer. On top of that was the war, that idiotic business with Spain, luring away most of his best men, and now he was probably going to have to assign McBride to this crap. It was only a matter of time, he was sure, before McBride would buy him a strong drink and announce that he too was joining up.

"Does he have a name?" Blakeley asked.

"Yeah. McBride did some digging."

"His name is Jacob Anthony Miller, Dr. Blakeley. We knew him better as Tony the Swordsman. Got drunk and cut up a prostitute in Wheeling and did a stretch in Moundsville. Later on he knifed a fellow wino in Pittsburgh in an argument over fifteen cents and did nine months in the county jail there. Another stretch, this time for sodomy involving a retarded girl, for which he served eight years in Graterford. There's more, but you get the picture. He's been in Philadelphia for the last two or three years."

Hudson shook his head and grumbled.

"Lucky us."

But it was good to have Blakeley along, and that was the first stroke of good luck Hudson had had in weeks.

When this most recent bum turned up in the alley behind Saint Malachi's Church yesterday morning and he noted the familiar signs, he seriously considered an early retirement. Granted, the pension was a bad joke, but he had invested wisely, quietly taking small savings out of his policeman's salary and buying railroad stock over the years. There was the little bungalow on a stretch of sand near Wildwood, a secret guarded carefully by him and the little woman lest they be invaded regularly by everyone looking for a cheap way to show the grandkids the Jersey shore. He meant it, he told the little woman—Gladys to others, Glad to him. He was all set to flip his badge on the commissioner's desk and go off to count sandpipers and sip his sarsaparilla. Only he knew he couldn't do that and still screw Jack Brown's wiener to the wall.

Then Blakeley told McBride that something about the bums fascinated him.

The man's face was, in a morbid way, fascinating. It was frozen in horror—mouth agape, tongue protruding, eyes bulging and yellowed by broken blood vessels. His photograph had caused a few gulps and gasps even among the jaded down-and-outers from Wharf Street to Kensington before McBride had finally established Tony Miller's identity somewhere in the foul cluster of tenements and tar paper hovels called The Sink.

"Certainly went out badly," Blakeley opined.

"They all did," Hudson replied.

"This badly?"

"The first one showed up a little after the New Year in a grave they'd just dug in St. Patrick's cemetery. The old guy who found it passed out and fell in, right on top of the corpse. He said the mutilation was the most shocking thing he'd ever seen."

Blakeley, however, saw no mutilation to speak of.

"Whoever did it shows some skill. Look there, Lieutenant, how the heart has been removed through a relatively small incision without much damage to surrounding tissue. I've seen clumsier work done in laboratories."

Hudson forced himself to look at the body.

"Yeah, they're getting better at it."

"Practice makes perfect," McBride said. "The first two had incisions the size of grapefruit. There were bones and severed muscle sticking out in all directions, and . . ."

He noticed Hudson turning the color of the corpse.

"Uh, sorry, Lieutenant."

Hudson remained stony-faced.

"Unfortunately, Dr. Blakeley, he isn't exaggerating. I had the privilege of investigating them. This almost looks like a different killer's work. I hope I'm wrong about that."

Blakeley stepped over to a table a few feet from where the body rested and poured himself a cup of tea. The laboratory and research library took up a substantial portion of his spacious home. It was in the basement where sunlight could pour through ground level windows and where it was possible to look out across the sprawling grounds and watch the Schuylkill flowing eastward into the city. He watched a sculling crew from one of the universities practicing for the spring races.

"If I could have a look at them for comparison, I might be able to determine that, but I doubt I'll get much cooperation from the coroner's office after the Beecham debacle."

Hudson smiled for the first time. He had never been fond of either the coroner or Judge Magwood, especially the latter, who had often derided the department in court.

"St. Malachi's church and St. Patrick's cemetery," Blakeley went on. "Are the victims always deposited on or near sacred ground?"

"Yes, and without any religious preference. We've found more of them on Catholic property because our precinct has a lot of Catholic parishes, but one of them turned up on the Methodist parsonage grounds a couple of weeks ago. Somebody has a grudge against religions, wouldn't you say?"

"But you've never found a body actually inside the church?"

"That's correct. They stop short of that kind of desecration."

The word desecration sounded strange in his own ear. It was the one uttered by Glad when he had first mentioned the bums on the church lawn. Hudson himself never went to church, rarely even thought about it. Ever since the day over 30 years ago when he lied about his age to get out of Camden and into the Civil War he had seen too many signs of how feeble the Ten Commandments could be when man had to choose between them and his baser drives. To him the churches in his precinct—and there were many—were no different from the markets and taverns and offices and stables in the precinct. They were just things to be protected, sometimes to be avenged. He had no animosity, of course. Glad was a churchgoer—every Sunday and Holy Day of Obligation at St. Canicus and marathons during the lenten season—and there were times when he would take her there, give her some change for Father O'Grady's many collections and sit patiently until the Mass was over. He never even complained about the dirty looks and self-righteous huffing of the old biddies as they left the church and spied him on a park bench reading his Sunday paper. Glad herself had long since despaired of his sudden conversion, and he knew she was praying and lighting candles that he would see it her way one day. She meant well.

"That may mean something," Blakeley mused.

"Yeah. I'll grab at anything right now."

"Seems a strange way to die in Philadelphia."

"I take it you're interested enough to take it on?"

"Eh?" Blakeley toyed with his beard and ex-

80

changed looks of conspiracy with McBride. "It is rather challenging . . ."

"All right, all right, you've got him—but only for a couple of weeks. I'm real short on detectives right now."

"But, Lieutenant," McBride gulped, "you still have Fatzinger."

But Hudson was already at the door and had paid no attention. It was just as well. He was not, obviously, in a jocular mood. Such illtimed humor had sometimes resulted in a lengthy assignment near a compost heap.

"May I offer you a spot of tea before you leave, Lieutenant? There's a slight chill in the air and you've not had time to dry off."

"Gotta get back to politics and papers, Dr. Blakeley. Thank you—and please try to wrap this up quickly."

He was out the door, and Blakeley and McBride were smiling. They had always worked well together.

"Nathan, this Miller chap, was he known to have unusual tastes in food?"

"In food, no. In other things . . ."

"I realize it sounds preposterous, but could he have developed an epicurean palate?"

Blakeley had put his tea aside and was reexamining the wreckage that used to be Tony Miller, as debased in death as he was in life. Before Hudson had obtained the writ and had the body taken to Blakeley's lab, an attendant at the morgue had inadvertently destroyed evidence by burning the victim's trousers and underwear. It was tempting to think it had been done to spite Blakeley once the coroner had read the order. McBride had said so.

"Honest to God, Sergeant, nobody ordered me to," the attendant had sworn.

"Well, what the hell were you thinking of? This is a murder victim, for Chrissake."

"Yeah, I know, but he . . . messed."

"They all mess."

"They don't mess like this one, Sergeant. I mean, he musta been scared, y'know, shitless."

And not long ago Blakeley had also observed dryly that Tony the Swordsman had been in an advanced stage of syphilis at his time of death.

"An epicurean palate in the Sink?"

"To be sure, to be sure. I thought it was a silly question, but let me show you some data."

There was a clipboard attached to the foot of the examination table with a forensic form on top. Blakeley's notes could be confusing, even to other pathologists, until he explained his shorthand. McBride understood many things that Blakeley had not yet decided to share with his scientific colleagues, mostly because he liked the young detective more than he ever had his peers.

"I was not unmoved by the look on his face," Blakeley said. "It reminds me of self-portraits painted by inmates of a madhouse. So just out of personal curiosity, I decided to look for traces of an anaesthetic—any kind of anaesthetic, legal or otherwise, though I'd hoped to find something traceable to a manufacturer or distributor. Nothing. Absolutely nothing. The people who did this are sadistic beyond belief. As you know, Nathan, even the poor wretches sacrificed in the Mayan temples were given opium before their hearts were torn out of their bodies. But there was little to be found in this particular wretch's bloodstream, save some residual alcohol. He died in extreme agony. So I opened his stomach, and again I found nothing resembling a painkilling drug."

The bruises on the arms, legs, shoulders and in particular the throat suggested he had been held down by some very powerful hands while the cutting went on. Three, perhaps four, people, besides the one wielding the knife, were involved.

Blakeley continued.

"But I did find something in there to pique one's imagination. The chap dies less than an hour after eating, and it seems his last meal consisted of roast goose, veal in mustard and parsley sauce, caviar and artichoke."

"Artichoke?"

"I thought you'd find that curious."

"I'm surprised he knew they were edible. They must have looked like weeds or something."

"Quite. Personally, I cannot abide the little devils. However, they fit our purpose admirably. They've become one of the fashionable foods lately, served by and to the conspicuously comfortable. I've no doubt that Jacob Anthony Miller was on the periphery of some very select gathering, found out that artichoke was a delicacy like caviar, and virtually gorged himself. Gulped down half-chewed as they were, they digest rather slowly."

"I'm sure I can find out which restaurants had them on the menu the other night," McBride said. "There aren't many suppliers."

"Preferably served with roast goose and veal salad."

"And then we may deduce that he broke in, ate a spectacular meal, was caught in the act, and executed by an outraged maître d! Excelsior! We've solved it!"

Blakeley's son, Ralphie, "Beef" to his friends, passed by the open window, pushing a lawn mower. Since his abrupt discharge from the army a few weeks before he had been on painfully good behavior. Whatever had transpired between the large, likeable Ralphie and the colonel's lusty and not-too-cautious wife during that beachfront rendezvous a few miles from the Tampa encampment might very well remain a mystery forever, especially from his mother. Blakeley himself knew the story well, and he tended to blush and turn away, disguising his mirth whenever it came up. Whatever the truth, the colonel had wanted to get Ralphie out of Tampa in a hurry, and only a clerical error had saved him from a hitch in the Everglades. Sooner or later, over a pitcher of beer, Beef would tell Nathan the whole story.

And, like everything else in Beef's history, it would not be a colorless tale.

His parents still clung to fond hopes that some school with an ambitious football program and hardly any academic standards at all would accept him soon. Someone had mentioned one in North Dakota.

Blakeley pointed to another item on the form.

"And this may or may not mean something, but I found a few samples of cat fur, most of them in his hair, but one stuck to his eyebrow. I checked it against some I borrowed from Thomas Aquinas."

Thomas Aquinas, resting contentedly beside his saucer of milk, rolled over and stretched, displaying a wide, snowy tummy, and made a squeaking sound, as though he understood that he was the topic of discussion. He had a set of white whiskers on a black background, which gave him a look of permanent astonishment.

McBride had found him one freezing night, buried up to his neck in a snowbank, barely visible but for his tiny black ears, but mewing loudly enough to be heard over the din of trolleys, hucksters, Christmas shoppers and Salvation Army bands. His first meal in days was a random selection from McBride's icebox— meatloaf, hard salami, and a chicken leg that they shared because McBride himself had missed a few meals that week. McBride named him after his favorite philosopher and they lived together in perfect harmony until the kitten was discovered by the landlady, who threatened to drown him or do worse at the first opportunity. Calla W. Allcock distrusted all living things. "Especially cats. They sit on yer face at night and smudder yiz! Everybody knows that! What the hell do youse think this is—the goddamn pound or somethin'? They give yiz the dropsy, cats. If I

catch the little sonofabitch, I'll stomp it flat!"
And so Thomas Aquinas became a member of
the Blakeley household and, like Ralphie, had
grown to impressive dimensions. This was especially true of his tail, a proud black plume which
could easily have graced a hat worn by Louis
XIV or his courtiers.

McBride studied the short, thin hairs in a Petri
dish and recalled some misleading evidence in a
case some time ago.

"Any chance his body was a warm bed for the
neighborhood cats that night? I mean after he
was deposited there among the piles of trash
where they gather. It was cold, as I recall, a full
moon."

"That did cross my mind, Nathan, but the fur
was much too elegant. Healthy, well-groomed,
no sign of its ever having housed a tick or a flea.
When I analyse it further, I suspect it will prove
to be from a special breed. I dare say, our
Thomas Aquinas there might very well envy it.
Very privileged creature."

Thomas Aquinas heard his name and looked
up.

Victor, the butler, entered without knocking.
He was out of breath.

"Sir, a gentleman on the phone for you."

"Victor, as you can see, I'm at work."

Victor noticed the body on the table, turned
greenish-gray and stepped back.

"I thought it sounded important," he sputtered.

"Did you ask the name?"

"Something like Sceptre. Or was it Spectral?"

"Bernard Spector?"

"That is it, sir." Victor collected himself. There was a thinly veiled hint of smugness now. "He told me I might call him 'Bernie'."

"Tell him I'm indisposed."

"But—"

"Victor?"

"But, sir, it's the press."

Blakeley glowered. Victor tried to look him in the eye but failed. He took another step backward.

"Yes, sir."

He turned and stomped out the door.

"He'll pout now," Blakeley said, grinning. "That's good. It will keep him out of the way."

"True. But Spector will know you have the body."

Blakeley sipped his tea and sighed.

"Oh, I don't doubt he'll know a number of things. All it will cost him is a few bottles of gin."

Chapter Seven

A gentle breeze from somewhere out in the Atlantic made its way up the bay along the Delaware and into the Schuylkill, drifting over the riverbanks and across the drive, climbing over the horse and cooling off the cab. The sun at eleven had already dried up most of the mud from that morning's cloudburst. It was a good day to have a canopy overhead.

Fatzinger kept the horse at a slow trot because he knew by the look on Hudson's face that he did not want to be jostled.

"Dr. Blakeley hass vun nice haus dere," he said, burping. "Wonderful good eadts, too."

"Yes, he does."

"Huh?"

Hudson was preoccupied again, mostly by something the magistrate had said on the telephone the other night. If he had indeed caused

Jack Brown to leave town in a hurry by tipping him off that he was a prime suspect, Hudson would never forgive himself. Neither would many of the parents in the precinct.

Goddamnit, he knew Brown was his man. The slimy bum had done it the same way the San Francisco people described it. He had got a job near a school, watched the little girls long enough to know when they came and went, where from, where to, when they were escorted, when they were not. Then he picked out a few favorites.

"Do you know if dott cook iss shpoken for?"

"What?"

"Missus Whosediss, da cook. Anybody got da hooks in her?"

"How the hell would I know? Anyway, I thought you had a girl friend up in Ebenezersville. Huckleberry or something."

"Strawberry Knockelknorr. Vell, dere's a lotta guys up dere dat got der eyes on dott cow. Und chust between you and me und da horse, she's prob'ly been gettin' diddled in da bushes."

"Bones, the cook is old enough to be your mother."

"Beauty ain't everyting, Lootenant," Fatzinger belched.

They turned off the tree-lined river drive and climbed a hill on a road that led to another, wider road and then onto a boulevard where the street noise drowned out Fatzinger and made it easier to concentrate.

Hudson should have been thinking about the burglar, he knew.

Just this morning there had been another message from City Hall, but this one contained a deadline. While someone was carving up Tony Miller, someone else was opening a safe in a wealthy merchant's home on Lancaster Avenue. Gone were a roll of fifties, a coin collection and a silver samover heirloom. Left were a Ming vase and a rare manuscript dated 1679. At least there was a pattern of sorts now.

He knew he owed it to his career to show some concern about injustices perpetrated against the rich. After all, they have feelings, too.

Shit!

One of the little girls, missing since March, bothered him a lot more than the others. She used to bring him wildflowers on summer days. She sang a Christmas carol in a church pageant last winter. She was a tiny creature, a porcelain doll with dark saucer eyes, the granddaughter of a close friend.

The friend, like the little girl, was gone now— shock, strain, grief, coronary.

He was a little surprised that he could become outraged again. It had been a long time. The Eleventh had just closed a case on its own Jack the Ripper. Two or three months ago one slum-lord had burned down another's tenement be-cause of a poker debt and 15 immigrants had been trapped inside to cook. Just last week an old woman had neutered her 70-year-old hus-band with a pair of garden shears because she was convinced he was unfaithful. Hudson had seen just about anything that one could do to another out of anger, greed and jealousy, and it had all become just part of the goddamn game. Somehow or other, it all balanced out, like a successful merchant being outsmarted by a low-life and losing his coins and samovars.

But something like this . . .

He nudged Fatzinger in the ribs to avoid hitting a dog that had just wandered into the street. The dog, a little mutt, brown with a bushy tail, put up his chin proudly, yapped at the cab and took his time crossing.

When they swerved and slowed down, Hudson started to swear.

"Holy Jumpin' Jesus."

"Vott iss?"

"I just saw the sonofabitch going down Friday's alley. He came out of that drugstore."

"Who?"

"Never mind. Stop the wagon. I'll see you later."

"Oh, now I get it. You're gonna chase down dott shtreet Chack Brown!"

"Listen, Bones, I stopped at that drugstore because my stomach was acting up and I was out of Beeman's, just in case anybody asks."

"Vell, I . . ."

Brown was his casual self, kicking an empty tin can along the littered ground and chewing on handfuls of jelly beans. If one fell to the ground on the way from bag to mouth, he scooped it up and tried again.

Hudson wondered if candy had been used to lure the little girls. He wondered if Brown might lead him to the children. He even wondered, desperately, if they might be living children.

He stepped carefully and stayed close to the sooty walls and rancid trash cans, staying about 50 yards behind Brown, ignoring the sometimes powerful odors. Friday's alley used to be Duckenfeld Street, but two generations knew it by its unofficial name because of the fish markets whose loading docks jutted into it. It was smelly but convenient, with many niches to step into should Brown decide to look around.

He watched him turn a corner and proceed down another alley where there were more open spaces, which meant he had to allow a little more distance to grow between them.

Then Brown saw another tin can, kicked and missed as he passed it, and turned around to try again. Hudson stopped in his tracks and stood still, hoping the dilapidated wooden backstairs leading up to a burned-out second floor would hide him.

Brown did not look up, concentrating instead on the tin can. When he had it lined up he kicked it ahead of him and continued up the alley. Hudson followed.

There were lots of abandoned buildings in this neighborhood, some turned to char, others discarded by enterprises fleeing the crime and blight for safer locations. There were lots of places where a bum could take his chances on the rats and feral gangs and get out of the storm on a bad night, places where bodies can get lost amid the other refuse, places where children could disappear as certainly as if it were quicksand instead of brick and rotting lumber.

And then suddenly Brown spied an unbroken

third floor window and turned around to look for a rock.

His face turned ashen when he saw Hudson almost within striking distance.

They ran down the alley, ducking under wooden slats and other pieces of building exteriors, in and out of piles of crates and more trash cans, scattering a group of crap-shooting children who cursed them like army sergeants, turning suddenly out of the alley and onto the main street then back into the alley.

Larry Hudson was still surprisingly fast for his years. Ulcers did not necessarily slow down everything. In fact, they had forced him to give up cigarettes ten years ago, and now he was almost as fast as he was when he lied about his age to get into the army and out of Camden. And he was twice as tough, a wiry, battle-hardened welterweight.

Brown shoved a pile of crates into Hudson's path and climbed over a wall that the city had put up years ago to keep pedestrians out of the way of the stone facing that fell at random from an old building.

He could hear Brown's footsteps as he climbed the wall, but when he climbed down the other side, Brown was gone.

He opened his collar and felt tiny streams of sweat trickling down his chest. He had lost his hat three blocks back.

It was cooler inside, chilled by the dank pool that had grown in the basement and which cast off rancid, deathly smells. Brown would be dangerous in there. It was his milieu.

Hudson held his breath and started in, moving carefully in the shadowy places but staying just close enough to the light to make himself a less than perfect target. Halfway into the cavernous shell he spied a large hole in the floor and heard the steady, muted dripping of water into the basement.

He also heard a faint noise behind him.

A hunting knife, the kind with a thick blade for gutting prey, sank into a wooden beam less than a couple of inches from his eyes. He hit the ground instinctively.

At least he had an idea now about Brown's general direction. There was a brief, scrambling noise, then silence again, but for the panicky squealing of rats in the basement.

He got up and started to move in. There was a chance that Brown had a second knife and it was unsettling to know he could throw it like a circus performer, but the odds were even better that Brown was scared enough to miss again.

Closer to the rubble in the corner where he was now almost certain Brown was hiding he spotted something on the ground and smiled as he picked it up. It was black, and at first he had dismissed it as something left by the rats. He looked again and saw a pink one, two orange, one green, then all kinds of them in a trail leading in a circle around the rubble. Praise the Lord for jelly beans, he thought, and jumped headlong into the rubble.

Brown screamed and tried to scramble away but slipped on something slimy and fell.

A left jab, a right cross, a foot in the crotch, and Brown was on the floor.

"Whattaya want, Hudson? Whattaya want?"

"The kids, assface. Where are they?"

"What kids? I don't know nothin' about no kids. I told you that at the magistrate's!"

After a right in the stomach, a left on the cheek and two more rights in the face, Brown was bleeding from the nose and mouth.

"Are they in here, Brown? You dumped them in one of these old buildings, didn't you?"

"You're outa your fuckin' mind, Hudson."

And that brought on a flurry of kicks and punches from the old Camden street fighter that left Brown on all fours, groaning and cursing.

"You're my man, Brown. You know it. You took those little girls somewhere, you violated them and you killed them. And you have a better chance of becoming the King of England than getting away from me. You hear me?"

He kicked Brown's face as if it were a football at the opening of a game. Brown fell backwards, then staggered slowly to his feet, a sick, bloody smile registering slowly in the sunlight.

"But you and me both know you can't do shit without the bodies, don't you, Hudson? The magistrate as much as called you an asshole for even tryin'." The smile became a taunting laugh. "And you ain't gonna find nothin', Hudson. Nothin!"

Hudson watched and listened for a few seconds. Then he knew what he had to do.

Chapter Eight

The docks were bustling that morning, and the channel seemed unusually crowded. A military band was playing a Sousa march as members of the Pennsylvania Sixteenth, impressive in their blue tunics and tan slouch hats, their shining Krag-Jorgenson rifles resting on their shoulders, marched up to the river's edge and stepped aboard the troop carrier. They were on their way to Puerto Rico, he heard somebody say. He recognized a few friends who winked and smiled as they passed. When the officers looked away, some of them even spoke.

"*Cuba libre*, Sarge."

"How's the ole hammer hangin'?"

"Don't let Hudson get on your nerves."

"We'll send you some *frijoles*."

McBride had a lot of friends in the Sixteenth, in the Twenty-eighth as well—college buddies, people he grew up with in Saint Canicus parish, fellow members of the Eleventh Precinct, even a few gents he once bested in the ring in his boxing days.

There were times, more of them recently, when he seriously considered joining up, seeing the Caribbean and maybe even the Hawaiian Islands, places that had been in his mind since grade school. He was probably cheating himself, friends had said. Detective work can get so boring, and in the army he would make officer's rank in no time.

Only Lieutenant Hudson would probably have a stroke if he even brought up the subject, and he had a massive respect for Lieutenant Francis Lawrence Hudson.

Horse-drawn carriages were parked three deep near another pier where passengers were disembarking a sleek liner just in from Hamburg. That had been the "in" place with the Main Line crowd until recently when the Germans wavered on whom they liked better in the war with Spain. Now they were coming home in droves, puffed up with patriotic indignation.

Reporters and newspaper photographers cursed and jockeyed for position at the same pier as they awaited the arrival of Miss Lillian Russell, home after a triumphant tour of the Continent. Last night's *Inquirer* had said she intended to put on the same revue in its scandalous entirety right here in Philadelphia, and already the righteous were mobilizing. At a safe but conspicuous distance there were lean, gothic men in black and stony, determined women in

gray carrying Bibles, crosses and ominous placards. They reminded him of the Beecham jury.

He really wanted to catch a glimpse of her, the
chesty, brazen redhead who was said to have
inspired so many highly publicized divorces,
who was supposed to have caused bankruptcies
in New York, duels in Paris and riots in London.
They were calling her the latest wonder of the
world—Salome, Cleopatra and Marie Antoi-
nette in good old American bloomers, the Gib-
son Girl with a potent sexual appetite.

But with a build-up like that, she would have
to be a disappointment, so he decided to get on
with it.

He did pause for a moment to look at a
horseless carriage, a shiny black Winton DeLuxe
with white and gold trim. It was only the third
driving machine he had seen in his lifetime, but
it was definitely the most striking. Whatever they
were saying about the decadence of the Machine
Age, this was a true work of art. And it was
probably worth two years of his salary.

The proud owner, posturing in white coat and
goggles, noticed the look on his face and cast a
patronizing smile.

He trudged on through the top hats and
parasols, and soon the smells of the waterfront
were much less genteel. Wagons of many descriptions lined both sides of the street where
the freighters were being unloaded, and pedestrians had to be cautious about the horse drop-
pings.

The pedestrians themselves were also of a
different sort.

"Well, I'll be dipped in dog vomit, if it ain't the altar boy hisself."

The voice was whiskey deep, almost mannish. She was leaning against a warehouse wall, one foot propped up on a coil of hawser hemp, gold tooth glittering in the bright sun.

"A little early for you, isn't it, Goldie?"

"It ain't every day I get the chance ta see the boys off, ya know. Where the hell's your patriotism?"

"It must be quite a challenge, what with your customers marching double file and some of their mothers looking on."

"Where there's a will, ya know . . ."

"Something tells me you're really working for the enemy."

"Go to hell, McBride."

She laughed and lit up a panatela.

Goldie Becker's smile never reached her eyes. Her mouth turned down quickly into a flat, hardened sneer. The perfumed rice powder was perhaps a week old and about six layers deep over skin that betrayed miserable teen years a generous decade ago. No heart-of-gold variety this! It would be less than intelligent to turn one's back on her for long.

"So, you know what I'm doin' down here," she said. "What're you doin' on the docks? You been demoted?"

There was no need to explain that he was looking for artichokes.

"Did you know Tony Miller?"

"That bucket a piss?" She bit off a piece of

tobacco and spat it into the gutter. "Yeah, Tony the Swordsman."

"Somebody mistook him for a sacrificial chicken the other night."

"Yeah? You ain't thinkin' a hangin' somebody for that, are you?"

"You had something better in mind?"

She blew a thick cloud of smoke into the air.

"You wanna know how I got this gold tooth in the first place?"

"Would I care?"

"You might."

She blew smoke against his chest, just enough to annoy him. It was a foul cigar. When he waved at the air, she found that much funnier than it deserved to be.

"About your gold tooth," he suggested.

"Yeah, well, what it was was a couple a years ago it got real cold one night—rain, snow, lousy. So I didn't wanna go downtown and work the streets. Ya know, where you ran me in that time?"

"I never wanted to work vice. Besides, that was two years ago and it was nothing personal."

"Only tryin' to do your friggin' job, right?"

"Right."

"But so was I, ya know."

"And you do it well."

"Thank you," she said and curtsied sarcastically. "Anyways, Tony drops by and he's, ya know, in need of it and we talks it over. 'Okay,' I says, 'but I want it up front' cuz he's a well-known deadbeat. He gives me six bits and I lifts up my skirt, and when it's over he wants his six bits back! 'Whatsamatter?' I ask, as if I give a fart. 'Wasn't it no good?' Then he starts callin' me names and slappin' me around. Jeez, a black eye, black 'n blue ribs, a tooth knocked out, lip all swelled up like a darkie's, and he even takes everything out a my purse. The putz!''

Somewhere in the channel a freighter sounded its horn. Goldie cleared her throat and spat against the warehouse wall.

"I take it you don't miss him."

"The putz . . ."

"Well, there must be a happy ending to this because that's how you got your trademark, right?"

"Yeah." She blew some more smoke in his direction and savored the memory. "I got a ex-prizefighter, a guy that worshipped the dirt under my feet, to pay him a visit. Almost killed the sonofabitch. Made him replace my missin' front tooth with a gold one. A cheap one, too, it turns out. Keeps comin' loose. My real name ain't Goldie, ya know. It's Eliza Becker.''

"No, it isn't. It's Edna. Edna Becker. Age . . ."

"Oh, yeah," she said, "I guess you'd know that from bookin' me. Anyway, Eliza's more classier. Shit, now my cigar went out.''

He lit it for her and weighed a few possibilities in his mind.

A company of marines came into view, at parade rest now as they awaited orders to board the troop ship. Goldie was obviously distracted by them with visions of greenbacks dancing in her head. It promised to be a very productive summer.

It was time to exploit Goldie's greed.

"Don't turn around right away, but there are vice people down here."

"Wha?"

He shushed her.

"I said, don't look around."

"All right all right."

"Now, you see the one in the rolled-up shirtsleeves leaning against the post over there? Gray shirt, woolen cap?"

With his eyes he indicated a dockworker who had wandered away from his gang to smoke a cigarette and cool off for a few minutes.

"Tight pants and big muscles?" she leered.

"Yeah."

"That's Flaherty from the Eighth. He averages three collars a day."

"How come I never heard of him?"

"A lot of the vice people have been reassigned because of the war. You probably never work the Eighth Precinct. Rest assured, he knows who you are."

She eyed the dockworker for a moment, then the marines, then the dockworker again—and McBride won the first poker hand.

"Where are the other ones?" she asked, her voice just a little above a whisper.

"In due time."

"What the hell . . ."

"Tony Miller, during the last few days—"

"I told you—"

"Did he do anything different?"

"—everything I know!"

"Did he say anything to anybody?"

Her mouth fell open and she looked away.

"Aaaah, shit!"

"Was he seen with anybody out of the ordinary?"

"I mind my own business, McBride."

"Have it your way, Edna. Your summer profits could look like Wanamaker's at Christmas, but if prosperity means nothing to you . . ."

"I hated the bastard! Who the hell cares who stuck him?"

". . . all I have to do is nod and you'll spend the next three months scrubbing floors in the women's lockup."

"McBride, you are one rotten sonofa—"

"Now, now, we mustn't let the commanding officer hear you. He might take a good look and place you off-limits."

She clenched her teeth, threw up her arms and walked around in a complete circle until her anger was under control. It was a grossly exaggerated gesture, obviously designed to draw the marines' attention. She gestured with her smoking cigar.

"All I know is, he left the Edwards Street Mission the other day sayin' he had some job. Nobody paid no attention cuz you know how them winos go on about nothin'. Whatever it was, he was all puffed up about it, actin' like he was some kind a celebrity. He took a trolley somewheres, and that's it."

"Did he tell anybody where he was going?"

She shook her head.

"Was he alone when he left?"

"I dunno. Now, if you don't mind, McBride, I'd like to get on with business. So where are the other vice cops?"

He was silent, the look on his face unchanging. She waited a while, and when he did not blink, she glanced again at the marines and sighed.

"Some do-gooder come around lookin' for a dishwasher—they tell me—and hired Tony. Y'know how them sissy boys like to hang around the flophouses hopin' to rehabilitate some stewbum? Well, Tony was wise to that kind a shit, so he usually only went along with them until he could get them into some alley and clean out their wallets. So it took a special kind a do-gooder to flush him outa the Sink."

"That's much better, Goldie. Do you know the do-gooder's name?"

"Sister Mary somethin'-or-other."

"You mean . . ."

"You're real quick, McBride. That's right—a nun!"

She let out a short laugh. The teeth surrounding the gold one were heavily stained with nicotine and neglect, making her trademark stand out almost grotesquely.

McBride was silent. A nun? Arrest a nun for the murder of a Sink bum? That's all Hudson would need. His ulcers would multiply, divide and explode.

She cleared her throat.

"Oh yeah, sorry. You want to know about the vice cops."

"Before the war's over, if it ain't too much trouble."

"Listen closely. There's one near the motor car." He pointed at the gent with the condescending smile. "Name's O'Shaughnessy."

"Oh yeah? Where the hell did he get the motor car?"

"It doesn't work. Just a come-on," he intimated. "The other one's standing near that street lamp. Don't stare."

"Who you tryin' to dick, McBride? That's an old lady."

"Shhhhh . . ."

"It's a friggin' little old lady!"

"Just don't let her hear you making a suggestive overture."

She muttered a number of oaths about his mother and his sex life. He tipped his hat, thanked her for the information and went on toward the import-export warehouses. She bared the gold tooth as he passed, and as he crossed the street her obscenities grew louder.

After about 50 yards he felt a stone whizzing past his head, not far from his right ear. It hit a water wagon and ricocheted into the street, narrowly missing a draft horse.

He turned. She made an obscene gesture, and there were sounds of embarrassment among the onlookers. He tipped his hat again.

The smells of the waterfront were not always

rancid. Sometimes when a freighter just in from some tropical port was unloading a shipment of fruit, they were downright pleasant. Certainly, it was preferable to being downwind of Goldie Becker.

The rain that morning had left some deep puddles where the paved road ended and the reddish clay began, and horseflies seemed to grow out of the shallow mud.

The company name had not changed. It was still the Gazzo Brothers' warehouse, although Guglielmo "Fatso" Gazzo was long gone. Fatso had disappeared suddenly and thoroughly over ten years ago. It was said he had seen a vision, returned to Sicily and became a Trappist. It was also said he had been rent, spiced, ripened and stuffed into enough casings to hold his 250 pounds, and then shipped to a grocery in New York.

The first three men he asked to direct him to Nunzio, the surviving and obviously smarter Gazzo brother, pretended not to understand English while several others scurried to get the barrels of stolen olive oil out of sight. By the time he reached Nunzio Gazzo everything was in apparent order, with all the produce crates stacked neatly wherever he looked.

"You shake-a-dem up real good when you drop in unexpected, McBride."

Gazzo was chuckling and waving his index finger like a short, squat schoolmarm. Then he waved his arms animatedly to suggest a lot of frenzied activity.

"Andiamo! Andiamo! Carabinieri."

"Take my word for it, Signor Gazzo, I haven't the slightest interest in olive oil."

Gazzo was still chuckling, now feigning solemnity.

"Needer do I, McBride. Needer do I."

"Of course."

"Have a cup a coffee."

McBride passed politely. Gazzo's espresso could be used as a tar substitute.

"What I'm really interested in right now are artichokes."

"Artichokes? Pretty tough to come by now on accounta da war. We usta get 'em from Spain."

"Pretty expensive then?"

Gazzo rolled his eyes and groaned something in Sicilian.

"Friend a mine in Palermo, he buys dem offa some guy in Portugal, den he sells 'em ta me for arm 'n a leg! Some friend, huh?"

Gazzo made a gesture of contempt.

"Is there still much of a demand?"

"Snob appeal, dat's all."

Gazzo shrugged and thought. Discussing artichokes seemed to cause him to wince. Times were tough. Deals required arcane and often heart-wrenching decisions, not like the old days when a man could do business without feeling as if he'd just made a pact with the devil. Nobody trusts nobody no more.

"I could get twenny, maybe even twenny-five bucks a crate for dem, but I only ask eighteen. I don't tink it's nice ta make a profit on da war. Know what I mean?"

He sipped his espresso and swabbed his forehead with a white silk handkerchief which he folded neatly and returned to the lapel pocket. The other lapel sported a red carnation. Nunzio Gazzo was a dapper little man—white linen suit with vest, gray silk tie, gray spats over shoes whose shine could embarrass the spiffiest of the marines a few blocks away. Even his mustache showed great care in the waxing and pointing.

The tidy office was an oasis in a corner of the loud, bustling warehouse. A window looked out on the Delaware toward the southern end of Windmill Island where goods tossed quietly overboard from passing freighters were quickly picked up and ferried across the river to the Gazzo Brothers' warehouse. Besides the usual olive oil, marinated peppers and the like, there were now tons of government issue that had just happened to get lost on the way to the war. It promised to be a good summer for Nunzio Gazzo.

The office was somewhat austere in its furnishings, but for a handsome walnut desk, a dark leather couch, and a gold-framed portrait of the late Fatso, set in an honored place between Christ and Pope Leo XIII. Fatso was staring at the camera, doing his best to look God-fearing, upright and mercantile, but he looked more like someone passing a kidney stone.

Gazzo opened the door, shouted something into the warehouse, and in a few seconds a worker came in with two shiny red apples. Gazzo tossed one to McBride.

"Good fer da bowels, an apple a day. I guess

you don't have no trouble like dat at your age. So anyway, how come you're askin' about artichokes? Da commissioner wanna impress somebody at dinner tonight? Hey, take a coupla crates an' give him my regards."

McBride smiled and shook his head.

"Nothing like that at all, Signor Gazzo. It's part of a homicide investigation."

"Uh?"

Nunzio Gazzo's mouth tightened and his eyes flashed. McBride hastened to explain the situation, editing here and there, stressing above all that there was no apparent connection between the death of the derelict and Gazzo's wholesale produce—except that no one else on the Philadelphia docks was known to import artichokes.

Gazzo's mouth loosened. The little waxed mustache drooped gradually, but the eyes remained wary.

"Only one dat ever imported zucchini, eeder," he appended. "I betcha you never even heard a dat, zucchini." He pointed the stubby index finger in McBride's face, close enough to notice that the nails had been buffed and manicured professionally. "Pomegranates, too, 'til dat crook Shapiro uppa da road cut in." He sat back. "So, what can I tell you about da fruit business, McBride?"

"I need to know who bought your artichokes in the last week or two. What restaurants, what groceries, canneries—that kind of thing. Can you help me with that?"

"I can get you dat information, McBride."

He opened the door again and shouted something in Sicilian.

"No kiddin', McBride, dey really can cut you open and find out what you et?"

"Even when you ate it, approximately."

Gazzo shook his head.

"Ain't nothin' sacred no more."

"There's something else," McBride said uncomfortably. "Did you, by any chance, give a crate to a church lately?"

"A church?"

"Or a convent."

"What da hell you talkin' about? A church, a convent . . ."

"Or were any artichokes stolen from you lately?"

"Nobody steals off Nunzio Gazzo."

McBride bit into his apple and chewed, looking into Gazzo's eyes. It was a good way to hide discomfort.

A man in a dark suit entered, handed Gazzo a list, waited for approval, then handed it to McBride.

"You're a very generous man, Signor Gazzo. On behalf of the entire police department I want to thank you for your cooperation."

"It's only a copy of some invoices we sent out."

"But everyone in the south end of the city knows of your generosity. The altar of Mater Dei Church, where you worship daily, is magnificent. And I'm told you donated the marble, imported at your own expense from Italy."

"From Soano in Tuscany. You never heard of it, but it's da best. In memory of my late brudder Guglielmo, rest his soul. Dat's him nexta Jesus. Da udder one's my good friend, da Holy Fodder."

"I recognized him. I, too, am a Catholic, Signor Gazzo."

"I didn't give away no artichokes."

"I see."

"Too goddamn expensive."

"Eighteen dollars a crate, and you could get twenty-five."

"You got it straight."

McBride tapped his knuckles on the desk and continued to chew. He had the list he wanted. Now there was the matter of a graceful exit to negotiate.

Gazzo frowned.

"What's-a convent got ta do wid it?"

"We have to check out all the leads, you see. And the victim was last seen in the company of a nun."

McBride tossed his apple core into the wastebasket. Gazzo's knuckles whitened on the head of his walking stick.

"You sayin' a nun mighta done it?"

"I said, we have to check out all the leads."

"You ain't said nothin' yet."

"We're not sure of anything yet."

"You ain't gonna arrest no nun, McBride. I, Nunzio Attilio Gazzo, won't stand for it."

"Look, it isn't as if we want to arrest a nun."

"Arrest a nun." Gazzo made a fist and raised

his arm. "I changed my mind, McBride. Gimme da list back."

Gazzo's voice was only slightly above a whisper. The little waxed mustache twitched slightly under flared nostrils.

"That would be very disappointing to the commissioner, Signor Gazzo. He said there's no one in Philadelphia for whom he has more respect."

Gazzo tapped his walking stick on the floor.

"*Pezzo di cornutu.* Don't-a you talk ta me a respect! You who would arrest a nun, a little sister a Christ. You don't know nothin' about respect!"

"Signor Gazzo . . ."

Gazzo stood up. His head was just below McBride's shoulders. He looked up and waved the stubby index finger as he shouted.

"I could say da word right now an' you'll sing falsetto for de rest a your life, McBride. *Secrezione della cullo!*"

"Signor Gazzo, I'm very impressed by your devotion to our Holy Mother, the Church. And if you don't want to cooperate, I don't suppose we can force you."

"What you doin'? What's-a dis all about?"

"Don't worry. It has nothing to do with olive oil, or even about the crates of guns and army issue medicines stacked against the wall in the corner behind the army issue canned goods."

McBride never took his eyes from the pad on which he was writing a citation.

"That will only come up if I should meet

113

with . . . an accident, say, while visiting your premises. Lieutenant Hudson and I discussed precisely that possibility when I left the station an hour ago. 'Don't worry, Lieutenant,' said I, 'Signor Gazzo may have some unorthodox business arrangements, but he's certainly not stupid enough to do physical harm to a police officer and draw attention to all the illegal goodies in his warehouse.' 'True,' said he, 'but just to be certain, I'll send a few of the boys down there to look around if you aren't back in an hour and a half. We wouldn't want any harm to come to you, Nathan.' That's what he said, Signor Gazzo, word for word.''

For someone who had never cared for poker, McBride was playing it well. Listening to the Monday morning chatter around the station must have taught him something. But bluffing Nunzio Gazzo was a lot shakier than toying with Goldie Becker, and he wondered just how long he could keep a straight face.

McBride tore off the citation.

"I happened to step in something on my way in, Signor Gazzo. I'd describe it, only you're about to eat your lunch. There are samples all over the place. You really ought to pay closer attention to the sanitary code.''

The sun was hotter as he made his way down the street to his buggy, parked under an elm tree where the horse could relax in the shade. The band was playing again, and the marines were almost all aboard the troop ship. At the foot of the gangplank where Lillian Russell had just departed her vessel, the newspaper people were

still pushing, shoving and calling each other
names. But now the words and actions were
more heated. He saw a few black eyes and
bloody noses. Whatever she was saying, they
were working frantically to record it.

He paused to look. No exaggerations had been
made. Actually, there had been understate-
ments. Lillian Russell was truly magnificent. If
wars really had to be fought, better for her than
for sugar cane and tobacco.

Unfortunately, the crowd was blocking his
view. And besides, the list he had just risked his
neck, or worse, for was long and would probably
take all day to look into.

He turned off the main road and into an alley,
hoping to avoid the crowd.

It was a big mistake. Two of Gazzo's men were
in front of him, and two behind.

Chapter Nine

Sophia Blakeley put aside her novel, the one she had been reading in secret for the past few days, and watched for a quarter-hour as Ralphie did his best to attract the attention of the cook's niece, who was ostensibly feeding the birds near the gazebo on the river bank. Eventually, when he stripped off his shirt and displayed his muscles, Olga Wojdzekevicz just happened to notice him. The bosomy Miss Wojdzekevicz had stepped off the boat only a fortnight before and spoke no English, but there are messages which require no nouns or verbs—only glands, body heat, and a flair for exhibition.

The Blakeley's teenage daughter, Rosie, was pleased to offer an interpretation.

"There they go again. First he takes it off, then she—"

"If you finish that sentence, you'll finish your lunch in your room."

"Really, mother, sometimes I think you shouldn't be permitted to enter the twentieth century with the rest of the world."

Rosie snapped a piece of celery and chewed, sulking.

Miss Wojdzekevicz was still something of a mystery in the Blakeley household. Her aunt, Mrs. Snopkowski, their cook, had finally coerced Blakeley into paying the Wojdzekevicz twins' way out of their unpronounceable village and into this country. The entire affair had not set well with Sophia. The cook had threatened to quit and go to work for the Quimbys on the estate across the river, and it was memories of Sophia's cooking that had made him acquiesce.

Olga's brother, Casimir, seemed docile enough, passing his days with a silly, vacant smile, trying his best to appease the implacable Snopkowski, giggling at the sight of two pigeons mating, then skulking off like a blushing simpleton.

But there was nothing quite so simple about his sister, unless it was the ease with which she handled Ralphie. There was a wealth of peasant cunning there, as a snob would put it, although Sophia tried very hard not to be.

It would be easier for her to accept if only the relationship had a hint of subtlety. This was, after all, 1898, and the human race had supposedly climbed a few steps up the evolutionary ladder—or so she had tried to tell Ralphie. Even in the most libertine of societies, she had informed him, there was a customary interval between introduction and . . . well, good heavens, this was little more than a reaction to scent.

"Ian . . . Ian . . ."

"Eh?"

"Do you think Ralphie might wish to start that program at North Dakota College this summer instead of waiting for the fall?"

"Sophia, dearest, they've not yet accepted him."

"Oh," she pleaded, "but surely they will."

Long before his military debacle, Ralphie had found ways to age his mother. After Princeton, where the welcome was over after his first football season, he had spent a term at the state university, then another at a school near Elmira. Since then only a remote agricultural college somewhere north of Rat Gulch, North Dakota, had seemed willing to talk to him.

"You sound anxious," Blakeley observed inanely, his eyes still fixed on his notes.

Olga was now flexing her biceps and giggling as Ralphie felt them. They were leaning against a chestnut tree about 50 yards down the lawn from the patio where lunch was soon to be served.

As Rosie made a gesture of pretended shock and Sophia's eyes grew larger, Olga puffed out her already bounteous chest.

Sophia gasped.

"To be perfectly candid, Ian, I'm concerned about Ralphie and that . . . that Slavic brood mare."

He looked up suddenly, thought, stroked his beard, then thought again.

"Now, do not try to pretend you've not noticed their—"

Casimir came out of the scullery and placed a tureen of clam chowder on the table. He smiled, bowed and backed away as Snopkowski, her arms folded, looked on. Sophia waited until they were inside the house.

"You cannot tell me you haven't seen the same things I've seen."

He removed his monocle and watched as Ralphie and Olga disappeared, ever so sneakily, into the spreading foliage.

"Sophia, my darling, it should come as no surprise that at his age Ralph has a healthy libido."

She arched a brow.

"I'll thank you to keep the language of that filthy Dr. Freud away from our food."

Sometimes she was more Victorian than at other times.

"I shall bring your concerns to his attention posthaste," he assured her, then returned to his notes.

Since McBride had left him that morning, he had come up with something in the laboratory. The breed of cat whose fur had been found on the victim's person was identified as a manx. If not very rare, it certainly was not commonplace. It was possible that it had been purchased at a local pet shop.

"Sir . . . Madam . . ."

Victor, the butler, had come out of his hiding

place in a clump of dogwood where he would retreat whenever Snopkowski was on the war-path, or if he suspected there was some heavy work to be done.

"Good morning, Victor," Rosie chimed, soup spoon in hand, "and how are the little pink elephants this morning?"

She slurped her chowder. Sophia darted an admonishing glance.

Victor ignored her. He was standing like an actor who was about to deliver a soliloquy—feet perpendicular, chin up, one hand at the side, the other gesturing grandly.

All three Blakeleys rolled their eyes.

"What is it, Victor?" Sophia volunteered.

"I regret that I must protest cook's unfortunate choice of expressions."

"With regard to you, I presume?"

"Precisely, Madam."

"But, Victor, Mrs. Snopkowski speaks very limited English."

"Madam, I know I am being insulted when she bares her tusks and screeches at me, and I am quite able to understand her jibberish when she threatens me with a meat cleaver."

"Pish-tush, Victor."

"Madam, this is no trifling matter."

"Victor, please go down to the chestnut tree near the gazebo and tell Ralphie to come to lunch. Thank you."

"But, Madam," he whined.

"Victor?"

"Yes, Madam."

An impish smile crossed her face as they

watched Victor walking on tiptoe, coming within a few yards of the chestnut tree.

"It's possible," Blakeley said, "that whatever he discovers behind that tree trunk will put him into a state of shock."

And sometimes Sophia was less Victorian than at other times. "Yes, my darling, I know."

Rosie giggled.

Victor Primrose, as he chose to be known during his best forgotten career on stage, was arguably the worst butler in Philadelphia—perhaps beyond Philadelphia—but except for a brief stint as a butterfly in a vaudeville act, the butler was the only role he had ever played. And when the producers finally grew weary of his hypochondria, marathon pouting sessions and hidden gin bottles, and he was about to be sent to Cleveland where a burlesque comic would throw cream pies in his face twice a day, Sophia stepped in. In a moment of terrible judgement she had hired him to play a butler in real life.

Since then there had been many nights when she had dreamt of Victor with his head protruding from a hole in a circus flat, staring ahead in his stuffy, fatuous way, as she took aim with a gooey lemon meringue.

"Your notes must be fascinating," she said, just to change the subject.

"Rather more like perplexing, I'd say."

Rosie eased out of her seat and wandered off for a better view of the scene near the gazebo. They noticed her, but preferred to avoid one more confrontation.

"Do they have to do with the derelict found in Lieutenant Hudson's precinct?"

"Yes, and there's precious little in them to inspire me."

It was a grim subject to be avoided at the lunch table, and he wondered how to do so gracefully.

Rosie was gone at any rate, off to investigate one of the mysteries of life that had been brought to her adolescent attention.

As for Sophia, he realized that the book she was reading, supposedly without anyone's notice and hidden at the moment inside a copy of the *Saturday Evening Post*, was about a Transylvanian chap who sucked the blood of young women and put them under a diabolical spell. Melodramatic drivel! But it was the literary rage of the day, and certainly it had not kept her awake at night.

Besides, when she ceased playing the beautiful mental butterfly, Sophia Blakeley had a shrewd perception that he had grown to respect.

So he told her everything.

"How awful," she said, shuddering.

"Yes, it is. Chowder?"

"Please."

"And the more that I study it, the more I must conclude that we have a cult on our hands."

"A cult? Here? Really, Ian . . . . Just one half of a bowl, please."

"It's not that far-fetched, my dear. We had them in our terribly civilized London, you'll recall."

"Yes, but London has pockets of odd sorts

from all around the Empire. Good heavens, Miss Wojdzekevicz is probably the most exotic type I've seen here in ages."

"I don't think one need wear a turban or decorate one's nose with a chicken bone in order to qualify as a sociopath. That Ripper chap dressed like a proper gentleman, and I dare say, if he's ever taken, he'll speak English like an Oxonian. Tea?"

"Yes, thank you."

He poured a cup. She bit into a dainty cream cheese and cucumber sandwich and chewed for a moment, thinking.

Snopkowski screeched in the background. Casimir scurried out of the house with a bowl of fruit, placed it uncertainly on the table, smiled haplessly and scurried back.

"Cook is in particularly horrid spirits this morning."

"Ian, the Ripper was—or so they believe—a member of the privileged class. More to the point, so was the Marquis de Sade and his friends."

"In other words, we may have some bizarre neighbors?"

They looked into each others eyes, thinking similar thoughts.

There was a sudden eruption of loud, indecipherable verbiage from the direction of the gazebo. They craned to see over the wall, the hedges and the Scotch heather. Olga was staring back defiantly as Snopkowski waved a big, beefy finger in her face. Victor was skulking off toward the dogwood, Rosie was hiding behind the chestnut tree where she could take it all in, and Ralphie, trying to rebutton his shirt, was running up the lawn, whooping with delight as he bounded over a hedgerow.

"I don't believe the cook's altogether pleased with Miss Wojdzekevicz either," Blakeley observed.

"I'm not surprised," Sophia snapped. "She spends a lot more time tempting Ralphie than she does in the scullery."

Ralphie disappeared around the other side of the house as the cook led a screaming, cursing Miss Wojdzekevicz away by the ear.

"Ian, do you think there's any chance at all?"

"I shall write to North Dakota immediately after lunch."

"Do."

She sipped her tea, gazing off at the river and beyond.

"And now, where were we? Oh yes, about that cadaver in your laboratory . . . Ian, did you happen to notice the marking below the left ear?"

"Hello?"

"There is a very small but very distinct signature of sorts just below the left ear lobe."

Chapter Ten

Do *you call that good work, child? Do you?*

The little girl in the dream did not answer. She stared at the floor. That above all infuriated him. He was not a very big man, but in that hot, smelly shop, he stood out like a monster in a fantasy.

It is certainly not, I repeat, not good work, child. Do you hear me?

The woman tossed in her bed. The child in the dream refused to answer, refused to let him hear the petrified squeak of her voice, refused to look up and let him see the tears gathering in her eyes. The others were silent and nervous, going about their monotonous work like so many half-grown robots.

The dream was vivid. In the depths of the drugged sleep she saw it all again in strange colors, but the terror and the little girl were quite real.

His voice rose above the clatter of the machinery.

I told you to answer me. Are you a rebellious little girl?

The back of his hand swept across her face. Her head snapped and her cheek felt numb. The little girl started to cry.

You know what happens when you do not clean them properly. You know, do you not? Look at me, child. You eat them—that is what happens.

The woman moaned in her sleep.

The little girl tried to get away, but he had her by the arm. She held her breath and clenched her teeth. It smelled so horrid that she felt herself getting sick even before he pried her jaws open and stuffed it into her mouth. She spat it out, and he hit her again. The others looked away. . . .

The woman sat up in bed, eyes fixed on some vague figure in the mirror. A draft rippled through the canopy over her fourposter bed. She shivered in the cold sweat of her night clothes.

Chapter Eleven

She was sitting at the top of the stairs when he opened the door, a rosy smile on her Celtic face, the face that used to launch ships for him, until one day, almost whimsically, it turned away and sank the fleet. The big green eyes were the same, as were the freckles that dotted the tiny nose. The hair was still strawberry, tied up in a fashionable knot, but the dress was a silken announcement of new prosperity.

He was far from pleased to see her now.

Mrs. Allcock, the landlady, stepped out of her first floor apartment, moved as quickly as her Clydesdale shanks could take her, and intercepted him as he approached the stairs.

"You look like hell," she said, her mean, pig's eyes squinting.

"Mrs. Allcock," he said, "if you don't like cuts

and bruises, then don't rent to cops. Or is that too abstract for you?"

"Don't you get flip with me, you pagan."

"Mrs. Allcock, I'm busy."

"I bet youse are. Who's she?"

"I haven't the foggiest idea. Do I owe you rent or something?"

"No, but it's due tamorra."

"I'll leave it under the bowl with your soup bone and water."

"Be damn sure ya do."

He started up the stairs, but her broad body was in the way. She nodded toward his visitor.

"I asked you, who's she?"

The visitor smiled sweetly and waggled her fingers.

"How about . . . my sister?"

"Your sister, my arse."

"My first cousin, then."

"McBride, if that's anything but a sinful acquaintance, I'll eat me foot."

"What an unbelievably disgusting thought."

"Damn well better not be no hanky-panky up there, or I'll toss youse out, cop or no cop. This here is a respective roomin' house!"

She slammed the door and waddled down the street to consult her crystal ball gazer as she did each week at this time. Madame Natalia, who knew a good mark when she saw one, had been promising Calla W. Allcock a handsome lover for the past six months.

"I thought we took care of all the loose ends."

"I was in the neighborhood," his visitor said, "and . . ."

He climbed the stairs toward her, hot, weary and somewhat embarrassed by his wounds.

"I wondered whose carriage that was outside with the white horse and the coachman."

"They're rented."

Approaching her, he could see the very thing he did not want to see—that Allison Meredith was lovelier than ever. He kept his sentences short and clipped lest he should stammer, but there was no way of cloaking the hostility. When it came to Allison, he had spent every last ounce of nobility.

"You wanted me to know how well you've done in a year, so now I know."

"A year, two months, three weeks, two days."

"More or less. I hadn't noticed."

That was childish, he knew. And he knew that she knew.

She got up when he reached the top, her silken skirt rustling.

"May I help?"

"You don't know the first thing about cuts and bruises."

"Want to bet?"

"You'll get bloodstains on your little linen gloves."

"I can take them off."

Nunzio Gazzo's goons had cornered him in the alley off Wharf Street, blocking the way and frightening his horse. Since it was impossible to turn around in the narrow space and since the horse and buggy could not get by the packing crates that had been piled in front of them, he had climbed down to settle things.

He decided to make a move on the two men blocking his exit because they looked a little slower than the two closing in behind him. One of them swung at him with a pick handle. When he ducked, the club had hit the other man across the bridge of the nose. Then McBride had come up with two quick shots, one an uppercut and the other a left hook, and the man with the pick handle slammed noisily into a cluster of overflowing garbage cans. But by this time the other two had caught up with him and the scuffle spilled out into the street, scattering Lillian Russell's admirers, most of her righteously angry pickets and all of the newspapermen. There were shouts, screams, angry epithets, the neighing of horses and the smacking sounds of fist against face.

It was really no contest. McBride was very fast and his boxing skills had never left him, and whatever needs those skills did not cover were more than compensated for by the street tactics he had learned from Lieutenant Hudson.

The goons were amateurs, just off the boat probably and much too eager to score a few points with their patron. He guessed that they had done it on their own, because if Don Nunzio had wanted him rearranged, he would have sent professionals, and now McBride would hardly be climbing the stairs on his own.

By the time uniformed help had arrived, Gazzo's people were limp and wheezing. The cut on McBride's cheek was more like a glorified brushburn, incurred when one of them had hit him with a knotted piece of hawser hemp.

But the sun was hot and the dockside alley was filthy.

"All right," he said after trying not to return her gaze, "but let me wash the grime away first."

"Running water?"

"Cool to ice cold."

"I'm impressed."

He opened the door and led her into his small apartment where she treated the cuts on his knuckles with alcohol and daubed some ointment on his cheek. Neither of them spoke for a time, waiting for the awkwardness to pass.

He was seated in a chair beside an open rolltop desk where she could tend to him conveniently. During pauses, while she discarded pieces of cotton, he glanced over the basin and medicine bottles and hoped she hadn't noticed the dust on the bookshelves and the unwashed coffee cup on the bedside table. Allison rarely missed a thing with her perfect journalist's mind. He remembered her as fastidious, too, compulsive in the hours they'd shared in a simpler time, so long ago. Fortunately, he had tidied up the place recently and made the bed that morning, so his quarters were not overly messy. There was no need to let her think he'd been depressed since she dropped him, not that that was any of her business either.

She had dropped him for a—what the hell was it?—some story about troubles along the Mexican border. And the damned revolution never happened anyway.

When she stepped closer he could smell the gardenia toilet water that was sprinkled somewhere between the layers of silk and expensive undergarments. It was subtle, but the room was warm, and the heat escaping through her pores brought it out, releasing long stifled memories and putting his already shaky personna in jeopardy.

Gardenia was special with Allison—that and the little splash of freckles.

She leaned in very close to him.

"Does it hurt when I touch your cheek?"

"Umm? Oh, no. No, it doesn't."

She had a very gentle, utterly feminine touch. It was important to her that he notice that. Unlike so many equally ambitious women she'd met along the way, she had not become hardbitten. She still disliked shrill voices as much as she had as a little girl in Fishtown, and four-letter words were not yet established features of her vocabulary.

First-aid was another of the many skills she had come by in her efforts to climb as far from her origins as possible. She had hoped it would help to convince her editors that she wouldn't just get in the way if they could find it in their hearts to assign her to the war zone. After all, she had learned to speak acceptable Spanish for the Mexican border assignment, and she just might be of some help in a field hospital when she wasn't filing reports on the exploits of Colonel Roosevelt or the workings of a Gatling gun. She wanted to write the kind of things Frank Norris was writing about—the plight of the Cuban peasants caught in the middle of the struggle, the hungry children, greedy men of influence, and an indifferent world. She wanted that very much, but of course it wasn't possible. Too dangerous, they had said, as if the Yaquis of the border had been tooth fairies.

But Maggie McInally had always been resourceful, even well before she'd become Allison Meredith or the score of male pseudonyms that she was often forced to write under. And if she had failed to persuade her stodgy old editors this time, she had succeeded more often than not, and she would succeed again. She also knew she would have to make more sacrifices, just like the one she had made a year ago when she left Nathan McBride with nothing more than memories and an apologetic note.

"There," she said, taking a small mirror from her purse and holding it before his face, "handsome as ever, Sergeant McBride."

He studied the face in the mirror. Bruised and puffy under one eye, it looked like the person attached to it could use about 12 hours of sleep. The mustache was badly in need of a trim, but the bandage was neat.

"Thank you," he said blandly.

"I guess I happened by at the right time."

He got up and stretched.

There was a very faint breeze blowing through the open window, but the elms along the sidewalk barely shivered. The rumbling and clopping of horse-drawn traffic and the clanging and rattling of trolleys drifted upward from the street as did heat waves off the brick roadway.

"I guess I happened by at the right time, huh?"

He didn't answer. She cleared her throat. His back was turned as he stared down into the street.

"I don't think it's reasonable to expect me to do a flamenco dance at the sight of you, Allison."

"But . . . you don't hate me, do you?"

He was silent for an uncomfortably long time, watching a pair of squirrels playing something like tag on the ground, then chasing each other up the large oak that sprawled over from the lot next door. They raced in and out of the shadows along a lengthy branch.

He shook his head.

She came over to him and rested her head on his shoulder, hugging his waist in a familiar gesture.

"It would be very kind of you to leave right now," he said.

"You don't mean that, Nathan, or you wouldn't have let me in."

"I was groggy."

She still clung to him. He felt the heat from her body against his back, and he knew the glib answer was not enough.

"All right, I was curious. I wanted to see if you were—"

"You wanted to see me again."

"—the same as I remembered you."

"I am."

"I'm not too sure I like that."

"I guess it would sound rather flimsy if I said I'm sorry."

"Yes, it would."

"But I am, Nathan. I am."

"You probably are, in your own way. But what could follow would take a much bigger toll on me than on you. So, please, let's keep our distance."

Suddenly her coachman became visible below them. He had just climbed down to stretch his legs and was mopping his brow in the shade of the large oak.

"Besides, Allison, I can't tell you anything about the case without Dr. Blakeley's permission."

She released her hold and stepped away.

"That was blunt."

"It was apt."

She might have told him then that she'd already been in touch with Blakeley, who had received her warmly, but she decided to hold that card for the time being.

He reached into a small cabinet and opened a bottle of Jameson's that Blakeley had given him on his last birthday. It was still three-quarters full because he used the strong stuff sparingly, but it had been and continued to be a very trying day.

When he poured himself a drop or two, she surprised him by asking if she might join him. He accommodated.

"I don't know why your readers would be interested in a bunch of dead bums anyway. It's certainly no Mexican revolution."

"I don't agree. Neither, apparently, does Bernard Spector."

He shook his head and smiled. No comment was needed.

"And we're *not* birds of a feather," she said. "And by the way, I didn't come here on business."

"You never used to indulge," he said. "Is this another sign of your progress?"

"I need the courage."

She turned and sat on the bed, sipped a little bit of whiskey and tried not to flinch.

"Actually, I've been in town for a week, and I've been trying to talk myself out of this visit ever since I learned I was coming back to Philadelphia. And then this morning I decided I just had to. So I sprinkled myself with the gardenia scent you always liked, and I put on a green dress because you always liked me in green, and here I am. I was lucky you came home early and even luckier that you'd been in a scrape. Otherwise, you might have tossed me out by the scruff of the neck, and I wouldn't have blamed you. But, oh God, I'm so glad you didn't because—"

"Stop right there, please."

"I can't, Nathan. I've come this far and I can't."

He stared at her with piercing eyes. A fool twice burnt is a fool indeed, he'd heard it said.

"Why the hell are you doing this to me?"

"I'm trying to make amends. I haven't liked myself much in the past year."

"You'll get over it. I have great faith in you that way."

"There isn't anyone else, you know, Nathan. There hasn't been and there won't be."

She put her whiskey on the dresser and got up. He knew what came next but did nothing to prevent it.

The kiss lasted a long time. Her lips had the familiar fruity taste, and her voice was husky and bated, coming from the depths as he remembered it in so many moments like this.

She took a step back and opened the buttons that ran down the bodice of her dress.

"You'll have to do the rest," she said.

He did, and in another half-minute she was stepping out of the silken green dress, and the memories were overwhelming. He held her in a tight embrace and looked for something to say that he hadn't said too many times before.

There was a rap on the door, but they barely heard it. They savored the heat coming off each other's body. There was another shorter rap, and the door swung open.

Allison turned and gasped.

"Hullo, sarge. Hullo, missus, or . . ."

Fatzinger blushed and babbled something apologetic. McBride stepped between him and Allison as she hurried back into her dress.

They went outside and spoke in whispers.

"Bones, when the hell are you going to learn how to knock?"

"I did, sarge. Vunce, tvice . . . . Vell, Cheez, I didn't know you vass in dere diddlin' or I would a knocked again!"

"We weren't diddling."

"Dott's right, und I won't tell nobody. Mit glue dese lips are sealed. Hey, issn't dott da dolly mit da typewriter you usta be goofy aboudt?"

"No, it isn't."

"Sure as shidt looks like her."

"Well, it isn't. What are you doing here anyway?"

"Huh? Oh yeah—mit a message fer ya da lootenant sent me."

"I was coming back to the station in an hour anyway."

Fatzinger rolled his eyes and giggled.

"Ya sure. Vell, anyways, diss here couldn't vait. Ya know dott Lillian Russell, da lady in the stage plays mit da big titties? She seen youze punchin' dose four guys' lights oudt, and so she vants you should her body look after! Und vott a body dott iss!"

"Is this a joke, Bones?" McBride frowned. "Because if it is—"

Fatzinger put his hands up, palms open, then crossed his heart.

"Da lootenant hassn't made no chokes all year. Dese here are orders from downtown. From da commissioner!"

He started down the stairs, stopped, and added much too loudly, "Better finish yer diddlin', sarge, before da lady mit da big titties changes her mind. Oudtside in da wagon I'll vait!"

He counted to three, opened the door and entered his apartment. Allison was fully dressed and putting the finishing touches on her strawberry blonde hair. The passion had cooled, but she was smiling.

"Well, it's reassuring to know I'm the dolly you 'usta be goofy aboudt'."

"I, uh, have to report in."

She started to chuckle good-naturedly. It built itself into a healthy laugh.

"Yes, I know. Well, if they should prove to be, er, less than the boys say they are . . ."

"You'll be the first to know."

"Good."

She kissed him on the cheek and started out the door.

"That's as good an excuse as any to come back."

Chapter Twelve

"**D**o you see it now, Ian, there, a few centimeters under the lobe?"

"Yes, of course."

"Nice work, isn't it?"

"It looks like a fish."

"Right."

"A bloody upside-down fish!"

"Do you think it means anything?"

"Possibly."

"Oh, good!"

"I said, possibly."

"Ian, you're not angry with me for discovering it, are you?"

"Certainly not."

"Yes, you are."

"No, I'm not, Christ blast it."

He lay his magnifying glass on a cabinet and

paced the room muttering to himself. She crossed her arms, tapped her foot and sighed.

"It was all quite by accident, you know. It isn't as if I've been snooping."

"I don't mind, really."

"Yes, you do."

He pinched the bridge of his nose and turned.

"Sophia, will you not permit me a moment to be angry with myself?"

"Well, of course, if that's what you wish. But it is quite unnecessary, Ian."

"Just one brief moment, please."

He glanced at the cadaver, feeling very much like an amateur. She understood. There was a great deal of professional pride there, all of it beyond question, earned in countless challenges thrown at him by a frustrated Scotland Yard. A bit of absent-mindedness was to him unforgivable under the circumstances.

"Ian," she explained, approaching, "I was becoming, as you know, suspicious of Ralphie and Miss Wojdzekevicz. I suspected they were sneaking off to somewhere on the basement level to, well . . ." She gestured toward an empty surgical table. "I asked Victor to investigate, but he turned green and informed me that there was a body in the laboratory, and that if he had to come down here he would no doubt faint and be bedridden for a week. So I had to do it myself. When I walked in, there it was, all packed in ice."

"The city is sending someone over this afternoon to tote it away."

"Then," she said, "it's a good thing I happened by, isn't it?"

He smiled sheepishly.

"Please forgive my childishness. It is a good thing."

"I suppose it's also a good thing I've been reading that book."

"Book?"

"You know, *Dracula*, the one I've been reading and you've been scoffing at for days. As it happens, the Count leaves two little red marks on his victims' necks. It inspired my morbid curiosity and *voila*, the fish."

"Looks rather like a pilchard, don't you think?"

"Certainly tiny enough," she agreed.

"I suspect it has some anti-religious significance," he said, again studying the marking on Tony the Swordsman. "The Simon Peter symbol and so on. Upside down, as if dead."

"Or caught in a net."

"Whoever did it used a tiny needle and used it precisely. I do think, Sophia dearest, this trademark will be quite useful."

"Too bad we can't check the other victims to see if there's a similar mark."

"True. Perhaps I can prevail upon the court to let me exhume one. Probably badly decomposed, but . . ."

"In any case, Ian, I doubt we'll have long to wait for the next one."

Chapter Thirteen

Alfred Peteroff of Peteroff, MacBirney and Schnurr was recognized, even grudgingly admired, by his peers as one of the oiliest attorneys in Philadelphia, which was quite a distinction in a city known to breed lawyers like microbes in a culture.

"My client has been harassed, victimized, terrorized and brutalized," he asserted in a trembling voice, pointing a finger of outrage at a heavily bandaged Jack Brown.

Brown was a pleasing sight indeed—one eye closed, the other resembling a multicolored knuckler marble, an upper lip that could pass for a small black-and-blue awning. And, of course, there was the leg.

When he looked up on cue, expecting a blush of shame from Hudson, he got instead a wink and a smile and looked away, muttering obscenities.

"My client has been hounded by this department despite the absence of any real evidence against him, evidently just because Lieutenant Hudson objects to his looks."

"Good point," Hudson said. "And who the hell wouldn't?"

"Lieutenant Hudson," the commissioner's aide intervened.

"And now that you mention it, Peteroff, I object to your looks, too."

"You'll have your chance to speak, Hudson," said the aide, a milky young man with puffy lips.

"*Lieutenant* Hudson, you rectal itch."

The aide blanched. They had met before, and Hudson had always intimidated him. They stared at each other until he realized he was in charge.

"Go on, Mister Peteroff."

Peteroff jabbed at his glasses which tended to slip over the bridge of his nose in the heat. Whenever he did that he snickered and looked like a large, angry rodent.

"These are bills presented by Dr. Van Arsdale, who treated my client's injuries, by the dentist, Dr. Seward, who did his best with my client's teeth, and by Mr. McGurk, who made the plaster for the cast on my client's leg."

It was the leg, above all, that brought a smile to Hudson's ruddy face. The painful, compound fracture would keep Brown from moving any faster than a constipated tortoise for the next few months, and Hudson had broken it himself.

"Give them to Lieutenant Hudson, Mr. Peteroff. He will be pleased to accept them."

Hudson was on his feet.

"Slow down, you turd. Where's your evidence? Where the hell are your witnesses?"

"The evidence is on display," Alfred Peteroff said. "My client is wearing it."

"How the hell do you know it wasn't some bookie who beat him up for nonpayment of debts? Some pimp, maybe. It could even have been an angry husband, for Chrissake, though I can't picture the infested floozie who'd bother with *him*."

"You'll have your turn," the aide reminded him.

"Shut up, you."

"Doesn't that say it all?" Alfred Peteroff said.

"Where are your witnesses, counselor? Show me one."

Peteroff rested an arm on a cabinet and let out a long, drawn out sigh. The aide picked up a tiny bell and rang it daintily. A patrolman entered.

"Bring in the witness."

The patrolman left and came back a minute or so later, escorting a nervous-looking gentleman.

Hudson looked up and laughed uncertainly.

"This is a practical joke, right?"

The nervous-looking gentleman shook his head in disagreement.

"Vell, dey asked me aboudt da monkeyshines, Lootenant, und . . ."

Fatzinger was dressed in his best Sunday clothes—plaid coat, striped high-top trousers, bowler and big bow tie.

"You look like the end man in a goddamn minstrel show."

"Tanks, Lootenant. Youse look real nice yourself."

Alfred Peteroff and the commissioner's aide smiled smarmily.

Chapter Fourteen

In the late afternoon heat the odors were almost visible in the tiny, cramped room—rank vapors from the seldom emptied chamber pot under the bed, the stale smell of beer, cigar smoke, and sweaty bodies that lingered long after last night's last visitor had departed.

The times had been good to Goldie. There had been a convention in town last week, a revival meeting at the Baker Bowl the week before, a couple of merchant ships in port this week, and of course there was always the war, God bless it. Every night before going to sleep, no matter how drunk and weary, she prayed that it would continue and thanked God for whatever the hell it was that made McKinley hate the Spanish. A few more months like this and she could afford a whole mouthful of gold teeth and retire! Maybe even buy a farm, get respectable, become a country gentlewoman like the ladies in the Sears catalogue. Raise pigs instead of entertaining them.

The cluttered rooms she rented in the rear of Gunselman's saloon were convenient. The entrance was dark, even in the daytime, so her lunchtime customers could come and go in privacy. But there were little problems, like the heat and the stagnant air because the breezes off the street rarely made it beyond the saloon on the one end and the maze of alleys on the other.

Goldie had often thanked heaven that her work required very little clothing, too.

Damn, the mascara was running again. So was the rouge. She daubed on more rice powder and grumbled at the face in the mirror.

She checked her stockings for holes and her lacy bloomers for stains and whatever. The silk stockings were almost new, a gift from a traveling lingerie salesman, and she had worn them only once when that creepy guy from Pittsburgh wanted her to dress up like Little Bo Peep and prod his behind with her crosier. And the bloomers, if not her newest, were at least her most recently laundered.

Her best and gaudiest velveteen dress was laid out on the bed. It was violet and shoplifted at great risk; she wore it only on very special occasions. It had a row of golden tassels dangling from a very low cut bodice that shivered whenever she laughed or took a deep breath. when she wanted to advertise or if she had to haggle over prices, all that was necessary was a little tug and she could display more cleavage. Tonight she planned to tug a lot.

She sat on the bed and forced her size eight feet into the size seven and a half high button shoes.

There was a shoeshine boy, a towheaded immigrant kid who worked the sidewalk in front of Gunselman's, and she had noticed a few weeks ago that his adolescence had so confused him that he'd become infatuated with her. It was touching, she thought, how every night as she set out on her rounds his mouth would fall open when she passed and his eyes would follow her as far as they could. Now and then she would stop, wink and wave, and he would all but swoon. One of these days, she reminded herself, she would have to invite him in for an introductory lesson.

Tonight she must be perfect, cuz tonight she, Edn . . . Eliza Amanda Becker was gonna entertain the friggin' swells.

She raised one arm and sniffed, then splashed on more rose water and waved her hands under her pits.

The burly guy had said they'd be around by five. The clock on the dresser, almost lost behind the clutter of perfumes and junk, told her she had ten minutes.

What a nifty break it was running into Fatso, just when she was about to call it a night. Not that he was really fat—chunky was more like it—but fat was her first impression, and like most of her casual acquaintances, he hadn't told her his real name, so Fatso would have to do for now. Earlier that evening, while entertaining a couple of slumming college boys, she had knelt in a soggy spot in an alley behind a dockside saloon where she'd usually been lucky with the merchant sailors, and a few hours later a cold wind had come up the river. She had the chills and her nose was stuffing up and nobody likes a damn whiner, so she was on her way back to Gunselman's for a bucket of suds and a half-pint of rye.

He came out of the fog as she started up Broad Street. She ignored him at first, but he was persistent, following her across the road, dodging horses and carriages and huffing as she stepped into a side street and hurried up the broken pavement.

He was only about ten feet behind her when she turned around.

"Whattaya want, Fats?"

"Jeez, whattaya think I want, ya dumb tart?"

"Yer givin' me the creeps, follyin' me in the dark. Who the hell are ya?"

"What if I gave youse a few bucks? Would dat make me skinnier?"

Maybe he was a cop, she had reasoned; some a them could look real shady—especially the vice cops, the bastards.

"You must think I'm a bum talkin' like dat," she had said, just in case.

"Look, ya dumb tart, I got half a sawbuck says ya probably are. Or was you on yer way ta church?"

She had followed him back to a carriage,

which he drove to a cemetery about two miles away, where they rutted in the fog behind a large tombstone with some old guy's face chisled on top. She remembered looking up and giggling because the old guy looked like he didn't approve at all. The noises they made were those of a pig attacking a chicken.

It was the biggest payoff Goldie had ever seen. That night she had dined on knockwurst and potato salad and ordered two buckets of suds and a whole pint of rye. Hell, she even tipped old Gunselman a nickel.

Fatso had reappeared a few nights later, this time with a friend, a sickly little twerp named Pluto who she was told to service as part of the deal.

"God of the dead and ruler of the underworld, Pluto was," he informed her.

"Lookin' at you, I could a guessed as much."

"And the planet of love 'n affection."

"Whatever ya say, sport." She lifted her skirt and lay back on the cemetery grass. "Giddee up—it's gettin' cold out."

He had wheezed and panted so much that she thought they might have to leave him behind in one of the freshly dug graves which was not a bad idea. She didn't like him much; his breath smelled like curds and whey, and he had a personality to match.

"Ya done yet, ya little piss ant?"

"Huh?"

"I said . . . are ya done yet? Or can't ya hear neither?"

"Maybe I am, maybe I ain't. I'll let ya know."

"Look, if yer done, then get the hell off, why don'tcha? The goddamn grass is wet!"

"Oh yeah? Well, maybe I wanna do it again!"

"Well, if ya do, then hows about borryin' somebody else's pizzle next time?"

He had muttered something and picked up a large rock, but before he could use it Fatso plucked him off her and sent him back to the carriage to button his trousers and curse under his breath. He made moronic gestures as he stomped up the hillside.

Soon he was coughing in the night air. His hacking and spitting echoed in the fog.

"You interested in ennertainin' a few big shots?" Fatso had asked.

"Like who?"

"You don't need ta know."

She swatted a mosquito on her forearm and brushed some mud off her ample buttocks.

"Big shots, huh? I heard that one a couple a times before, y'know."

"I ain't much of a kidder, lady."

She eyed him coolly. These were funny times, and everybody knew it.

"They ain't Spains, are they?"

"Huh? . . . Jesus, what a dumb question."

She blushed, rearranged her skirt and fussed with her hair nervously. Maybe it was a dumb question, but somebody once said there were Spains all over the place. Spies. Especially down around the docks where they could figure out how to sail right up the Delaware and blow us all to hell, and which was where she had met Fatso in the first place. So, who the hell was he to call her dumb anyways?

"I don't need no extra work," she pouted.

When he made a gesture of disgust and started off, she changed her mind quickly.

"Wait a minute, Fatso."

"I prefer to be called burly."

"They really got lots a money?"

"Lots a money."

"I ain't playin' horsey or nothin'. No whips 'n stuff."

"Nobody ast ya to."

She rolled a cigarette, lit it and weighed the offer.

"Lots a money . . ."

"Y'know somethin'? I oughta let Pluto slap ya silly, ya dumb tart. Awright, whattaya charge? I can pay half of it right now."

She blew a smoke ring into the air and thought. It was no time to underbid one's self.

"This here's my goin' rate, Fats. Half a buck for a hand job, a whole buck for missionary, two bucks for what I done on you tonight, and three if I gotta, y'know, take it like a man."

"Izzat it?"

"That's it," she said flatly.

He chuckled. "You drive a hard bargain."

"Take it or leave it, Fatso."

He handed her a ten and slapped her on the backside.

Ever since then Goldie had been in a daze, envisioning a new career among the swells out on the Main Line, down at the shore, out on a boat, up in the Poconos, Jeez, anywhere. Maybe she could even become some high mucky-muck's mistress, go to Europe, eat snails and drink something better than Tess Gunselman's rotgut.

And she was all prepared to do whatever was called for—dance naked, pose for loonies, paint blue circles around her things, let them pee on her, make the rounds under the poker table, turn herself into a goddamn one-woman band!

She was so excited that she'd almost forgotten to record her adventures in her diary.

Jeez, it was hot. She added another layer of powder on her pockmarks. Wherever they were going, she hoped it would be cooler.

There was a knock on the door, loud enough to be rude and presumptuous.

"Jist a minute. Jeez . . ."

She put on some lip rouge and squeezed into the gaudy violet dress, struggling to button up the back.

Another knock was louder and more assertive.

She raised her skirt and dusted a strongly scented talcum powder between her legs. Some of it got on the velveteen and she slapped at it angrily. Then there was a third very loud knock.

"Keep yer pants on, lardass!"

She opened the door. He was standing outside, chewing on a piece of salami from Gunselman's free lunch. The tubercular little twerp stood about ten feet away, munching on a hard boiled egg.

"I told ya, I don't like to be called dat. Name's Grover."

They might a said somethin' about how nice she looked, Goldie thought, after all the gussyin' up she just did. Instead, they was only lookin' her over, like she was some kind a meat hangin' on a friggin' rack. That really got her goat, but she stayed calm. The night was too special to be ruined by a pair of ignorant assholes.

"Well, will I do, gents?"

"Ya smell nice," Grover acknowledged.

"A lot nicer than the last time," the twerp said through a mouthful of egg.

"Do we gotta have him along? He gives me the chills, hackin' 'n spittin' all the time."

"I don't have ta take that from a dime-a-dozen," said the twerp.

"C'mon, let's go," Grover intervened. "It's hot in here."

On the way out they passed through the saloon where some of the regulars whistled and hooted as she went by. She walked gingerly around wads of discarded chewing tobacco and other unsightly things that threatened the shine on her shoes. When she raised her skirt to avoid gathering sawdust on her velveteen there were more whistles and she hoped the display of admiration did not go unnoticed by Grover, but he was stuffing himself with whatever he could scoop up as they passed the free lunch.

She was halfway to the carriage when she spied the shoeshine boy and paused to give him a thrill. As usual, his mouth fell open and his eyes were wide.

Pluto buttonholed Grover a few yards behind her and spoke nervously.

"You think it was smart, bein' seen with her by all them guys?"

"Nothin' to wet yerself about. They was all too drunk to see anything. Besides, they was lookin' at the tart."

"Ah, Jeez," Pluto whined, "I dunno . . ."

"Here," Grover said, "have another egg."

He stuffed the hard boiled egg, shell and all, into Pluto's mouth and forced the jaws shut. Pluto gagged and started spitting out pieces of egg white as Grover guffawed and strolled away.

"This here's Bogdan, my number one beau," Goldie announced. "He sees to it that my shoes are always real nice."

"That's cuz he gets to look up yer skirt when he shines them. C'mon, I don't like yer neighborhood. Let's go."

"Bogdan," said Goldie in a strange, affected, remotely British accent, "I'd like yiz to meet two a my friends from Gay Paree."

Bogdan stood up and reached out to shake Grover's hand. He smiled and nodded his head eagerly. Grover looked at the bootblack on the fingers and waved him off.

"My name is John Jacob Astor, Bogdan. Remember that."

"But you could jist call him 'Fatso'," Goldie said, giggling.

Grover frowned but smiled again as he pointed at Pluto, who was removing the egg from his mouth.

"And this here's the Sultan a Hong Kong. Hey, Sultan, c'mere!"

"Huh?"

"Shake hands with Bogdan."

Bogdan was still grinning and nodding his head. "Zoltan . . ."

"Yeah, sure," Pluto said, stepping forward.

He shook hands vigorously, pressing the soggy, half-chewed hard boiled egg into the shoeshine boy's palm.

Bogdan turned red, cursed in a language that none of them recognized, and smeared the gooey, yellow pulp all over Pluto's coat as Goldie and Grover roared approval. Pluto let out an adenoidal bellow of outrage and threatened to strangle him, but the shoeshine boy knocked him down with one punch.

"Get op, Zoltan, swine."

He stood poised with blackened fists and waited for Pluto to get up because nobody was going to make Bogdan look foolish in the eyes of his muse and goddess, the Lady Goldie.

"Get op, Zoltan, and fight!"

Pluto got up and pulled a knife, but Grover yanked him by the collar and dragged him, cursing and struggling, to the carriage as Bogdan, fists still poised, looked on.

"C'mon, ya dumb shit, yer lucky the kid didn't kill ya."

"I wish ta hell he would a," Goldie added.

"I dropped my knife, damnit! When ya grabbed me, I dropped it!"

"Get in—before I knock yiz inta next month, ya dumb arsehole!"

As the carriage passed, Bogdan continued to scowl.

Goldie winked and blew him a kiss. Pluto

made one of his customary idiotic gestures. The carriage disappeared around a corner and the few who had paused to watch the skirmish staggered on into Gunselman's.

Bogdan's scowl faded gradually. He knelt beside his shoeshine stand and picked up his trophy. The switchblade knife gleamed in the late afternoon sun.

Chapter Fifteen

She sat in the large picture window, brushing her hair absently, giving it the obligatory 100 strokes and watching the sun fade behind a distant thicket. Nestled in the slight fold where her legs parted beneath her dressing gown, a gray manx was sleeping peacefully. A snifter of cognac, half-empty, was on the dresser.

The moment should have been serenity itself, but she dreaded such times. The memories were inescapable then, in solitude at sunset.

'Ow long since you saw a thigh like that, eh? White as snow but a good deal warmer, I can guarantee. Just imagine 'avin' 'em about you. . . .

They came by every night at this time, the first of them, the odd assortment of haughty, faceless gentlemen with their quirks and often strange demands.

I'd 'ardly call these common tits, would you, sir?

You may touch them for a shilling. Go a'ead, sir. They won't fall off. There, there, now. I'll wager you won't feel nothin' that nice at 'ome. . . .

She put the brush aside and opened a small wedgewood box. She selected two pills. Her hands were shaking as she swallowed them and took another sip of cognac.

Oh, but sir! You mean, you want me to . . . ? Oh, sir, you've a devilish imagination, you 'ave. That'll cost a bit more, you know. . . .

There was a knock at the door. She turned suddenly and dropped her glass. The manx leaped off. She got up and paced the room.

Was it good, sir? Did you like it? Did you like me? . . .

After another knock, she put her hands to her ears and screamed.

The chambermaid thought it best to wait a while.

Chapter Sixteen

Blakeley toyed with the contents of his bowl and tried in vain to avoid detection. No sense in triggering Snopkowski's wrath, but he knew by the pained look on Casimir's face that he had triggered it anyway. Dash it all, it was impossible for a man of his dimensions to be inconspicuous, especially when he was seated at the head of the table. Perhaps he should have forced himself to ingest some of it, however difficult, when he sensed she was watching and lurking like a bloody assassin in some shadowy recess of the dining room, waiting for an insult to her creation. She preferred to look down through the openings in the railing on the next floor. Perhaps he should have made a bigger fuss when the large tureen was wheeled in by poor Casimir, who would suffer her wrath.

Pots and pans would clang that evening.

He felt a twinge of guilt watching Casimir's nervous hand as it poured the Bordeaux. The poor chap was walking a tightrope on wobbly legs. What with Snopkowski screeching, Victor, as usual, shirking, and his sister Olga up to whatever it was, God forbid, that she was up to, it would not be long before the lad would be cutting out paper dolls.

But there was little Blakeley could do about it this time. The day's events could have taken away the appetite of a billy goat.

He complimented it for the third time, just in case she was still lurking, but even a faint whiff of her prized bouillabaisse caused legions of nasty, taunting, imaginary things to grow in his stomach.

And when he forced himself to look at the bowl there were tiny, veinous, shell-colored shrimp curled up in the fetal position, dull gray oysters that seemed to smile like putty-faced sycophants, and mussels whose gaping black shells evoked a feeling best undescribed.

He cleared his throat and tried to make small talk.

"I see Lord Kitchener is going to take Khartoum back from the dervishes."

Sophia was nibbling on her customary dainty portion. Ralphie was finishing his third helping. Rosie, as usual, was pouting. He thought it was over something Ralphie had said earlier about her latest beau, Fred Shuster, looking like a turtle, but he could not be sure.

"I wish him Godspeed," Sophia announced, raising her glass.

"Here, here!" Blakeley agreed.

"Yeah, gooluck," Ralphie said, gulping down another mouthful of the aromatic stew. "What's all that about a cartoon, Dad?"

His parents paused in the midst of their toast and exchanged long-suffering glances. Rosie looked at him and huffed. Fred may look like a turtle, she had answered, but he didn't think an optimist was an eye doctor.

"Your ignorance is appalling," she said.

"And you have sprackle on your dress," he replied.

Sophia hushed them and turned to Blakeley.

"I'm on holiday this evening, Ian."

Well, it was better than eating the bouillabaisse.

"Khartoum," he lectured, "is in the Sudan, part of the Empire that's been violated by a chap called the Madhi."

Ralphie chewed on a piece of French bread and listened politely. Rosie watched him and rolled her eyes.

"It's where your third cousin Neville Blakeley of the Lancashire Blakeleys fell in the Queen's service. He was commanding a troop of horsemen during Gordon's heroic defense of the city. It's been over a decade since then and the Mahdi has passed on, but his successor is another devil called the Khalifa. And now General Kitchener is coming down from Egypt to rectify the situation. As your Teddy Roosevelt would say, 'Bully!'"

Ralphie put his hand over his mouth to stifle a mild belch and broke off another piece of bread.

"He's hopeless, Daddy," his sister claimed. "He doesn't know where Ohio is, much less where the Egyptian Sudan is."

"It's a good thing nobody ever listens to Rosie," Ralphie said.

"Ralphie," Sophia interrupted, "this is not, I suspect, the most appropriate time to bring it up, but I've found a job for you."

Ralphie's chewing slowed down. He looked confused.

"Bully," Rosie said.

Victor made a brief appearance, entering quietly, removing a bottle of wine from the ice chest and replacing it with a full one. He bowed and limped off.

"What is Victor's affliction this evening?" Blakeley inquired.

"Our sturdy manservant's been stung by a bee," Sophia said.

"We'll give you three guesses where," Rosie said.

"Hush," her mother said without conviction.

Blakeley sipped his wine and looked off toward the door where Victor had made a hasty exit.

"I don't believe that bottle of Bordeaux was more than half empty. Or is my judgement impaired?"

"He does that all the time, Daddy," Rosie informed. "You just never looked before."

"He must have quite a collection."

"The bee that stung Victor's backside must be pretty drunk itself by now," Ralphie said, buzzing and making erratic circles with his spoon.

Sophia covered her mouth and giggled. That was risqué for her, downright bawdy. The Bordeaux was going to her head.

Blakeley squinted through the candlelight and saw the dewy-eyed, tipsy smile that he loved but saw only rarely. He wanted to sweep her up and hold her in his arms, but there were Ralphie and Rosie, and the latter was arching a brow smugly, knowing her mother had transgressed.

Blakeley was about to toast the bee when Ralphie lifted the cover from the tureen and scooped up a large fish head. It stared through empty, sunken eyes, like some time-blackened decapitated thing.

"Oh, there you are, Victor," Ralphie said in Victor's pompous tones. "We were just talking about you."

"Yecckk," Rosie said, overreacting.

Blakeley felt a nest of moths coming to life in his stomach and fluttering as if they were desperate to escape. He excused himself and stepped out of the room through the wide doors, out onto the terrace and down the lane through the hedgerows. Behind him Sophia was half-heartedly shushing Ralphie and Rosie was making exaggerated noises.

When their voices faded eventually, he muttered something under his breath and kept going.

There was a statue of an Arthurian knight, made to look somewhat eerie in the glow of a gas lamp. He paused there to take a couple of breaths, still queasy, then two more big gulps of air.

That was better. The moths were getting pacified.

Damned witty of Ralphie, he thought. Victor precisely!

Sometimes he had to remind himself that he sought out remote grounds for praise where Ralphie was concerned, and often these morsels were miniscule.

But the fish head did have Victor's vacant stare. One could almost expect it to complain at any moment.

He lit his pipe and decided to stroll about the grounds.

The Blakeley estate was, like its owner, large, meticulous and impressive. The house was rather more medieval than Victorian—solid stone and mortar where there might have been ornamental bric-a-brac, a battlemented rooftop above instead of a widow's walk and gaudy gables. There were plum trees and ivy, shrubs and creepers and climbers in the finest Kentish tradition. There was a long, winding drive that began on the main road and ran uphill to an archway, a fountain and a circle in front of the huge house.

It was beautiful there at any time of the year, but he had always thought it especially so in April with warm, scented air, the river running freely and everything in color.

Mostly there was Sophia. She, too, tended to bloom in the early spring.

The river was calm that evening, of a manner to soothe one's dyspepsia. He leaned against an elm tree, puffing on his Turkish and Virginian and gazing across the water at the lights from a church bazaar where the tuba in a German band oom-pahed faintly in the breeze.

The morning had begun with a call from the coroner's office, the dull, self-important voice of a bureaucrat informing him that permission had been granted to exhume the bodies of the last two victims and that there were forms to be made out in triplicate if he wished to enjoy any further cooperation from that or any other office in the city or county.

He had rejoiced over breakfast, putting away a meal that would have challenged Ralphie, a meal that he heaved up only a few hours later.

The first of the bodies was that of a vagrant discovered on the green outside the Methodist parsonage two weeks ago. There was no way to identify him and only a few had remembered him as a pathetic half-wit who used to panhandle on the docks near Bainbridge and Water, so he remained suitably anonymous in Potter's Field.

"Sure stinks, don't he?" said the gravedigger, himself a half-wit who grinned through broken, brown, eroded teeth. "Smells like a bucket a doggie diamonds."

The ten o'clock sun was punishing the hillside with almost midsummer ferocity, and the breeze, though slight, was wafting over the field through the grave and up into Blakeley's nostrils as he forced his hands into the rubber gloves. While the gravedigger stood by, whistling and scratching, he covered his face with a handkerchief and parted the soiled linen cover to study the remains. The cheap wood of the coffin had already begun to rot.

The familiar hole in the chest was wide and jagged, a primitive incision growing wider as the leathery, foul-smelling flesh puckered, stretched and cracked. The body had been emaciated long before death. The look on the face was also familiar, caught in the throes of brain-numbing horror.

"Whatcha lookin' for, Doc?"

He turned the body over and checked the other side for the tiny trademark but found nothing. The smell was becoming unbearable.

"Hey! Whatcha lookin' for, I ast ya."

He rolled the body onto its back and opened the linen cloth the rest of the way, holding the handkerchief a little tighter and pressing it against his nose and mouth.

And then he found it, the tiny, upside-down fish, visible in the magnifying glass on the callus of a big toe.

He stood up, gasping for breath.

"Cover him quickly, Mr. Jordan."

"You still ain't told me what you was after."

He coughed into the handkerchief and waved at the odors which were hovering near his head.

"Fish, Mr. Jordan."

"Fish?"

"Fish."

Sometimes it was difficult to suffer a fool politely. Jordan kept asking stupid, impertinent questions, and Blakeley felt his patience wilting in the heat.

The other body was in a grave about a half-acre away in a corner shaded by a clump of chestnut trees, and it had to be lifted out of the ground and into the sunlight for examination. Jordan complained of stiffness in his back and let it be known that the coroner never expected him to do anything but dig graves.

Blakeley fumbled angrily with his rubber gloves and pulled a piece of paper out of his vest pocket.

"See here, Mr. Jordan, this signed agreement guarantees your cooperation."

"Can't read, Doc."

Blakeley gritted his teeth and smiled. They were bare and wolfish behind the dark beard.

"In that case, Mr. Jordan," he said coolly, "I shall have to throttle you."

Jordan looked up, smiled back and expelled gas.

"The old woman made pig's knuckles 'n sauerkraut last night. Better out than in, I always say, don't you?"

It took a second or two for Blakeley to react. There are some gestures so fundamental that they actually require an interpretation.

His face turned florid, but the corners of his mouth were tense white zones where saliva might have run an eon ago on the Darwinian ladder. His eyes became angry little slits, taut at the creases, the brows forming a large black V. He picked up a shovel and snapped the handle across his knee while the gravedigger looked on stupidly, disturbed but not disturbed enough.

So he took a lead pipe from somewhere inside the hole and bent it in his hands.

Jordan grumbled as he tugged nervously at the lid of the coffin and pulled the linen-covered corpse out of the grave.

"The coroner's gonna wanna know who the hell's gonna pay for the damn shovel."

Minetta MacVaye was a young mulatto woman who disappeared from one of her favorite dockside haunts some time ago and was found lying naked amidst the shrubbery that adorned Transfiguration Church. There had been a freak snowstorm overnight, an inch or two which melted by late morning. Her body was discovered by a group of school children at lunch time when they noticed a trickle of red and followed the bloody little stream to its frightening source. One of the children, a little girl, was said to have gone into shock at the time.

Beyond that part of it, her death had attracted little attention. Practitioners of her arts were more or less expected to fall into such disasters. Her pimp was sought without enthusiasm because he was as good a suspect as any. An older brother had spat in the dirt and the rest of her family had expressed vague relief at her passing, and only a distant relative, a deacon in a down river revival camp, had cared enough to sign the necessary papers. It was hard to believe just now that, according to the vice detectives at least, she had been a rather striking woman.

The incision in the chest was especially crude this time; it looked as if it had been made as the victim struggled desperately. It might even have been made with a broken bottle.

The face was too shrunken and skeletal to discern the terror, but it was not difficult to imagine Minetta MacVaye's last minutes on earth.

Blakeley held his breath and peeled off the linen as flies from a nearby slue started to swarm around the body, buzzing close to his face as he readjusted the rubber gloves and picked up his magnifying glass. Her flesh was like cold parchment stretched tightly over a mass of pulp. The gravedigger was silent for a change. A variety of subterranean vermin sought the mouth, eyes, nostrils, anywhere that the putrid matter oozing from the body might collect. The stench was dizzying.

There was nothing on the neck, the arms or the torso. The damned insects had found the hole in the chest.

He gripped the hands and tried to turn them outward. They moved reluctantly.

The palms and soles of the feet were unmarked.

Nothing on the other side either, on the back or on the buttocks. He turned the stiffened body over twice, cursing to himself and trying not to breathe.

The gravedigger seemed mesmerized.

Blakeley turned away, took another deep breath, turned again, and placed the glass closer to the skin.

Nothing on the ankles, calves, either side of the knees . . .

And then, yes, there it was.

The familiar little pilchard was rather well-preserved and located somehow appropriately inside the thigh.

He stood up quickly and used his handkerchief to shoo away the flies, but they persisted. He felt his stomach starting to rebel. For a diabolical few minutes the breeze refused to blow.

"Cover her, Mr. Jordan," he said, gasping for air.

"Izzat the lady they found in the bushes at Transfiggerashun?"

Flies were landing on the gravedigger's face and crossing his forehead.

"I say, cover her, damn it!"

Blakeley could stand it no longer. He draped the soiled linen over the body, lifted it into the pine box and replaced it in the grave. And as the gravedigger grumbled about having to work with a broken shovel, not to mention a bad back and no breakfast, he climbed over a pile of graveside dirt and hurried to a cluster of bushes where he could be violently ill in private. He thought he heard Jordan laughing in the background.

Perhaps in a year or so, with patience and cooperation, his normal appetite would return.

It was peaceful here now with the river breezes in his face, the clean scent of new-mown grass in the air, and all of that hours behind him. He had instructed Olga to burn his clothing and had soaked in a tub of hot, soapy water before feeling free of the terrible stench. A heavy dose of cologne and a walk in the rose garden had helped. So had the four ounces of Bushmill's in the late afternoon.

"Reach fer the sky, yuh varmint, or git set tuh meet Ole Nick."

The voice did not fit the words, not even remotely. He raised his arms anyway and did his best to reply in kind. His accent was equally bad.

"Yuh got me dead tuh rights, Sheriff. Now jist don't git trigger happy."

She jabbed him in the small of the back where she knew he was ticklish, and while his hands were still raised, she threw her arms around his considerable waist and squeezed.

"Been reading Ralphie's dime novels, I see."

"Reckon so, pardner."

"May I drop my arms now, Sheriff?"

"Only if you put them around me."

He picked her up and hugged, gently, because he was damnably strong and she had the delicate beauty of a spring blossom. Whenever he did that, Sophia seemed to disappear for a moment. Such unVictorian displays could only occur in absolute privacy, but when they did she squealed like a nymphet in wildest abandon. He kissed her long, patrician neck, whispered something softly that concerned only them, and gradually let her down.

She rested her head on his chest and patted his stomach.

"And how are we getting along?"

"Admirably now, only please do not surprise me with a midnight snack."

"You have my solemn word."

"Quite a lot of activity over there," he remarked as some fireworks splashed in the night sky across the river. "Father Hertzog's parishioners are certainly enjoying themselves."

A loud, reverberating thud followed. She held him a little more closely.

"The fireworks got the better of Ralphie. He insisted it looked like the attack on Fort Assiniboin, so he saddled up 'n hightailed it fer the church bazaar."

Thomas Aquinas, who had been chasing squirrels by the river's edge, came out of the shadows and rubbed against their legs. She picked him up and tickled him under the chin.

"He'll be disappointed when he finds out they no longer hold up stage coaches out West."

"Not enough to make him 'hightail it fer Philadelphia,' I hope. This is, academically speaking, his last round-up."

Another splash in the sky was followed by another thud. Thomas Aquinas tensed his perfect muscles and threatened to jump out of her arms. His fur puffed out slightly.

"Well, that's a problem for another day."

"He wanted us to go along to the church bazaar, but I thought you'd prefer a peaceful evening, and I was sure he'd wish to be unencumbered. He begins his new employment tomorrow."

"Yes, I recall that being mentioned."

"It's nothing much, but it will keep him occupied for the summer and he ought to enjoy working around the stable. Besides, they'll see to his lunches."

"They've no idea," he said wryly.

"They can afford it. It's the West farm out on Lightcarn Lane."

"That fellow who's running for governor?"

"Yes. His wife goes horseback riding along the same trails where I exercise Gladstone. She's English, from Penryn in Cornwall. A lovely person.

"Her husband is a buffoon."

"You've met him?"

"I've followed his campaign."

Sophia shrugged noncommitally. She had never fathomed enough of American politics to become interested. She knew there was a silly war that served some political interests, just as the Crown and Parliament had gotten Englishmen into some assinine predicaments over the years, but beyond that she had only a vague recollection that the governor's name was Stone, and she had never cared to find out who the mayor was.

And then a cold breeze came off the river, Snopkowski could be heard screeching in the distance, another rocket exploded in the sky, and Thomas Aquinas started to crawl up her chest.

"Now, hang it all, Ian," she said in mock disgust, "I did not come out here to catch some rheumatic disorder in the damp and chill. The river will be here tomorrow, whether we stand guard or not."

He was chuckling again at Ralphie's caricature of Victor.

"Eh?" He squeezed her gently. "Actually, I flattered myself that you'd come out here to be alone with me, not to look at the river."

"I did."

"And so you have, my jewel."

"Ian."

"Sophia?"

"Ralphie is out, Rosie is in her room, secretly reading about Count Dracula, the servants are either asleep or pretending to be, and save for Mrs. Snopkowski, the house is quiet. There is a very friendly fire in the bedroom hearth, and I've a magnum of Dom Perignon, perfectly chilled, that has somehow escaped Victor's attention."

"Oh?"

Sometimes Blakeley was irksomely slow.

"Really, Ian."

She started up the lane toward the house.

He tapped the tobacco from his pipe and smiled.

"Would you mind very much if I joined you?"

Chapter Seventeen

She soaked for quite a while in a hot bath and scrubbed with Yardley soap until her body was pink and white.

The smell and the look were part of her now, infused and symbolic.

Scroob thaself clean now, loov. The gen'mens won't have no truck wi' no randy bawds.

Yes, mum . . . .

The room was cluttered but refined, a planned mixture of Victorian and Edwardian, with the space and comfort demanded of a well-ordered life. Across the shiny parquet floor was a fringed fourposter bed, large and baronial, with a quilted satin spread and big eiderdown pillows.

And the sheets, loov, must be fresh as a daisy at all times, lest the gen'mens fear the cooties.

Of course, mum . . . .

A pink dress with green floral designs across

the bodice and the evening's delicately scented undergarments were draped over a chaise. Like the other furniture, it was made of dark oak and upholstered in blue velvet. There were lamps with stained glass shades and beaded fringe. They were lit at the moment because the drapes were closed.

Not too bright and not too dim. Nice 'n cozy like . . . .

It was always cozy there in its own way—in its own awful way.

The warm light spilled over the Persian rugs, over the William Morris wall coverings, the Dresden figurines, the carefully polished hardwood, over all the trappings of her new station.

And it spilled across her own beautifully sculpted body.

And most especially down there, dearie. Down there's tha meal ticket. Tha must maintain it like a flower garden. Remember.

Yes, mum . . . .

She squatted awhile longer over the bidet that evening, closing her eyes and smiling through clenched teeth as the warm soapy water lapped at her, made love to her, and perfumed suds trickled down her ivory thighs.

Chapter Eighteen

"He's drivin' me nuts, Nate. Any day now they're gonna find me skipping down Broad Street in my birthday suit, tossin' daisies to the wind."

"Careful with those fish hooks."

"If I don't get out a here soon, I might just stuff a handful up his ass."

He felt a barb prick his fingertip, muttered an obscenity, and put the bleeding finger into his mouth.

"You don't know how goddamned lucky you are to be anywhere else right now."

"Oh, I think I do," Nathan McBride said.

When at first he had been assigned to be bodyguard to Lillian Russell, McBride was a lot less enthusiastic. It struck him as another one of the many fatuous, self-serving things dreamt up in City Hall with no regard for real priorities, like the time the commissioner transferred six patrolmen out of the Eleventh to tend bar at the Odd Fellows picnic while some maniac was dynamiting buildings all over the precinct.

But that was before he had actually met the lady.

A sudden northeastern front had come into the Delaware Valley overnight, bringing heavy April showers. McBride had arrived at the plush, new Berwick Hotel that morning during a downpour. There was a grim gathering of righteous souls at the main entrance, and in the doorway a wan-looking manager was pacing nervously. He recognized some of the picketers from the episode on the dock. Their clothing looked darker, more funereal in the wetness and their angry placards drooped soggily, but they plodded along and chanted their monotonous demands with Old Testament determination. Word had leaked out that Lillian Russell intended to include the infamous feather dance— the same routine that had caused such a furor in Vienna and St. Petersburg—in her Philadelphia revue, and that was just too much.

On his way through the crowd McBride noticed a gothic-looking figure seated in a carriage across the street, watching the activity on the sidewalk. The Reverend Ezekiel Twombley, their field general, looking like a cross between Lincoln and a scarecrow, seemed to approve.

McBride knew him better than did the newspaper editors who had given his hellfire tirades so much space. There were some around the town who actually gave him some credit for starting the war. McBride knew him for much less august things; the reverend's police file was bulging.

They made sudden, brief eye contact. Nathan winked and nodded. Rev. Ezekiel Twombley remained sphinxlike.

Lillian Russell's suite was the penthouse on the sixteenth floor.

He showed his badge. Talking through the partially opened door, he got the immediate impression that certain parties weren't anxious to welcome him in. Specifically, there was a man named Al, in an expensive but rumpled suit, business manager or press agent, obviously, and one named Whitey, a large, inbred type, obviously the regular bodyguard.

"Who're you?"

"McBride."

"Somethin' you want, mister?"

"Yeah, for you to open the door."

"Hey, Al. It's the wonder boy! Hello, Wonder Boy."

"Hello, cretin."

"Huh?"

"Open the door you festering pile!"

"You gonna make me, Wonder Boy?"

Just when it was getting truly childish, the press agent's natural timidity had taken over.

"Better open the door, Whitey."

Whitey opened the door and gestured for McBride to come in, then just as childishly, decided to stop it at halfway. So McBride had kicked it open the rest of the way.

Sooner or later, if he had to stay on this dumb

assignment, he knew that territories would have to be established, just like what happens among kids in a schoolyard.

Whitey backed up, covered his eye with his hand and emitted a wounded bellow.

"Don't touch him, Whitey," Al interceded. "She'll have a fit."

"But look what he done, Al."

"Yeah," said McBride, mocking Whitey's stupid tones, "look what I done. Now, I'd like to see Miss Russell. She's expecting me."

"I'm gonna kill ya," Whitey promised.

"Your fly's open, Whitey."

Whitey stared down with his good eye. It was indeed open. He was fumbling with it as McBride walked by. Al nodded toward an archway across the spacious living room. The entire downtown, rain clouds and all, was visible through the bay windows.

He stepped through the arch and rapped on the door. A maid with a thick French accent opened it and demanded an explanation.

He cleared his throat and crossed his fingers. *Je suis ici pour visiter ta maitresse*, he answered. *Elle m'a invite. Je m'appelle McBride*.

The maid, fists clenched and resting pugnaciously on her hips, looked him over. It was a studied, icy stare.

"Officer McBride," said a voice from a few feet away, "do come in."

The maid's fists unclenched. She smiled, curtsied and took his rain-soaked bowler hat. He smiled back and stepped into Lillian Russell's boudoir.

He had been by no means prepared for what came next. He paused and blinked.

Miss Russell was soaking in a bathtub and sipping a demitasse, scented soap bubbles floating just above the level of what—if one were to dismiss her singing voice—had made her most famous.

"Welcome," she said.

Her smile was beyond disarming; it was enchanting.

"Thank you," he sputtered.

"Fifi—that's not her real name, but the newspapers like it—will probably love you forever. She seldom meets a man who speaks French nowadays."

"I'm glad you spoke up when you did. My French is on the kindergarten level."

"Please sit down. Have some demitasse. You look chilled."

He took a chair a respectful distance from her tub.

"It's all right, Sergeant McBride. I promise not to splash you."

He smiled awkwardly and took another chair closer to the tub.

There was something surreal about the whole thing, as he recalled their meeting—the finery, the jasmine scented vapors rising from the tub, the magnificent Miss Russell in the buff.

Hidden by soap bubbles, of course, but in the buff!

"Dreary out there."

"Philadelphia isn't noted for its climate."

"Nor, I gather, for its Lillian Russell fans."

"Fringe loonies, Miss Russell. Nothing to be concerned about."

"I'm glad *you* feel relaxed about it," she said cheerfully.

There had not been much time to study her background, but he recalled a birth date that would make her 33 years old at the time. Add another year for vanity and another two for press agentry and one arrived at an age that gives new meaning to the term "well-preserved." The place of birth was somewhere in the Middle West, but her speech was New York. The coppery hair, now piled atop her head and wrapped in a girlish blue bow, had been expected, but as for the eyes, big, emerald green, and dancing as she smiled, no one had adequately described them.

"I understand you didn't want this assignment."

"We're badly understaffed at the Eleventh," he said, clearing his throat. "The war and all."

She dabbed some suds over one shoulder.

"I should have thought of that. Sorry."

"No reason why you should."

"Oh, I don't know, Nathan. Do you mind if I call you Nathan?"

"Please do."

"It's Lillian, or even Lil, unless that makes you uncomfortable. Anyway, as I was saying, the war was all the Europeans could talk about during my tour. Frankly, I expected to come back and find it had taken all the best men. Glad I was wrong."

"Thank you. But the fact is—"

"Don't you care about what happens to me?"

"Certainly, but we've had a lot of—"

"I'm getting death threats in the mail."

"You get death threats everywhere you go. Jealous women, crazy Bible-thumpers—"

"Not just in the mail, Nathan. In person. Would you mind soaping my back?"

"Not at . . . not at all. What do you mean, in person?"

"Oh my, that feels good. You must have soaped a few backs in your time."

"You mean to say, you've been approached and threatened?"

"I mean to say that yesterday, shortly after watching you disposing of those hooligans at the pier, I encountered a wild-eyed woman—"

"I'm sure you encounter many—"

"—a wild-eyed woman who uncorked a bottle and threw water in my face. Later on a note was delivered here by a street urchin, and the note said it could just as well have been acid, and that next time, who knows? Forget that! I have too much fun with this face, and I don't care how sinful it looks. Say, don't be afraid to rub below the shoulders. I won't get overheated."

He put the soap back into the dish and started to massage her back and shoulders. He had read somewhere that the best way to handle a strange dream was to go with it and not fight it; an abrupt awakening was not good for the heart.

She closed her eyes and purred.

"Do I know my bodyguards or what?"

"I'm glad it was water."

"Not as glad as I am."

"I don't really know how to do this, Miss Russell. I'm just improvising."

"Lillian."

"Lillian."

"They're making cops better every day. Anyway, I don't intend to become a martyr to the cause of show biz. So, how about it?"

"Did they get the wild-eyed woman's name?"

"I guess so. They arrested her. Al said he wanted the whole thing hushed."

"I'll look into it."

"Thank you. I'd appreciate it. And thank you for the back rub."

He dried his hands and tried to appear calm as she sank into the tub, rinsed the soap from her shoulders, and raised a shapely leg out of the water. She studied her toes as if they were jewels and repeated her question.

"So, how about it?"

"Miss Russell, Lillian, in all due respect, you already have a bodyguard who's as big as a house."

"Whitey? He yelped when he got splashed with what missed my face and ducked under a wagon into a pile of manure. Listen, when I told you the war had caused a shortage of good men, I meant it. Whitey is so dumb, he'd lose a spelling bee to a ragweed. The army turned him down because he couldn't tell the difference between 'at ease' and 'about face'. The man has the brain of a milk cow. You must be wondering about how all this happened to me, right?"

She leaned against the side of the tub and spoke secretively, just above a whisper, so that he was forced to lean closer.

"I had a very good manager cum press agent named Harvey, whose only flaw, besides an occasionally overactive carnal imagination, was a tendency to tipple. So, one day in Liverpool, as we were about to embark for the States, I was informed that he'd been at a party with some Americans the night before, got very drunk, and was on his way to the embassy in London to sign up. The feather dance, by the way, must have been his idea. I know it wasn't mine because I've no idea what it is. Honest! Anyway, poor Harvey hired his cousin Al, also no doubt while under the influence, and since I was also out one good bodyguard—lost to the marines—Al hired his friend, Whitey. He likes Whitey because Whitey makes him feel intelligent. And if I ever catch up with Harvey, I'll fry him in animal fat. Would you mind getting me that towel, please? The red one with the pink and white hearts."

"Right."

He turned and took the thick towel from a rack. There was a slight, splashing sound behind him. When he turned again, she was standing, wearing only a few bubbles which were disappearing quickly.

"Would you be a dear and dry my back, Nathan?"

Oddly enough, he grinned; at least now he had the answer to Allison Meredith's question.

He had told himself many times since then

that it was the tale of the acid scare and certainly not the sight of her *au naturel* that had won his loyalty. Naturally, his sense of propriety prevented him from telling the story, so he believed what he chose to believe. But he did tell the entire tale to ex-Lieutenant Hudson, if only to cheer him up, and when he got to the part about his actual motives, Hudson gave a little chuckle.

He knew he'd made a permanent enemy of big, dumb Whitey when, as he was leaving, Fifi the maid, who would henceforth refer to him as *le beau gendarme*, gushed as she handed him his derby. Whitey crossed his arms and glowered as Nathan passed.

He probably should have left it at that, but something about abject vacancy in a human being's eyes inspires tackiness in others.

"Chin up, Whitey. Low foreheads are coming back into style."

And when he had agreed to be her bodyguard, Lillian Russell had pecked his cheek then gasped at the quality of his clothing. If he was going to be seen with her, that would have to change immediately. See the hotel tailor on the way out. She would have it put on her bill.

So now whenever he entered the station house there were good-natured howls and comments about his sartorial trappings mixed with the usual off-color questions about the body he was guarding.

"How much longer?" Hudson asked, still sucking his wounded fingertip.

That was also before the commissioner had decided that the best response to the Jack

Brown incident was to demote Hudson and replace him with Officer Wilmer P. Fatzinger. Ever since then Fatzinger had come up with a number of irritants designed specifically for his former boss. This morning's menial task was the worst so far. It was trout season up in Ebenezersville, so Hudson was tying fishing flies for Bones' girlfriend, Strawberry Knockelknorr, and her eight brothers.

Hudson scowled at Fatzinger, who was sitting in bovine splendor at the desk that used to be his, and challenged his own imagination to come up with a proper vengeance when this ordeal had passed. And it would pass, he swore mightily.

"Patience," McBride advised.

It was close to noon. Fatzinger was engrossed in an interview with a very pretty complainant who had entered in tears shortly after McBride arrived.

He interrupted their conversation to bark another order to the back room.

"Keep dose flies tied up good! No shleepin' back dere on da chob!"

When he turned his head the girl winked at McBride, who nudged Hudson, who gritted his teeth.

"She did it," McBride said.

"God bless her."

Hudson had a hunch, based on some evidence, that he thought might lead him to the burglars—if only he could get out of there and pursue it. He might even get himself out of this fix because, after all, many of the burglary victims were the commissioner's close, personal friends.

"Sometimes I gotta yell, missus. Udderwise, dott filibuster back dere would shtart hiss high jinks. Now, where vass we at?"

She fought back the tears.

"He . . . opened his coat and, and . . ."

"Oh, yeah. He showed you hiss baloney."

She bit her lip and covered her face.

"That's about . . . it."

"Vell, missus, you haff come to da right man. Dott's how come I got diss here chob, ass da boss, fer flasher catchin'!"

She batted her tear-filled eyes and spoke in a whisper.

"Praise God."

Emily, the woman before him, was a schoolteacher with an unfortunate prolivity for shoplifting It was hard to estimate how long the practice had been going on or how extensive her gleanings, but one day last month she'd been caught with her entire Easter wardrobe stuffed into a large purse as she departed the most exclusive shop in the precinct. The owner, a vindictive old crone named Madame Sylvia, was determined not only to press charges with all deliberate vigor, but also to notify the ever choleric headmistress of Miss Fudderman's Latin School where Emily taught third grade. For no good reasons, other than Emily's great big China doll eyes and sublimely innocent smile and the fact that Madame Sylvia was one of the most notorious whiners in the precinct,

McBride had decided to come to the accused damsel's aid.

But Madame Sylvia was implacable.

"Look at her, a schoolteacher, for Chrissake. An educator of our precious youth— shopliftin'! Robbin' me blind!"

"Madame Sylvia, you have your garments back."

"They're wrinkled."

"She'll get them pressed."

"Stuffed 'em into that cheap lookin' purse."

"She's been humiliated, Madame Sylvia. They can hear you from here to Wilmington."

"Don't get smart with me, you. I'm a tax-payer."

"I know. Everybody in City Hall knows."

"Listen, you, I want the little sonofabitch screwed into the ground, and that's that! What the hell was she doin' in my shop in the first place?"

That last comment probably established a kinship of sorts. There were quite a few places where a cop was deemed unworthy, too.

So McBride had called his lieutenant, and Hudson, his ulcer just happening to be acting up at the time, had asked to speak with Madame Sylvia.

When he reminded her of a raid on an Atlantic City opium den last summer, where Madame Sylvia was found in the company of three gentlemen, not one of them vaguely resembling Mr. Sylvia, a sudden, much more amicable settlement was reached. Emily could go in peace, never again to come within a block of the flowery yellow awnings that adorned Madame Sylvia's Shoppe de Haute Couture. But Emily would still be employed.

She was grateful, and in her words, this was a marvelous chance to return the favor. She was clearly enjoying herself, fascinated by Fatzinger and keeping a straight face for the most part.

She was also very good—so good, in fact, that they were sure they'd helped to liberate a felon. The skill with which she opened the bottom drawer, removed Fatzinger's lunch, closed the drawer, and hid the lunch in her big, cheap purse was a sleight of hand worthy of Harry Houdini.

"Youse must a heard a da Lordly Lilywaver what shtruck inta da hearts uff ladies terror all over Philly."

He sat back and rested his hands on his suspenders, while she gasped at the reference.

"Vell, missus, youse are lookin' at da fella dot wrung dott turkey's neck, by Cheesuss."

"I'm overwhelmed."

"Ya, so am I."

He checked his pocket watch. It was one minute to twelve, one minute to liver pudding and chow-chow relish on Miss Knockelknorr's best buns, a half a apple pie, and a jar of stewed prunes.

"Und now youse can tell your friends dott Inshpector Wilmer P. Fatzinger iss on da case, und he won't be showin' hiss baloney to nobody no more if he can help it."

Emily blushed, pecked his cheek, blushed

again, thanked him primly, picked up her purse and left.

Hudson and McBride watched as he opened the drawer and reached for his lunch. Hudson made evil little laughing noises under his breath.

Fatzinger looked up, momentarily stunned.

"Vott iss . . . ?"

He opened the drawer again, opened another, checked under his desk, then checked the nearest waste can. Hudson remarked how like a big, manic bird he looked as his head went down then up, to then fro, his Adam's apple prominent and his eyes showing confusion, ire and indescribable alarm.

"Don't nobody move!"

Activity slowed down. Heads turned. Weary looks were exchanged.

"Somewhere in diss room dere iss a criminal!"

Since there were two thugs and a suspected poisoner being booked at the time, everyone took it for a trite attempt at humor and went back to work. Some who were near his desk smiled politely; for good or ill, he was the boss now. Those at a greater distance smirked, rolled their eyes and made masturbatory gestures.

Fatzinger roared.

"Who shtole da liver puddin'!"

In the confusion that followed Hudson slipped out the door, secure in the feeling that Fatzinger would be preoccupied for some time.

He walked down the broken pavement and crossed the street toward an island where trolleys stopped every ten minutes. The heat rising from the concrete and cobbles burned through the soles of his shoes, but his feet were ready for it. Larry Hudson had pounded out thousands of miles on these pigeon dappled streets in his beat cop years, and the calluses can grow thick enough to dance on porcupines.

Mustn't forget about the burglars.

It was a measure of his anger and of everything else that Larry Hudson stood for that his thoughts returned to Jack Brown.

Chapter Nineteen

The diminutive Father Sigmund Herzog started to climb the 21 steps that led up to the great door of Saint Fidelis Church. He paused as usual at the first landing, looked up, blessed himself, repeated the act on the second landing and a third time outside the great door itself. It was a ritual of his own making, devised over 40 years ago when he first saw the church and dedicated the rest of his days to the Trinity.

Nowadays it was as much out of respect for his aging knees as it was for his vocation that he paused and prayed. There was a price to pay for grandeur.

He loved this church. It was a statement of man's devotion. It reminded him of cathedrals in another time and place, pieced together stone by stone by devout guildsmen. It was smaller, of course, and the Schuylkill, which ran past it, was no Danube. But it had a magnificent door. Hand carved in Salzburg and donated by Sigmund Herzog's family as a gift to his American parishioners, it was of eight-inch-deep oak decorated with cherubim and seraphim arranged around a large Roote of Jesse, and the men of the parish treated it as if it were a newborn.

It was not hard to imagine a passion play on these steps. It had crossed his mind before. He could see the settings along the way, with Calvary in front of the door. At the right moment the doors would open and the brilliant light from within would become the Celestial Paradise, a wonderful touch of the Old Faith. He would discuss it with the Bishop soon, because the days of Sigmund Herzog's life were counting down.

Perhaps next Easter they could afford it, he would inform the Bishop. This year's bazaar, like that of the past ten years, had been a great success. All the knockwurst, beer, sauerkraut and potato pancakes were gone.

He paused before the door and squinted into the morning light, shielding his eyes with a missal. There was about a ton of refuse either in the trash bins or still being gathered up by the men of the Holy Name Society, knotted old fellows like him, united by language.

The springtime birds had been singing since dawn. Now they were waging a noisy war over the stale crumbs around the trash bins. Beyond the bins and the grumpy volunteers, on the green overlooking the river, there were multicolored shrubs in bloom. The sky promised a gentle sun.

He breathed deeply and entered the church. It was approaching time to say the seven o'clock Mass.

There were more steps inside, just after the holy water font, but they were not quite so steep, and since none of the other old fellows could see him, he used the iron railing. After climbing them there was another door, this one of less imposing design, open for anyone who wanted to visit and pray.

He was just beyond the vestibule, on the way to the sacristy, when he spotted it, the puzzling form. It was slumped in a corner, like a pile of rags, near the bank of votive lights. It was anything but frightening at first, just an amorphous blob, something to bring up the next time the sacristan grumbled about his wages. A pile of rags in the flickering illumination of the little candles posed a fire hazard. Sigmund Herzog's eyesight was as dubious as his creaking joints.

He stepped closer. The lump was soft, fleshy-soft and white.

He blinked it into focus. The votive lights often threw off mysteries of their own.

"Are you . . . are you ill?"

And then, after a few more steps he asked, "Who are you? Do you want a doctor?"

But he realized as soon as he said it that the question was inane.

The eyes were not eyes; they were little black holes staring up at him. He stared back. He had seen such looks before on etchings of martyrs, heretics and the possessed. People tied to the stake, alone with an unspeakable horror as flames engulfed them until their bodily gasses exploded, had looks of that terrible dimension.

He knelt and looked away as he hastened through the last rites. Sweat started to drip from his face and he could hear himself breathing as he recited the prayer and made the gesture of the cross.

It might have been comical, the form, lying there propped against the kneeling bench, its dead limbs spread grotesquely, its mouth slack-jawed and stupid.

But for the eyes—and the gaping hole in the chest.

He got up and stepped back. Sweat had soaked his cassock. His eyes saw little dancing spots that split apart and made chaotic little circles. He felt heavy stones against his chest.

He started for the altar, but it was too far away.

His mouth turned to dust. He could not breathe.

No one heard him call out for help as he staggered down the vestibule steps, grasping his throat and tearing the Roman collar away. He fell against the great oaken door and burst through into the morning sunlight.

Some of the men looked up, astounded by the gestures of the very dignified old Father Sigmund Herzog. Buttons popped off the front of his cassock and bounced like tiny black marbles off the stone steps. The noises he made were like deep, desperate croakings.

CEREMONY IN SCARLET

He tumbled down the first seven steps and came to rest on the landing, just as Lucifer would have fallen from heaven in his passion play.

Chapter Twenty

"**Y**ou knew him, Dr. Blakeley?"

"I did. A superb fellow."

"Is it true that he was related to the Hapsburgs?"

"Possibly. They say that everyone in Austria is, somehow or other."

"You knew him well?"

"I was his physician. He thought it best the relationship be kept secret."

"If his heart was in such terrible condition, couldn't someone have orchestrated the fatal attack?"

"Certainly. He had extensive holdings in Austria. There was some aristocratic lineage, as suspected."

"You were . . . ?"

"Yes. I was his lawyer, too. And if I didn't know that all of his estate would revert to Saint

Fidelis Church, and that I was, I'm reasonably sure, the only one privy to the desperate condition of his heart, I'd think we have a perfectly dramatic murder here. Only that is not the case."

"I met him once," she recalled aloud, "back when we were working on the West Philly Butcher case. He translated some documents for me."

Obviously, the topic of discussion as they hurried down the hallway and entered the laboratory was not the person whose wretched remains lay on the table under bright lights. That was the corpse of Goldie Becker. Father Herzog inspired more serious mourning.

Allison Meredith was dressed in boots and jodhpurs and carried a pith helmet under her arm as the door opened and closed with a thud. On Saturdays when she was in Philadelphia she and Sophia used to take long rides in the country. Blakeley preferred to see them in long skirts for side saddle, but he had ceased protesting months ago.

The timing of this morning's ride had been fortunate.

"This will be most unattractive," he warned.

"When I met you, Dr. Blakeley, you and Nathan were fussing over a headless corpse."

"Very well, then," he said, "forewarned is forearmed," and he undraped the corpse.

She gasped and took a step back, feeling wobbly for a moment. She looked away, swallowed with difficulty, then slowly turned back to the subject on the table.

"I'm terribly sorry," he hastened. "One grows callous in this business."

"It's . . . the eyes, Dr. Blakeley."

"Rather defy description, do they not?"

There was a quiver in her voice.

"Like a soul in purgatory."

True. There was something feral in the eyes, a special kind of horror imprinted on the big yellowed pupils. It was not unlike what he had seen before in the eyes of Tony Miller or in similar cases when death was most painful.

"The heart's been torn out—if you will forgive the metaphor—as if someone had merely cleaned a chicken. It probably was a purgatory of sorts. Odd that you should bring up a religious concept just now, Miss Meredith."

"I must have been thinking of the late Father Herzog."

"This represents a new wrinkle. Heretofore the bodies have been deposited at a more respectful distance. I shouldn't be too surprised to find one on the altar soon."

"Do you mind if I take notes, Dr. Blakeley?"

"Not at all. I've some information here, by the way," he picked up a notebook and flipped it open, "for which I am indebted to Detective McBride who stopped in on his way to, to—"

"—to Lillian Russell's hotel suite. I know. It's quite all right."

But he knew by the studied cadence of her voice and by the overly cheerful smile that it was by no means all right. A curious relationship, theirs.

He adjusted his monocle and went on.

"He identified her as one Edna Becker, called Goldie after her prominent gold tooth."

She glanced at the gaping mouth and nodded.

"A prostitute," he went on. "And like the other victims, she lived in the dockside area."

"The Sink."

"Yes. I've been thinking of paying a visit there. You're welcome to come along, Miss Meredith."

The initial shock had worn off, but there was a weakness in the knees and a surge of something in the tummy, and she knew there would be no horseback ride this morning.

"I'd appreciate that very much, Dr. Blakeley."

"Splendid. We'll leave just as soon as I find something that's been eluding me."

He had removed his monocle and was bent over the corpse, scanning it with a magnifying glass. She watched as he ignored the terrible hole in the chest in favor of random parts of the body.

It was large and flabby, a heavy drinker's body, badly neglected and carelessly groomed. He had to exert some effort to turn it on its side. The smells of death were sadly appropriate to the form. It was easy to feel a great distance, easier still to feel pity.

"There it is," he muttered with some relief.

And there it was, whatever it was, at the juncture where the ripples of the upper thigh met the bounteous left buttock. It seemed almost a special act of derision to put it there.

"A tiny upside-down fish," he explained, stripping off his rubber gloves. "A perverse signature the murderer leaves."

Suddenly, her curiosity outweighed her disgust. She lifted the linen sheet and studied the little mark with obvious fascination. But for the glib comment tossed out to the gravedigger a few days ago, it was the first time the signature had been brought to anyone's attention since Sophia had noticed it.

"Good heavens."

"I must ask you to keep this matter in confidence for a while. It's our best clue to date. The rest of it you may report as you wish."

"Thank you. It will be more dramatic that way."

He checked his pocket watch. It was 9:30. The police had wasted no time in getting Goldie Becker's body to his laboratory.

"We should be off, Miss Meredith. The Sink will be coming to life soon."

"I'm all set, unless you don't approve of my riding apparel."

"It will do. We shall take the motor-wagon."

"Motor-wagon? I had no idea you owned one."

Blakeley's reluctance to embrace the things of the coming century was well-known by his friends and closer associates. Even the telephone, which he despised as an intruder in his very private world—a world where one was received generously, but where genuine invitations were extended to a worthy few—was adopted only after Sophia had argued its usefulness for months. To this day he despised the contraption, finding little of value in it save for the simple-minded moments it afforded Victor.

The motor-wagon was probably there because Blakeley was curious about its engineering.

"It arrived last week," he said sheepishly. "I've a devil of a time keeping Ralphie away from it."

There was an uncertain rap on the door. Blakeley recognized it and rolled his eyes.

"Come in, Victor."

Victor entered carefully, aware that a body had been brought in that morning and hoping to avoid anything that might disturb the gin that lingered in his bloodstream.

"Sir."

"Victor?"

"There is a gentleman to see you."

"His name?"

"A Mr. Spector. Bernie to his friends. He desires an audience."

Blakeley and Allison looked at each other; word must have traveled quickly.

"I think not, Victor."

"But, sir . . ."

"Please do not whine, Victor."

But he did anyway.

"Sir, he said he'd introduce me to James O'Neill."

"James O'Neill wouldn't let him in the back-yard, Victor."

"He said he has friends in New York who are looking for a gentleman's gentleman for a new play. Sir, he can give me publicity! All I need is a little puffery and, oh Gawd, stardom is surely not unimaginable."

Blakeley was momentarily still, considering how a revived career might take Victor away for good. But he would probably return, as he usually did, after a week or two.

"Tell him I have a communicable disease or something."

"But that would be an untruth."

"Yes, it would."

Victor whined something and stomped out. Blakeley shook his head and chuckled.

"Shall we?"

"I can't wait."

"After you, Miss Meredith."

The motor-wagon was a Haynes-Apperson surrey, a beautiful machine whose black and silver finish gleamed in the morning sun as he assisted her over the running board and past the steering tiller. It was not her first ride—that had been in a German Benz on assignment for a Chicago newspaper—but for the sake of politeness she pretended it was. He tried to hide his own ebullience as he described the 12 horsepower engine and the reverse and two forward gears. She knew from her research that it was expensive, around $1200, but that he would never be so bourgeois as to mention that.

Sophia bade them a happy journey and rode off on her horse Gladstone, secure in the knowledge that a horse would not overheat or lose the air in a tire.

They were chugging along the scenic river drive, keeping apace with a practicing skull crew and drawing occasional looks of awe and bemusement.

His eyes were fixed on the road surface, actually noticing its imperfections for the first time.

Now and then he muttered "Hrrumph" or the like when the cab shimmied over a rough spot.

She broke the silence.

"Did, uh, Detective McBride say he was pleased with his new assignment?"

"Eh?"

"Sorry. I should let you concentrate on your driving."

"Quite all right, Miss Meredith. I have it under control. Now, what was the question?"

"Small talk, Dr. Blakeley. I was curious about Nathan's assignment, though I guess it's not exactly an assignment."

And then she added, again a little too good-naturedly, "More like a reward."

Blakeley smiled. Ever since he and Sophia had orchestrated an introduction, the relationship between Nathan McBride and Allison Meredith had been a source of some pride to them. They fit each other well—he with his bright, brooding handsomeness that the ladies found so charming, she with her chiseled, slightly freckled face and proud bearing.

But they were creatures of the time, stormy and independent, quick to estrange lest they find themselves apologizing for breaking commitments.

"He doesn't say much about it," Blakeley fibbed.

"I'm told she's really as beautiful as her publicity says."

"I've never seen her in person."

"Hasn't Nathan said . . . *any*thing about her?"

"I believe he said something like, 'all right, if you like the type.' Something of that nature."

This time she smiled. Blakeley was not a very good fibber. They were silent again as he eased the carriage over a bump and dodged a horse deposit.

Only once during the rest of the drive did the subject of Nathan McBride come up again. That happened along a placid stretch of roadway after they'd cut through a park, and for a time it was not necessary to shout.

She still spoke in a bogus devil-may-care attitude.

"You mean, that's all he said?"

Blakeley was uncomfortable with the line of questioning; it would be much too easy to find himself in the middle of a lovers' squabble.

"No," he said after thinking it over. "He also said it was a lot better than tracking down artichokes."

And he left that thought to be juggled and deciphered in her journalistic mind.

The Sink was yawning, slowly waking up when they arrived. The unlucky shopkeepers who had not been able to get out of there chattered in doorways, mended recent damages, and drowsily swept the broken pavement that fronted their places of business. The hard core Sink gentry— the drunkards, addicts, feebleminded, pimps and midnight madonnas— were only beginning to stir.

But the sun was warm enough to bring the smells of the neighborhood to life.

They did their best to ignore a lanky bum who was routed from his sleeping quarters under a stoop when the landlord noticed him. There were curses and a shaky fist in the air as he staggered across the street a few yards in front of them. Then he stopped, muttered something to himself as he fumbled with his fly, and urinated against a broken beer keg that housed another drunk. The occupant seemed not to notice, waving away whatever happened to splash near his head, never waking up.

Miss Meredith handled the situation well, he thought, but he never looked to see how deep a shade of red her cheeks had turned as she struggled to control a giggle.

He knew as soon as they encountered the hostile, jagged brick road littered with debris that taking the motor-wagon that morning was a decision which bordered on senility. Red-eyed stares followed them, and he could only guess that the words of assessment exchanged on the rancid streets were less than complimentary. He tried not to look like Henry VIII making a royal entry into a leper colony.

They stopped in front of Gunselman's Saloon. He was silent for a moment. What were the odds that the motor-wagon would remain intact if he left it there unattended? What were the odds of harm coming to Miss Meredith if she were left unattended? What were the odds of both the vehicle and Miss Meredith being absconded with if both were left unattended?

"I'll stay," she said, reading his mind.

He studied her eyes and found nothing indecisive there.

He reached into his coat and slipped something quietly into her hand.

"I don't know if I can even hold it, much less fire it."

"Just keep it hidden in your purse. If anything should warrant it, all you'll have to do is pull it out. Use two hands, if necessary."

It was a heavy, six-shot Colt .45, of the kind increasingly carried by police officers. The late Captain Regis Tolan, a very close friend, had willed it to him, and he'd kept it in impeccable condition. She slipped it nervously into her purse.

"I shan't be long," he promised, "and should anything dramatic turn up, you'll be the first to know."

The saloon door was unlocked, but the toothless crone running a filthy gray rag over the bar extended no welcome.

"We're closed. If yiz need an eye-opener, try the Polak across the street."

"Is this the residence of one Edna Becker, also known as Goldie?"

"If she's in, she's sleepin'."

The crone looked up for the first time, looked him over and passed judgement.

"There's better'n Goldie around. Try the lady upstairs. A few years younger and a helluva lot cleaner."

"And when I wake her up and she comes to the door, who may I say sent me?"

She grinned and cackled, her gums showing. "What do I gotta do then? Put it in fer ya?"

He handed her a five dollar bill and repeated, "Who may I say sent me?"

She laughed a little more, then shrugged her shoulders.

"What the hell. Tell her Tess sent ya, and ya better be smilin' when ya leave. Tell her dat, too."

"Thank you, Tess."

He took something else from his wallet. She smiled again, expecting another five, but instead it was a badge.

"Ah, shit!"

"It's all right. I don't want it back."

"Take it anyways."

"No, no, I insist."

"Ya sewer scum! Finaglin' an old lady like dat. Yiz oughta be shamed!"

"Of course. And I certainly am, Mrs . . . ?"

"Gunselman—and ya knew it when ya walked in, ya puke bucket!"

"A pleasure, Mrs. Gunselman. And now, if you would please—"

"A widow, too, a poor old widow. Gunselman's dead these fifteen years from the drink, and there yiz are, finaglin' a poor old widow!"

"Show me to Miss Becker's quarters."

"I said, she's sleepin'."

"I know."

She led him down a musty corridor where a dying oil lamp was the only illumination.

"I ain't no madam, y'know. I was jist lookin'

216

out fer yiz. Ya look like a real proper gent. The tootsie upstairs won't give yiz da crabs or worse."

She rapped on the door and called out.

"Yo! Goldie!"

There was no response.

"Get yer ass outa bed. Time is money!"

The crone shook her head.

"She ain't answerin'."

"I'm not surprised."

"Whyncha try later on?"

"Why don't you open the door, Mrs. Gunselman?"

"Shit! Ever heard a privacy?"

"Open the door, Mrs. Gunselman."

"Jeez, knowin' Goldie she could be doin' almost anything."

She opened the door and he stepped in.

"Nice smell, huh?" she said, waddling off.

The badge was Lieutenant Hudson's idea; it deputized him for months at a time and got him past many idiotic roadblocks.

The crone had been right; the smell in Goldie Becker's room was almost overpowering. He went right to work.

There were bugs in the bed and dust and litter everywhere. Among the few things of value he uncovered were several photographs which verified Goldie's identity. Unless this, too, was just another form of aberrant exercise, one of them suggested that she had been married at one time; there was a picture of her in a wedding gown, younger, thinner, not quite so coarse as in later portraits. Next to her stood a dull-looking man in an ill-fitting suit, presumably the husband and probably someone the city should notify.

Beyond that there was nothing much, other than confirmations of her late career. Under the bed, unsettlingly close to a poorly scrubbed chamber pot, were a pair of red boots. Silk and fishnet stockings, lacy undergarments and other tawdry finery spilled out of one dresser drawer. In another there were strange leather and rubber devices that might have been designed for medieval tortures.

He was beginning to feel the same sort of taunting sensations in his stomach that he had felt in the cemetery yesterday. The stench was not quite so bad this time, but close. He had heard it said in his university years that only madmen pursued this branch of science.

There were much more civilized pursuits, like cautioning the upper crust against overindulgence, monitoring their pregnancies, lancing their backside boils during polo season—all for palpable sums. He thought of accepting a boring albeit sanitary position at Swarthmore next year. But there were madmen in the Blakeley line.

Hello? There was something under the whips and paraphernalia.

It was thick and hardbound, sealed with a faded, dirty ribbon pulled to the verge of snapping. He opened it, scanned its ungrammatical contents and departed the small, overheated room.

In the saloon Tess Gunselman was haggling with a group of soldiers who insisted it was time that any respectable saloon was open, and that anything else was unpatriotic. They were going off any day now to be shot at by savages, crazy Spaniards down in Africa. There were different accents and slightly different issues, but it was much the same set of lines he and his mates used to utter in the Fleet Street pubs years ago while in Her Majesty's service. One or two of them eyed him curiously as he went by.

They seemed an amiable lot, youthful and impressive in their spiffy uniforms even after a night of debauchery. The crone was going to hold out until a suitable monetary settlement was reached, but they would win the moment. Youth had a way of doing that.

He felt a twinge of jealousy, but it passed.

"Got what you was after?" asked the crone as he caught her eye.

"All that and more," he replied.

Outside the building there were two or three more soldiers admiring the Haynes-Apperson and, of course, the stunning woman who had arrived with it. She, however, was paying closer attention to a young street tough who was shining her riding boots.

He approached. The soldiers tipped their hats to her and drifted off toward the saloon.

"Dr. Blakeley, I'd like you to meet my friend, Bogdan."

"Good morning, Bogdan."

"Dr. Blakeley's a famous detective, Bogdan."

"Gud mornink. You want shoeshine, boss?"

He glanced at Blakeley and sized him up in one or two blinks, his eyes showing only street-wise indifference. He was finishing the job on Miss Meredith's boots, snapping a rag as it passed over heel and toe.

She made a gesture with her nose, a kind of tiny tweek which pleaded lightly on the boy's behalf.

"Very well, Bogdan. A shoeshine it is."

A tranquil moment was to be desired just then. That morning he had eaten a hearty breakfast of sauteed kidneys, soft boiled eggs, oat meal, and rye toast with ginger marmalade. It was one of his favorite means of starting the day. Unfortunately, he had eaten all of it just before being summoned to Father Herzog on the church steps. His digestion had troubled him since, and after breathing the soiled air of Goldie Becker's bedroom it was threatening to erupt. Hardly a time to subject one's stomach to a ride over broken cobbles.

"Bogdan is very good," she said, tipping him 50 cents.

Her riding boots were indeed shining like a Prussion general's. The street tough pocketed the coins, watched Blakeley and the fancy lady admiring his work, and for the first time cracked a little smile.

"You next, boss."

"Any luck?" she asked as Blakeley propped one foot atop a soap box.

"I think so."

"All privileged? Or do I get to see any of it?"

"I have to decipher it first. I got out of there as quickly as possible."

"Decipher what?"

"Oh, forgive my fogginess, please. The late Miss Becker kept a diary."

Bogdan looked up, thought, then returned to work.

"Good Lord, naming names?"

"I've only glanced, but, yes, a few."

She rolled her eyes. "Oh-ho."

"Most of the time, I suspect, they were nameless or used false identities, but the descriptions might help."

"When do I get to look?"

He smiled.

"Remember, we're concerned only with her murder."

Bogdan's pace slowed. Normally, he was indifferent to his customers' conversations.

She smiled back.

"All I want to know is who she entertained most recently."

He nodded wisely. "And you shall."

She sighed.

"Well, it isn't very likely that Goldie Becker ever entertained the Secretary of State, Dr. Blakeley."

Neither of them noticed the shoeshine boy reacting to the second mention of Goldie Becker's name, but his eyes opened wide then narrowed suspiciously.

Blakeley took the diary from his coat pocket, opened it and thumbed through the last entries. Even at a glance, it could have been a blackmailer's treasure. Though the actual names were seldom logged and Goldie's descriptions were hampered by near illiteracy, the late prostitute had shown a flair for drawing. The sketches were often grotesque, reminiscent of the pornographic caricatures used as evidence in the Christopher Beecham trial, but often she had caught the essence of the shadowy men and women who passed through her life.

Allison had just cleared her throat for the second or third time. He looked up abruptly.

"No sign of the Secretary of State?" she asked.

"I promise you, Miss Meredith, should anything of importance to national security appear on these pages, you shall know immediately."

"Rather interesting art work."

He arched a brow and smiled as she peered over his shoulder. The shoeshine boy strained to understand their interest in his Goldie.

"Now here's something in the last entry about a quote shindig unquote she planned to attend that evening with some chap called Fatso."

"Goldie's last shindig, I'll bet. Anything else on Fatso?"

He scanned the pages, squinting now and then at the phonetic spellings and arcane references to lollipops and so forth. Suddenly, the shoeshine boy looked up.

"I'll have to go back a few entries and—"

"Dat's my Goldie book. Why you take?"

Bogdan was standing. His tone was panicky, and he dropped his brush.

"Did you know her, Bogdan?"

"What you do my Goldie?"

"Nothing. Can you tell us about her, Bogdan?

"My Goldie dead, huh?"

"I . . . I'm afraid so."

"You kill Goldie!"

"Of course not."

"For why you got book den?"

"Because—"

Bogdan swung at Blakeley, who blocked the wild punch and pushed him back.

"Now then, calm down and we'll discuss this!"

But this time Bogdan's eyes flashed with a mad dog's ferocity, and in a second he produced a switchblade knife.

"Bogdan!" Allison demanded. "Put that away!"

He clicked it open and took another step, muttering something in his own language. From listening to Snopkowski's tirades against Victor, Blakeley picked up a few words, vaguely, presuming they were anything but complimentary. The few that he could make out with any clarity at all, as he watched Bogdan's eyes and the knife and waited for the youngster to make a move, sounded like "Jake a bastard" and "Zoltan honk-honk," and he wondered if he was facing a new form of criminal dementia.

Bogdan lunged again, this time getting close enough to put a small hole in Blakeley's dress coat.

Enough was enough. Youngster or not, Blakeley put his fists up and made ready for a set-to.

But as he did so, he dropped the diary.

"Bogdan!" Allison repeated. "Please put that knife away!"

But Bogdan intended only to put it somewhere in Blakeley's stout body.

This time, instead of lunging, he reverted to the form of the streets, circling, looking for an opening, and shifting the knife from hand to hand, as if intending to mesmerize the opponent. It was a typical method of fighting in the back alleys of immigrant neighborhoods, but fairly remote to Blakeley. He had heard it described years ago while on duty in the Khyber Pass where a friend had witnessed a fight between two Afghans. He recalled something the same friend had told him, so when Bogdan made his next move, he stepped aside, used his leverage, and shoved the youngster into a foul mound of garbage outside Gunselman's. When Bogdan landed he let out a cry of outrage and disgust more than anger.

Blakeley was grateful for the sudden recall; never had he expected anything worthwhile to come of his time spent in that remote, God-forsaken piece of the Empire.

As Bogdan got to his feet, the look in his eyes was every bit as wild as any Afghan's. And unfortunately, he still held the knife.

A crowd was gathering. One could sense an ugly mood from lowlives with hangovers and a deep down hatred for his class. They seemed to come from every fetid nook and cranny.

He peeled off his dress coat and rolled it around his forearm, which was something else he'd learned in the Khyber Pass. But he knew it was of limited value as a shield because the switchblade in Bogdan's hand was like a stiletto.

Two of the soldiers stepped out of Gunselman's carrying mugs of beer. "What the hell's goin' on?'' one of them said, and the others followed.

The crowd closed in, forming a small circle for the two combatants. Bogdan inched forward and prepared to lunge again. Blakeley looked around for a weapon, any weapon, but none was forthcoming. There were shouts from the crowd, surly, sadistic suggestions for where Bogdan should insert the knife and how to twist it. Something seemed to change in Bogdan's eyes just then, a look less fierce that Blakeley caught in passing. The business between them was private. Bogdan's anger was his alone. The outside forces were unwelcome. But the Sink had rules of its own, a prison yard code that took away free will and, in its own way, reaffirmed Darwin.

Bogdan's next move was more a dive than a lunge. Blakeley blocked the swing, twisted the street tough's arm, and slammed him against a rickety wooden pillar that held up an equally rickety wooden roof in front of a pawn shop. He knew he was hurting the boy, but twist as he may, the knife would not come out of his grasp.

"Now see here, Bogdan," Blakeley grunted, "give it up and we shall talk this out like civilized human beings. I did *not* harm your Goldie!"

The crowd did not like the way the struggle was going. It grew angrier and noisier. The circle around Blakeley and the shoeshine boy narrowed. There were voices urging others to kill the swell.

And a shot rang out.

The crowd noise fizzled.

There were isolated oaths muttered as Bogdan's grip weakened and Blakeley took the knife. But the voices were suddenly subdued, lost in the distant sounds of the city.

"If I have to, I'll shoot anyone who takes another step."

Miss Meredith held the .45 in both hands and aimed it at those in the forefront. Smoke wormed out of the barrel after the shot she had fired in the air. From her vantage point atop the motor-wagon she could shoot almost anyone who made an unwise move. Only Blakeley realized with what trepidation she handled the weapon.

"Back off, all of you," she demanded, and the circle widened.

Gesturing with the knife, Blakeley shoved a path through the crowd and cranked up the engine. It started with a bang and a puff of smoke that sent some of the riffraff on their way.

"Excellent thinking, Miss Meredith. I'd quite forgotten the revolver."

"Thank you. May we go now?"

"Immediately."

But as he climbed aboard the carriage, some of the toughs who took exception to being shoved by a swell and threatened by a skirt started to make their way forward.

"I meant that, mister," she snapped, aiming the .45 between the eyes of their ringleader. "I'll use you for target practice."

The wolfish sneer remained.

"You ain't shootin' nobody, lady."

Blakeley noticed others easing around behind the motor-wagon, and he knew that he and his companion would be in serious trouble should their tires be slashed.

Damn, he thought. This was hardly a situation for Miss Meredith, resolute as she was. It was just the sort of mischief that Ralphie reveled in, and he was off somewhere mucking a stable.

He took a deep breath and put all of his considerable weight into a roundhouse right. The punch landed and knocked the sullen ringleader halfway into the street. Two more jumped him and tried to wrestle the knife from his grasp. He took one punch near the eye, landed one in return, and tossed the other over his shoulder. And all of a sudden it turned into a first-rate donnybrook. The soldiers gulped down their beer and jumped into it on Blakeley's side, and for a brief moment the numbers were even. Grunts and groans and curses mingled with the crunching sounds of bodies crashing into other bodies. Allison wanted to take notes, but there was no time. She stood up in the carriage, waved the pistol overhead, and cheered Blakeley on. For a man of his girth, he seemed to move almost balletically. And he was very strong. When he hit them, they got up slowly or not at all. He would protest, she knew, that this was hardly fitting for a middle-aged thinker, but she also knew that he was enjoying it. Now and then a body would crash into the carriage and it would sway, and she would teeter unladylike for a second or two.

Another crowd was gathering, joining in and swelling the sidewalk. They shook the motor-wagon even worse as two or three bodies at a time crashed into it. This time she lost her balance and fell backward. A couple of toothless hags out of Dickens seemed intent on pulling her down by the hair. This, she thought, was better than the fiction she was reading about Teddy Roosevelt and his so-called Rough Riders. This was the real thing. She gave one of the hags the back of her hand and was called a "pig's arse" as the hag lost her grip and fell to the ground.

Above the noise she heard a clanging and the rumble of horse-drawn carriages over the broken roadway. She looked around to see a small contingent of uniformed men rounding a corner and approaching in a hurry. First there was a paddy wagon, and then a buggy with a bad spring.

In the front seat of the buggy, next to the driver, she recognized a figure in a garish suit. Next to him, holding on to a flat straw hat with one hand and clinging for dear life to a rail with the other, was a gentleman in an even gaudier outfit. From a distance they could have been clowns at a circus.

The paddy wagon slowed down and policemen jumped out, charging into the melee with nightsticks. She counted no more than five, but to the Sink people, with their many reasons to avoid the law, they must have seemed like hundreds. The first to flee were the two hags nearest the motor-wagon. Somebody shouted "Raid," and in a blink of the eye the crowd was much smaller.

In another minute, but for those on the ground and a groggy few standing, the street was empty.

Blakeley looked quite unlike himself—torn vest, stained shirt, tie askew, classic black eye. He was smiling as he helped one of the soldiers to his feet.

Allison returned the .45 to her purse discretely and climbed down from the carriage.

"Are you all right, Miss Meredith?" he asked.

"I am. But you look a sight."

"Yes, yes, I suppose I do," he said absently, wondering how to explain it all to Sophia.

"Don't look now," she said under her breath, "but the morning's about to go from bad to worse."

"Good Lord!"

Crossing the street were the two gentlemen from the buggy, the first one looking greenish-gray after his manic journey and walking with a familiar, high-stepping gait, the second wearing a familiar noxious smile and carrying a large leather satchel and an instrument on a tripod.

Suddenly Blakeley turned the same color.

"Where's the book?" he whispered.

"I thought you had it."

They looked around frantically, then quickly stiffened as the two men approached.

"Good morning, Officer Fatzinger, Mr. Spector."

"Call me Bernie."

"Look oudt fer da doggie-doo, Bernie. Vell,

vell, Doctor Blakeley, diss here musta been some minny-ha-ha youse got yerself into."

"Hold still, Doc," said Bernard Spector as he fumbled with his camera. "My readers will want a look at this. Maybe if you'd put your arm around Cutie here, I could get both of you in it."

Chapter Twenty-one

"Let's just pay him off."

"I don't think that would be a good idea."

"What the hell, it gets him off my back."

"Maybe it does."

"All I want is to be able to come and go without having to dodge rotten eggs."

"I can understand that."

"It can't cost much."

"Want to bet?"

"Find out, okay?"

"In all due respect, Miss Russell, you aren't acting very much like a worldly businesswoman right now."

"Nathan, this is standard operating procedure in my business. Morally indignant people have been making money on show people for centuries. Don't you think Shakespeare ever had to make his peace with the preachers and politicians? If it was good enough for him . . . trust me."

"He'll only want more, probably every night."

"Look at it this way. The publicity he's given me is probably worth ten times the bribe. We're already sold out in Pittsburgh and Baltimore, places we won't even get to for weeks. Hell, I ought to fire Al and hire the reverend."

"You ought to fire Al anyway."

The conversation ceased for a moment. She got up, lit a cigarette and paced, looking more girlish than glamorous in a slate gray skirt and prim, high-necked blouse. She could have been Allison, he mused, or a schoolteacher, but for the scent of Parisian perfume and Turkish tobacco.

"You're sure you saw him? Really sure?"

"I'd know that handsome devil anywhere."

Nathan's morning had gone almost as well as Blakeley's had. The Rev. Ezekiel Twombley lived on an estate of some size, palatial in fact, for a man of professed moderation. It was Tudor, complete with stable and servants' cottages, and was located about three miles south of the city line, off a highway that led to the Delaware seaside resorts. For the third straight day, Nathan had staked out the main entrance, wondering if a hunch he had had about Al would pay off. Sure enough, at about 9:30 someone who looked a lot like Al drove up to the entrance in a two-wheeled cart, but his face was obscured by the fringe that hung from the roof, shading the cab. Nathan had scaled the high wall and followed the cart onto the reverend's property, moving carefully through the blooming laurel bushes until he had a clear view of the house.

Al—and this time there was no doubt—had knocked and entered and spent about a half-hour inside. Nathan had circled around to the rear of the house, guessing that any serious discussion would have to take place in the study. To get there, he had to wait until the gardener looked away then dash across an open space and hope above all to avoid the watchman he'd spotted yesterday. He was a large lumberjack type, as humorless as the reverend himself, with an even meaner looking Staffordshire straining on a leash, and he seemed to prowl without any regular itinerary. The shotgun he carried in the other hand looked like it could bring down a dinosaur.

The room was where Nathan had expected it to be, but the window was too low and the voices too muffled, so he had pulled himself up into an apple tree and leaned forward for closer inspection.

For two people on opposite sides in a struggle for the souls of all good Philadelphians, Al and the Rev. Twombley were quite chummy. Whatever they were saying had caused the reverend to laugh uncharacteristically, drape his arm over Al's anemic shoulders, and toast the subject with a glass of cognac. Yes sir, there it was on the Chippendale desk, a fifth of Martell Cordon Bleu, the very best—and at 10:00 in the morning yet. So much for moderation.

And then the bough had snapped.

Eyes flashed toward the window. Nathan

could swear the reverend had uttered the foulest of foul words as the tree shook and Nathan landed on the perfectly manicured grass. It was Al's voice, he was sure, that had screamed for the watchman and demanded that the dog be sicced on Nathan—and it was, accompanied by the loud, reverberating crack of the shotgun.

Nathan had seen the dog bearing down on him at a pace that ruled out any chance of outrunning it, so he cut through a begonia patch, drawing howls of obscene rage from the gardener, and jumped into Al's rented two-wheel cart. The old draught horse, moping happily in the shade, had looked up listlessly until it spied the dog and was startled out of its daydreams. They charged down the driveway with the Staffordshire yapping close behind. A second shotgun blast tore away part of the seat a few inches from Nathan's right ear, scattering shards of wood and chunks of padding through the cab. This seemed to give the old horse new life, and for a time they outran the dog. Nathan was shouting encouragement when he suddenly realized something that made him utter language twice as foul as what the reverend had said. The main gate was closed and there was no time to get out and open it.

The dog was bearing down on his left. He jumped out through the other side and ran along the wall, sprinting like an Olympian as he looked for a chance to scale it.

The Staffordshire got around the cart, spooking the old horse and snarling as if the ruse had made him even angrier. He was the perfect breed for this kind of duty—fast, strong, and vicious, with the jaws of a python and the tenacity of a gila monster. As a rule dogs reflect the personalities of their owners.

He spotted another apple tree and prayed that it was sturdier than the last. It shook but held his weight as he climbed as high as it would allow.

The dog leaped, and the seat of his trousers, underwear and all, were torn away.

Another shotgun blast put a deep scar in the brick wall. He saw the watchman across the lawn, reloading and taking aim. The dog was leaping and growling, its jaws making contact with the sole of his shoe, gaining height with each effort. Nathan distracted it for a few seconds by offering up his brand new bowler hat, which was quickly torn to pieces.

He leaped from the tree, used the hole gouged out by the shotgun pellets for footing, and propelled himself over the top just as the watchman fired again.

There was a loud yip and a brief, sickening whimper, and he realized that the blast had caught the Staffordshire, probably in mid-air. Under the circumstances, it was hard to feel sympathetic.

Nathan had spent the time that it took to drive back to the Berwick and sneak through the lobby in his bottomless pants thinking of what might have been the case if the dog had jumped just an inch or so higher, especially remembering what its teeth had done to his hat.

He also considered a score of things he wanted to do to Al.

"But what's a girl to do?" Lillian Russell asked. "I can't be without a manager and press agent in this business."

"You don't seem to understand. Al is worse than no one at all."

"I suppose so," she sighed. "Maybe I can get someone to come in from New York. God, I wish my Philadelphia days were over."

"You'll miss us."

"Think so?"

She picked up a letter that was lying on a coffee table.

"This is a polite note from the hotel's management saying that, though they appreciate my business and realize that I may be a victim of some misguided zealots, blah-blah blah-blah, they'd be grateful if I'd find lodgings elsewhere. No offense intended, of course. I guess I don't bring the kind of notoriety they want in the long run."

There was a knock on the door and the maid entered, a pair of trousers draped over her arm. When he thanked her, she winked, curtsied, and left.

"Excuse me, please," he said, backing into a screened area to change.

Lillian Russell snuffed out her cigarette and marveled at the hole in the seat of the pants he took off and hung over the top.

"My, my, a closer call than that and I'd have another tenor for the chorus."

"It's nice to know there are alternatives."

"If I know Al, he won't come within a mile of you unless he has Whitey with him."

"That's understandable."

He stepped out from behind the screen adjusting his tie and shuddered as he inspected the trousers. She put her hand through the hole and wiggled her fingers playfully.

Less than five minutes later Al burst in, demanding that Nathan be fired for interfering in his negotiations with the Rev. Ezekiel Twombley. The best defense is a good offense. Only in Al's case it was a pitifully feeble offense; he sputtered in impotent anger.

Arms folded and eyes peevish, pretending to follow the proceedings with his one-watt mind, Whitey stood a few feet away.

"I don't recall sending you out there," she said.

"I wanted to spare you the trouble. I'm your manager, fer Chrissake. That's what managers do. Keep the boss from gettin' her hands dirty. And I had the old geezer all set up when this, this maniac appeared in the window like some goddamn monkey in a tree and wrecked it!"

"Monkey, yeah," Whitey reacted. "In a tree."

"Wrecked everything I've been workin' on for the last two weeks—and now it's gonna cost us a real bundle!"

"No, it isn't, Al," she interrupted.

"And then, just to ice the cake, the sonofabitch even killed a dog!"

"We aren't paying a cent. And you're fired."

"The guy's a walkin' disaster!"

"I said, you're fired, Al. Get out and take your trained ape with you."

"Trained ape," Whitey laughed, then scowled uncertainly.

Al stiffened. "Fired? Me?"

The maid entered carrying Al's briefcase and hat and handed them to him. Nathan stood up. It was about time for Whitey to make a move.

"Show them out, Fifi," Lillian Russell instructed.

"*Oui, madame*."

"Whitey," Al pleaded, "do somethin', fer Chrissake."

The maid jerked her thumb toward the door and shoved Whitey.

"*Allez!*"

Al's eyes showed near hysteria. The French maid scowled, and Whitey left in a hurry. Something about her—the language was a fair guess —intimidated him. Al followed him out the door awkwardly.

She brushed imaginary dirt off her palms, curtsied and went on to her next task.

"Now, wasn't that a lot easier than brawling, Nathan?" Lillian Russell suggested. "No mess, no damage."

"Al got off too easily, but I guess you're right. I've had enough fun for one day."

She sat back on a sofa and rested her feet on the coffee table.

"Well then, Officer McBride, what are we going to do next? At this point we're still stuck with the Reverend Twombley, and I'm afraid you're really stuck with me."

Chapter Twenty-two

It was not what was taken so much as what was not taken which had inspired him. Missing were cash, baubles, spare change, anything gawdy and uncomplicated that could be easily banked or fenced. Either the method of operation was especially streamlined and utilitarian, or it was engineered by a moron. Hudson suspected the latter. Not missing were a Ming vase of perfect jade, a Johsua Reynolds original, a rare stamp collection, and a document whose watermark dated it to 1679 and connected it to the court of Charles II. In all the wealthy homes victimized by the burglars the pattern was the same—unimaginative.

Getting the victim's cooperation was difficult, and it confused him at first.

"You say the references were good?"

A bored Bryn Mawr voice answered.

"We didn't question them."

"Beg pardon?"

"I believe I said, we didn't investigate."

"Oh."

"It's a tedious formality, Officer."

"The girl in this photograph has dark hair. She could have worn a blonde wig. Can you see that?"

"No . . . .Well, yes."

"This is the chambermaid then."

She took another look at the girl in the picture, holding it at a distance, pinky finger curled outward.

"Could be. Certainly looks cheap enough."

"And she was in your employ for about two weeks?"

"I didn't count the days."

He returned the photograph together with his notebook to the scuffed, well-traveled satchel in which he carried them and removed his reading glasses.

"Mrs. Worthington, I just want to catch a burglar."

"I want you to."

"And when I catch the person who opened your safe, I won't ask any more questions than I have to. I promise."

"Don't be dreary, Officer Hudson. We have nothing to hide."

"Lieutenant Hudson, Mrs. Worthington. We have our little pecking order."

"You, sir, are no gentleman," she cawed. "I would remind you, we know the commissioner."

"You needn't remind me. You've said so twice."

"I would not hesitate to call him and complain."

"I'll try to remember my place. Now, about the girl in the picture, was she or was she not the one who worked here for two-and-a-half weeks prior to the burglary?"

"I thought I told you."

"No. You just said, 'could be' and 'certainly looks cheap enough'."

"Are you mocking me?"

"Do you need another look, Mrs. Worthington?"

She glared at him for a moment. A pale, pretty woman in her late forties, she had high, delicate cheekbones, eyes of gray to match the few strands that showed along the light brown temples, and the sensuality of a rock on the bottom of a cold mountain lake.

"Show it to me again."

He reopened the satchel and removed the photograph, holding it in front of her like a maitre d' presenting a bottle of fine wine.

She looked, sniffed and passed judgement.

"It is the cow. Now, if—"

"I can show myself out, Mrs. Worthington."

She made no effort to get out of her Louis Quinze chair, dismissing him with a simple wave of her fan that could have been intended to clear the air of something foul. In those few moments when Mrs. Worthington seemed less determined not to notice him, she had a way of making one feel he should check the state of his armpits.

He smiled a bit at his cheesy little victory, forcing her to look once again at the crude girl who had hoodwinked her so easily. The rich need that sort of thing now and then, just to keep them off-balance.

Mrs. Worthington had not been the worst of them. A Mrs. Marbury, whom he had visited earlier, had insisted he remain outside, giving minimal replies through the latticed door of the servants' entrance. Some had refused to speak at all. They, too, were friends of the commissioner. And then there was the swishy young man dressed for squash who stopped him on the street and asked if he'd mind removing his shoes and stocks because he wanted to know if cops were really flatfooted. Hudson wanted to stuff the socks in his mouth and let him suffocate as his fruity friends looked on. Cardboard people every goddamn one of them!

His hunches were paying off, though. Mrs. Marbury, Mrs. Worthington and a Mrs. Dinwiddie yesterday afternoon had all identified the picture of Jennifer Zebers, whose method was quite simple because she was quite simple. Had she stolen a vase it would have been for serving beer to a client, and the only portrait that could have caught her attention would have been that of a hunting dog. Just get a job in a ritzy house, preferably as a chambermaid because that put her in the best position, get close to the man of the house, find out where the valuables are kept, and take it from there. Because nature had endowed her with overwhelming attributes, the whole thing seldom took very long.

Mrs. Dinwiddie had sneered something about her husband's brokerage house on Chestnut Street.

"An Officer Hudson to see you, sir."

There was a hint of shock on Dinwiddie's face as the secretary announced him but no suggestion of refusal, just a cautiousness in the smile at first.

"Come in, Hudson."

"Lieutenant Hudson, Mr. Dinwiddie."

Dinwiddie sat back and scratched his head with a pencil.

"I simply cannot imagine the theft of a few hundred dollars requiring the services of a police lieutenant."

"City Hall tends to overreact."

"You're just in time for lunch."

The chairs facing the wide desk were deep and comfortable. He chose the one offered.

"This won't take long. Just a few questions."

"Which I'll be happy to answer."

He was a big man with a ruddy, round face atop a large, well-dressed body. He was confidence personified.

"Damned irritating business. Had the theft occurred here, my insurance would take care of it. At home only the furnishings are covered, not the cash and shiny trivia. Excuse me, won't you?"

He pressed a button and Hudson heard a buzzer sound faintly on the other side of the

243

wall. Within seconds the secretary, a drab little woman with thick glasses and a witch's nose, entered.

"Keep me up to date on that Philippine business. I have a few people watching the rubber market. Don't hesitate to interrupt."

"Yes sir."

"You play the stock game, Lieutenant Hudson? . . . No, I don't suppose you do. Well, there are grand things coming and you should." He drew himself up in his massive chair. "Take rubber, for instance. Bright men are actively engaged in perfecting the horseless driving machine. Soon those contraptions will crowd the roads and the fellows who purchase them will need rubber for their pneumatic tires. Out there where we have the Spaniard on the run there's a helluva lot more than bananas. There's tobacco for your cigars, coffee for your cup and sugar to sweeten it, and copra for the gunpowder we'll need if we intend to keep it all. Think about it."

Hudson had read all that in the *Wall Street Journal*.

"About the shiny trivia, Mr. Dinwiddie, was there anything of any real value in it?"

"Not really. In fact, it was mostly costume jewelry that Mrs. Dinwiddie was holding for her drama club. They do a show every year for the Radnor Valley Botanical Gardens. They drape their fat asses in oldtime clothing, charge too much, and embarrass themselves and their husbands."

"Mr. Dinwiddie," Hudson thumbed through

the contents of his satchel, "I came here on a slightly delicate matter."

"I've been expecting this."

"Ever see this lady?"

He showed Dinwiddie the photograph. There was a brief, throat-clearing moment and a wry smile.

"I, uh . . . I'd hardly call her a lady."

"And by that you mean . . . ?"

"What the hell, Lieutenant. You know what I mean, so let's get on with it. A little slap and tickle never hurt anyone."

"True. But where did you slap and where did you tickle?"

"In the guest rooms, the library, once or twice in my study."

"Where the safe is located."

"My big mistake. But I cannot for the life of me figure out how she got in there. The double lock was intact, so the burglar had to get in from outside. The rear of the study is just below ground level and nobody with a pair of melons like hers could ever squeeze through the tiny window. Damn, for a little while there I thought I was a real Casanova. Too soon old and too late smart, as they say."

There was a peremptory knock and a concierge entered, wheeling in a cart full of food. Dinwiddie got up and poured them each a glass of mineral water.

"Have some lunch, Lieutenant. There's enough here to feed my wife's drama club."

"Don't mind if I do," he replied, making himself a ham and Swiss on rye. He was starting to feel a grudging sense of amicability, despite the surroundings. "Thank you."

"Ever have an artichoke heart, Lieutenant?"

"I don't believe so."

"Here, try a few. Full of exotic properties, they tell me. It'll keep your old putter from flagging —just in case you run into the girl in the picture."

Chapter Twenty-three

It was one of the most perplexing days of Blakeley's life, but it was also one in which the world of Casimir Wojdzekevicz was improved measurably.

To begin, Bogdan knew the dank, jumbled topography of the Sink well enough to lose himself there forever if necessary, and the natives were far from eager to help Blakeley find him.

As soon as Fatzinger, Spector, and the police were gone, he paid old Gunselman enough for several rounds for the soldiers, then set out with Miss Meredith to find the boy with all deliberate speed. He had the book. She had seen him carrying it as he disappeared while Blakeley was doing his best to break a camera over Spector's head. They had to get it back. God only knows what could happen to their case if the book fell, for instance, into Spector's hands.

Twice Blakeley slipped money into grimy palms only to discover soon that he'd been sent on a fool's errand—first to an empty lot, then to a rat-infested dump. Mostly they were totally ignored or met with cold stares, and suddenly nobody in the Sink understood English. At last they approached Kapuznik, who owned the saloon one block up the street from Gunselman's, and were threatened with the contents of a slop bucket. As she dodged it, Miss Meredith stepped into a rotten spot in the wooden sidewalk and sprained an ankle.

Blakeley was furious. He picked up the bucket and flung it at Kapuznik, who ran inside and locked his door.

Miss Meredith gritted her teeth and muttered an obscenity under her breath that he must have heard but chose to ignore as he picked her up and carried her to the motor-wagon. They drove off in a puff of blue smoke, and along the way he stopped in a shady spot miles from the Sink to cut away her riding boot and see to the ankle.

"You're quite the trooper, Miss Meredith," he assured her as she winced and apologized for becoming a casualty.

One hour later he returned in a horse-drawn vehicle with Casimir, who was pleased to get away from Snopkowski and overwhelmed by the trip through Philadelphia. Blakeley noticed, not without admiration, that the young man had been working on his English in the few free moments Snopkowski allowed him, but since it was still in its primitive stages, they used sign language whenever possible to supplement it. Now and then Casimir got carried away.

As they rode into the heart of the Sink he held his nose and waved at the air. Some passing ladies saw him, held their noses and waved in his direction.

"This is a very unfriendly place, Casimir."

"Hah?"

"I said, this is . . ." He let his voice trail off. "Never mind."

He spied an old woman in a babushka scrubbing a stoop in front of a narrow house and pulled up nearby.

"Ask her, please, about Bogdan."

"Hah?"

"Bogdan." He pantomined a shoeshine and spoke very slowly. "Shoeshine boy. Bogdan. Ask her if she knows him."

Casimir looked confused as usual. "Shushinkboy?"

"Shoe . . . shine . . . boy."

The old woman looked up and shook her head.

"I ain't no Polak, mister, and I don't know where the hell the kid is. And if I did, I wouldn't tell yiz anyways."

After another half-hour of similar futility it occurred to him that he had one ally in the neighborhood. There was a church nearby with a soup kitchen that served the tenement children. The curate was Polish. He knew that because every year on Christmas Eve Snopkowski would prepare boxes full of delectable things that Ralphie would deliver to the church. One year Ralphie had even volunteered his father to play Santa Claus when the local fellow who usually played him got too drunk to say ho-ho-ho.

The priest welcomed them, quickly reminding Casimir that he heard confessions in his language. Casimir blushed and grinned.

"Bogdan is very sad boy, Dr. Blakeley. Is orphan. Mama, Papa die in big fire when he is maybe one, two. Always I ask him, come to church on cold night and sleep with other kids. But Bogdan got head like mule. Eat, sleep his own way, thank you very much, Father Wladislaw."

"Where does he usually sleep, Father?"

"Kid like Bogdan live like alley cat."

"Please concentrate, Father. I have to find him."

The priest mumbled to himself for a moment and looked upward for inspiration. He was a young man in his mid-thirties with the lean, chiseled look of a boxer. The hands were big and marked by hard work. For some reason, it was easy to picture him in an upstate coal mine.

He thought of something, vaguely.

"Bogdan know some color people up Nigger Hill. He go dere play hooky from school. Hooky playink all the time. You go ask for John Henry."

John Henry lived in a patch about two miles from Father Wladislaw's church. It was one of those places that belonged to no particular town or city. It might have been thrown together by a once-promising enterprise as a place to house workers, then abandoned during one of the financial panics of the past. Or its original residents may have settled there simply because a living of sorts could be had off the nearby city dump. John Henry's people had trickled in about a quarter-century ago, gradually swelling the population with friends and relatives coming up from the Carolinas. It had never been incorporated and no one had ever cared to lend it his name. Hence there was the unflattering title it was now known by.

"What fo you wantin' John Henry? He done suppim wrong?"

"Not at all."

"Ain't nobody evuh lookin' fo John Henry ceppin he do suppim wrong."

"It's not like that, I assure you. We're looking for someone, and we think John Henry can help us."

She was a dark, doughy woman with big hands resting on her big hips as she challenged him with her eyes. Behind her a small army of children scampered in, out and around a freshly hoed vegetable garden. The first person he had asked for directions, a gray old gent leaning on a walking stick, had burst out in laughter as he pointed over the hill. "Is something the matter?"

"You'll see when you gets dere, mister."

"I say, are you sure you don't want to tell me something?"

"You'll find out soon enough, mister."

"All right, will a dollar help?"

"Oh, it'll hep some," he said, accepting it, "but it won't hep you none when you gets dere. Oney duh Lord can hep you den, cuz dat woman be duh evilest creature fum her to Biloxi 'n back.''

"What woman? I'm looking for John Henry."

The old man trundled off, pocketing the dollar and giggling.

Casimir's eyes were wary as they made their way over the nob of the hill, down the slope past the shanties and through the acrid smoke of dump fires. It was obvious he had never seen, or perhaps even heard of, the dark-skinned people. Blakeley hoped he would not do or say anything too silly before they could get Bogdan out—*if* Bogdan was there.

"Who you lookin' fo? Somebody rob a bank?"

Something told him she knew. Otherwise the conversation would have ended by now.

"A boy named Bogdan."

"Ain't no Bogdan here. Bogdan? Thass a fool name."

Perhaps sentiment would help.

"That's unfortunate, madam. You see, this is his brother who just came here from across the sea. They were separated years ago by a war."

She shrugged and turned back to her hoeing.

"Jess tell 'im to keep on lookin'. Cain't be mo'an one Bogdan hereabouts."

Casimir nudged him and made a wallet-opening gesture.

"What? Oh, yes, of course. Madam, I'm prepared to pay for information."

"If I got it, you'll get it," she said without looking up. "How much you payin'?"

He handed her a dollar. She stuffed it into her apron and continued to prod the ground.

"Seen a kid named Bogdan about a hour ago. Haid like a jug. Could be his brother all right."

"Madam, where was he?"

"I woke up dis moanin 'n said, 'Sweetonia'— dass my name, Sweetonia—I said, 'know what? You jess as poo as you was yesterday'."

He smiled and handed her another dollar. She smiled and put it with the other. Then the smile disappeared.

"How come I still feelin' poo?"

"Perhaps there's a hole in your apron." He peeled off one more dollar, but his smile had also disappeared. "This is it, madam. Invest it wisely."

She leaned on her hoe and snapped in the direction of the tar paper shanty. "John Henry, come out here!"

There was no response, and her moon face darkened.

"John Henry, I axt you once. Ain't gone ax you no second time."

A door flew open and clapped against the shanty wall. John Henry loped downhill and skidded to a nervous halt on the gravel a few feet from his mother. His form belied his legendary name. Watching him stepping cautiously closer, Blakeley was reminded of a big, popeyed praying mantis, as if the heroic appellation had been a practical joke.

She glowered at him.

"John Henry, you lookin' sheepish."

His eyes opened wider, darting left and right.

"You 'n dat white bum been lookin' at duh book wif duh dirty pitchers in it?"

Book? Blakeley's eyes also popped open.

John Henry mumbled something unintelligible and she slapped him across the ear. He yelped and backed away.

"If thine eye offend thee," she bellowed, "pluck it out! Halleluiah and amen."

He was rubbing his ear and muttering as he led them uphill to a ramshackle coal bin. Several of Sweetonia's urchins tagged along and delighted in climbing ahead of them. They heard the shuddering rumble of a coal pile being disturbed within and knew that Bogdan was escaping to the far recesses as they approached. He really was an alley cat. There was no sense in trying to coax him out with the words of a rational, reasonable Englishman, which was why he had had the foresight to take Casimir along.

"Hah?"

"You . . . him . . . talk." He pointed at Casimir then at the coal bin with one hand, and with the fingers of the other made a flapping talking gesture. "Talk Bogdan Polska."

Casimir felt important. He stepped up to the door, cleared his throat and spoke through a crack. The urchins giggled.

Casimir said something, and Bogdan yelled something back. The answer was long and threatening. Casimir blushed and replied in kind. The urchins giggled and made grunting sounds. Blakeley began to consider more radical measures, like kicking in the coal bin door.

"It ain't locked, mister," John Henry said. "Jess open it."

There was more sign language, and somewhat apprehensively, Casimir tugged at the door. It opened with a jerk and a clank. He looked even more apprehensive as he squeezed through the narrow opening. The urchins laughed so hard that some of them had to hurry behind the building. They laughed even louder when they heard the strange, muffled words of Casimir and Bogdan arguing inside. Blakeley found it much less amusing.

Time passed slowly. He was in no hurry to join them in the dampness and the anthracite dust, but the negotiations were dragging. The voices lowered. There were occasional laughs and long pauses.

The door opened and Casimir emerged, a silly smile showing through his coal blackened face. Bogdan, looking sullen but resigned, soon followed. He was the color of tar. Sweetonia's tots found this especially hilarious.

They walked past him, chattering in their language. Casimir's hand rested reassuringly on Bogdan's shoulder. He winked when he saw Blakeley.

"Where's the book?" Blakeley whispered.

Casimir tried to mouth the word.

"Book," Blakeley repeated, opening an imaginary volume and making grotesque writing and reading gestures.

Casimir shrugged, his apologetic eyes pleading incomprehension, and the two proceeded downhill toward Blakeley's carriage.

Blakeley stepped inside and groped around. It was cool at least, but the footing was most precarious. The coal, gathered up from wherever the cars had stopped along the Reading or Lehigh Valley tracks, was an uneven assortment of pea and walnut. It would give wherever he stepped. There were brackish puddles where rainwater had seeped through the many little rents in the roof. The bin was long and narrow, an ideal hideout for Bogdan. One would have to have the senses of a mole, however, to find anything there. He ran his hands over the roughly cut stones and sought, cursing, any source of light. But of course, any damned fool knew that one kept fire away from anthracite until one had to light it for a purpose. So whatever was illuminated came from scant rays of sunlight through those same holes in the roof and through an occasional knothole in the wall. But those, he guessed, were now blocked by the urchins whose tee-hees were audible over the crunching of the coal. Damn! He knew by the odors that some real alley cats had spent many a night there. That suspicion was quite rudely confirmed when he felt what appeared at first to be a handful of moist pea coal, but it was much too soft.

An eternal ten minutes later he emerged. He had to kick the door open because the urchins had closed it and thought it riotous that he should remain there forever. He and his Seville Row serge were scuffed, sweaty and the color of charcoal—but, by George, he had the book.

It was torn, sooty, and dog-eared where Bogdan and John Henry had marked off certain pages, but it was again in his possession.

But the little beggers with their hysterical giggling and the sound of his foot slamming against the door had summoned Sweetonia. She met him halfway down the hill as he trudged carefully through the freshly tilled ground and made his way back to the carriage. Her fists were on her hips in that familiar challenging stance and her eyes were fixed on the prostitute's book.

"Lord have mercy, but the perverts be comin' in all shapes 'n sizes nowadays."

Chapter Twenty-four

It was an awkward evening. No, awkward was too frail a word; disorienting perhaps, or better yet, byzantine.

Allison's only triumph that day was a petty one. That was when, as she hobbled into the house in tattered clothing on an ankle that resembled classic gout, Sophia had said the horse had thrown a shoe and Allison had realized that the motor-wagon hadn't failed them. It was a shabby reaction to smile and say "ah-hah!" and it had only occurred because she was feeling as shabby as she must have looked. There was Sophia, fresh as a morning flower, while she smelled something like a camel. Later, after a thorough scrubbing and being told that Dr. Blakeley thought it best she remain there until he was certain that it was only a sprain, she felt terribly guilty as Sophia offered her clothing for the evening. In fact, she had almost had to fight back tears. But the guilt had passed quickly when she discovered she had to leave a few stays unbuttoned. Sophia must be the tiniest, trimmest woman in Christendom, and if she were not so wonderful a human being it would be oh-so-easy to hate her.

It was much easier to hate Nathan and easier still to hate his companion.

"He didn't have anywhere to put me, so here I am!" Lillian Russell had said.

How blithe!

He could have had the decency to blush when Allison appeared, but he simply nodded, said hello, then introduced his guest. There was a little gracious hand kissing, and as Victor took Miss Russell's wrap he stammered and blanched, verging on apoplexy.

She thought she even detected a hint of nervousness in the usually unflappable Blakeley. So did Sophia, who smiled behind her fan.

No doubt the most embarrassing reaction belonged to Ralphie, who kept dropping hors d'oeuvres in his lap as he stared at her bosom—and it was a prodigious bosom. "Pre-Raphaelite" was the term Sophia used later as she smiled and acknowledged that Lillian Russell was every bit as described in the papers. Only they had not prepared anyone for her disarming friendliness. She, too, was difficult to dislike.

At least the wine was comforting. Allison felt a bit like a dowager as she sat in a deep chair with her swollen foot resting on a stool and received assorted condolences. After her third glass she felt loose enough to dart icy glances at Nathan whenever he erred and glanced her way. Sometimes he would smile or give her a vaguely wounded reaction. Poor misunderstood Nathan who just wanted to do his duty was looking good, she thought wistfully. The shiner was fading and was nothing at all compared to the one around Blakeley's eye. The new clothing became him and must have been tailored to fit because men with his form could seldom buy suits off the rack. He had a muscular upper body with too little waistline. How well she remembered. Somebody should tell him that his tie is crooked. She liked him in light blue, which matched his eyes. Evidently, Lillian Russell did, too; what the heck, she had bought it. What's that word? Gigolo? Stop that right now—it's cheap and unfair. But the tie *was* crooked, and the hair was mussed a bit, and there was a tiny smudge of scented powder on the light blue lapel.

"Pre-Raphaelite." She seemed to recall that the term was once used to describe Olga the maid.

But Lillian Russell was, as everyone observed to the point of inducing nausea, really lovely. Allison wondered if it was because she had a truly solicitous nature, or if it was because she had seen the icy exchanges and wanted to defuse things. Time and again she floated over in her tastefully lascivious gown to ask if Allison wanted anything. Caviar? Smoked salmon? More wine? It was also a bit hard to dismiss the thought that the visits were intended to display her assets. After Miss Russell's second trip across the room, Allison noticed that Ralphie would appear, as suddenly as a moth to a light, behind her chair to get a better glimpse of the lovely guest's lovely bosom as she bent over to talk to Allison.

Actually, Lillian Russell was just a guest. The guest of honor that evening was Casimir Wojdzekevicz, scrubbed pink, dressed in his best shirt and knickers, and looking like the proud groom in a village wedding.

For retrieving Bogdan and thus helping to rescue the prostitute's diary, he was being treated to a feast the likes of which he had had but rarely. The menu was appropriately exotic, and everyone seemed to find it delectable. It was fun to watch Ralphie and Casimir in an unannounced eating contest.

Only Victor, as predicted, had sniggered.

"Madame, what manner of wine does one serve with . . . kielbasa and halupki?"

Sophia drew a blank.

"No wine," Snopkowski insisted. *"Piwu!"*

"Beer?" he sniffed. "How quaint. And then I suppose we shall all remove our shoes and sing about fat people."

She snarled as he pranced off, one prominent tusk standing out in a fleshy field. Despite herself, Snopkowski beamed with pride at her nephew, though Casimir's tactics had been questionable. After convincing the shoeshine boy that Blakeley meant him no harm, what had drawn him out of the coal bin was a photograph of Olga that a friend had snapped in the old country, a candid shot of her stepping naked out of a fish pond on a hot summer day. For a time it seemed as if his aunt Snopkowski would have his pale head on a stick, but Blakeley had calmed her down.

She pinched his cheek and smiled.

"*Dobrze kielbasa, Casimir?*"

"*Dobrze, Baba.*"

"*Pirogi?*"

"*Smaczne!*"

And so it went until someone inquired of Olga's whereabouts because Victor had been whining all night about his work load, and Victor, knowing a perfect cue when he heard one, had observed with a vicious little grin that, "Mistress Olga is giving Master Bogdan a bath."

"But . . . he's fifteen years old," Sophia gasped.

"Yes," Victor minced, "he is." And Snopkowski stomped off to find them.

Pre-Raphaelites must have all the fun, Allison thought as she excused herself and started to hobble off toward her room. The Blakeley's owned a Victrola, one of the best she'd ever heard, and so the air was filled with romantic Strauss waltzes. Across the table Nathan and Miss Russell's billing and cooing was not settling well with the Slavic repast.

Nathan tore his attention away from his companion and asked if he could assist her, but she waved him off politely.

But Ralphie jumped up and refused to be waved off. He swept her up, misused Sidney Carton's line from *A Tale of Two Cities*, "a far, far better thing that I do," and carried her upstairs to the guest room. Naturally, she protested that she was too heavy, the obligatory line of the not-too-heavy, and naturally, he insisted he could carry three of her and the lamppost, too. When her feet were firmly planted and she realized what a task it would have been to climb the stairs, she decided impulsively to peck him on the cheek before saying goodnight. It was a harmless, thoroughly Platonic little peck, given out of gratitude, even though she fully understood that he had done it as a show of some sort for Lillian Russell, but he turned a deep red.

He was delightfully embarrassed, whistling and gushing "Wow!" as he bumbled down the hallway. She took heart.

Had the evening been better up to that moment, she would have excused herself nonetheless. She was anxious to get on with the more important part of it. Blakeley, impressed by her performance that morning, had graciously reconsidered, and the prized book was now in her possession. Of course he could be confident that she would not abuse the information, but it was tempting.

The late author's powers of description were surprisingly effective. It read like a primitive— very primitive—novel at times. It reminded her of one of those works translated from the French supposedly and smuggled at great risk into the country because it was a matter of principle, usually finding its way into finishing school dormitories and other adolescent bedrooms, where it was read by future sophisticates strictly out of homage to the First Amendment. It made her feel very naughty as she perused the early pages. She slipped out of her clothing and into something lighter and looser, seldom taking her eyes from the book, poured herself a drop or two of Napoleon brandy and settled into an easy chair by a Tiffany lamp, telling herself that this was a strictly professional matter. Only she wondered if she could have been so absorbed by something of greater literary quality.

As Blakeley had hinted, Goldie may not have named names, but it was hard to miss the identities. And if words failed her, as they often did, there were the drawings.

When words didn't fail her, she had a tendency to exaggerate, and that also helped.

For example, the man with a face like an alligator and a breath twice as bad, who used to invite her to visit him at his Elm Street address whenever his mother was away, insisting that she enter after dark through a rear entrance, and who used to make her dress in his mother's undergarments and spank his bare backside with a yardstick—he just *had* to be Dr. Blakeley's old nemesis, Judge Magwood. She wondered how Blakeley would deal with that little story.

There was a prominent member of the mayor's staff, a man often caricatured in the newspapers for his prominent big nose, who liked her to accommodate him in a coffin. There was an unmistakable bank president who enjoyed dressing as Jesus and washing her feet, a one-eyed diamond merchant with a famous shop at Sixth and Samson whom she would tickle to the point of incontinence and who paid her in cheap costume jewelry, and a famous baseball player who used to visit her for physical and verbal abuse whenever he was in a hitting slump. Best of all, she found the identity of what had to be the insufferable editor at *McClure's Ladies' Magazine* who kept refusing to let her cover the war in Cuba. But something prevented her from reading on about him; the self-indulgence was bothering her.

Business had gone down abruptly. There were fewer and fewer allusions to the affluent and recognizable and more and more tales of conventioners and college boys. And after she had wound up in the Sink, there were the dregs of the docks.

There was a noise on the driveway below. She closed the book instinctively as she sat up, then caught herself chuckling at her own reaction. She hobbled over to the window to see.

A little round man dressed in an officer's uniform was trying very hard to look like Teddy Roosevelt. He was very familiar, but she couldn't remember the name. Yes, he was an eccentric running for governor on some third party ticket. The United States should expand its empire throughout all of Latin America, purchase Indochina from the French and Australia from the English, and invade Russia through Siberia. Then we should renounce the constitution and become a monarchy. That fool! What the dickens was his name? Sophia had mentioned it, but Allison had been too preoccupied with her ankle and the events of the morning to pay much attention. Sophia said they had seen to Gladstone after he'd thrown the shoe, and that she had felt compelled by etiquette to invite them over for dinner or whatever. Blakeley had grumbled something about having had all the lunatics he needed for one day, thankyew. A stunning woman started to step down from the coach. She was younger than he by about 20 years and quite beautiful. As if Allison had not been depressed enough, here was another good reason to stay upstairs. She was fashionably, expensively dressed, too, right out of Paris.

The little round man looked up toward her window. Probably all he saw was a blur behind gossamer drapes in a frame of warm light, but she took a quick step backwards anyway, forgetting her tender, swollen ankle, biting her lip and holding her breath until the pain went away.

West. That was it.

The room was suddenly stuffy. She switched on a fan, watched the light pink bedspread billow in the breeze and returned to her research.

She reminded herself once again that it was cheap, lowbrow and infantile to wallow in the world of Goldie Becker and her erstwhile clients, and she swore to seek only the identity of Goldie's murderer or murderers. But there was one very interesting piece of information on the page she was reading when the clatter of horse and carriage had disturbed her. There was one great big juicy morsel she might share with Nathan, with Dr. Blakeley's permission, of course.

There was a knock on the door and a clearing of the throat. She clapped the book shut and looked up.

"Yes? Who's there?"

"Ian Blakeley, Miss Meredith. May I come in?"

She hoped she had not sounded too breathless or guilty.

"Yes, of course."

She tightened her robe and hopped over to the door on her good foot.

"Are you sure I'm not disturbing you?"

"I'm sure. Please come in."

"I want to have a last look at your ankle. If it's broken we shall have to set it first thing in the morning."

He helped her back to her chair and planted himself on a footstool, untied the bandage and loosened it gently. She had already made up her mind that no matter how much it hurt she would insist she felt nothing, because she had no intention of spending the next month or more dragging one of those monstrous casts wherever she went. And just in case she caught herself about to wince or groan, she would look at Dr. Blakeley and think of Goldie and the Biblical bank president.

It was an evening to think like a teenager.

"You left the gathering abruptly," he said.

"I was anxious to get to the book."

"Quite a collection of ribaldry, eh?"

"I noticed that the T's are never crossed, but she took great pains to dot the I's with navels and valentines." That ought to sound clinical enough. "You left rather suddenly yourself, I see."

"I spent my daily quota of patience, I'm afraid. Sophia will no doubt call me boorish, but I had to leave."

"West, right?"

"Jeremy West. Proof positive that there is inbreeding among Philadelphia's elite. Does this hurt?"

He probed. She bit her lip.

"No. Is that his wife who arrived with him?"

"Yes, it is. She and Sophia have become acquainted on the riding trails."

"She's very beautiful."

"Mmmm, I suppose," he mumbled. "Something strange about her, though. Does this hurt?"

"No. I suppose you'd have to be strange to marry an oddball like Jeremy West."

"Quite. Now, I'm going to turn it ever so slowly, and I want you to tell me if the pain becomes intense, please."

"I will," she said as breezily as possible.

He gripped her foot and bent it outward. It hurt, but it was not what she had expected. Then he turned it inward and it was more painful, but it could have hurt much worse. She grimaced but felt no need to cry out.

"So . . . far . . . so good, Dr. Blakeley?"

"Splendid."

He released it and she let out the breath she'd

been holding. For the first time since he'd unwrapped it, she looked. It had not turned color, a good sign, but it was swollen to almost twice its normal size.

There was a jar of liniment on the table. It had a pleasant eucalyptus smell, and he rubbed it on gently.

"I guess I won't dance the cancan for a few weeks."

"You should be fine within a week if you treat it sensibly. It's a very ladylike injury, and you'll have no reason to put any pressure on it. We'll see to your every need."

"I'll get fat."

"Nonsense." He finished rebandaging the ankle, sat up and smiled. "Now then, have you found our murderer?"

"I found out why any number of people may have wanted to murder her, but I found nobody in particular. I got up to the Reverend Ezekiel Twombley, who must be in dire need of Ehrlich's magic bullet by now."

"Isn't he the one giving Miss Russell fits?"

"The same. He's the fire and brimstone preacher who Goldie used to visit backstage at revival meetings, the one with the—well, they all have strange tastes. He continued to see her long after even she had ceased pretending she didn't have . . . you know."

"The pox. The great avenger."

"His brain must resemble a fried oyster by now."

"That's certainly worth filing away, Miss Meredith."

"Otherwise, it's mostly ancient history."

He poured himself a little brandy, gestured toward her glass, and she accepted a refill.

"I had time to read it in its entirety this afternoon while soaking away the day's filth in a tub of very hot water. I'd no idea how much coal dirt I was wearing until I got home and saw what could have been a blackfaced minstrel when I looked in the mirror. I came across several references to the fat gentleman. She met him, as expected, near one of her dockside haunts. He had an accomplice, a sickly chap whom she despised, but who usually tagged along. As usual, they are unnamed, but on one occasion when she persisted in questioning him he must have told her sarcastically, 'John Jacob Astor.' That may account for something Bogdan said this morning during our altercation. It sounded like 'Jake, a bastard' and I gather he thought we were acquainted. Perhaps he observed my stockiness and thought we were related. He drove an impressive carriage, according to one description, and he must have spent money freely enough to impress her, and when she left with him on that last engagement she fully expected a profitable evening."

"Do you think she ever got there?"

"Are you certain you want to hear the rest of it?"

"It's my ankle, not my stomach that's bothering me."

"I performed an autopsy. She had sexual relations with someone, but it wasn't quite the orgy she was expecting when she jotted down

her last page. That part of her evening was only
incidental, I suspect. What is more germane is
the stomach full of expensive food. Just like Tony
the Swordsman, she had eaten heartily only a
short time before her death, as if it were the
condemned's last meal. It was all there, scarcely
digested—chateaubriand, salads nicoise, artichoke hearts, dessert of Spanish flan, coffee—"

"Artichoke hearts? You mentioned them this
morning and I thought you were being glib."

"I was. Then."

There was another clatter on the driveway
below. He huffed, made a gesture of futile protest and got up to look.

Fatzinger, accompanied by a uniformed officer and the ubiquitous Bernard Spector, was
pulling up outside the front door in a police
department buggy.

"I think this day will go down in history with
the day they invented taxes. Excuse me, Miss
Meredith."

When Victor had opened the door, Spector
had already dashed in before Blakeley had a
chance to stop him.

"I couldn't help wondering how you'd like
your picture—the one in tomorrow morning's
paper. Take a gander at this, Doc."

There was a picture prominently displayed on
the front page showing Dr. Blakeley, black-eyed
and disheveled, charging at the camera like a
mad bull. Rosie, who had been quite subdued
throughout the evening, studying Lillian
Russell's every word and gesture and wondering

if she could get away with wearing a padded brassiere, saw it and squealed.

"Daddy, is that really you?"

"That's him, kid," said Spector. "Keep your hands off."

"I thought I'd destroyed that contraption over your head."

"Not exactly, Doc. Hey, ain't that Lillian Russell in there? Something going on between you and the Red Hot Mama?"

"I must remember to purchase a large dog to guard the door."

"Oh dear," Sophia said, obviously amused, "you've looked better, Ian. And who is this across the page?"

Fatzinger puffed up. He had wondered how long it would take to be noticed.

"Good evenin', missus. Like good eadts dott shmells."

"Good evening, Officer Fatzinger."

"Dott pitcher is on accounta diss here shtuff."

He showed her an official document and handed it to Blakeley.

"Good Lord, you're not going to arrest Bogdan!"

"Diss here's da warrant. Fer murderin' the late Tony Miller 'n den Goldie Becker. Chust a minute. I almost forgot . . ."

He reached into his vest pocket and pulled out another paper.

"Diss here's da bill fer breakin' Bernie's pitcher box over hiss head."

Chapter Twenty-five

It was a warm night, close and sticky, especially on the streets where the heat escaped the ground reluctantly. There were halos of humidity around the street lamps, and open collars were seen everywhere.

But he was chilly most of the time, except for those moments when he would feel so hot that his chest was on fire, those flashes that Grover said came because he was a woman, a goddamn snivelin' old lady. To hell with Grover. He's an asshole anyways, and who needs a second asshole? That's what he said. Well, that's what he would a said if he hadn't been aware that Grover was drinkin' and probly didn't mean it.

He needed him. That was obvious. Without Grover to back him up, the bartenders along the row were not nearly so hesitant about tossing him through the door for his barmaid pinching, his obnoxious mouth, his disgusting coughing fits and his generally hateful deportment.

Grover had told him to beat it. Said that with him around the women stayed away. The only thing that'd come near him would hafta be toothless 'n feebleminded 'n probly slept in a trash can. With him along the bartenders always put out the glasses with the chips and cracks because he was always dropping them and because who the hell knows what kind a scum he was coughin' up? Thass what he said. Thass what his ole buddy Grover had said. Told him to hit the trail cuz Grover wanted to spend his bonus, his finder's fee on his own. Piss on Grover.

He pulled a cigarette out of his shirt, part of a pack of expensive ones he'd snitched earlier from the Madame's purse. Madame leaves all kinds a shit layin' around. Grover says he'll break his friggin' elbows if he ever catches him taking anything, but screw Grover anyways. Screw Madame, too.

Jeez, wouldn't he like to.

He could a stole a lot more. People like her don't pay a lot of attention to people like him. Friggin' cigarette was strong. Too good for good ole American butts, the Madame.

He paused to cough again. He was hot from the neck up. He leaned against the wall of an old building which housed a sweatshop where people who didn't speak English worked 20 hours a day making shirts and leggings for army uniforms. He stayed there for a few minutes, closing his eyes and struggling to catch his breath while passers-by crossed the street to avoid him.

A stray dog, black with a bushy tail, yapped a few feet away.

There was a salty taste in his mouth.

Somewhere up the street there was a gin mill where he got lucky once and met a real good looker. Li'l beefy but good. The drinks cost more cuz they wanna keep the riffraff out. Classy place. Shit, he could afford it. Got his bonus, too, just like Grover. His finder's fee was 50 bucks a stiff. Not bad. He could drink all night, hey, 'n still have enough for a good-lookin' dollie.

He coughed again. He shivered, was hot from the waist up, then shivered again.

Carried her right up the steps and into the church, and Grover bet he'd never have the balls to do it.

His lungs were on fire. Oh, Jesus!

The little dog kept yapping, following him up the street. He turned and flipped the cigarette at it. It shut up, but it kept following him, only at a safer distance.

Somebody was approaching. Looked like a couple a big tough guys with dark suits.

"Get outa my way, assholes."

They stopped and looked him over.

"Don't I know yiz, mac?"

"I dunno no cops."

"What's the matter with your mouth?"

"Whatsamatter me, whatsamatter you. Get outa my way. I got an appointment."

"There's blood all over your chin and down your shirt. Where you been, mac? Somebody kick your ass for you?"

"Whattaya talkin' about?"

He felt his shirt which was soaked. He wiped his mouth and blinked at his hand with bright red splotches on the palm.

"What the, what the fu—"

He collapsed.

One of them broke his fall, eased him to the ground and propped him against the wall. The other whistled for help. Across the street an audience was gathering.

"Get Gro . . ."

"Who?"

"Don't talk, mister. We'll get yiz to a doctor."

"I know who he is, Pat, I think."

"You don't know me. I dunno no goddamn cops, I toldja. Get Grover 'n get the hell outa here."

But by that time his voice was too weak to be heard. All they heard was a rasp and a gagging noise. The policeman whistled again. He coughed again. The little dog was sniffing the uneven trail of crimson spots that led up to him. He coughed in spasms and the onlookers cursed the crimson spray that flowed out of him.

His chest was molten lead. His eyes were shattered windows.

Chapter Twenty-six

"This is preposterous."

"Is anyone laughing?"

"Not yet, but when word gets out, the public will."

"It's oudt, it's oudt," Fatzinger proclaimed triumphantly. "Mit mein pitcher even."

Zimmerman, from the district attorney's office, had a long, lumpy face and basset hound eyes.

"What was he doing with the victim's switchblade knife then?"

"Shtickin' it in people, dott's what."

"I'd like to know how you connected the knife to Bogdan when it was in my possession."

"Dr. Blakeley, in all due respect, I don't know where you got that idea. It was found in the street after yesterday's minor riot and identified

279

as the weapon with which he attacked you."

"By Mr. Spector it vass found, right by da doggy-doo."

"Spector? Good Lord."

"And it bears the initials, J-A-M. Jacob Anthony Miller."

"I see. So a fifteen year-old boy took Tony the Swordsman's knife right out of his hands, held him down and surgically removed his heart. Good luck with that one in court."

"Since you'll be acting as his defense attorney at that time, Dr. Blakeley, I suggest we wait and see."

"Dem shlum kids can cut off yer knockwurst und have it et before ya know it's missin'."

Fatzinger was wearing a rather conservative suit this morning, two-tone blue stripes with a red and green bow tie, just in case the press should want another picture. He was peeling a hard boiled egg as he offered his sapient observations.

"Did anyone, Bernard Spector perhaps, say why he did it?"

"Dr. Blakeley, growing up the way he did can make anybody vicious. For all we know the state will hand him over to a team of psychologists after the trial instead of sending him to the gallows. Who can say? Personally, I'd like to see him swing. He's made us look like a town full of witches and warlocks."

"But he did, as you put it so compassionately, rid you of some trash."

"Indeed. And at least in the case of the hooker we don't need a psychologist to figure it out. He was in love with her, she was a bum, and he couldn't stand thinking about all the gentlemen she entertained. Big mystery, huh?''

"And he asked her to lie down for a moment while he opened her chest and took out her heart. Do keep up the good thinking.''

Zimmerman relit his cigar and recrossed his legs.

"All right, Dr. Blakeley, you've made your point that you stand for truth, justice, and western civilization, while we're a pack of sleazy, publicity-seeking morons. But I think you should remember that he was also responsible for the death of that priest yesterday. It strikes me as uncommonly malicious that the body was left in that place at that time, and if we can screw his ass to the ceiling for that one alone, it will be worth all the Victorian arrogance you plan to throw at us.''

Blakeley relit his pipe and recrossed his legs. He tried to sound unruffled—such attacks were far from rare—but there was a distinct edge in his voice.

"He's only fifteen-years-old, Mr. Zimmerman. You cannot try him for a capital felony. Even Uriah Chidsey knows that.''

Zimmerman smiled a toxic smile.

"Uriah Chidsey won't touch this case. The D.A. has decided you've humiliated his office for the last time. It will be you and me and twelve people who detest street hooligans.''

"I shall look forward to it.''

"As for the suspect's age, that's all hearsay. Where are his documents?''

"There are no documents in the Sink. You know that."

"Most unfortunate."

"But the boy can count. If he says he's fifteen, who can prove otherwise?"

"In a tub mit a poopsie he vas diddlin'."

"Doesn't sound underage to me, Dr. Blakeley."

"Ya! Chust ask da poopsie!"

The discussion was taking place in a hallway outside the chambers of the Hon. Winston Ezra Livingston as they awaited a ruling on a technicality. Ordinarily Blakeley hated such things; making the law a self-mocking body of pomposity. But this time he was grasping for whatever legal inanity he could find, because it was easy to imagine what Bogdan must think of him after all his promises and assurances.

The faces of most who passed by the shiny wooden bench where they were sitting reflected his renewed notoriety. It was depressing to consider how many otherwise intelligent people read the trash in the morning gossip sheet that employed Bernard Spector.

The article accompanying his picture contained some amazing details. There were more casualties in the street brawl than any reported lately in the war news; patrolmen from three precinct stations had been called out to quell the disturbance; windows had been broken and businesses set afire; a number of weapons had been confiscated, including a primitive Gatling gun; someone fitting Allison Meredith's description and who was evidently in Blakeley's company had lifted her skirt and bared her backside in defiance of a desist order; and Blakeley's quoted comments could have shocked a Turk.

He wanted to strangle Bernard Spector slowly.

How the devil did Spector get the knife?

How the devil did Bogdan get it in the first place?

Where the devil would he find the time to prepare a defense for Bogdan?

Fatzinger also noticed the attention. He gulped down his hard boiled egg, sat up straight and readjusted his bow tie.

"Know something, Dr. Blakeley?" Zimmerman spoke a little over a stage whisper. "I'm really anxious to joust with you in court. You are what they call one hot property."

"And when you make an ass of yourself, Mr. Zimmerman, the whole world will know."

"I guess you'd know what that feels like."

"Mr. Zimmerman—"

The door opened and a courtroom aide motioned for them to enter the judge's chambers. He had the ruddy rims and morning palsy of a man who lived his evenings to the fullest, a style of behavior he shared with his superior. Mornings, especially hot, humid mornings like this one, were hellish times to face Judge Livingston.

"Just remember," Zimmerman whispered on the way in. "Since you plan to become his defense attorney, you'll have to turn over all your heretofore confidential findings. No man may be a servant of two masters."

But Livingston surprised them. He and

Blakeley had never been close, but apparently the district attorney's office had irked him most recently. When they entered he nodded without warmth at Blakeley but scowled at Zimmerman.

"Who is this person?" he inquired of Fatzinger.

"The arresting officer," Zimmerman muttered.

"Wilmer P. Fatzinger, Chudge. I guess you seen my pitcher in—"

"Then *you're* the damn fool who's responsible for this."

"Huh? Oh, schidt . . ."

He looked at Zimmerman, who avoided eye contact.

Livingston's snowy beard and bourbon-flushed face were unusually intimidating. Blakeley had decided years ago that in pince-nez and black judicial robes he resembled an evil Santa Claus. He would remain ferocious until noon when three or four belts would mellow him somewhat.

Zimmerman was starting to look more like a basset hound puppy just caught leaving a deposit on the Persian rug.

"I don't understand, Your Honor. We have material evidence and the district attorney—"

"Who the hell authorized this warrant for the arrest of Bogdan Doe?"

"Bogdan Doe?"

"Git out of my sight, Zimmerman, and take Fattinger with you."

"Fatzinger. Mit a Z."

Zimmerman took Fatzinger's arm and hustled him out of the chambers, hissing and demanding an explanation.

"It vass late! Mr. Spector said he knew a guy! Shtop dott!"

"The district attorney will boil me in oil for this."

As Blakeley got up smiling, Livingston stopped him.

"I wouldn't look so fat and sassy if I were you, Dr. Blakeley. If there's any substance at all to that story in the *Morning Sun*, I'll have you disbarred at least and deported at best."

"It's good to know you keep up with the important news, Your Honor. Good day."

It occurred to him in the hallway that his reply, though apt, was downright dumb. A terse, falsely humble "Yes, Your Honor" would have been much better. Sooner or later someone would come up with a proper warrant and Bogdan would be rearrested.

"Psst. Hey, Doc . . . Dr. Blakeley."

"Lieutenant Hudson, good morning. Why are you lurking in the shadows?"

"To avoid Bones Fatzinger. I'm supposed to be home with a bad case of runs. I know, I know, I could have picked something more genteel, but the runs he can understand. I need the time away from his madhouse to conduct an investigation of my own. Long story."

"It's a relief to see a friendly face."

"Are you still on the lookout for artichokes?"

"Most assuredly."

"I fell into something yesterday that you might use." He tore a sheet from his pocket notepad and handed it to Blakeley. "This is the name and address of a grocer, the only one carrying them right now."

"Bless you."

"Use it well."

"I shall. And good luck with your investigation."

"Piece of cake."

Another nod, another smile, a few steps through a doorway, and Hudson was gone. The stairwell he chose was far from Fatzinger and the deputy district attorney.

Blakeley noted the name of the grocer.

JOAO SOARES-DASILVA, SPECIALTY FOODS, 23 JUNIPER STREET.

It was close to noon by the time Blakeley and Casimir arrived at the Eleventh Precinct. The turnkey at the lockup was a pleasant gentleman, his white hair signaling near retirement and his bad feet telling why Hudson had taken him off the street. He admitted quietly that he was pleased to release the shoeshine boy. "Niver should a been here in the forst place, between you 'n me, but ye know how it goes." As soon as the cell was unlocked, Casimir stepped over its other occupant, a sleeping wino, and threw his arms around Bogdan. There were shouts of joy and triumph unheard since the Chmielnicki Uprising.

And then, over Casimir's shoulder, the boy saw

Blakeley. He stiffened and went silent, which was no surprise of course.

As rehearsed, Casimir apologized for the inconvenience and embarrassment, and hastened to add that Blakeley had brought about his release. Bogdan remained rigid.

He left them to their negotiations. Casimir, he presumed, was explaining his plan, and Bogdan had little choice but to cooperate with it if he wished to stay out of jail.

Blakeley was on friendly terms with the men of the Eleventh. Any friend of Hudson's was a friend of theirs, he guessed. They seemed to regard Fatzinger with amusement mostly, and their experience told them to let politics take its own strange course.

"D'ye iver see Sergeant McBride, Doc?" asked one of them, a big, freckly lad named Patrick Carey.

"Frequently."

"I came acrost an old friend of his on me shift last night. At least I think it was. A pimp name a Pluto that the sarge was tryin' to nail on a whole pile of charges. Opium traffickin' mostly."

"Is he locked up here now?"

"He's on ice, waitin' for the embalmer. Dropped dead in the street last night. Might a been the hick, might a been a cancer. We put him in the morgue, and I didn't make much of it because it's really the sarge's business and I don't want the, uh, interim management poking its nose in to bollix up the works, if y'know what I mean."

He winked and Blakeley winked back.

"I know what you mean, Officer Carey."

"If ye don't mind, I'll show ye the deceased."

"But I know how to find the morgue."

"But I can get ye past the coroner's red tape. Besides, I'd like to be elsewhere when Emperor Fatzinger gets back from lunch. The man can drive ye daft."

Blakeley borrowed a phone, called Lillian Russell's suite, struggled through the French maid, and suggested that McBride meet them at the morgue.

Where they were going was hard to explain to Casimir. He drew a building, then a body being taken through the front door."

"Dronk? Saloon?

He shook his head and drew a body on a slab. Casimir gasped, giggled, then waved his finger and clucked his tongue.

"Aha! House of whores! I tell missus."

Chapter Twenty-seven

She guided Modock along the narrow path leading downhill from the stable, past the laurel and forsythia and splashes of wild roses, careful to avoid the bramble bushes that encroached on both sides. At the bottom of the hill she and the horse paused on a footbridge where Modock stood proudly, sweat glistening on his muscular frame after his morning workout, and she watched a small stream flowing into the pine forest. There it would join a larger stream and meander down to the lake. The trout were large and plentiful this year. There would be poachers.

The gamekeeper must be warned about that —about that and other things.

She ducked under a low hanging limb that had broken off a sumac tree during a storm a week ago. He should have seen to that, also.

The narrow, winding path approached the gamekeeper's cottage from the back. It was a cozy little Hansel and Gretel place in a clearing. All the fairy tale setting needed was a thatched roof and talking animals, but the smell drifting out of the cottage was not boiled porridge.

She followed the aroma into the kitchen where she found a skillet on the stove with rabbit simmering in suet gravy.

"Mr. Kalinka."

He might have run off when she came along.

"Answer me!"

The falcon was pacing nervously, his eyes darting around the cage as if he awaited his execution. His feathers covered the floor. His beak was open and his tongue protruded. His chest puffed out and contracted. She could imagine how his heart was racing as she knelt beside the cage.

"Calm down, my friend. Please."

She opened the cage and started to reach inside to comfort him, but she knew immediately that it was a foolish gesture. The falcon was in a mood to attack anything that moved.

And she was just as furious.

"Mr. Kalinka!"

This time there was a response of sorts, a wooden door creaking and closing. She turned to see the gamekeeper walking down the lane from his outhouse, straightening his suspenders and stuffing his shirt back into his trousers. If he had heard her commands, he was certainly indifferent to them. As he approached, Iago started to squawk. She slammed the side of the cottage with her riding crop.

"I've been calling for you, Mr. Kalinka."

He grunted and walked past her.

"How dare you ignore me? How *dare* you?"

She followed him into the cottage and grasped his arm. When he turned, she caught a staggering whiff of cheap rye. He shrugged her off and went to stir his stew, humming in a raspy monotone.

"You disobeyed me, Mr. Kalinka. That rabbit was for Iago, not for your lunch."

He dismissed her with a simple wave.

"Bird eats good enough. Someday maybe I eat him, hah? Ring dat bugger's neck and cook in pot."

"Get out of this cottage and off my property, Mr. Kalinka, or you'll pay a dear price."

He turned and looked at her. The unctuous squint was gone and had turned into a deep drunken sneer.

"Princess Lady, hah?" He laughed. "Dirty slut dat go naked in woods like bum lady. You tink I no see?"

She gasped. He forced a sneering, taunting laugh.

"Like bum lady on horse!"

Her eyes narrowed into piercing satanic slits. They were the eyes of a questing cat. He picked up a jug and took a big gulp of the cheap rye. Some of it dripped from his mouth as he gestured.

"Uppity Lady Shitpot got big titties. Go flippy-flop in wind. Up down, up down—"

She brought the riding crop down across his face with a slap that was loud enough to startle the falcon. A deep gash showed on his cheek. Blood ran along his lower jaw. He felt it, and his eyes fixed on hers, his mouth contorting.

"You are dirty godless bitch."

When he stepped toward her, she picked up the jug and smashed it over his head. Cheap rye whiskey splashed around the room as he broke his fall against the table. Pots and dishes clanged and clattered, and the falcon started to go mad in his cage.

He struggled to his feet, cursing her and anything that should ever issue from her womb.

On top of the hill the stable hands heard a shrill cry. Work ceased abruptly. They were silent as they waited for another. It was the kind of wail that conjured thoughts of souls in hell. Somebody said in a nervous voice that it was just a cat.

"They do make a nize like dat when their dander's up."

"A cat, me arse," somebody jeered. "It's a damn big cat makes a nize like dat one."

"Ye niver know what the hell you're gonna hear next in dis damn place," said another.

"Sometimes I tink it's a loony bin and no house at all."

"Cease yer prate," the foreman said.

And then there was another cry, long and agonized. Then another.

"Bejaysus," said the foreman, and the men followed him down the long narrow path through the wildflowers and bramble.

The cries grew louder.

"You will tell them you were drinking and should have known better."

The old man was on his knees, bent over in pain. A small pool of blood formed under him as it oozed through his hands and onto the ground.

The first man to get there suddenly stopped in his tracks.

"Jaysus, Mary 'n Joseph," he said, making the sign of the cross.

"Ye snotgreen noserag," the foreman growled, "it's a doctor he needs, not a bluddy church blessin'. Get the wagon."

"Tell the doctor that I shall take care of it," the mistress instructed.

He started uphill toward the stable, shouting for someone to hitch up a wagon. The foreman knelt beside the old gamekeeper and tried to calm him down. The cry had become a pitiful keening.

"Poor Mr. Kalinka," she observed sadly. "Whiskey does make one notoriously foolhardy."

One of the men was staring at the falcon's cage. Soon there were others. The foreman looked up, annoyed.

"What're ye lookin' at?"

"That, that . . ."

"That what?"

"The cage, damnit to hell, look at it!"

They were watching from a safe distance as the falcon pecked at something it held in its talons. The little gate was still open. She noticed that and fastened it tightly. Some of them started to disappear into the brush where they could be sick in private. Those who remained could only guess at what it was—the bloody, gelatinous, seed-coated thing on the floor of the cage.

"Weren't you, Mr. Kalinka, foolhardy?" she reminded him. "It is never wise to tease a predator."

Chapter Twenty-eight

"That's our boy, all right. Richard Albert Snyder, Pluto to his few friends. He won't be missed." McBride drew a line through a name in his notebook. "I appreciate this, Pat."

"Don't mention it, Sarge. Pluto did all the work."

"Wasn't much left of him," Blakeley said, looking at Pluto's wasted body. "My guess is that he had any number of problems, all of them fatal. How do you like that for a scientific diagnosis, gentlemen?"

Their subdued voices echoed through the melancholy steel and concrete chamber. Across the room a white-robed attendant was showing a mesmerized Casimir and Bogdan the wages of sin, trying his best to describe the violent manners of death which had befallen the street types on the cold slabs that he pulled out of the wall.

Red tags fixed on big toes meant that soon they would be transported to the University of Pennsylvania where medical students would dissect them. Blakeley had decided, for lack of a better choice, that the session might be good for Bogdan, but Casimir was turning whiter than some of the cadavers.

"But you might have stumbled onto something more important than you think, Pat," McBride added.

Officer Carey lit up. "Yeah?"

"Yeah. Pluto was a little twerp, but an exceedingly nasty one, the kind whose head you want to squeeze just to see what comes out. He was a so-so narcotics dealer until he got too heavily involved in his own merchandise, so he turned to pimping. Get the girls hooked on something and they'll do just about anything for it. And he'd get them hooked when they were barely out of diapers."

"He looks like someone we might have found among the ritual victims," Blakeley said.

"Which brings me to why I was looking for him," McBride said. "One of his ex-hookers turned up with a hole in her chest."

"Oh?"

"Very early on. The Tomlinson woman."

"I recall the name from your files. January, correct?"

"Right. At the time we had no idea we'd be seeing so many more. We didn't have much on Emma Tomlinson except that she was a drug user and prostitute who worked the docks and who used to work for Pluto. We had no success looking for him then, and after the next few bodies turned up he just became part of a confusing heap of slimy connections."

"Do you think he's actually connected to our case, Nathan?"

McBride chewed a little piece of skin from his thumb near the nail and thought about it.

He was happy to be free of Lillian Russell for a time, though he decided not to bring that up lest the entire precinct think him terminally bewildered. Miss Russell was beautiful, charming and playfully lusty, and the assignment was every man's fantasy, but he still preferred detective work to babysitting. He had made up his mind that if it did not end soon, he was going to enlist in the army and see all those exotic places.

An hour ago he had put Miss Russell on a train for New York where she was going to hire a new manager and press agent, and there was absolutely no reason to fear for her safety because with her there was a very protective and starry-eyed Ralphie "Beef" Blakeley.

"I'd like to think so. I was convinced of it last January, but I guess I have a weak attention span."

Blakeley removed his monocle, steamed it with his breath and rubbed it clean with a white handkerchief.

"He was a Sink resident, was he not?"

"No. He came from somewhere upstate, Williamsport, I believe, and he lived across the river when he was in the money. But he knew the Sink well enough."

"Then a wretch like that could have known all the victims."

"Or where to find them. But I still don't—"

Officer Carey remembered something.

"He kept tryin' to say somethin' before he died, sarge. It sounded like 'clover' or 'gopher'. Any sense to that?"

"Clover. Clover . . ."

"More like 'gopher,' I think."

McBride made a pensively pained face. "Doesn't ring a bell either."

"It seemed important to him."

"Gopher . . ." McBride started to focus on something, a flimsy recollection of a flimsy personality. "Damn, that sounds—"

"Maybe just 'go for help,' sarge?"

"Gopher . . . Gopher . . ."

Suddenly Blakeley became aware of Casimir and Bogdan who, with the helpful attendant, had made their way down to Pluto's slab. Casimir was so tense by now that he refused to look upon another corpse. His eyes wandered everywhere else, but Bogdan was staring fixedly down at Pluto.

Blakeley saw him just as he started to yell.

"Zoltan Honk Honk!" The name reverberated through the building.

"Stop that nonsense at once!" Blakeley demanded.

The boy pointed at Pluto's face and repeated, "Zoltan Honk Honk! Him! Him Zoltan Honk Honk!"

"It's distracted, he is, poor lad," Officer Carey said dolefully.

"Casimir," Blakeley said irately, "I insist you control him."

But McBride pointed too and snapped his fingers.

"That's it, damnit—the Sultan of Hong Kong!"

Bogdan repeated it carefully. "Zultan of . . . Honk Honk." He and McBride shared a laugh and a big handshake while Blakeley and Officer Carey exchanged quizzical looks.

"They used to call him the Sultan of Hong Kong," McBride explained. "Back when he had money he used to dress in outlandish costumes to attract attention whenever he visited the racetrack or a better restaurant. He wore turbans, long flowing robes, golden slippers. One afternoon he walked into the St. Regis Room looking like something out of a side show and the manager asked if he had a reservation. He said he didn't need one. He was the Sultan of Hong Kong. They threw him out and the name stuck with him."

"Sultan," Bogdan sneered and spat on the corpse. It was a very accurate shot, splattering across the open mouth. The attendant hastened to roll Pluto's slab back into its niche.

"That explains something else. The name he was struggling to get out last night must have been 'Grover.' Grover Stanhope, a goon type, was Pluto's usual companion. He used to do Pluto's head knocking, but lately he just sort of let Pluto tag along out of habit. Whenever Pluto called himself the Sultan of Hong Kong, Grover used to introduce himself as John Jacob Astor. They fancied themselves—"

"Jake a Bastard," Bogdan interrupted.

"Eh?"

Chapter Twenty-nine

There are times when a case, like a symphony or a great drama, builds to an emotional crescendo and then relaxes into a denouement when everything makes sense. The hints and foreshadowings are all there intermingled with the complications. Gloucester lost his eyes, Lady Macbeth her mind, the Valkyries appeared as threatened, something about Lincoln bothered John Wilkes Booth, and there was unhappiness all over the land. There are other times, more frustrating than dramatic, when each step forward is met by a bright but slimy lawyer, a crooked or obtuse fellow on the bench, or a cast of shaky witnesses. They never could convict that Mellon chap; no one dares challenge all that money. Sometimes a case just piddles down to a seemingly eternal watch, and the winner is often the one with the lower intelligence quotient. Jack the Ripper was laughing sardonically somewhere in London.

And then there are those in which luck plays the greatest role and small links simply fall into place; a chain forms, grows taut and tugs the principals closer together.

Blakeley had sent McBride off to question the grocer Soares-DaSilva. McBride had congratulated, thanked, then sent a disappointed Officer Carey back to the Eleventh with orders to keep silent about all recent developments—specifically from Fatzinger. The young patrolman had hoped to become a member of the team, but the team had grown too large and unwieldy as it was.

Sooner or later, he knew, Fatzinger and that salivating deputy district attorney would put together a workable arrest warrant, and Bogdan would wind up back in the keep. So the task at hand was to prevent that.

They were taking a scenic route over a highway that ran along the ridge overlooking the city from the northwest. It was a peaceful ride for a while, until the music started. After some effort at explaining to Casimir where they were going, Casimir had explained it to Bogdan. Now he was teaching the boy songs of their native land. Neither could sing; together they sounded like a small herd of wild jackasses braying at a full moon. But since he had no idea of what the words meant it was fairly easy to ignore them, and they in turn ignored him. After a while he looked at them out of curiosity and the brief glimpse of their eyes told him the probable gist

of the lyrics. Wonderful things, adolescent hor-
mones, he thought enviously and concentrated
on the horse and the uneven roadway they
negotiated together.

They had let the word out that Pluto Snyder
was dead, hardly the sort of thing to make the
front page, but perhaps Pluto's friend Grover
would show up to claim the body. And where
they would go from there was anybody's guess.

They would follow him, of course, but the trail
would probably just lead back to the Sink. He
reminded himself that it was foolish to get too
excited by one dram of encouragement, but the
boy *did* identify them.

Philadelphia was due for a cloudburst. The
heat was visible on the ground again, rising in
rubbery vapors from the bricks and concrete,
searing the top of the cab, making it feel like an
oven inside whenever the breezes grew faint. He
wanted to be indoors when it came; a Philadelphia summer storm could conjure memories of
the rains in Ranjipur.

Phidd-a-delfyah—that was how she said it,
that affected West woman, as though it were still
part of a colony. In their brief time spent in civil
conversation, before his sudden retreat to Miss
Meredith's room, he had almost thought he was
listening to a parody of himself.

"The cit-eh of Phiddadelfyah is sew teddibly hott in summah, don't you agree, Dr. Blakeley? And sew teddibly provinshul in any season."

A firm glance from Sophia ordered him to
respond.

"We muddle on, Mrs. West."

"Jeremy had quite misrepresented it when we met that day in Paris—I was shopping in a favorite little place of mine on the Rue Richelieu —and I cried all month when we arrived heah. I'm afraid it cost Jeremy a minor fortune to silence me, did it not, Jeremy?"

"Yes, no—yes."

What a silly sight he was in a military uniform, that Jeremy West.

"Well, if you'll excuse me, Mrs. West, I've—"

"Sew soon? But we've only just—"

"I'm afraid it's been an exhausting day, and I've some work to do before retiring."

"Detective work? You know, you've disappointed Jeremy, Dr. Blakeley. He quite expected to see you in deerstalker, Inverness, and lowslung pipe, didn't you, Jeremy?"

"Not exactly."

"Oh, you did. Admit it."

"I put them away for the summer. Now, if you'll ex—"

"We shan't be tardy next time. Do forgive us, won't you? My poor Jeremy has a simply beastly shed-ule, what with his campaign and all. Do say you forgive us. We're teddibly sorry, aren't we, Jeremy?"

"You're both forgiven. Good night, Madam, and good night, Jeremy."

"Good night, uh . . ."

"Blakeley."

"Yes."

And no doubt there were some who would

vote for him, signifying the ultimate failure of the democratic process.

The uniform was interesting. It was National Guard, of course, where a dolt like Jeremy could obtain an officer's commission through the patronage system. But the suntan tunic was regular army bedecked with many mysterious medals. A fair guess would say they were part of a family collection. Colonel Roosevelt would be justifiably outraged.

And she had practically ordered poor Jeremy to say "bully bully" at every opportunity. Hyper women like that always unsettled Blakeley and made him despise the Jeremys who encouraged them.

Well, they had been helpful to Sophia, and they had allowed Ralphie to muck out a barn.

Mrs. West's interest in Ralphie had been noticed as well. Watching him as he watched Lillian Russell seemed to bring out something visible in the dark eyes and pouty little mouth, something hungry and primal as she bit on the heavy underlip. "As if he were a plate of Yorkshire pudding," Sophia had complained that night at bedtime.

Sophia's huff had ended abruptly with the appearance of Officer Fatzinger and that ridiculous Spector chap when she was mortified by the suggestion that she was, so to speak, harboring a fugitive.

"Ian, you must stay and be charming. I order you in the name of all that's decent to be civilized." And so he had, mostly because it had never been easy to deny Sophia a serious wish. And after all, it had been his idea to bring Bogdan home in the first place. Mrs. West was, moreover, very beautiful and English, Sophia reminded him, both of them qualities which had usually met with his favor. "The poor dear is probably nervous meeting you," Sophia had said, "since you are a celebrity of sorts. She probably compensates by overplaying her English roots. Has that ever occurred to you?" Truthfully, it had not, but Sophia had created just enough guilt to persuade him.

He had listened intently to the stuffy prattle, stifling every temptation to yawn, now and then trading quick, weary glances with Nathan McBride and his companion, both of whom soon apologized and left.

But for him there was no escape, so he studied her and blocked out the words. After her first brandy she had taken a seat where the warm light from a decorative lamp bathed her from the waist up.

He noticed the eyes—deep, piercing emeralds and very beautiful. In fact, they were captivating, but . . .

She went on after a time about her days in Paris, where, she confessed, she had spent more of her adult life than she had in their dear England.

"Except in springtime. 'Oh, to be in England, Now that April's there,' quoth the poet."

The wine was getting to her a bit soon, he had thought, and Sophia had nodded to him that it was time once again to stop looking like a mannequin, so he recited, "And after April, when May follows, and the whitethroat builds, and all the swallows."

It was a favorite poem of his, one which came to him in moments of homesickness. Ralphie had covered his mouth and snorted, the first noise out of him since Lillian Russell had left.

The sun was getting hotter and Casimir and Bogdan's singing was getting much louder. He gestured for them to tone it down.

Jeremy, of course, had said nothing all night, except when ordered to. He seemed totally enthralled by her which was not surprising when one considered her beauty—skin like vanilla icing, dark little ringlets on her forehead, the ink black hair.

Her speech grew less affected as the evening wore on. Her eyes actually sparkled as she decided that he, who was so "happily involved in crime," would enjoy hearing of her visits to the Grand Guignol, that "delectable celebration of perversity which only the Gallic mind can truly appreciate!" He had heard of it over the years. In truth, he had wished to see it someday but had never quite decided how to do so in secrecy. It was Madame Toussaud's museum taken a grim step further, and he was certain it was not good for Sophia's digestion to hear of it just now. But Mrs. West insisted, relishing every detail of how "pahfectly realistically" the French had reenacted the bloodiest, most ghoulish, most celebrated recent crimes on stage with all the screams and gore as the madmen carved up their victims, leaving Sophia horrified and Ralphie's jaw hanging open.

They did sparkle, those big emerald eyes. And suddenly he understood. It had been some time since he'd gazed into those of an opium eater.

And why, he asked himself as they rattled over another rut, had he allowed her to linger so long in his thoughts?

Simply because, he answered himself, it was better than dwelling on Pluto and Grover.

He shushed them as they turned through a broken archway and into a narrow drive, stopping outside an old rundown building.

"Father Wladislaw, I've a favor to ask of you."

"For my good friend Blakeley, there is nottink for say no."

The big, knuckly priest was in shirtsleeves, biceps bulging as he mended a rain barrel whose top hoop was loose, letting water seep through the staves.

"Dis here hold enough water for whole bunch a kids go wash up Saturday night. Gotta fix before da rain comes down. Busy busy day."

"It's quite a large favor, Father."

"I told you, anytink for my friend." He waved a good-natured finger in Blakeley's face. "You tink I am kidder?"

Blakeley scratched his head, then cleared his throat loudly. Casimir stepped through the gate first, followed by Bogdan. Father Wladislaw stared.

"*Jezu!*"

"I can understand your ambivalence, Father. I am prepared to offer inducements."

"You kill dat lady, Bogdan?" the priest asked.

There was no answer. He asked again, this time in Polish, and Bogdan shook his head.

"Lyink is big sin too, Bogdan. You lie to Father Wladislaw, I slam you good three four times on da wall like bag a shit."

"I can vouch for him, Father," Blakeley intervened. "If I really thought he were guilty, I surely wouldn't have brought him here."

Father Wladislaw was unenthusiastic but resigned.

"Both of dem?"

"No, no, just Bogdan. I shall be keeping Casimir quite busy. You see, he and his sister Olga will have to help their aunt, Mrs. Snopkowski, with the food that will be delivered here daily for as long as you offer Bogdan sanctuary."

The priest thought about it and smiled.

"Is dot indootsment?"

Blakeley winked. "Do you think I'm a kidder, Father?"

Father Wladislaw laughed and brought his big hand down on Blakeley's shoulder with a loud plop. "You got one deal den!"

They shook hands and Blakeley was more convinced than ever that the priest was an ex-coal miner. It was like gripping a lump of pig iron. There were tiny black marks near the eyes where anthracite splinters had come dangerously close to blinding him, but they had probably settled too deeply beneath the surface to bother removing. Besides, Father Wladislaw was clearly not interested in impressing anyone with his genteel appearance.

"Got big party down in Sink! Everybody get fat!" he roared.

Just then an old woman in a babushka who could have been Snopkowski's twin sister burst through the gate, catching her breath and shouting frantically. The priest tried to calm her down, but the more excited she became the more she had to gasp and finish her sentences painfully. Whatever she was trying to say caused Casimir to wince. When she gestured toward her face, he did also.

"I gotta go, Dr. Blakeley," the priest said, buttoning his Roman collar as he ran off. "Old guy get drunk, do dumb ting and lose eye. Dey send for priest."

"I'm a doctor. I'll go along."

"Dey got one." Father Wladislaw stopped and turned to Bogdan. "You go for house and don't come out. You got dis or jailhouse."

Bogdan ran up the broken wooden steps and entered the rectory without a comment. The priest hopped into a carriage where a burly driver awaited him, and they rode off at a gallop.

Chapter Thirty

Hudson was getting irritable in the heat. For all his years of detective work, he had never gotten used to waiting. The nearby elm tree afforded just enough shade for either the horse or the buggy, and the horse was the logical beneficiary.

There were storm rumblings in the distance, far enough away to offer no immediate break from the sun but close enough to bother the horse.

He fanned himself with his newspaper and spoke gently.

"Calm down, Nellie. This is a nice neighborhood. The horses around here whinny with English accents."

Nellie brushed a fly off her rump and settled down.

Traffic went by placidly, proud coachmen

driving proud beasts with heads high and tails bobbed, two-dimensional passengers staring straight ahead. There were freshly painted gas lamps along the immaculate sidewalk, perfectly groomed plots of grass and colorful flower gardens visible through the wrought-iron gates that spanned the high brick walls. The elms hung at carefully measured intervals, but he could not climb down to take shelter under any of them because he did not wish to be seen.

He unfolded the newspaper and scanned it absently.

He really wanted to get this over with and take a day off, maybe a whole weekend with Glad at the shore or just a trip to the ball park. The locals were playing pretty good baseball in the early season and had beat the Baltimores again. Ed Delehanty, two home runs . . .

And then he realized he had read that twice before.

He put the paper aside and removed his coat. To hell with propriety. If they have a complaint, they can call Fatzinger. He folded the jacket carefully and laid it on the seat beside him. When he looked up he saw a carriage round a corner about 100 yards ahead and pull up in front of a prim and proper gabled mansion halfway down the street.

He grinned.

"Didn't I tell you, Nellie? Do I know my stuff or what?"

A tall, flaxen-haired Viking type pecked the driver on the cheek and climbed down carefully, then swung her weighty breasts around and followed them up the walk and into the house.

The carriage proceeded toward him. He chuckled and hid behind his newspaper until it passed.

Chapter Thirty-one

"**I** got the sign outside. Do you think it means anything?"

Joao Soares-DaSilva nodded toward the window, took a large slice of salt cod from the scale and slapped it on a block. Nathan McBride had caught him at a bad time.

"If you're busy now, I can wait," he said, sipping a cup of strong black coffee.

"Busy ain't the problem, my friend." He wrapped the fish in a newspaper and handed it to a customer, a young man in knickers and tie, obviously running an errand. "I could use a lot more business. It's been down at least fifty percent ever since they sank the Maine. Excuse me. Hey, listen, kid—be sure to tell the cook to soak this fish in cold water for a day before she serves it. I don't wanna get blamed if your papa's poker goes flat. Now, where was I? Oh yeah, business is lousy."

The young man stared at the package for a few seconds, decided its mysteries were beyond him and left. In another part of the store a plump woman was picking out some sausage. Farther away, toward the back, an elderly foreign gentleman was opening the barrels and sampling the marinated vegetables.

"I go so far as to put a damn flag of Portugal on the sign last time and the ignorant bastards didn't even look at it. They just broke the damn window again. Windows that size cost twenty bucks installed. That's a lot, my friend. So I call you guys and ask if maybe I could have some cop stand around here for a while, so's they get the idea it ain't funny, you could go to jail and etcetera, but all I get is a we'll-see-what-we-can-do. I'm all set to get the old fishin' boat out a drydock and quit this goddamn business."

McBride thought about trying to explain that the department was too short of men to put a guard on his business, too short because of the war, but he quickly reconsidered because that would only cause the grocer to repeat the story he had already told twice before. "Portuguese aren't Spaniards. Portuguese are Portuguese, right? I wish to hell somebody would take a geography lesson around here!" He felt for the big, likable man, as furry as a bear and probably half as strong. He wondered what would happen if Soares-DaSilva ever got his hands on one of the fringe morons who tossed bricks through his window and painted threats on his door then ran off like true patriots. And he wondered if it would be prudent to get in the way if he did.

"I'd like to tell you I've been sent here to solve your problems, Mr. Soares-DaSilva, but you know better."

"Me? What do I know? You want some more coffee?"

"Thanks."

"I know you from something, don't I?" Soares-DaSilva studied his face. "You're the cop they call 'Flying McBride,' ain'tcha?"

The reference was to an earlier, well-publicized episode. He no longer bristled at the reference but just smiled and bobbed his head.

"You work with that Dr. Blakeley, don'tcha?"

"Sometimes. When I'm lucky."

The grocer laughed. "Some pitcher in the mornin' rag, huh? He looked like he was gonna wrestle a crocodile. Anyway, what can I do for ya?"

"We're interested in artichokes."

"Artichokes?"

The plump woman waddled over with her hands full of sausage. Soares-DaSilva weighed and wrapped it as he spoke, winking as he handed her the change.

"You and Dr. Blakeley are pretty high caliber for artichokes. I expected maybe a murder at least, or maybe some kind of spy stuff. Artichokes?"

"Afraid so."

"Well, I sell them, but I guess you know that."

"Who buys them?"

He shrugged and gestured into the air. "People with gourmet appetites. People who don't mind spending too much money for some fancy little weeds. Snobs and dummies. Mostly people who live in Society Hill or out on the Main Line."

"Can you name names?"

"Names and addresses, because usually we have to deliver. But what's this all about anyway? You guys investigatin' Gazzo again? Look, I buy the stuff in good faith. Where he gets it, I don't know and I don't ask. Just a minute."

The bell above the door sounded and a thin gentleman in tweed and salt-and-pepper goatee entered tapping a walking stick. Soares-DaSilva gave a wary, warning look.

"Name's Watkins," he said *sotto voce*. "He'll rob you blind if you don't keep an eye on him. A college professor, no less."

"I know him. Good afternoon, Professor Watkins."

The gentleman stopped in his tracks, his face registering surprise, then shock, then horror.

"Nathan. How good to see you, dear boy."

"I gather you like Portuguese food. Nice to know we have something in common, Professor."

"Yes, isn't it?" he replied, mustering aloofness. He made a tight little smile and turned to the grocer. "I'm looking for Torre del Oro panatellas. Fresh, preferably."

"For eats you come here. For cigars you go to a tobacco shop."

Professor Watkins huffed, snickered mildly and started to exit.

"Do keep at your Caesar, Nathan," he said, pausing in the doorway. "You never did quite grasp the periphrastic."

The little bell sounded as the door closed. The elderly man shuffled over and placed a tin of anchovy paste on the counter for Soares-DaSilva to put on an account.

"He looked like he saw a ghost."

"He was my Latin teacher in college," McBride said, finishing his cup of coffee. "Later on I had to pick him up a few times for selling things that didn't belong to him. A very small-time Gazzo."

"Good. He'll stay away from here for a while now. One more problem I didn't need."

"Do you think I might see your artichoke list now?"

Soares-DaSilva scratched the black bearish hair that protruded from his open collar and thought about it.

"Why the hell not? I'm gettin' out a artichokes anyway. The sign's gonna read 'Joe Silver' and I'm gonna sell knockwurst and scrapple. My papa will roll over in his grave, but at least I won't have to deal with crooks like Gazzo no more."

The grocer produced the list and McBride studied it, copying into his notebook occasional names and addresses that showed vague promise. It was not very long, about 20 well-heeled families in and around Philadelphia, some in nearby New Jersey communities. It was in alphabetical order, and he was up to the L's, Henry Arthur LaFontaine, 140 Ithan Avenue

South, Villanova, when Soares-DaSilva finished taking care of the elderly man. He told McBride to keep the list since it was a duplicate.

The sky was very dark when McBride stepped out of the grocery and headed for the nearest trolley island. The rumbling in the clouds was louder, exploding like cannons from the northwest. He wondered how the boys of the Twenty-eighth were doing. Should be in Cuba by now.

The early afternoon pace seemed to pick up as shoppers, merchants and casual strollers hurried to finish their outdoor business. Street vendors along Market were gradually battening down their covered pushcarts.

He spotted Professor Watkins across the street, pausing to investigate the window of a haberdashery. The professor turned, saw him and hurried off, holding his top hat as the wind buffeted him from behind.

A sad case, McBride thought, certainly more to be pitied than despised—toiling in the thankless, barren acres of academe where the frontal lobes slowly atrophy, where one learns too late that the surly, ignoble forces of the real world are intractable and merciless. On quick but closer inspection the tweed suit was threadbare and the French cuffs frayed. And Professor Watkins well understood that if McBride caught him just once more the university would have to hear of it.

"Hey, McBride."

"I don't have time to look at dirty pictures now, Al."

"Always quick with the smart mouth, ain't he, Whitey?"

"Dat's cuz he's a smart man, Al."

"Smart enough to hoodwink the boss lady."

"Yeah, the boss lady and Fifi, too."

No one had noticed them yet. Frankly, if he could ease out of this quietly, he would. Nothing like a fistfight in the center of the city to attract the wrong attention. Besides, he was wearing a brand new Brooks Brothers gray summer suit that he hated to get dirty.

"Well, gents, no sense standing in the rain. Look me up at the Eleventh sometime."

Al's teeth were brown as he sneered, and tobacco juice ran over his lip as he shouted an order.

"Jump him, Whitey."

"Oh, for Pete's sake!"

Whitey flew at him, but he ducked behind an iron lamppost which went clank when Whitey's head hit it. Whitey stood wobbly-legged, staring at the post as if he were about to ask it to dance. He had his familiar stunned look of a steer in a slaughterhouse after the first blow of the sledge-hammer.

"C'mon, Whitey," Al insisted. "Go after him."

McBride decided there was no need to get dirty after all. He reached around the post, grasped Whitey firmly by each wrist and yanked him headfirst into it.

"Whitey, c'mon, get up!" Al pleaded. "Oh, jeez!"

They exchanged cat and mouse eye contact. Al

backed up, unaware that McBride would just as soon let them go, provided they had tickets to Buenos Aires or beyond, but a small crowd had formed, observing the sleeping Whitey. As Al backed up he tripped over someone's foot, fell backward and panicked.

"Stay away from me, McBride." The voice was high and quivery. "I ain't a well man!"

He took the slimy brown plug out of his mouth and fired it at McBride. It landed with a putrid splat on the front of the Brooks Brothers jacket. The crowd gasped. A little boy made retching sounds. McBride growled.

Al was half a block away when he caught up with him. Heads were turning and people were darting out of their way as Al's screams and curses warned them that it was possible to get very badly bruised if they did not. The words became louder and more obscene as he felt McBride closing in. Finally, after slowing down to avoid colliding with a trash barrel, he let out a loud adenoidal screech as McBride jumped over it and brought him down with a flying tackle.

The crowd was twice as large back at the lamppost, some still gawking at Whitey, others now pointing at the tobacco plug on the ground where it had slithered off McBride's coat.

He sat Al down facing Whitey and handcuffed them together around the iron post.

"There. Now you can comfort Whitey when he wakes up."

"Whattaya gonna charge me with, McBride? Assault with a gooey weapon?"

"I'll think of something good, Al."

And then he noticed the ugly brown blob on the sidewalk. He looked at the stain on his coat, felt the moisture on his fingers as, without thinking, he tried to brush it off, and he became furious again.

"How about indecent exposure, Al?"

"Hey! Whattaya doin'? Hey, there's ladies lookin'!"

Some of them blushed, some of them turned away, and some of them just stood there looking on brazenly as he pulled off Al's suspenders and tore away his trousers, leaving him in only his faded red underwear from the waist down.

"Longies? Al, you're supposed to take them off in the summer."

"I'll sue you for this, McBride. It's police brutality! Hey, where you goin'?"

"Somebody will be around with a paddy wagon eventually. There was a gigantic clap of thunder and everyone started to scurry away as the raindrops speckled the sidewalk. "Better hope it gets here before the big St. Bernard does. You're lounging around his favorite water closet."

He jumped on a passing trolley going westward. Al's howls grew fainter in the din of the car and the giggles of the three young girls who jumped on with him, ducking the sudden deluge and holding their bonnets in the wind.

"McBride! We're gonna drown! McBride! I'm scared a lightnin'! Hey, McBride, wait! It was Whitey's idea! McBr . . ."

It was not going to get the ugly stain out. Probably there was no solvent ever invented that could do that. But as he took the jacket off and looked it over sadly the disappointment ebbed a bit as he looked out the window at the two wretched forms on the distant dark gray ground, the one sleeping peacefully, the other howling in vain into the rain-soaked wind.

And a devilish grin crossed his usually impassive face as he uttered a silent prayer that the mythical St. Bernard would really appear.

Chapter Thirty-two

It was a pleasant evening. The rain in the trees, in the new mown grass, in the honeysuckle and lilac, brought out the glorious springtime smells, drifting gently over the veranda where they sat with their after-dinner Benedictines. The moonlight was scarce, easing through the dark clouds at infrequent opportunities, but when it did it lit up the river with splashes of silver. Inside the house the Victrola played the *Treues Liebes Herz* of Strauss just loudly enough to be heard above the crickets and wild canaries. There was a lull in the conversation. They watched Thomas Aquinas chasing lightning bugs on the lawn.

To a visitor it would have seemed serenely and perfectly Victorian. Two couples, one younger, the other somewhat middle-aged, enjoying the fruits of a well-ordered life. Dinner itself had been Victorian—oysters in a bed of watercress, lamb chops, parslied new potatoes, and a proper wine. Prior to that there had been two rounds of Madeira to inspire the palate.

However, the discussion, if overheard, would have seemed most inappropriate to the setting.

"I cannot help thinking, Ian darling, that you are just a trifle too eager to think ill of her simply because you don't like her."

"Sophia, my dearest darling, I assure you that I'm . . . we are only going where the map directs us."

"To Lightcarn Lane."

"Presumably. Unless you've a better idea."

"I'm sorry, Ian. I cannot appreciate the possibility of a nice, albeit a trifle eccentric, English-woman being responsible for such a sum of calamities."

"A quaint little Englishwoman named Mary Ann Cotton was hanged in Liverpool twenty-five years ago for poisoning sixteen people," he reminded her soberly.

She took a tiny sip from her snifter and frowned.

"Poisoning is one thing, and I am certainly not dismissing it, but . . ."

"But," Allison intervened, "didn't you both agree that the accent was phony?"

"You noticed it also?" Blakeley asked with a sudden smile.

"No. I was upstairs, remember? But I thought I heard you say—"

"My point exactly," Sophia said. "Ian's been

campaigning. I suppose he had a word or two for you as well, Nathan?"

"How would I know the difference between Devon and wherever?" Nathan answered lamely. "If you decide it's phony, it's phony."

"And you said so yourself, Sophia darling. Before you decided to play defense attorney for English womanhood."

"Oh?"

She blushed. Even in the imperfect light of the coal oil lamp it was obvious.

"Sophia, you've an excellent ear for this," he pursued, "and you remarked that the speech pattern was no more that of Stoke than of Texas."

He lit a cigar, hoping that the smoke, together with what was coming from the coal oil, would keep the mosquitoes away. But the Blakeley estate was simply too close to the river.

"Or did you say Brooklyn?"

"I was being facetious, and you know that."

She pretended to pout, very briefly, then smiled, much to the relief of Nathan and Allison. Seldom had they been present when the Blakeleys disagreed, though they frequently jousted in private.

"Very well, then, it was fraudulent. Well, actually, quite fraudulent."

Blakeley lifted his glass and grinned. "The prosecution rests."

Victor stepped onto the veranda, poured some more Benedictine into each of the snifters, made a great to-do about a mosquito bite on his neck and hurried back inside.

"You see," Sophia explained, "I come from Lancashire—as Ian likes to say, 'famous for its witches'—but as a girl I spent many a month in Devon. Father was in Her Majesty's foreign service, as were most of the men of the family, and whenever mother had the opportunity, she'd go off to visit him on the Continent or wherever. At such times we children would be shipped off to Auntie Meg in Northam: she'd been widowed in one of those African tribal uprisings and Uncle Colin had left her a huge estate on the coast. We used to look forward to such holidays, romping barefoot on the beach like a small band of savages, watching the tall ships out at sea, building bonfires in the moonlight like a tribe of Druids, lying awake and telling gothic tales during those many stormy nights—all manner of things that mother would have felt conditioned to disapprove of. But I'm digressing."

"Auntie Meg was a bit eccentric herself," Blakeley tattled, bussing her playfully on the forehead. "It was rumored she held seances at midnight."

"During which Uncle Colin would appear and give her financial advice," she replied, waving him off. "Very sound advice, I might add. But to return to our discussion, I actually thought I heard something else in her speech. A hint of the islands off Land's End. Difficult to describe, but it's quite distinctive."

Nathan was listening closely. He had developed a sudden fascination with the strangely beautiful woman who had been in their company the night before.

The trolley had been a tin drum in the hands of an angry child for several blocks. Faces had turned pale green and knuckles white on the straps in the crowded car as sweaty bodies tumbled against other bodies, feet stepped on feet, and the wet floor became a long slice of liver. Too many had squeezed in, the doors had closed too late, and the crowd was ill-tempered. But about halfway back to the Eleventh the hail and rain had let up, and in another couple blocks enough of the riders had chosen to take their chances in the heavy mist to allow some breathing space.

He had found a seat in the back, just behind the two giggling young ladies and beside a scowling old woman who kept looking down at his knee, daring him to make unwelcome contact with her person.

At the risk of inspiring a virtuous tirade, he reached across and opened the window. Her nostrils flared.

He mopped his brow and folded the crinkled paper. She looked at him quizzically, her mouth tight and her eyes narrow.

When the car stopped the next time he hopped off, jumping a swollen gutter and dashing down the block to another island and a trolley that was going back downtown.

But for the paddy wagon and a scurrying few who must have had no choice, the streets were deserted as he jumped off at Juniper and Market. He paused briefly to sign a citation ordering Whitey and Al off to the lockup. The rain was coming down in sheets again and the two seemed to blend in with the sodden refuse sweeping past in the runoff. They went along gratefully.

"Mr. Soares-DaSilva?"

"I bet you came back for some salt cod."

"I came back because of a name on your list."

"Lessee . . . Oh yeah, good customers."

"Have you ever met them?"

"No. They have a regular delivery. I send a kid out. He drops it off in the kitchen."

"You've never seen the mistress of the house, Mrs. West?"

"No, but I hear she's a real poopsie. One of my delivery boys got a look at her. Just a minute . . ."

He went to the back and brought out a young man about Casimir's age who eyed Nathan nervously as he wiped his hands on an apron.

"This here's Sergeant McBride, Nico. Tell him about Mrs. West."

"Whattaya wanna know?"

"Tell him what you saw."

"Why's he wanna know?"

"Yeah, why *do* you wanna know?"

"It's like this. Umm . . . A very important person died the other day, and she may have inherited a bundle. Only she doesn't know it yet. We think she's the Countess of Shmeckfenster."

The boy still eyed him suspiciously.

"She'll probably be grateful to anyone who helps us to clear this up," Nathan added.

"G'wan, tell the man," the grocer said. "It has nothin' to do with what you did. It's a little embarrassin' for him, Officer McBride."

The boy took a stubby cigarette from his shirt and lit it.

"Okay, well . . . I was makin' this there delivery once. Kinda early, still dark when I left here. I seen her as I was unloadin'. She had a bird—it looked like a hawk, but Mr. Soares-DaSilva said it must a been a falcon—on her arm, and she was ridin' a horse. Great big sonofabitch with a black mane. Beautiful. Only she, the lady, was even more beautiful. The most beautifulest lady I ever seen. So I unhitched the horse from the cart and followed her."

"And?"

"G'wan, Nico, tell him."

"She rode off over a hill and down into a valley by a lake. Nice place. Lots a nice trees 'n stuff. I was real careful, not because I was gonna do nothin', jist that I didn't wanna get caught lookin'."

"Get to the good part, Nico," the grocer said. "We ain't got all afternoon."

"Anyway, she must a stopped somewheres where I couldn't see her for a minute, cuz when I seen her next she was naked. Nothin' on, y'know? I thought she was gonna go swimmin' in the lake, but it was kinda cold fer that. Anyway, she stays on the horse and I hears this terrible screech off somewheres in the distance, and pretty soon the bird comes back with this dead animal in its hooks. A rabbit, I think. She takes the rabbit off the bird and looks at it, follow me? There's blood runnin' down her hand, down her arm, and next thing I know she's rubbin' it all over her tits. Honest to God, I don't lie! I thought it was real weird, so I beat it out a there as fast as the old draft horse could go."

"Yeah, and everytime he talks about it he still can't stand up straight." The grocer laughed. "Look at him."

Before he left the grocery, Nathan McBride had gotten not only an excellent description of the woman in question but also a list of dates when artichokes had been delivered to her home. And all it had cost him was two dollars for the salt cod he had to buy which eventually ended up with Father Wladslaw's orphans. He had had to take it with him back to the Eleventh, suffering the disdainful sniffs and gasps of those unlucky enough to be near him on the hot, crowded trolley.

The tale had been carefully edited in the telling, a token of consideration for the ladies' sense of propriety, but Allison had smiled sheepishly, knowing Nathan well enough to read between the lines.

For a time she had lost the anger which was growing with every hour of forced inactivity. Indolence did not become her, she hoped. She had spoken to him without an edge in her voice, and he had had the good sense not to mention Lillian Russell.

332

"So there you have it," Blakeley was beaming now. "Quite a coup, I'd call it."

But Sophia was getting back into her trench.

"You needn't be so smug, gentlemen. All you've established is that the woman is probably a social climber, and if the delivery boy can be believed, she engages in rather bizarre behavior when she has every reason to believe she is alone. Hardly savory, but I don't think it qualifies her as a homicidal maniac."

Allison caught Nathan's eye.

There was a brief effort at mute communication. She tilted her head toward the large fern near the glass doors. He squinted in that direction. He noticed the shadowy figure and tapped Blakeley on the knee. "Eh?" He nodded and Blakeley caught on.

"He's been taking notes, I think," Nathan whispered.

"He's been particularly vigilant lately."

There was a distant roll of thunder. Thomas Aquinas abandoned his pursuit and scurried up to the veranda and onto Sophia's lap, purring as she tickled his chin.

"Don't lower your voice too much," Blakeley advised. "We don't want to frighten him off."

"Am I missing something?" Sophia asked.

A breeze came up the river and shook the wetness in the nearby trees. Droplets spattered the grounds.

"I think it's going to rain, my love." He offered her his arm. "Perhaps we ought to go inside."

She took his arm and they led the way with

Thomas Aquinas, his proud plume waving, dashing ahead.

Nathan and Allison were a deliberate few steps behind. He assisted her up and she stepped carefully.

"Does it still hurt much?"

"It's turning a lighter shade of purple. Less than mauve but more than lavender."

"It's nice to have an excuse to get closer," he said as she took his arm and held on tightly for support.

"Is it?"

A few feet ahead, Blakeley stopped as he approached the door, leaned into the fern and spoke cheerily.

"Well, hello, Victor. How are you and the mosquitoes getting along?"

Victor stepped out from his hiding place. On closer inspection it was obvious he'd found the new key to Blakeley's private liquor cabinet, the third new key in as many months.

"Terribly, sir."

"Hmmm. They must be gin drinkers."

"That was cruel, sir."

Victor left hiccuping.

Inside the house a fire was lapping gently in the hearth, and there was more Benedictine on the mantle.

"Yes, it is. It really is," Nathan answered eventually as he helped her into a chair.

Her eyes told him she agreed, but she let it pass without comment or gesture. Confusion was much worse than anger. Something told her he meant it; something else told her it was only the wounded bird syndrome. As soon as she was ready to fly again, he'd just as soon pretend she was a bad memory. And then she had a very confusing moment when she wondered why she was angry at all.

"Would you like some more brandy?" he asked. "The butler seems to be indisposed."

He smiled. Nathan's smile was special in a way because he did not flash it frequently. She smiled back.

"If you'll have one with me."

Blakeley's day had also been quite eventful.

"I suppose then, you've dismissed the importance of my discovery this afternoon?" he asked Sophia rhetorically.

"Not at all. Provided the man you saw was the man you think he is."

"Oh, he's the real thing, Mrs. Blakeley," Nathan joined in. "It was Grover Stanhope. We've had him on our books for a long time."

Blakeley had been waiting at the precinct station when Nathan arrived. The plan had called for a meeting with Fatzinger, a little effort at conciliation aimed at getting him to slow down his pursuit of Bogdan. Perhaps when the case was concluded, Fatzinger's name could be dropped as someone instrumental. And it was, after all, a trifle brutish to pick on a poor immigrant boy. If the legal and humanitarian arguments failed, there was always the threat of looking like an ass when the real killer was found, especially looking like an ass on the front page of his friend Bernard Spector's newspaper.

But Fatzinger was still at lunch.

Blakeley had said hello to a few acquaintances and started to leave. Except for Fatzinger's little work space, the station was crowded and busy. A patrolman explained as he and his catch awaited their turn at the booking desk that the rain often brings out the petty types. Pockets can be picked in crowded trolleys or in the swollen masses huddled under awnings, and purses can be snatched as women hurried for shelter. Al and Whitey, looking saturated and wretched, were standing at the desk where an officer from the paddy wagon was booking them, Al for indecent exposure and Whitey for vagrancy. He had been sleeping in the street, and there were witnesses. It was easier than charging him with assault. Al had been shouting about the lawsuit he was going to bring against Nathan McBride, the mayor, the city street cleaners—against everyone involved for a broad assortment of indignities. There was a fairly wide perimeter around them, and when the breeze drifted the wrong way it was impossible not to notice that a sewer must have backed up while they sat at opposite ends of the lamppost. Grudgingly admitted, Al may have had a point, but his tirade quickly ended when McBride appeared.

"Dr. Blakeley, would you care for some salt cod?"

"Nathan, I thought you were looking for artichokes."

"I have a story that will have you doing cartwheels."

"Hey sarge," the desk officer interrupted, "there's some guy on the phone for you. Says he's from the morgue."

They had to hurry. The morgue attendant was doing his best to delay Grover with official forms to read and sign. Luckily, Grover did not read well.

McBride handed the cod to a patrolman who was eager to get away from Al and Whitey. He knew a shortcut over a curving, unpaved road which began in a back alley, ran parallel to a railroad for a mile, cut through a vacant lot, then led over the tracks and down another alley, narrower and muddier, ending right at the rear entrance of the morgue.

"So much for my new suit," he grumbled as they climbed down into a pond of brackish water, forded some mud, and entered through the creaking metal door.

"I can't believe our good fortune," Blakeley had said, barely able to contain himself after hearing McBride's report. "It's enough to make one believe in horoscopes."

The attendant had intercepted them, ushering them into an alcove and gesturing for them to speak in very soft whispers.

"The sound carries, as you know."

The attendant, a pale, prissy type with a squint, was a student at a nearby mortuary college who planned to open a place of business in the Eleventh Precinct and was naturally eager to make himself known to those who protect property. "Snodgrass, Marcellus A. Snodgrass," he said twice, although no one was taking notes. Snodgrass was clearly aware of his role and of the favor he was now doing.

"Where is Grover Stanhope?" Blakeley whispered.

"Follow me."

They tiptoed up a stairwell and across a hallway into another alcove where they had a good view of Grover on the next floor down. He was leaning over a desk with a small pile of papers in front of him. His mouth moved slowly as he read.

"That is your Mr. Stanhope, I presume?" Snodgrass asked.

"Nathan?"

"Grover Garfield Stanhope, Jr. All two hundred fifty pounds of him."

"He looks familiar."

"I don't doubt that," the attendant said.

"Did you say something, Mr. Snodgrass?" Blakeley asked.

"I said he should look familiar. He looks like you."

"I fail to see that."

"Listen, we put faces together with putty and spit. I should know faces. It's perfectly obvious. Somewhat younger, of course."

"I think you've been sniffing too much embalming fluid."

"Why don't we get on with it?" Nathan advised.

"Yes, why don't we?"

The attendant left them. In a few seconds he was down at the desk. His voice broke the silence unpleasantly.

"All signed and satisfied, are we?"

"I don't understand this shit. Where's Pluto?"

Snodgrass sorted the papers into a neat pile and gestured with his index finger for Grover to follow. They walked across the floor to the assembly line, heels clicking on the hard surface. The attendant found Pluto's slab, pulled it out and lifted the linen sheet for Grover to look.

"I know I've seen him before," Blakeley repeated in a soft whisper.

Nathan nodded but said nothing.

"Is this Mr. Snyder?" the attendant asked.

"Yeah, that's him. What he die of?"

Snodgrass gave him a bored, monotonous answer.

"He stopped breathing."

Grover looked up from the corpse. Whatever the attendant saw in his eyes had an immediately chastening effect. Snodgrass tried to smile but it was more like an imitation of a mouse nibbling on something dry. For a fleeting few seconds it was possible to like Grover.

"They say tha's goin' around."

The attendant laughed too hard, causing a shrill echo in the halls. Grover's expression never changed.

"Well," the attendant said, catching his breath and collecting himself, "I take it you're claiming the body."

"Yeah. Wrap him up and I'll be around in the mornin' with an undertaker."

"Very well, Mister . . . ?"

"John Jacob Astor."

Again the laugh was too quick and too shrill, but Snodgrass never challenged the answer.

"There's a small fee," he said, returning the slab and locking the vault.

"Huh?"

"It's a little something the city wants us to charge for services rendered. You see, we—"

"How much?"

"Five dollars. That includes the—"

"Shit. He wasn't worth that much on his best day."

"You mean, you don't want him?"

"I mean, you can use him for fertilizer. How do I get out a this cave?"

"Around the corner, to your left, and straight ahead," Snodgrass pointed.

"Five bucks for Pluto." Grover shook his head and chortled on his way out. "Next thing ya know they'll be chargin' for cat shit."

"Gawd! You wonder where they come from sometimes," said the attendant as they thanked him and hurried after Grover. "They must breed in mud. Now remember, it's Snodgrass, Marcellus A., and I'll be setting up shop at . . ."

They had followed a discreet half-block behind him, picking him up as he passed a side street not far from the morgue. He was in no hurry. He paused once or twice to whistle at pretty passers-by and made lewd comments when they ignored him. When he turned a wide corner in Overbrook and Blakeley had a better look at the carriage, he remembered where he'd seen him.

"This morning, Nathan. He came for Father Wladislaw. I am absolutely certain."

"Grover and a priest?"

"I admit it's strange. Something to do with a medical emergency. Let's stay with him for a while."

They followed for as long as they could feign innocence, north along City Line and west along Lancaster for several miles into the next county, through the first few towns and villages of the picturesque Main Line, but stopped when he took a less traveled road leading off to the countryside.

To Lightcarn Lane.

"I tell you, we have our prime suspect," Blakeley now repeated as Sophia sipped her Benedictine quietly, "and she was sitting in this very room last night."

Sophia started to speak, changed her mind and sighed.

She, too, had been wondering about the strange Mrs. West ever since the tales of the Grand Guignol. She had seemed much too involved in the telling. There was something about the eyes. Ian had said she was an opium eater, which was certainly possible, but it went beyond that.

"I must speak to Father Wladislaw tomorrow," Blakeley thought aloud. "I'd like to know where he went with that chap."

He had gotten up to change the spool on the Victrola. He was in rare spirits.

"The Blue Danube," he announced and bowed to Sophia, who demured momentarily then got up to dance.

Nathan and Allison watched them floating off into the next room, she a lovely glass figurine in his arms, he moving with the same kind of ease and grace that had surprised everyone in yesterday's donnybrook. My God, she thought, was that only yesterday?

"I'm sorry we can't join them," she said.

"I'm not. I'd feel like a yokel out there."

She smiled. True, waltzing was not Nathan's forte. He was, by his own admission, a klutz.

She wondered if he felt the same pangs of envy that she did in the Blakeleys' company. Their relationship was so perfectly complementary that it was as if their souls were fused. It was hard to imagine two people happier with and more suited to each other, and watching their eyes as they moved in stately circles told that to even a casual observer.

"He must have been furious at that attendant for likening him to such a loathsome creature as Grover Stanhope."

"He bristled a bit."

"Was there any—?"

"Resemblance?"

He thought about it then bobbed his head slightly. When he spoke, it was cautiously.

"Shave the beard but leave the mustache, take a little gray out of the hair . . ."

Actually, Blakeley himself had remarked on the way back that, much as he hated to agree at all with the morgue attendant, Grover could be a distant cousin. Later on that was amended to someone closer. He did, however, take exception to the comment about his age; on the shady side of 40 one becomes sensitive about such things. But he was laughing about it shortly thereafter.

The music continued and their conversation became more relaxed. It was too bad, he thought, that the weather and her ankle did not permit a walk in the garden. The roses were out, and there was a small, somewhat isolated bench surrounded by shrubs and tall hedges. There was also the walk down to the gazebo where they had spent hours in the evening stillness playing the game of guarded amorous dialogue.

Oh well, there were the mosquitoes there, too.

"Dr. Blakeley and I have a little surprise for you, Nathan."

"Hmm? I'll bet I know what it is. A certificate for dancing lessons."

"That will come later. If you'll look behind McCabe's *Illustrated History of the World* over there, you'll find it."

He walked over to a bookcase filled with assorted reference material, and behind the huge volume he found a ratty, dog-eared collection held together by a leather strap.

"A book?"

"Not just *a* book."

"All right, a beat-up, falling-apart book."

"Open it carefully."

"I will, first chance I get."

"Open it now—please."

"All right, all right. Now just in case this isn't a joke, thank you." He opened it and scanned a few pages.

"Good Lord!"

She shushed him gently. "It's not for Sophia Blakeley's eyes, obviously."

"Obviously. What are *you* doing with it?"

"Nathan, I collect that sort of thing."

"This is," he read it more closely, "this is Goldie Becker's diary."

"And she names names."

"Shame on you, Allison. I never took you for a voyeur," he teased.

"I'll have you know, it was all in the line of duty. We—"

She suddenly realized that the music had stopped and the Blakeleys could be heard chattering exuberantly, drawing closer. She motioned for him to hide the book, so he returned it to the shelf, dropping it behind the large volume.

"You were magnificent," Blakeley said, a little out of breath as he escorted Sophia to her chair.

"And you were dignity itself," she said, fanning herself with *The Saturday Evening Post*. "As always."

"I tell you, friends," he raised his glass, "this is the most perfect evening I've spent in months."

Thomas Aquinas followed them into the room and hopped onto Allison's lap. They'd become good friends. It had been a very good evening for her as well. She was wondering if Nathan would decide to spend the night there, it being rather late and the weather being so threatening. It would be the prudent thing to do.

"Nathan," Blakeley said, as if reading her mind, "you must be our guest for the night. The storm is returning. Hear?"

As if on cue, a loud crack rent the air. Thomas Aquinas' tail puffed up. Nathan looked at Allison and she tried not to react.

"I have an early meeting with a few people who owe me a favor. I want to set up a network to watch Grover."

"We've no intention of allowing you to sleep in," Blakeley replied, and there was a second loud crack.

Nathan smiled and started to agree. "It sounds like a good—"

"Good evening, Father. Mother. Miss Meredith." Suddenly, Rosie appeared across the room, dressed in a lacy, low-cut gown. "And Nathan, how utterly divine to see you again."

Sophia's jaw dropped.

"What are you doing with that chest?"

Rosie smiled, frowned and blushed at the same time.

"Why, Mother, whatever do you mean?"

"I mean," Sophia sputtered, "they will progress at a natural pace."

The fireplace cracked and hissed, and Nathan and Allison wished they were anywhere else. Rosie glanced at her mother's chest in unspoken but undeniable counterstatement.

Sophia's eyes narrowed.

"And what is that?"

"Oh, this? It's a cigarette, but it's unlit. Really, mother, I—"

Sophia stood up. "Leave this room, and do not

return until you are wearing your *own* chest."

Rosie stomped off, muttering. Sophia followed, waving an angry finger. Blakeley watched, unperturbed, and for the first time it dawned on his guests that the evening's libations had gotten to him slightly; usually, his collar remained stiff.

"I have an uneasy feeling that I'm partially responsible for that scene," Nathan confessed.

"How do you figure that?" Allison asked frostily.

"Well, I—"

"Nonsense, my boy." Blakeley hesitated until Sophia was well out of the room. "You've seen our little surprise, eh?"

"I had a brief look and put it back."

Blakeley chuckled, reached behind the massive history book and pulled out the diary.

"Miss Meredith and I have a page or two to show you."

Chapter Thirty-three

The rain came down in torrents on his slicker, boots and skin. The sharp loud bolts resounding somewhere not far away—and in his mind, even closer—would have made a lunatic happy. He looked around for a lunatic and saw only his reflection, a silhouette shimmering under gaslight in a mud puddle. He had an urge to sneeze, but it passed. He was certain he had pneumonia. The urge came back suddenly. He turned his head, held his breath and fought it off for as long as he could, cursing to himself. When it happened, he smothered it in the crook of his arm and cursed again for forgetting his handkerchief.

He could hear the busy noises on the other side of the little window, faint under the steady drumming of the rain in the knotty pines and over the stone walk. There were even fainter flashes of lighted matches, one after the other as they burned out. He had been there for over an hour, listening and observing from a shadowy distance.

The window opened with a creak and a satchel came out. It was bulging with expensive things. He could only guess what.

Another satchel appeared, this one open because the booty was both larger and waterproof.

He stepped back behind the trees, encouraged now.

A little figure protruded. Once in his childhood he had seen a ewe giving birth. Head first the lamb had issued, struggling and making little muffled sounds. And when it succeeded, it had been a dreary, wet little thing.

The dreary little figure emerged, squeezing through the tiny window and into a deep puddle. When he stood up, he was slightly higher than the average man's hip. He tugged at a cloth sack, so full of goods that it barely fit, until it was out on the lawn with him.

"Don't forget to shut the window, Wally."

The little figure turned with a gasp. "Wha—?"

"You don't want to flood the man's basement, do you?"

"Hudson?"

"Uh-huh."

"Ahhh, shit . . ."

"Wally, please, you'll disturb the neighborhood."

"How the hell did you know it was me?"

"You have an almost unique style."

"Yeah, it is, sorta," he said proudly. "It ain't

everybody that can get through a little hole like that and still keep Jenny smilin'."

"By the way, she's waiting for you around the corner. A lady could catch a cold on a night like this."

"Not that cow, Hudson. It'd take a real blizzard."

Chapter Thirty-four

The mystery of the knife that turned up in Bernard Spector's hands and just how Spector always happened to know where Blakeley and friends were had required no Scotland Yard expertise to solve. The trouble with the Victor Primroses is how easily they're overlooked. They are the kind who may collapse in the middle of a crowd and the crowd would merely step around them politely. And in the specific case of Blakeley's vapid gentleman's gentleman, many no doubt had. But sometimes it pays to keep an eye on them because the bite a Victor Primrose inflicts on one's heel or toe can be filled with venom.

And so, after taking notice of the information that Blakeley and Allison were so eager to show him, Nathan McBride just happened to leave the prostitute's diary next to the Boodles and Plymouth in Blakeley's liquor cabinet.

And then the Blakeleys, quite exhausted by the busy day, the waltz and the Benedictine, had retired, leaving him alone with Allison. There had been awkward silences followed by periods of nervous prattle. And some time later he had assisted her to her room, she had invited him in for a nightcap, and the rest of the evening was nobody's business but theirs.

Such were his thoughts as he later climbed the stairs to his apartment.

"You're givin' this place a bad name, ya know."

"Mrs. Allcock, you look stunning this morning."

He had hoped to sneak into his quarters, change clothes and sneak out without meeting her. She wore a bulky robe over a tentlike nightgown. A man's stocking cap rested unevenly on her bulbous gray head. He had seen prettier faces on punch-drunk fighters.

"Don't smart-mouth me, you. What's dis here horseradish about yiz in the paper?"

He meant to ignore her as usual, but instead he did a double take and looked at the artist's rendering on the front page of the *Morning Star*.

"I never knew they called you 'Flyin' McBride'," she sneered.

"It's probably a misprint."

The drawing was of a savage, almost salivating McBride making a diving tackle on a frail, terrorized Al while good citizens looked on in horror.

"Misprint, my butt. It says here they're chargin' ya with salt 'n battery."

He scanned the report as she ranted on. There were witnesses. He had used excessive force, endangering and humiliating Al and Whitey, and had committed a lewd and lascivious act in public when he pulled off Al's trousers. There were lawyers involved, most notably Alfred Peteroff of Peteroff, MacBirney and Schnurr, who said it was "high time the mayor took a good look at the hooligans in the Eleventh Precinct."

"And if yiz ain't fartin' around with some play actress tart or ennertainin' some floozie in yer room, it's dis here kind of bullsh—"

He shut his door and locked it.

Her yammering faded as he splashed cold water on his face and soaped it up to shave, one of the amenities he'd neglected when he got up early, scribbled a thank you note to Sophia and another to Blakeley of a business nature, thought about awakening Allison then reconsidered, and left in the morning fog off the Schuylkill. It was no time to look like a lout. He trimmed his mustache, brushed his teeth with baking soda and gargled with a strong mouthwash.

When he was out of the expensive clothes and into a suit more appropriate for where he was going, he opened the door, looked for his landlady, then tiptoed down the stairs. The day would be difficult enough without her.

It was late morning by the time he had set up his team of Grover watchers, a sleazy but hawk-eyed assortment of opportunists. A few had admitted to recognizing his picture, but most had made a point of promising nothing, pretending that only a miracle would help and that they would expect a favor of the same magnitude. He made no promises in return, offered no rewards, leaving only the unspoken understanding that all of them had been in trouble in the past and would no doubt be in trouble in the future.

When he was finished he caught up with Blakeley at Father Wladislaw's rectory.

"Father has some enlightening news, Nathan."

"Good morning, Father."

"Good mornink, Sergeant. I tink maybe Dr. Blakeley must tell. Bogdan and me gotta fix roof now. Rain come in like I was Noah."

He made a gesture of mild disgust and climbed the ladder to join Bogdan who was busily replacing wooden shingles on the sloping roof.

"I wish they wouldn't pound so hard," Blakeley said as hammers made loud contact with nails. "Curse me if ever I drink that much brandy again. Well, Father Wladislaw not only confirmed my suspicions that I'd seen him with Grover Stanhope in that carriage, but that there was a connection between Grover and the people on Lightcarn Lane. It seems the old fellow . . . Hello? What's this?"

A paddy wagon rounded the corner and pulled into the drive, splashing through a deep puddle in the unpaved road. Fatzinger sat next to the driver, ducking under some low hanging branches that threatened his bowler hat.

He spied Blakeley and waved a piece of paper, presumably the corrected arrest warrant.

They shouted at Father Wladislaw, who looked up and saw Fatzinger. He ordered Bogdan down the ladder and into the church as the wagon's doors opened and a small squad of patrolmen hopped out.

"Mornin', sarge," some of them said, loosening up their joints after the ride in the bumpy, confined space. "Mornin', Dr. Blakeley."

"Nice day for some flyin' tackles," one of them quipped at Nathan and there was a round of laughter.

"No laughin', youze." Fatzinger climbed down from the paddy wagon, his face still pale after the ride. "Get dott kid und arrest him dott come down from der rooftop!"

"But he's goin' inta the church, Bones," one of them noticed.

"Den hurry up den."

But Bogdan was at the church door before any of them could take a step. When he stopped in the doorway to thumb his nose at Fatzinger, the priest grabbed him by the ear and pulled him inside.

Fatzinger was rabid.

"Come back, youze!" He shook his fist.

The church door closed. Fatzinger ran up to it and pounded.

"Bejaysus," one of the patrolmen said, "I do think the pressures of command jist got to him."

"The lad niver did take disappointments well," another remarked.

"The priest must think he's one horse's arse."

"I ain't goin' in dere if he says."

"Neither am I."

"You?"

"Nope."

"You?"

"Riskin' hellfires fer Fatzinger's career? Ye must be dumb to ask."

"Get in der und chase him oudt!" he ordered. Nobody moved.

"Ye notice he ain't makin' a move hisself," one of them whispered.

He stamped his feet and paced around, eventually pointing a finger at Blakeley and McBride.

"Den youze go in. He knows youze."

They looked at each other and shrugged. Blakeley spoke up.

"Officer Fatzinger, have you considered the notorious implications of what you are attempting to do? Insulting the tradition of sanctuary will hardly improve the image of the Eleventh Precinct." He nodded at a sheepish McBride. "Temperance should be your watchword just now."

"Ye ought a walk on eggs for a while, Bones," someone explained.

"Ecks?"

He ordered the men back to the paddy wagon, stopped, turned and issued a parting threat at Bogdan and Father Wladislaw.

"Youze'll be sorry youze cheated. If youze tink I'm dumb, I'm schidt!"

"He'll go see big boss next," the priest suggested as the paddy wagon left. "Go see beeship and yell like hell."

"Probably."

"Which means we won't be able to do that again."

"Pretty good guess for you, my friend. Big boss already know about kid."

Both of them looked at him quizzically.

"Kapuznik," he explained.

They were still confused. He looked exasperated, since there was still work to do.

"You know Kapuznik. He throw garbage and make reporter lady cripple leg? Couple times I go in saloon, tell him no more sellink booze for make little kids get drunk. I tell him maybe I come back and put big bald head in shit pot. I say no more lettink bum ladies do pootsie-pootsie upstairs. Kapuznik say nottink. Just look down at floor and shake head like great big mistake I make. So den somebody tell him about kid and he run to beeship like big sissy tattletale. Big boss send some milkey-faced guy come see me dis mornink. 'Father Wladislaw, beeship is unhappy.' I chase him out, but big boss is big boss."

"Damn!"

The priest laughed.

"Gotta fix roof. By da way, tank you for fish."

He climbed back up the ladder and shouted for Bogdan to stop malingering in the church and help him on the roof.

"I wish I could be that philosophical," Blakeley said.

Some children were playing hopscotch on the

sidewalk outside the churchyard. A dog was barking at a drunkard who was staggering across the street. A trolley came down the tracks and scattered the pigeons. Some old ladies, waddling close to the ground, paused to make a sign of the cross almost in unison as they passed the church with their shopping bags. Somebody was cooking cabbage in the area.

They climbed aboard Blakeley's carriage and got on with it.

Chapter Thirty-five

On May 1, 1898, Commodore Dewey, commanding the Asiatic squadron of the navy, arrived in Manila Bay where he met the fleet of Admiral Montojo and completely destroyed it, suffering the loss of neither a ship nor a man. The defeat was so devastating to the Spaniards that their 7000-man garrison in Manila was left without any hope of support or reinforcements by sea. General Merritt's infantry and cavalry forces were moving across Luzon Island, approaching the city from the northeast, and the conquest of the Philippines was now only a matter of time. In Cuba the Spaniards were digging in at El Caney and San Juan Hill, expecting an invasion at any time. Major-General Schafter told war correspondents he was all set to leave Tamps, where the Pennsylvania Twenty-eighth was based, and attack the island. Commodore Schley's Great White Fleet was steaming toward Santiago Harbor to engage the six ships of Admiral Cervera there.

These stories made the headlines on the front pages of the *Inquirer* and the *Bulletin* on May 2. The headlines of the *Morning Star*, however, read:

DEAD HOOKER FINGERS PREACHER FROM GRAVE

The story under Bernard Spector's byline was so good that Nathan McBride thought he could have written it himself, except that it had Spector's patented smarmy solemnity.

"The *Morning Star* has been made privy to one of the most shocking documents ever perused by these weary, jaundiced eyes. We warn you that this story is grim. It is about deceit, disenchantment and wholesale debauchery.

"The litany of pathetic and hypocritical gentlemen whose untrammeled passions drove them to the busy bed of the late Edna Becker, 'Goldie' to her countless customers, is both long and depressing. In the interest of propriety and to protect their unfortunate loved ones, the names of the deceased will be ignored on these pages. May they rest in blissfully ignorant peace. They have already been shamed in the presence of Him whose blessed Name will not be defiled by inclusion here.

"It is the names of the living, those smug survivors, whom we shall accuse.

"It should be a cause of particular chagrin to see the name of a man of the cloth, a self-proclaimed guardian of our city's adherence to the sixth and ninth commandments, printed on these unhappy lines. The Rev. Ezekiel Twombley, well-known to all literate Philadelphians for his fire and brimstone outbursts, is prominent among the fallen, prominent because the craven Miss Becker took great pains to describe the reverend's odd, indeed unnatural, obsessions. These preferences will go unexplained for obvious reasons; suffice it to say she called him 'Dr. Diaper' and he used to call her 'Nursey.'

"Perhaps the saddest note of all is that the unfortunate Miss Becker was quite ravaged by the wages of sin, and her clientele will no doubt suffer the flames of more than figurative fire and brimstone. That is, if they are not at this very moment.

"The Rev. Twombley is best known nowadays for his outspoken opposition to the Lillian Russell review opening tonight on the stage of the Erlanger . . . ."

McBride could hear snickers all around him, from the readers who shared the trolley. It was depressing to realize how many actually read Spector's gossip strip, many who looked to be of normal intelligence, too, with clean cuffs and collars and civilized demeanors. Only a few days ago they had read and believed that he was a "self-serving sadist," as Spector put it.

But it was nice to know that the Spectors of the world could also be used. He could only imagine the uproar now taking place at the Reverend Twombley's estate.

It had taken longer for the diary to fall into Spector's hands because Victor had wanted to read it himself.

Poor Victor. Bernard Spector had yet to mention him. No wonder Victor was drinking more gin than ever.

Anyway, the delay had worked to their advantage, getting the scandal out on the day of Miss Russell's opening. Nathan hadn't seen much of her lately; she was busy, of course, and so was he, and Ralphie had become her constant companion and bodyguard. There was no happier man in all Philadelphia than Ralphie Blakeley, and that was fine with Nathan McBride. Apparently, it was fine with everybody, especially with Allison, though it was impossible to tell by anything she said or did.

In the meantime, Allison's ankle had healed, and on her first day of freedom from Blakeley's supervision she had mounted a beast the size of Gladstone and rode out shortly after sunrise.

It was not an ideal morning for a ride; the fog off the river was heavier than usual, the breeze damper and chillier. But Allison and Sophia had been planning this outing for days, especially since Nathan had told his bowdlerized story of the lady on horseback. They paused to admire the yellow roses in the garden and took the riding trail that went west by northwest.

The trip to Lightcarn Lane was long, circuitous and, as Allison remarked at one narrow turn, appropriately dark. The tall evergreens blotted out much of the morning sun and the trail was in deep shadow for miles at a time.

"The Black Forest in miniature."

"Watch out for robber barons."

"And other goblins and ghoulies."

Allison was careful of her conversation, steering clear of any references which might trigger memories of a few nights ago. The guest rooms were only a short walk from the master bedroom—not that Sophia would have tiptoed down to investigate, but there was the inquisitive Rosie. Not that there had been anything happening that either would have found interesting, she reminded herself.

The horses grunted occasionally, almost as if they were making small talk. The road rose and fell like a tattered brown ribbon. There was the sweet smell of wildflowers drifting down from hillside clusters. They forded a stream and followed the trail uphill through a stretch of charred woods. They both recalled the lightning storms and the fires of last autumn and talked of them in sad but clinical tones for a while, then concentrated again on the ground.

They came to a main road, unpaved but much less threatening, and followed it for a mile. When it met Lightcarn Lane they came to a halt and Sophia dismounted.

"Look at this little curiosity, Allison."

She picked up a piece of wood, green around

the edges, rotting where it had been partially covered by creeping foliage. Sophia's eyes were unexpectedly sharp.

"Swine Hollow Road?"

The lettering was faded, barely readable.

"I wonder just when this became Lightcarn Lane," Sophia mused. "Not that I do not applaud the change."

"A good guess would be the day Mrs. West moved in."

"A very good guess."

"Something else?"

Sophia studied the old sign, looked at the new one, then returned to the old. Allison patted her horse on the neck and watched.

"Would you say it's been here on the ground for three years?"

"At least," Allison guessed.

"Lightcarn Lane. Lightcarn Lane . . ."

"Ring a bell?"

"A distant one, Allison, but I can hear it faintly."

They continued down Lightcarn Lane, approaching the estate as quietly as the horses would allow.

Now and again Sophia repeated "Lightcarn Lane."

It was a magnificent estate, reminiscent of great chateaux on the Loire. From the hillside they could see the mansion, the statuary along the drive, and the fountain in the circle. Groundskeepers were moving lazily through their early morning tasks. They and the rest of the picture came and went in the fog. The birds and cicadas were in loud cacophony.

They spied a figure on horseback, tiny in the distance but distinct, even in the mist.

The tiny figure galloped down the drive, under the arch and up the hill on a road that snaked toward them. They directed the horses into the shadows.

The clopping grew louder, and a minute later she rode into view. In silhouette against the morning sky she and the horse were quite imposing, like one powerful unit.

"That's quite a horse," said Allison, catching herself speaking too loudly.

"Yes, it is," Sophia whispered. "She adores him. His name is Modock."

"Modock? As in the secret society?"

"As in the elitist ruffians who terrorized England during the last century."

"Didn't they single out poor wretches for brutal treatment?"

"Yes, it was a celebration of arrogance."

They were silent as she rode past, her dark hair trailing like a pennant, as poised as the falcon that nested on her wrist.

"That bird must be the one that injured the gamekeeper. Look at those claws."

"Let us follow her very, very carefully."

She led them over the hilltop and down into a valley where the fog drifted upward from a lake. The evergreens grew taller, the shadows darker. The trail grew more serpentine, coiling and slithering downhill. Then they lost her.

"Where is she, Allison?"

"I don't know. Wait a minute."

"Wh—"

"There—on that ridge. Look."

"Where the devil are her clothes?"

"Where the devil is the bird?"

Suddenly it appeared, fluttering angrily in the branches overhead. They froze.

"Don't . . . even . . . breathe."

"I'm not."

They saw feathers floating to the ground and getting lost in the clutter of dead leaves. The horses started to balk slightly but made no sounds above a loud grunt.

"Good boy, good boy."

The falcon perched on a nearby branch and seemed to eye them for a moment. They agreed later—as Blakeley, listening to Sophia's admonitions, wrote a letter to Scotland Yard requesting any possible information on Mrs. West—that it had been for only a half-minute or so, but it was long enough to cause unladylike responses. Allison would always wonder if Sophia had also felt the perspiration trickling down from her own armpits, running along the ribs and over the belt, dripping into her navel. Unconsciously, she may have glanced at Sophia's blouse to see.

Sophia felt uncomfortable. Sweat was dripping from her armpits like a sudden summer rain. She felt it on her rib cage.

The falcon gave no signal. It sprang like a flying shark and sailed overhead, close enough to cause the horses to lurch and the riders to turn ashen.

There was a pitiful screech, and something small and furry, its flesh torn and its body writhing in the falcon's cruel grasp, flew close to them. Splotches of blood showed on their clothing. Gladstone moved, as did Allison's horse, whose name was Galwegian after one of the Blakeleys' favorite places. But they remained under control for the moment.

"Was it a rabbit?"

"A squirrel, I think. How ghastly."

"He's making a circle. See?"

"Let us do our best to follow him."

The falcon made some wide, graceful patterns, as if proclaiming his superiority within his sphere, and started his descent, appearing to be about to land not far from them. They could see the small animal—now dead, thank God— hanging limply in his talons. They told themselves that there was nothing to dwell upon. The falcon is a hunter; the squirrel or rabbit or whatever, a natural prey. Such events were not uncommon in their wild estate.

It found its place and landed.

And what they saw next seemed to both of them uncommonly unnatural.

A pink shade of embarrassment started to creep up the flesh that showed on Sophia's neck where her hair had been swept under her bonnet.

"He wasn't kidding," Allison thought aloud. "She really did that."

They eased the horses out of the woods and back onto the trail. Neither spoke for most of the ride back to Blakeley's stable, not until they were a mile from their destination, in a spot where the riding trail came close to the river. They rested the horses under some Dutch elms and fanned themselves with their riding bonnets. It was nearing nine o'clock. The sun had burned the fog away.

The heat trapped inside Allison's boots had caused her ankle to throb. She removed the boot, inspected her foot and found a little swelling, as expected. She found a comfortable spot on the river bank and soaked it in the cold water, letting the waves massage her gently. It felt so good that she removed the other boot.

"Lightcarn Lane," Sophia repeated after a time.

Allison looked up. The horses had noticed the water and were taking a drink. Sophia joined her on the bank, slipped out of her own boots and cooled her feet in the same fashion.

"I think I've just arrived at a rather sinister conclusion."

"Hey, Hudson, no hard feelings, huh?"

Hudson simmered in silence and thought about all the reasons why he should quit the department then and there. There was his health for one; certainly, his sanity for another; and then there was the imminent danger of his committing a capital crime at any moment.

The place was, it seemed to him, infested with lawyers at the time. Zimmerman from the D.A.'s office was conferring with Fatzinger. They wanted another chance at the shoeshine boy. Zimmerman sat some distance away because Bones had just eaten one of his favorite limburger with onion sandwiches for lunch. Their conversation was animated, and their voices carried over the others. The pompous Alfred Peteroff of Peteroff, MacBirney and Schnurr was at McBride's desk doing his best to avoid Nathan's unsettling gaze as he spoke. Two thugs and a dull-eyed fellow from downtown were also there. Peteroff was going on about something or other that Hudson was too preoccupied to notice.

And then there was this asshole, the one whose name kept escaping him, the one at his desk.

He represented Jennifer Zebers and the midget Wally Dorman. The latter's legs did not quite touch the floor as he sat in a chair next to Hudson's desk.

"The mouthpiece here says we could probly sue yiz fer false arrest, but what the hell, we ain't holdin' no grudges. Are we, Jen?"

Hudson turned his head slowly and looked up at the attorney, who gave him a mousy smile.

"They could, you know," he said. "It isn't as if you haven't had the time to get someone, anyone, to press charges."

"Yeah, count yer blessings," Wally said.

Jennifer Zebers said nothing. She sat next to Wally, legs crossed, arms folded over her breasts, clicking her chewing gum with deepseated indifference. Jennifer never did say anything, not from the time he surprised her as she waited in the rain for Wally and his overflowing satchels. He knew she could speak; her victims had said so, the same victims who now refused to come forward and admit they'd been snookered by a midget and a cow. Wally had said on the way to jail that night, "The gossip sheets will have a field day with this," and his sentiments must have echoed throughout the neighborhood.

"My clients have decided—quite magnanimously, I'd suggest—to avoid further unpleasantness. All they want now is to leave town and pretend that you and your ilk do not exist."

"Translated—you reached a nice settlement with the bigwigs they burglarized. 'We'll pay you to go away. No questions asked.' Am I right, Keester?"

"It's *Kess*ter, Lieutenant, for the last time."

"I don't know nothin' about no settlement, Hudson," Wally Dorman interjected. "Jenny here has folks out in Pittsburgh she'd like to see, that's all. Ain't that so, Jen? Jen?"

Jennifer's jaw slowed down. She looked up, thought, then nodded seriously.

"Pittsburgh? Christ, Wally, you could've made a better deal than that. Or is that the only town where the cops don't know you yet?"

"That's below the belt, Hudson."

"If it's all the same to you," said Kesster, their lawyer, "we'll be on our way now."

When Wally hopped down from the chair and snapped his finger, Jennifer got up. Since his arm could not reach around her waist without effort, he simply rested a hand on one buttock.

"Ah, c'mon, Hudson. Like the guy says, ya can't win 'em all. Wanna rub her tit fer better luck next time?"

Jennifer leaned over his desk, chewing gum still clicking, but he declined the offer.

They followed Kesster out the door, Wally pinching her behind, she yelping and giggling.

"Jesus."

Hudson shook his head and realized how much time he had wasted.

There was a pile of correspondence on his desk that had accumulated as he pursued the burglar. Somewhere in there, no doubt, was a note from the commissioner's office telling him to mind his own business and stay out of nicer neighborhoods.

He started to work at it, finding a token pleasure in tearing envelopes apart.

A seedy-looking man entered and paused as he passed Fatzinger's desk.

"Would you kindly direct me to Sergeant McBride?" he said.

He smelled of stale whiskey and one or two eye-openers. Neither Fatzinger nor the man from the district attorney's office looked up. Someone—Blakeley, they guessed—had gotten word to the bishop that turning Bogdan in would not be well received by the public; indeed there was a chance that the irritating Father Wladislaw would become a celebrity of sorts because the press was starting to show an interest in him. The bishop's advisors had suggested that the priest's unorthodox methods could appear heroic to the uninformed. So His Excellency had rethought his position and was now willing to bide his time before transferring Father Wladislaw to the far reaches of the diocese and letting Bogdan's fate be settled later.

And that was giving Fatzinger indigestion.

Across the room, Nathan was not certain whether to laugh, to scream, or to commit a really serious case of assault, but at the moment he was leaning toward the latter.

The seedy-looking gentleman asked again.

Fatzinger looked up. The lawyer, Zimmerman, was clearly annoyed by the interruption. He looked away and blew a large puff of cigarette smoke. Fatzinger tilted his head toward Nathan's desk and quickly returned to his conversation.

Whitey and Al, all cleaned up and dressed in their Sunday best, sat with hangdog expressions as Alfred Peteroff's harangue continued. They, too, were about to be released. The dull-eyed fellow from downtown checked his pocket watch repeatedly. He wanted his lunch; people from downtown treated lunch like a religious obligation. This meant that there would be neither time nor tolerance for anything Nathan might wish to say in his own defense, and when the dull-eyed man eventually went to lunch, it was a sure thing that Alfred Peteroff would buy it. His report to the commissioner on the charges being brought against Detective Sergeant Nathan McBride would read like something out of the Salem witch trials.

"I suggest that the so-called celebrity cops, like Sergeant McBride here, be made to understand that they cannot get away with whatever comes to mind simply because they're celebrities," Peteroff concluded. "Frankly, I think it most inappropriate that he was assigned to bodyguard a wanton showgirl while—"

"The assignment came right from the commissioner. It wasn't my idea. Why don't—"

"You'll get your turn, Sergeant McBride," said the dull-eyed man from downtown.

"She fired him cuz he was so violent, y'know," Al chimed in.

"What the hell are you—"

"Sergeant McBride, I said, you'll get your turn."

"Will I?"

"Go on, Mr. Peteroff."

"Naturally, I'm not here to condemn the entire force."

"Naturally."

"Naturally," Nathan mimicked.

"He isn't exactly cooperating, is he?" Peteroff asked.

"No, he isn't."

Nathan had wasted enough time on this. Less than an hour ago he'd gotten word that one of his Grover watchers, a bartender in a dockside saloon, had observed him patronizing a strange, probably feeble-minded woman who pretended to be a palm reader and fortune teller. He had been seen with her at least three times, and Nathan was sure he had a nibble. And then Peteroff had arrived with the dull-eyed man.

"Why don't you guys just go to lunch," he said, getting up. "Talk it over and get back to me. Right now I—"

Peteroff had spied someone approaching, and his eyes lit up.

"Ah! It's our witness."

Nathan's jaw went slack.

"Professor Watkins?"

"Nathan, dear boy. You've been naughty, I see."

The voices in the precinct station were loud and angry that afternoon. Sometimes in the welter of charges and countercharges, there seemed to be a competition for whose was the most strident, the harshest, the most piercing. Gentle ladies passing by held cupped hands over their ears or quickly crossed the street. There were threats and allegations couched in phrases which strained not only one's patience but one's eardrums.

But in a quiet corner where Larry Hudson preferred his desk to be, there were no words spoken. The lieutenant sat in silent, self-imposed isolation and read the letter a second time.

Chapter Thirty-six

"**N**ot a-gain, 'again.' It should rhyme with 'hen'."

"All right . . . . 'Do dat again, and I'll press yiz like a pimple'."

"Better, much better. Now, try to be a little less precise with 'and.' It should sound like an N, that's all. Don't enunciate the D."

". . . 'n I'll press yiz like a pimple."

"Good."

"What about the voice? The vocal quality?"

"Closer. But he has more gravel in it. You're still sounding a little too Oxonian."

"Cambridge."

"Sorry."

"Perhaps when I shave the beard I'll get a little closer to character."

He was getting there quickly, assuming the

persona of Grover Stanhope. It was not supposed to happen so soon.

"Uncle Nigel trod the boards with the great Macready and was Iago to his Othello, Gloucester to his Lear, and so on. Unfortunately, the family disowned him for philandering and similar offenses, so I am not supposed to have inherited his mimetic abilities."

"But you did."

Blakeley smiled. "Evidently."

Nathan smiled with him. They had just spent five intensive hours working toward the same elusive goal.

A lot of things had happened since his suspension for bloodying the nose of the dull-eyed man from downtown and for chasing Al and Whitey and a babbling Professor Watkins down the steps, out of the building and up the street, followed by Alfred Peteroff of Peteroff, MacBirney and Schnurr.

For one, Lillian Russell had opened her show to rave reviews and a very crowded house, thanks in part to Nathan's vigilance, but in greater part to Bernie Spector's verbal abuse of the Reverend Ezekiel Twombley.

And the reverend's disciples were there in full force, chanting their protests.

"Nice language for a reverend."

"This was all your fault, McBride."

"Thank you."

"You slimy string of vomit, when I—"

"Probably, when all the facts are known, Reverend, you will—"

"You were trespassing on my property, too, you sonofabitch."

"Sightseeing. That's all."

"And when I'm finished with *him* in court, I'm coming after you. And my lawyers are going to cut your balls off."

"Are you putting me in the same category as Bernard Spector?"

"Like two pigs in shit. You'll sing soprano together."

"You have an unlimited list of cliches, Reverend."

"Give me that sign, McBride."

"This? The one with the obscene message regarding Miss Russell?"

And he did, apologizing to the reverend because, after all, the people of the fourth estate had already recorded their quotes and pictures.

Besides, he was no longer a cop.

He had to come to grips with that. A very righteous judicial board put together by ashen-faced functionaries downtown would determine in time whether or not he would ever be one again.

That would be somewhere around the time when he would also learn how serious the lawsuit would be, the one that was certain to come for losing his temper that afternoon. The Peteroffs of this world never slept.

But he was quite willing to put all of that behind him. Ahead was the army or maybe the marines, and something called a combat zone where the knaves and scoundrels were clearly identifiable and where hostilities were settled in a simpler fashion. Privately, he was hoping never to have to fire a gun. But he had already decided that if ever he met a Spaniard, and the Spaniard's gun were trained on him and his on the Spaniard, and it came down to the fateful split-second decision, and said Spaniard looked too young, nice, cherubic and puppylike, he would merely imagine a Watkins or Twombley or Fatzinger or Peteroff and . . .

Oh, well, that was someday, but now there were other things.

The tip on Grover and the fortune teller had captured Blakeley's imagination enough to make him forget his pique at the obvious similarities, and the plan now was to follow the fat man until the precise moment. Since the past victims were discovered during full moon periods and since the lunar cycle was winding down, that moment was not faraway.

The full moon business made sense, especially after Sophia's argument on the origins of Lightcarn Lane.

"The Carn of Light, Ian, don't you see?" she said, dabbing a lotion over the welts on her hand caused by poison oak when she and Allison hid in the woods as the falcon circled overhead. "It was a place of Druidic worship at Land's End, just below Sennen. A place of human sacrifice."

They had already discussed whether the accent which sneaked through the veil of pretense was Cornish, and they had agreed that it very well could be, though there was a better chance that it was from the nearby Scilly Islands. One way or the other, it would put her in the area. And so Blakeley had wired Scotland Yard by submarine cable for information on the strange Mrs. West and was now eagerly awaiting a reply.

"I ought to have done that long ago, damn it."

"Ian, please . . ."

"Sorry."

What made the operation more interesting to Nathan McBride was the fortune teller.

Ida Tempesta was a half-wit with a long history of vagrancy, fraud, petty theft, shoplifting, public intoxication, corrupting the morals of minors, and various crimes against nature. She was tolerated in some of the dockside saloons where she spent days and nights panhandling because the managements considered her a form of cheap entertainment. She was a little something, however demented, that the next guy didn't have. There were always a few drunks wandering in and staying to buy a few more while she mumbled over their palms. By 10:00 or 10:30 she was usually talking to herself and by midnight her face was usually resting on the table amid the cards and tea leaves. She was natural prey for Grover.

Ida Tempesta made it more exciting, but he would have been more than pleased just now if she had no part in it at all, because Allison had siezed the opportunity to play fortune teller to Blakeley's fat man.

He had to admire her commitment. The strawberry blonde hair was now dark and dirty, the teeth that could have been a tooth polish advertisement in the Sears catalogue the day before were now dulled by licorice, and somehow she had managed to capture the "deses and doses" and flat, suspicious tones of the fortune teller.

It worried him. She was going into the bowels of the beast, and he felt a gnawing sense of helplessness about it.

Not that he had needed a shove, but that night, after Lillian Russell's last triumphant curtain call, as she and her vast party of admirers sipped champagne, the star had said, "You know what, Nathan? I have a great intuition about people, about couples, I mean. You're daffy about her, aren't you?"

"About wh—?"

"You know. About the girl you keep jousting with and losing."

"I have no idea what girl you have in mind."

He had lost this jousting match, too. He was winning his case, he thought, almost convincing Allison that her charade was foolish, until Blakeley caved in and agreed with her.

"Not without some trepidation, of course, but it does seem a logical tactic, Nathan."

"Logical?"

"Miss Meredith won't be in any real danger," Blakeley explained, then he hedged. "Well, that's not quite true, but—"

"See?"

"But if and when danger appears, we shall be nearby."

He was leafing through Ram's *Unrivaled Family Atlas of the World*, searching for the site of the Carn of Light at the southernmost tip of Cornwall. Their argument did not actually involve him anyway.

Allison tried to lighten the situation because she realized that Nathan's point was well-taken. There were safer means of covering the story, and many women with more street experience could be hired as decoys. This was a price she had to pay for having kept him in the dark about all the times she had stepped into harm's way for a story. Someday they would sit down and talk about everything.

" 'Beware the Jabberwock, my son!' "

"Oh, please . . ."

" 'The jaws that bite, the claws that catch!' "

She stuck her face into his. He tried to look away, but she got in closer.

" 'Beware the Jubjub bird, and then the frumious Bandersnatch!' Nice teeth, huh?"

"I always hated that verse," he replied.

"You don't like my teeth?"

He was having a hard time with this. Say too much and she'd know she had him doing tail-spins again.

"I didn't say anything about your teeth. I just said I hated the verse . . . oh, all right, let's get on with it."

The fortune teller left the saloon early that evening, blinking as she stepped out into the brilliant 6:00 sunshine. She paused to loosen the undergarments which had bunched up under her gypsy skirt as she sat for the past two hours drinking, shook each leg vigorously, and went off a bit wobbly across the street and into an alley. In a moment, the now familiar carriage came out onto the avenue, turned a corner and proceeded up the busy thoroughfare.

The beat cop signaled the bartender who was watching it all through the big smoke-stained window. The bartender ran to the back of the room and cranked up the telephone.

"North on Broad. Remember, McBride, it was my tip."

"You'll get it back."

"I better."

The next time the phone rang it was a call from a bookie who told him the carriage had turned off Broad at Market, heading west.

"The fat guy, all right. I seen him before. And everybody knows that screwy fortune teller. She's into me for ten in old bets that I'll probably never see."

"Probably."

Hudson, heretofore never seen by Grover, picked up their trail at Sixty-eighth Street and followed them out along the Lincoln Highway. One block behind him there was a squad of men from the Eleventh, all of them dressed in civilian clothes.

When he had answered all of the calls, Nathan McBride took a shortcut and caught up with them. For a while he, Hudson, and the men from the Eleventh hopscotched and leapfrogged as they followed Grover's carriage into the suburbs.

Hudson had been acting strangely in recent days, very strangely for him because he was so quiet. In fact, he said so little that what came out resembled the product of an amateur ventriloquist. Once or twice McBride had started to broach the subject, but someone had always walked in. And if the conversation threatened to enter a second minute, the subject of the case would take over. Hudson seemed to prefer dealing with it instead of with his own troubles anyway. It was he who had arranged this network since McBride was not supposed to be seen in the precinct station for the time being.

It would have surprised both of them to discover that Wilmer P. "Bones" Fatzinger was well-aware of that, and his long absences from the station house were not simply long lunches and long walks in the park.

The route was the same as Grover had taken before when followed—across City Line and out Lancaster through the hamlets and villages running parallel to the Pennsylvania Railroad's main line. The land was painted in stark tones. The sun was still hot, even after seven, and it came at them with blinding strength, but there were cooler stretches where the tall trees shaded the road.

Soon the carriage turned off Lancaster and onto a private road, and the men in its pursuit went off in different directions, with only Nathan following a leisurely quarter-mile behind. As he passed an access road, Blakeley, Allison and Ralphie met him on horseback.

He shook his head as he studied Allison in full costume.

"I know, I know, but it washes off, Nathan."

"I certainly hope so. Shouldn't you be speaking in Ida Tempesta's voice?"

"Yeah," she said with the fortune teller's gutteral edge. "So where da hell's dis dump yer tellin' me about?"

"That's better."

"We been practicin' all day, me 'n da skirt," Blakeley said in Grover's gravelly tones. "What're ya waitin' for? Let's go."

"Much better."

They followed the carriage for another mile and a half until it came to a halt beside a tall Dutch elm. They maneuvered their horses a little closer, staying in the pasture where they could hide behind hedgerows.

Grover got out and then helped the fortune teller to climb down. They hopped over a ditch and trudged through the tall grass toward the other side of the tree where the hanging branches gave them some privacy. They moved with singleness of purpose, evidently in a hurry because Grover was fumbling with his trousers and the fortune teller was lifting her skirt as they ran.

Blakeley, McBride and Ralphie blushed in unison and refused to look at Allison. No one spoke for a moment, then Ralphie suggested, "Whatever it is, I guess we ought to give them a little time to do it."

There were several possibilities, all of them indelicate, running through their minds.

"Well, uh," Allison cleared her throat quietly, "shouldn't we find out? I mean . . ."

"Yes, I, um, suppose you're right," Blakeley said, and he looked at Ralphie.

"Me?"

"Well, we can't very well send Miss . . ."

"Oh, all right."

Ralphie dismounted and dashed up the road to Grover's carriage where he paused to look back. When Blakeley made an impatient signal, he tiptoed over the ditch, through the high grass, and around to the other side of the tree. After a long minute he tiptoed out of there and raced back to them.

"I . . . they're . . . Oh, Jeez, excuse us, Miss Meredith."

She watched them for a second then looked away as Ralphie whispered that it was probably the best time to attack, but there was no time to waste if they intended to.

"If you know what I mean, Dad."

"I know what you mean, Ralphie."

They climbed down from their horses and circled the tree, crawling through the long grass as they approached from three sides. Grover and the fortune teller were engaged as expected. The sounds they made were like two hungry dogs rooting through a rubbish heap, occasionally whining, occasionally snarling, he grunting, she staring at the sky, mouth agape as if about to bay. Ralphie fought off the urge to giggle, while Nathan wondered absently whether Allison could hear them and hoped she could not. Blakeley was reminded of a scene from Hogarth taken one step farther.

When the fortune teller's face contorted and she looked as if she were about to let out a long, wrenching primal scream, Blakeley stood up and shouted, "To it, men."

Grover heard them eventually, three sets of feet trampling the ground, coming closer by the second. He looked up with confusion and near panic, his body demanding one thing, his addled brain another.

"You bastards," he muttered.

He rolled off, leaving her prone, hairy and froglike on the ground, her skirt still bunched under her chin.

"What the hell are . . . ? You sonofabitch, get back here!"

Grover ignored her. "Oh, shit!" He had left his pistol in the carriage. He tried to run and get into his trousers at the same time. He tripped and cursed again, his broad white buttocks momentarily naked in the twilight sun. He got up and pulled the pants on just in time to brace himself for Ralphie who was the first to arrive. He caught him coming in with a good counter-punch that landed solidly on Ralphie's cheek. They collided and separated, hitting the ground at the same time, while the fortune teller scrambled away on all fours, cursing. Ralphie was shocked and dizzy, pastel dots and cruel red and black splashes of sunlight blurring his eyes as he got up groggily. When he threw his next punch it was at the wrong Grover.

"Ralphie, damn it, *I'm your father*."

"Oh Jeez."

Grover was already dashing away, with Nathan, who had approached from the far end, chasing him.

He started for his carriage and the pistol, but the wagon carrying Lieutenant Hudson and the contingent of men from the Eleventh was coming down the road from the opposite end, a large cloud of dust trailing in the sunset sky behind it. He turned away, still holding his trousers up, and spied their horses.

Nathan was drawing closer, so close he could smell Grover's perspiration and hear his desperate huffing and puffing. There was a big chestnut stallion from Blakeley's stable—the one Ralphie had ridden—grazing under an apple tree only ten yards away. Grover seemed to pick up speed at the sight of it.

McBride lunged at the fat man's legs, sure that he could bring him down.

He missed.

He felt his hands slipping down along the sweaty shirttail and over the pants, grasping frantically for any piece of cloth or flesh to hold on to. His knees hit the ground just ahead of the fallen apple branch that had tripped him at the last second, and he felt ligaments tearing, bringing back the pain of an old injury. Then the cloth in the fat man's trousers gave way, and he fell on his face.

"You're real tough, McBride," Grover hooted, climbing into the saddle with his trousers hanging loose. "They said you were real quick, too!"

Nathan struggled to his feet and limped after him. When he was close enough, Grover brought his foot up and caught him under the chin. The kick sent him reeling backward.

"Next time I'll kick yer teeth out," Grover sneered. "I'll slam yer nose through the back a yer head!"

Nathan tried to get up, but nothing in his body would obey. He tasted blood and thought he saw spots of it in the grass. When he was able to focus, Grover was turning the big chestnut stallion and starting to gallop away.

But as he took off he rode directly into a low hanging apple tree branch.

None of it was very clear to Nathan. He knew he heard a loud smack when the branch intercepted Grover's face. No doubt the fat man's head snapped back and he was stunned as he tumbled out of the saddle, and something about the incident must have unnerved the always jumpy thoroughbred.

It was the kind of scene that returns to memory with sickening regularity for some time, until something more sickening eclipses it. The big stallion raced down the dusty road, dragging the fallen rider like a twisting, writhing, bouncing, screeching lump of disintegrating flesh. Grover's hellish screams echoed across the valley as some of the men from the Eleventh tried in vain to overtake the swift chestnut in their clumsy wagon. One trouser leg had gotten caught in the stirrup, someone would explain later, after tracking them down by following the long, bloody rut in the road gouged out by Grover's body. Most of the men who came upon Grover's remains beside the tree stump where he'd been jolted free on impact tried not to speak until their stomachs were more settled.

When McBride limped back to the others, spitting out blood from the cut inside his mouth, Ralphie was trying to see out of a very black eye which had almost swollen shut. It could be, he thought aloud, that they had really underestimated the fat man.

The fortune teller was pointing her handcuffed hands, making a strange gesture with thumbs and little fingers as she cursed at Allison. She hissed and spat as one of the men lifted her onto a horse. The sight of Allison had thrown her into hysteria.

Allison had tried not to notice, but she had.

"Just out of curiosity, Nathan, would you happen to know what she's saying?"

"Hard to tell. I think it's something like . . . you're going to make love to a pit full of venomous toads."

"Oh."

"All set?"

"Yes, but it doesn't look like you are."

"I'll survive."

"I certainly hope so. I'd rather have you than a pit full of toads anyday."

"Ever kiss a man with a swollen cheek?"

"No," she said, wiping blood from his lips, "but I'll bet the fortune teller has."

Blakeley, waiting in Grover's carriage, whistled impatiently.

Chapter Thirty-seven

They stared at the naked statuary adorning the driveway of the Jeremy West estate. It was downright obscene. Allison observed clinically that it must be portable, placed there for special occasions, because she would have remembered it had it been there a few days before. They rumbled over the bridge that spanned the trout stream and under the archway with the impressive coat of arms, with *dieu et mon droit* above and the family name below. Blakeley glanced at her with unvoiced concern, estimating the odds that her eyes would give her away. They were fair and Celtic, not much like the madwoman's dark and rabid beads. Like the others, he had noticed Ida Tempesta's outburst and had heard the superstitious threat. The road was loud but straight, then it curled around the building and rendered the servants and other subordinates properly invisible.

They could no longer look back. Who knew how many eyes were watching?

At last sighting, Hudson, Nathan, Ralphie and company were a cautious half-mile behind. Ralphie was still mortified by the ease with which he'd acquired the black eye. Next time he wouldn't yell as he approached.

The sky was still bright, but the air was cooling and the fog off the nearby lake was dulling the sky. Soon the dust they kicked up would not be so obvious, so they were taking their time.

"They're waitin' fer yiz, Grover," an older woman in a maid's uniform said peevishly as they pulled up near the scullery. She had a face like a mean flour sack, Allison thought.

"So what?" Blakeley answered in Grover's voice.

"So, yer late, that's what."

"Drop dead, ya old goat," he said appropriately.

She left, muttering that things would go downhill for certain now that Pluto was gone.

Funny, Allison mused, how relationships fall into place. It made sense that Grover and the old frump would hate each other, he with his off-color personality, she with her holier-than-thou attitude. As they stepped out of the carriage, another maid, a puffy teenager, squealed, waved wildly and blew a kiss. That also made sense.

They followed the frump into the house.

"She looks like she could use a good bath," she said.

"You look like you could use a good undertaker," Allison replied in the fortune teller's voice.

"All she's gonna do is gaze in a crystal ball," Blakeley said. "How clean you gotta be fer dat?"

"Just a word to the wise, Grover. Y'know how the mistress hates body odor."

"Who're you callin' smelly?" Allison said, chin out.

"Yeah, maybe you got a point," Blakeley cut in. "So where's she gonna get cleaned up?"

"Same place as last time. You a stranger here all of a sudden?"

"Pluto must a took care a dat," he said with downcast eyes.

The frump became suddenly reverent.

"Yeah. You take care a the horse 'n buggy. I'll see to her."

She led Allison to a far corner of the first floor, past the kitchen and a decorated ballroom.

"You ain't gonna ennertain in there. They want yiz upstairs later."

"I know that," Allison lied. "Whereabouts upstairs?"

"Jist somewheres upstairs. I dunno. I get off at ten and all that stuff goes on later."

"What stuff?"

"What're you tryin' to do?" she chortled. "Act innocent? Here's the room. Go in and scrub yourself. We got nice people comin'."

It was austere, almost like a Carmelite cell—white walls, a chair, table, wooden tub, and in a discrete corner, a chamber pot. One window with open curtains let the light spill in from outside, and as the sun declined the contrasts were stark. She found some candles on a shelf and lit one, suddenly realizing that it was black.

She was only slightly surprised. Probably, she guessed, that were she to take a tour of the premises, she would find an occult smorgasbord.

There was a brief kick at the door and the puffy teenager entered carrying a bucket of hot water in each hand.

"There's soap 'n perfumy things on the shelf where you got that candle," she muttered irritably, pouring the water into the tub.

The air was chilly enough for steam clouds to rise. She placed the candle near the tub and started to get undressed.

The teenager left, returned with two more buckets, entered this time without an announcement, poured and left, muttering, "That's all yiz get."

"Next time knock before enterin'," Allison said.

The teenager turned and scowled. "Afraid I'll see your fleas or what?"

"Get your fat butt out a here before I kick it to New Jersey."

The teenager took a half-step but stopped to reconsider. Allison stared her practiced toxic stare, the one Nathan had called the fortune teller's *malochio*.

The girl backed off, muttering something about an unnatural act that Allison should perform on herself.

As Nathan was telling her about it, Ralphie had joked that he thought a *malochio* was a little wooden kid with a big nose and she had been tempted to laugh with him. But there must have been something in that hard, cold evil eye, and if the teenager had taken a good description of it back to the frump in the scullery, so much the better.

She started to get undressed, stopped, closed the curtain and turned her back to the door before removing the rest of her clothing. As the last garment fell on the uncarpeted floor, it occurred to her that she'd never felt quite so naked.

She tested the water with her big toe. Though a bit too hot, she chose to get in anyway, wincing as she eased her body into it, feeling a warmth crawling over her skin. Part of her preparation for playing the role of Ida Tempesta had been allowing herself to take on the appropriate redolence. Since it had been recorded in the nostrils of the old frump and the puffy teenager, it could now be washed away. Praise the Loard and rub the soap.

The door opened, and she looked up.

The frump entered carrying a tray with food and a bottle of wine. "I don't know what yiz did to her and I don't wanna know, but the goddamn kid won't come anywheres near yiz. Which means a lot more work fer me." She placed it on the chair and moved all of it closer to the tub.

"What's this all about?"

"It ain't my idea, girlie. It's called hospitality. They do it in good homes."

She left. Allison glanced at the label. A nice,

dry white from the Côte d'Azur. No cutting corners in this house. The tray was filled with petit fours, orange slices, cherries, cheeses, mushrooms, cauliflower florets, and oh yes, artichoke hearts. She wondered if she should touch it. Blakeley had said there were no real poisons or opiates in the victims' bodies, but . . .

She thought a sip of wine might feel good under the circumstances, but the bottle was uncorked.

She eased herself further down into the warmth of the water until her knees were almost even with her eyes. The night was decidedly cool, a true full moon period. She dabbed soap over whatever she could reach and soaked, letting the water find its way into and over whatever it could reach.

The door opened again, this time noiselessly, and when she looked up, Mrs. West was standing near the tub. Allison must have appeared shocked.

"Please do not be alarmed. I knocked, but you must not have heard me. I'm Mrs. West."

She was dressed in a well-tailored, high-necked dress of dark brown satin and exhibited a demure but friendly demeanor. She held a gray manx cat which she stroked gently as she spoke. One of Blakeley's lab reports, the one on Tony Miller, mentioned the presence of manx hairs, she recalled.

The voice was gentle, almost dulcet. "May we visit?"

"It's your shack."

"Her name is Honi, with an I."

"Cats give me a rash."

"She promises to keep her distance, don't you, Honi?" She petted the cat on the top of the head and put it down. It trotted off. "May I join you in some wine?"

"It's your booze."

With a slightly condescending smile she poured two glasses, gave one to Allison, and sat cross-legged at the table. Allison waited until she sipped and swallowed before joining her.

"Not quite chilled, I'm afraid," the visitor observed.

"What do I know from good or bad?"

Allison had a strong impulse to cover her breasts with something, but it was hardly what the fortune teller would bother to do. There was something about the woman's eyes, something beautiful but feral, and she sensed herself being studied in an unusual manner. The thought crossed her mind that perhaps Mrs. West had abnormal inclinations, and she wondered how the fortune teller would deal with that kind of thing.

"You aren't exactly one to flatter our humble offerings, I see. Would you care for an hors d'oeuvre? The mushrooms are especially delightful."

"I don't trust anything that grows in the dark."

After another condescending smile she selected something from the tray and nibbled, but Allison noted that it was not a mushroom.

"I presume you've been instructed in what to do this evening?"

"Yeah, Fatass told me. Big surprise—I'm gonna tell fortunes."

"Later on, after the dinner party, upstairs in a smaller, more intimate room."

"Intimate, huh? I sure hope Fatass told you that's all we talked about, tellin' fortunes. Anything else and the price goes up. Way up."

"Grover. His name is Grover." The tone became tepid. "And I've no idea what other business you have in mind."

Allison emitted a brief, cheerless laugh.

"I guess it ain't worth discussin'. Down the hatch."

She gulped down the wine and belched. Her visitor sipped and stared, smiling. The eyes never blinked. It was disturbing.

"You got my money?"

"It can be delivered to you here, if you prefer."

"It can wait, I guess."

"Whatever. Are you quite sure you don't want a canape or something?"

"If you insist. What're them things there?" She pointed.

"Artichoke hearts. Exquisite little morsels. Devilishly hard to come by these days, what with your wretched war with Spain and so on. Want to try one?"

"Expensive, huh?"

"Quite."

"Maybe I will. Mind my fingers?"

"Not at all."

Allison took one from the tray as the woman poured her another glass of wine.

"Not bad," she said, chewing. "Not much kick to them though."

"Do you like bath oils?" the woman asked, as if to continue the small talk.

"Never used them."

"Would you like some?"

"You think I need them?"

"I think you might enjoy the feeling."

She got up and selected a jar from several atop the shelf.

"I always thought the reason for a bath was to get the oil off," said Allison stupidly but in character.

"Here is an essence which a Parisian chemist created expressly for me. He's a dear little fellow with a shop on the *Rive Gauche*. Jean-Claude is his name, I believe. He called it *eaux d'enfer*. I shall share it with you."

Allison knew French fluently, and she thought the woman's accent was a trifle overdone. The R came from so far back on the palate that it might have been German, which was rather incongruous for a properly schooled Englishwoman.

Eaux d'enfer—the name bothered her much more than the accent. The waters of hell!

Mrs. West opened the jar and sniffed appreciatively. Then she sprinkled it into Allison's bath water. It had a pungent, exotic scent, not unpleasant but not easily identifiable.

"Slightly jasmine, is it not?"

Her visitor seemed to await a response. Allison looked up. Her eyes were somehow different.

"Yeah, if you say so."

Other things changed vaguely. The ceiling did something, something slight. She thought it was lower, or did the shelf seem higher? She blinked and tried to focus.

"You do like it, though, don't you? The essence?"

It was hard to hear her at times. Her voice seemed to slow down, like music on the Blakeleys' Victrola when it needed to be cranked again.

"Huh? . . . Yeah, I guess."

"Of course you do. What if I were to sprinkle a little more?"

The voice was dreamy and distant. It seemed to fade in and out. The eyes grew larger, like eyes in a child's picture book, like doll's eyes. Blakeley had said she was an opium eater, but there was something more—much more.

"Just a smidgen will do. There you are, my darling. Nice and warm and bubbly."

The scent coming up in the steam from the hot bath was strong now. She felt the glass of wine slipping from her hand, spilling over her breasts and submerging between her legs. Her jaw became heavy. She looked down at the sinking glass, then looked up with the annoying realization that she must appear terribly stupid just then with her legs spread and mouth agape. She wondered if she were smiling. It was humiliating, but she felt helpless to correct it. She had the worse feeling that her body was losing all feeling, beginning at the toes and crawling upward, like Socrates' after drinking his hemlock.

But at least Socrates could speak as his body departed. She hoped, prayed, begged in silence that she was not befouling the waters of hell into which her own body was sinking.

"It's not nice to struggle with one's destiny, to try to outthink the forces which control it. Naughty girl, refusing to test the mushrooms, insulting the hostess. Fortunately for all of us, there are subtler things than mushrooms. Naughty, naughty girl . . ."

The voice was deeper now and farther away, laughing a derisive maniac's laugh. The words seemed uttered in another time and place. It was someone else's voice. Even the accent had changed.

"Certainly a fortune teller should understand that. Tha fate is beyond tha ken. Think of it as a grand design, inexorable and, for lack of a better word, divine. Tha shouldst be flattered, fortune teller. That is, if tha truly art a fortune teller. No matter. We've all had our little stage plays in life, haven't we? Tell me, dost tha read palms as well?"

There were several voices, several in one, Allison thought, but her mind was too foggy to sort them out.

The eyes had a feral look. They were cat's eyes, the cruel eyes of a questing cat. She tried to stare back with the evil look that had so unnerved the teenager, but all she saw this time was a scornful smile.

"Look at me palm, loov. Tell me what tha sees . . . Oh! that's much better. Tha mustn't fight it now. You are quite loovly. Just relax, me loov . . ."

The palm grew larger, massive, then suddenly disappeared. Dark clouds covered her eyes.

"This shouldn't hurt, dear . . ."

She was doing something to Allison's body, some sort of ritual. Allison wanted to fight it, but her arms would not move. She felt vague little pricking sensations in her chest and knew there were tears flowing from her eyes because somewhere in this house, she knew despite the fogginess of her mind, someone had torn the hearts out of other visitors. She cursed her brave ambition and whatever else had conspired to put her there, but felt her courage deserting her quickly.

"Sometimes they arrive here wi' great expectashins," the voice went on, *"just like tha hast, and I size 'em up in a wink and send 'em on their merry way. This is a business, after all, I reminds 'em, and I'm not runnin' a home for ha'penny harlots. There, there, me loov, I told thee there'd be no pain . . ."*

At times Allison heard only a few words as the voice drifted in and out of her brain. The words were especially cruel, chosen as if to reassure, but uttered with sinister pleasure. The voice became harsh and old.

"Now, first we've got to scrub tha clean, dearie. Remember, it's tha bread 'n butter now, so tha must treat it like a bleedin' treasure. Think of it as a flower garden, all fresh 'n prettylike in the springtime—especially down there. Keep it smellin' like a bleedin' rose—instead of a bleedin' fish!"

An eerie laugh echoed through a cold dark cavern.

CEREMONY IN SCARLET

She saw a dot. Or was it the cat's eye? The cat's eye dancing around the cave?

There was a sudden blinding light and the world was black and white.

And scarlet . . .

Chapter Thirty-eight

The chubby little arms were strong. They wrapped around his neck like a voracious boa constrictor and clung with life or death determination. Warm, wet lips were leaving strange little marks on his throat.

He had not expected this, and he was sure he was coping rather poorly, trying very hard not to react with monkish fright and Victorian stiffness.

"Grover, you big fat sonofabitch, give us a big fat kiss."

"I, uh, I been eatin' garlic."

"Who gives a poop? I been cleanin' chickens."

She tightened her grip and pursed her lips. He held his breath and gave up. The kiss was deep and sloppy, and when it was over she squealed again.

"Hey, no need to wake up the neighbors."

"Piss on them. You got my cigarettes?"

Cigarettes?

"I must a left them in the buggy," he gambled. She frowned playfully.

"What the hell good are ya? Probly lost 'em when you was horsin' around with that weird fortune teller."

"Don't be disgustin'."

The fewer words, the better.

"I betcha did. I bet ya diddled her in the bushes on the way," the teenager teased. "Otherwise you'd have me on the floor by now."

"Quiet. The old bag is probly listenin' at the door."

They were in a pantry just off the entrance to the kitchen. The teenager had lured him there with a soft whistle and a finger gesture. It was roomy enough for whatever she had planned, and no doubt it had served her and the late Grover well in the past. He was grateful for the dim lighting.

There was no chance that the old bag was eavesdropping there or anywhere else at the moment. He had chloroformed her gently and eased her into a well-ventilated linen hamper only a few minutes before.

"Piss on her. Gimme another kiss."

She planted another bigger, sloppier one on his mouth before he had a chance to reply."

"I know you did, Grover." She rested her head on his vest and kept a firm hold on his arms. "Ya cheated on me again. Jeez, how the hell could ya? That fortune teller is so strange! I can't go anywheres near her without gettin' the bejeebers in my pants. Y'know how the mistress's eyes look sometimes? Scares the arse off a yiz."

"You scare too easy."

"Cheatin' on me after all the lovin' I give ya. And all I ask is a friggin' pack a cigarettes and yiz probly lost 'em in the bushes when you was—"

"I told ya, we didn't do nothin'," he said with gutteral finality.

She looked up suddenly and gasped.

"Jeez, I almost forgot! I brung you a present, even if you did lose mine. It's hid in this room."

"Where?"

"I told ya, it's hid."

Good Lord, how long would she keep this up? He was looking for an opportunity to open a remote back door where Nathan and the others could quietly enter. Soon Fatzinger and his men would also arrive.

"I don't wanna play no games," he said.

"Hey," the teenager said, "you mad at me or somethin'? What I do, huh?"

"Nothin'." He softened, feeling in his pocket for the bottle of chloroform. "Maybe later."

She giggled, took something from a shelf where it had been hidden behind a row of jars, and placed it on a crate.

"All right, here it is. I snuck it out a the kitchen where they was makin' one up fer the weird fortune teller."

"You're good to me, kid," he said, glancing at the plate of hors d'oeuvres. "Thanks a lot."

"I shouldn't a, cuz you're a big fat cheater. Here, try one."

There were assorted cheeses, fruits and vegetables. He chose a slice of cheddar. She chose a handful of mushrooms.

"You oughta try one a these," she said. "They must be special cuz I seen the mistress comin' in from somewheres near the stable and puttin' them on the fortune teller's plate."

"Better hope they ain't toadstools."

"Yeah," she giggled.

She stopped suddenly.

Her eyes popped open and stared at him with surprise and ferocity. She started to breathe heavily. The changes in her were visible even in the shadowy room. Her chest heaved, and he wondered if in fact she had eaten a toadstool. But her face took on a strange, contorted smile, and there was no sign of her strength leaving her. On the contrary, she seemed to seethe with it.

"Let's do it now, Grover."

"I told ya, I—"

"I said, let's do it now!"

Her eyes grew wilder. She seemed to snarl as she spoke. She started to gasp and tear her clothing off with great howls of triumph. Someone was bound to hear.

He reached for the chloroform and had to fight to get close to her. He was reminded of wrestling matches he used to indulge in with Ralphie, only there would be no gentlemanly rules here. She cursed and wept and grappled with the strength of an ox. He had to grasp her in a choke hold until the chloroform took effect and she started to fall limply into his arms.

He eased her to the floor and hid her ragged, sleeping form behind a stack of boxes, struggling to catch his breath. There was a noise outside, and he froze.

"Yoo-hoo," a voice announced. "Iss diss da place for da party to be heldt?"

"Officer Fatzinger?"

"Vott iss?"

"Thank heaven."

"Somebody left dott door open."

"Good. Please whisper. You're supposed to be someone else."

Fatzinger spied the puffy teenager behind the crates.

"Und chust who iss diss?"

"I don't know. She's had too much party." Blakeley whispered.

"I don't see no party."

He had never imagined Fatzinger in tie and tails, but here he was, an even sillier version of Victor.

"I say, Officer Fatzinger, such regality."

"Hausknecht, the undertaker up in Ebenezersville, owed me a favor. Hey, dose look like good eadts."

"Don't touch the mushrooms. There's something the matter with them."

"Ah-hah," said Fatzinger through a mouthful of cheese and fruit.

"Not what you think. They contain a narcotic, not a poison." Blakeley was feeling their texture and sniffing them carefully. "I believe they're of the *amanita muscaria* variety. It can be grown around here."

"Huh?"

"Amanita. A-mann-ee-ta."

"Hmm, dott's chust vot I thought ven I seen dem."

There was an alcove upstairs where, one by one, the special guests could be intercepted on their way to the intimate room where Allison would be the featured entertainment. As Grover, Blakeley was able to move about freely with occasional light nods and cursory smiles from the guests who recognized him. In keeping with Grover's personality as he understood it, he just winked back sullenly.

He thought he recognized some of them, members of a certain affluent coterie. Some, he also thought, were in Christopher Beecham's corner during the trial. It was not hard to guess who among them would be there when the others departed and which ones would climb the stairs to join in the bloody ritual. They had credentials of sorts, an odd cast to the eyes, as if depravity were a natural next step.

He took a second, more careful look. He had not been imagining it; the eyes said they were using narcotics.

Between aperitifs and the first course the mistress beckoned to him.

"You've done extraordinarily well this time, Grover. I shan't forget you."

"I try," he answered as she flitted off.

She, too, had the look—a heavy-liddedness and a strange vivid aspect to the pupils.

Fatzinger ordered his men to stay away from

the mushrooms then retreated to a room in the basement to await the proper signal. At the rear of the group, looking more like wartime casualties, a bruised and angry Ralphie helped a bruised and limping Nathan down the stairs. He had suggested they stay behind with Hudson, whose men were portioning themselves around the estate grounds, but they would hear none of it.

The evening was not without its genteel moments—fine wine, vichyssoise, roast pig, flambeau, demitasse, all in subdued lighting while a small orchestra played selections from Mozart somberly. The mistress had taste.

Around ten o'clock Jeremy West yawned, excused himself to his guests and retired to his room, leaving them to snicker about his uniform and other idiosyncracies. Blakeley gathered that this was the usual routine. Evidently, running him for governor was just one more grim joke dreamed up by the jaded little group, something to keep the silly old goose occupied while they indulged in things of a more colorful nature.

Soon the orchestra concluded and packed up its instruments. The chattering of servants and the sounds of dishes being washed drowned out the few voices that remained in the dining room. Outside, Hudson took careful note of the guests who left. Some of them, he recalled, were faces he had seen as he investigated the burglaries.

The mistress approached Blakeley at a little after eleven.

"Bring her to us at midnight," she said.

"Where is she?"

"Where you left her, I presume."

She looked slightly surprised.

"Right. Midnight," he hastened.

She smiled. He looked at her eyes. Probably the mushrooms, he decided, were taken in gradual doses by people who had developed a great tolerance for them. The drug was called bufotenine which takes away inhibitions and any sense of compassion the user may possess. Warriors had used it as far back as the Bronze Age.

And the Druids . . . . Yes, they used it in human sacrifices, sacrifices at places like the Carn of Light at Land's End.

"You are a dear boy, Grover. Rumors have it among the servants that you're quite the stallion, too. I'm very much the horsewoman, you know."

He smiled back appropriately lewdly. She chuckled.

"But you know how the servants lie." She started to drift off. "Or do they?"

Take her to us at midnight . . .

Where you left her, I presume . . .

Good Christ . . .

He noticed a few of the guests climbing the red carpeted stairs and found a rear staircase leading up to the next floor. There he hid behind a medieval knight in armor and watched as they entered a room. It was then that he discovered the convenient dim alcove and hurried down to the basement to summon the men.

"Use this chloroform," he instructed Nathan,

"and try to keep the scuffling to a minimum. No need to alert the prey, wherever she is."

"Where is Allison?"

"I've no idea. I'm about to look for her."

"I'll come with you."

"You're lame, damn it."

"I'll come with you," Nathan repeated.

"My dear boy, I fully realize—"

"Hey, Dad, I can chloroform them for you," Ralphie said. "It sounds like fun. What the heck, Nathan won't be much help anyway while he's worrying about Miss Meredith."

"Christ blast it, very well then."

"Thanks, Beef."

"Don't mention it. It'll cost you two tickets to the ballpark when the Baltimores are in town."

"Don't let's dally now," Blakeley said.

The men went upstairs by way of the rear staircase. Fatzinger gulped down the last of his plate of roast pork, smuggled somehow out of the banquet, and followed them.

The two searched all the rooms on the first floor, including the closets, and returned to the basement to look for an out-of-the-way utility room. By 11:45 they had still not found Allison Meredith.

"Why don't we just arrest the lady," Nathan said finally, "and have the men search the entire property for Allison?"

"Let's keep looking."

"Why?"

"Because I don't have any proof that the woman is anything more than an eccentric yet.

Do you realize that? Unless I can arrest her in the act, the most we can do to her and her friends is charge them with a breech of the narcotics laws. And I'm not altogether certain even that would hold up."

"What about your cable from Scotland Yard?"

"All they were able to say was that they suspect she's a common prostitute from St. Ives who murdered a man in Beverley and fled to the Continent. Doesn't mean a damned thing, Nathan."

Nathan made a fist and clenched his teeth.

"All right . . . the old lady you chloroformed earlier. Where is she?"

"Yes, of course."

They found the closet and opened the linen hamper. The maid was snoring as they lifted her out.

"Please, woman, please."

"Wha?"

"Wake up, confound it!"

"Gethellouthere . . ."

"Try some cold water, Nathan."

He found a tray full of melting ice, dunked his hand and sprinkled water with his fingers. Nothing. "Oh, hell."

He poured the tray of ice water over the flabby jowls, and the hag sat up with a snarl.

"You sonofabitch!"

"It's nice to hear your voice. Take us to the fortune teller at once."

"Grover? You ain't Grover? Who the hell—"

"At once, I say."

She moved on wobbly legs, but led them

through a darkened hall to a recess at the far end of the first floor opposite the scullery where she opened a door and showed them in.

The room was very dark, lit by only a small, flickering black candle. There was a strange cloying scent in the air. It lingered just about at their nostrils and Nathan thought it was so sickening that he tossed the stool which had just made contact with his shin through the window.

"Whatcha do dat for?" the frump snapped.

"Are there any other candles? Quickly!"

"Jeez," she muttered as she took a handful from the shelf and started to light them, "the guests get stranger every time."

She gasped. They turned to look in the other direction.

A figure lay on a bench. It was draped in a cloak which had fallen open to reveal a naked form in moonlight. Nathan knelt beside it and felt for a pulse.

"She's alive, thank God."

"Cover her. It's cold in here."

Nathan started to but noticed something.

"Look at this mark on her breast, Dr. Blakeley."

It appeared like a little red welt, tiny dots of dried blood in a pattern.

"The little fish, Nathan. Another link in the chain."

"That ought to be enough, shouldn't it?"

Blakeley wanted to think so. He was silent for a moment, trying to weigh the odds. He checked his pocket watch. Only a few minutes before midnight.

"Look at her eyes," Nathan said. "Do you think she's been drugged?"

Blakeley opened one of her lids and studied the pupil.

"I'm sure she was."

"Let's get her out of here."

"Yes. That smell is making me woozy. It must be coming from that tub. The bath water's been doused with something."

They got up, Nathan lifting her carefully and holding her with obvious affection. The torn ligaments in his knee made every move excruciating, and Allison's body was a dead weight.

They noticed that the old woman had made a hasty exit. It passed without comment.

"Nathan," Blakeley said at length, as they left the room, "if our Miss Meredith were able to answer now, and if we were to ask her whether or not we should take the next step, what do you think she'd say?"

Nathan started to answer but he stopped as he studied Allison's face. It was soft and lovely, even in the harsh light of the full moon. Though frail now and devoid of the coquettish pugnacity that had always charmed him, it was Allison's face, and he knew that eventually it would awaken and that he had better have a very good answer. He nodded.

"I shall protect her with my own life, Nathan," Blakeley said solemnly as the body was transferred to his arms. "As God is my witness, I shall."

"I know . . . I know . . ."

It was a matter of seconds before midnight. It

was warm in the room as he entered. Fatzinger and his men looked strange in their formal wear. Stranger still were the cowled monks and nuns in ill-fitting habits. He tried to avoid eye contact because, for all he knew, one of them would be unable to stifle a giggle. The crowd parted as he walked through it, careful of any false step which might cause the cloak to slip and reveal the naked Allison.

He worried about her. The dead weight especially bothered him. He had not told Nathan that a tap on the knee and a pin prick on the heel had both failed to elicit a response. The paralysis, he could only pray, would pass in time.

Ahead of them was a curtain. As they approached, it opened.

A tall statue of Lucifer stood against a bay window. It was a strange night; the fog off the nearby lakes hung like a thick silvery blanket in the light of the full moon. It shone like a halo around the statue. Lucifer seemed to grin approval. His eyes were burning anthracite coals.

In front of him was a mound of stones, his altar, illuminated by torches which threw off a dark, acrid smoke. And behind the mound stood another devil, this one with its back turned.

He stepped forward and placed Allison gently upon the altar.

When he did, the figure turned and raised its arms.

The mistress of the house was magnificent in her nakedness. He was reminded of the statuary he saw on the way in. She was ivory in firelight. Her black cape made it all the more explicit, and he could sense a hush of astonishment behind him.

She looked down at Allison and started to chant.

Te Diabolem laudamus. Lucifer, dominus moscarum . . .

He and Nathan understood it. "We praise thee, Devil. Lucifer, Lord of the Flies . . ."

She picked up a chalice filled with deep red wine and drank. It ran from the corners of her mouth like bloody rivulets.

In honore tuum nunc bibimus . . .

"In thine honor now we drink . . ."

She chanted in a very high pitch, like a nun in a medievel priory—or a bat in a deep cave.

Muscarias tuas consumamus . . .

"We eat thy fruit . . ." He wondered if the crowd should be chanting with her, but she seemed to pay no attention. She was in a deep trance and the mushrooms would drive her even deeper.

In honore tuum peccatores sumus . . .

"In thine honor we sin . . ."

And she opened the cloak to reveal Allison's breast, took up a knife and raised it overhead.

In honore tuum interficiones . . .

"In thine honor we kill . . ."

Lucifer! Ecce agnum tuum!

"Behold thy lamb, Lucifer!"

Blakeley lunged at the figure and seized her arm, stopping the knife as it plunged downward. She had the strength of madness, and when he tried to wrest the knife from her hand she met his force with her own surprising force as he called for help. The others rushed in, and she snarled and fought like a cornered animal. When she bit his hand he recoiled as if he had just met a mad dog and for a split second she half-sneered, half-laughed.

"I hope tha hast a slow death, tha scum a the gutter."

Blakeley was stunned as he looked at her. The face changed. It was older, a hard, almost cronelike face, and she had a Yorkshire accent. And then it changed just as suddenly back to the beautiful Mrs. West, the mistress of Lightcarn Lane.

"It's not the first time I've been surrounded by gentlemen, you know," she mocked sweetly. "Can't you chaps just get in line and do this like proper gentlemen? I've appetite enough for all."

The face was hers, but the voice was not. It came from somewhere else. London, he thought. Then it became cockney.

"A quid gets yer a real good time, me friend, and tuppence for me arse'ole."

And then came the cultured voice again.

"Oh, pardon me. One mustn't speak vulgarities in mixed company."

They had forced her to back into the statue where they were trying in vain to slip handcuffs on. But a number of them had long since lost interest in subduing her and were fascinated by the many faces and voices that were leaping like demons to the surface and just as suddenly disappearing.

"Mes amis, lentement, s'il vous plait. Le plaisir est plus fort quand ce n'est pas rapide. Ah, bien . . . je vien, je vien.

Her mouth opened and the smile that crossed her face made the translation unnecessary. This must have been the woman of the Montmarte. Hers was not the only mouth which had opened as they listened to her heavy orgasmic breathing.

Good Lord, Blakeley thought, this was the closest thing to demonic possession he had ever seen. Never again would he scoff at the mention of such things.

It was the Yorkshire crone who first noticed that their grips had loosened. She looked up and saw that they were distracted by whatever they were seeing and hearing, and she spat in the face of the one nearest her.

"Tha won't take me, tha won't," she said, springing away from them. "Not this night, not any night."

She tilted the statue of Lucifer which fell into the first three men to come close. The others were just a second too late.

"I'll see tha mothers in hell," she cursed and dived through the big bay window.

It was Ralphie who reached her just as she plunged. He grasped but all he held was her cloak. It gave way, and the beautiful ivory form fell backwards. It landed with a cracking noise that was followed by a long gasping sound, then the form went limp.

The men on the ground were the first to see the body, pinned to one of the statues that lined the drive, one of the many with long phallic symbols, this one reclining on the grass with its own proud erection jutting through the ivory chest of the mistress of Lightcarn Lane.

Hudson looked on for a moment, then turned to one of the men.

"Better cover her. She looks chilly."

Epilogue

It was a nice day for baseball. Only the outfielders minded the bright sun, which made shagging fly balls, especially those hit to the right, a trifle difficult. Butch Donahue had pitched an almost spectacular game. Sooner or later, anyone with an ounce of baseball sense knew he'd pitch a no-hitter, and for eight and a half innings that Sunday afternoon he had baffled the Baltimores. This was the same Baltimore team that had lost only eight games since the season opened six weeks ago. Today they had managed only a dribbly infield hit in the third inning, and two of them had reached base on walks, and another had done so on a throwing error in the fifth, but he had been left on base when Donahue struck out the side for the second time. Since then it was as if he were conducting a pitching clinic, but so was the Baltimore pitcher, so the ninth inning had come around quickly and neither team had scored.

The Baker Bowl was packed and noisy. The spring rains had finally let up, leaving the field, like the rest of the unpaved areas of Philadelphia, soggy. The gentlemen were, for the most part, in straw hats and shirt-sleeves, the jackets resting on their laps and their forearms turning pink in the rejuvenating sun. The ladies, like summer flowers, were clad in their Sunday softness, a few of them actually interested in the game.

They were seated in the shade of the grandstand midway between home plate and first base, where Ralphie had easy access to the ice cream and hot pretzels.

The crowd quieted as the leadoff hitter for Baltimore in the ninth, Wee Willie Keeler, stepped up to the plate. Someone behind them bet someone else that he'd lay down a bunt, hoping it would die in the saturated grass. Once on first, Keeler was a definite threat to steal second because if there was one thing that Donahue lacked it was the ability to stop runners.

"You're full of it," someone said.

"Hey! The way Crawford's pitching, the Orioles only need one run. We ain't gonna get nothin' off him."

Another voice said that Donahue is smart enough to expect a bunt, so he'd throw fast balls with a lot of spin.

"He'll bunt anyway," someone else insisted, and there was good-natured laughter when Keeler, instead of leaning in to bunt, swung away with home run intentions.

"There's your bunt for ya."

It was a fast ball with a lot of spin, as predicted. Keeler fouled it off and Nathan had a chance to catch it, but his knee still ached when he stood up and he could not stretch far enough. Ralphie made no effort lest he spill his bag of peanuts. It fell a row in front of them, where an old fellow caught it in his bowler hat. The crowd applauded as he bowed triumphantly.

Even Hudson smiled that time. Had anyone been counting, it would have been only the third or fourth time in the past month that he'd done so.

Had he caught it, Nathan would have given it to a goldilocks in lacy blue whose eyes had met his with almost predictable regularity since the last pop foul had landed in their section five innings ago. She was one of a small group of Bryn Mawr belles seated nearby with some gentlemen in dinks and school sweaters whom he took to be their beaus. He would wait for the right moment to reach behind the young man beside her and press it gently into her hand. The young man wouldn't notice; he yawned and posed in profoundly affluent boredom throughout the afternoon. And she would take it and smile modestly, but with a smile that was as sunny as the tiny imitation sunflowers that decorated her bonnet.

No doubt she'd studied Shakespeare. All the Bryn Mawr ladies studied Shakespeare.

"Thy eternal summer shall not fade, nor lose possession of that fair thou ow'st."

Words he might have said to Allison.

Keeler took a pitch low and inside. The crowd grumbled, but it was a good call. Honest John Kelly knew the strike zone.

His friends had long ago ceased asking Nathan McBride about Allison Meredith. His silence was eloquent. When, if ever, he was ready to talk about her, he would, and then to only a select few—Hudson, Ralphie, Blakeley and the like. The others were courting a punch in the nose.

At least he could take comfort in the fact that she had left a note this time. "Dearest Nathan," it had opened, "You will, I'm sure, find it hard not to hate me," and he had known before reading what followed that she was disappearing again, as if on the white puffs floating in the sky over the left field bleachers.

Another one inside, and the count on Keeler was two and one.

He knew that whatever had happened to her during those hours leading up to the death of the strange Mrs. West could not be shrugged off like a bad dream after a heavy meal.

The memories weighed heavily on Blakeley, too.

As they looked down through the shattered bay window into the surreal light of the fog-draped full moon and listened to the death rattles emanating from the beautiful white body with the giant erection protruding grotesquely through its torso he had muttered his customary "damnit." He knew he'd lost a rich vein of opportunity. Rita Mudd, as Scotland Yard had finally identified the wife of the ridiculous

Jeremy West, had certainly looked possessed. By any description Miss Mudd had been beset by demons for years, and since that bizarre evening the newspapers had done their best to fuel that rumor. Bernard Spector had interviewed and quoted every mountebank in three states and seemed to know where Blakeley was no matter how one tried to lose him. But Blakeley was convinced it was something else, something just as arcane but much closer to this world than to the other.

He was tempted to make Rita Mudd the subject of intense study, even if it had to be after the fact. Orphaned or deserted, evidently the child of a Cornish woman and a passing fancy, cleaning fish in the pilchard canneries of St. Ives at five or six—that much Scotland Yard could offer without any depth of detail, and it was that which intrigued him the most. Something in those melancholy formative years had predisposed little Rita Mudd to become the beautiful monster whose death bore an ironic resemblance to something he'd read in that silly Dracula story. The little fish, no doubt, was her taunting trademark, perhaps a means of pointing an angry finger at a cold, dark, uncaring world. And everyone knew the tales of the Carn of Light at Land's End, had known them for centuries in that still mysterious corner of England where history is as proud of its sea rogues and highwaymen as of anything else—tales of miserable souls sacrificed on stone altars to angry, insatiable gods. It was the sort of thing a lonely, resentful and obviously intelligent child might dwell on, dwell on to a point beyond morbidity, to a point where it becomes part of the sublime macabre in the mind. And then there was the part of Rita Mudd's life that Scotland Yard had reported in finer strokes—a prostitute at 13, working the dockside dens of Cornwall, a murderess and a prostitute in Beverley where a madam had lured her from London at 16 and where she had murdered a lover, a fugitive at 18, a prostitute in Paris where Scotland Yard had lost track of her for a time. The information was as exciting as it was elusive, and Blakeley had been enthralled by it. Time and again he had told Nathan that he was sure he'd just seen something that no one else in the history of criminology had actually identified. Crazy as he admitted it sounded—and Nathan had shown no reaction as he heard it—Blakeley believed he was looking at a whole cast of characters in one, devils if one had to call them that because they certainly had possessed and tormented her, but he saw them more as people. The child, the child whore, the cockney, the crone, the *femme de nuit*, and only God knew how many more—they were there in the strange Mrs. West and the different stages of her life. What he would give to have taken her alive, to have put her in a strait jacket and talk to them!

"Damn," he had said as Nathan had seen him and Sophia off at the pier, "I shall return with the answer if it's the last thing I do," and Sophia had chided him gently for his use of profanity. And the two had departed for England. Halfway up the gangplank, Rosie had stopped, and hastened back to kiss Nathan on the cheek as the liner's whistle sounded. It was not a little girl's kiss anymore, and he well understood why they'd decided it was better that she go along.

There were Bernard Spectors everywhere these days, hounding Blakeley like a band of Greek Furies in striped sport coats. Some had even shouted questions as the gangplank was raised and the big ship floated out into the Delaware, and Blakeley had waved from the railing with an impish grin. The neatly trimmed beard was back, as was the ubiquitous monocle. Nathan would miss him.

The city was abuzz with tales of the Witch of Lightcarn Lane, as the newsmen were calling her, and of the strange collection of acolytes who had joined her. About three dozen of them would stand trial for varying degrees of homicide and other crimes, a bonanza not only for the gossip sheets but for the legal profession as well. For a time, Blakeley had even seemed to enjoy it, the aftermath of the case and all the attendant publicity, but the ringing of the phones and the strange assortment of publicity seekers who sought him out soon jangled his nerves, and it was only a matter of time before he would feel that Allison was well enough to do without him. Shortly after that he was gone.

Donahue must have been expecting Keeler to bunt because he threw another rising fast ball. Keeler leaned forward in a bunting stance then stepped back. Ball three. The crowd groaned.

The inebriate a few rows back started to taunt the umpire. No one joined him.

Allison's note had continued:

"I don't suppose this will make much sense to you, you with your philosopher-detective's logic, but I'll try to give you some idea of the confusion I'm running away from. Even if you cannot forgive me this time, it's the most important thing in my world that you at least understand.

"Do you remember a summer evening when you took me to the Beethoven concert at the Academy of Music? We arrived early, planning to take a walk in the park, but there was a sudden downpour which drove us inside. The orchestra was tuning up as we entered the hall and we both remarked at the terrible, almost maniacal cacophony of the string section. You said it could be part of some special level of hell, reserved for people like your landlady perhaps, where the sinners would have to listen to the cellos and violins for eternity. Think hard. Try to hear the sound. Then let it build in your mind into something so loud that you're afraid your brain might explode.

"I hear that every time I try to recall what happened to me on that evening. I hear it now even though I'm trying desperately not to think about it. I know there was a moment there when I was surrounded by what seemed like a horde of men and women—the latter, mostly—who were speaking to me in many voices. They seemed to be trying to make me join them. Their hands were on me, I know that much, but I don't even know if the feeling was unpleasant. I seemed to be floating most of the time. Maybe the fortune teller wasn't too far off.

"But whatever happened, it fills me with horror. I can't sleep. I awaken in cold sweats and hear them. They seem to know me, to know things I've never told anyone, and they speak in rushes, sometimes in unison, sometimes severally. And I have to purge myself of them. I simply have to, even if it requires the help of a Viennese physician.

"Just a little time, Nathan. I won't forget you, and I trust that, although you'll try—and I cannot blame you for it—you won't be able to dismiss me so easily. I do need you, darling— dearest darling. Someone has to be there to warn me against diving into shallow ponds or skating on thin ice. This time, though, I think it best I take care of my own things that go bump in the night.

"Funny, I look at the tiny mark that she, or they, left on my breast, and I know—that is, my mind knows—that it's only the product of a profoundly disturbed woman. But I still cannot help feeling that I've been somehow initiated into the Damned.

"It's barely noticeable now. It will be gone entirely when next we meet. I'm praying for it. It's the first time I've prayed in a month of Sundays.

"And we *will* meet again, Nathan. Because it's supposed to be that way and you know it.

"Love always, Allison."

What the hell! He was going into the army anyway, going off to join the Twenty-eighth wherever it was. China sounded pretty good, the moon even better.

Keeler swung away on the next pitch and hit a line drive over the head of Batty Abbaticchio, the third baseman. There were obscenities muttered in the crowd as the left fielder, playing him like a pull hitter, looked confused as the ball rolled down the left field line. "He lost it in the sun, damnit," Hudson observed as the man chased it out of left center then slipped on the wet grass as the ball ricocheted off the fence just in front of the sign advertising Bull Durham tobacco. Keeler never slowed down. He was rounding second by the time the center fielder, backing up the play, picked up the ball at the 345-foot marker that separates the TastyKake and Gretz Lager signs, and was closing in on third when the ball came in from the outfield. "Jesus," Ralphie growled as the ball hit a pebble or something and squirted past Abbaticchio, "they won't catch him now, that's for sure," and Keeler crossed home plate standing up.

"Whattaya say we have a beer?" Hudson suggested.

"It isn't over yet," Nathan said. "We still have another at-bat."

"We can stand by the gate and stick around to watch if anything happens—which it won't."

"Where are you gonna get beer on a Sunday?" Ralphie asked, and the others just smiled.

They had to squeeze past the Bryn Mawr belles and their beaus to get out. Goldilocks made eye contact, demurely at first, then as

Nathan winked, she blushed, smiled and winked back.

They stood near the gate as the Orioles finished their half of the inning and Philadelphia came to bat. Others had had the same idea, so a small crowd was forming.

"I can't imagine you wanting to have a beer with Bones Fatzinger, Lieutenant," Nathan said, continuing the conversation which had begun several innings ago when Hudson had first grown antsy.

"Huh? Well, Bones isn't the worst guy in the world."

"I didn't say he was the worst."

Hudson relit his cigar and spat a small piece of tobacco into the dirt.

"I'll tell you something, Nate. When you take a look at the real knaves and harlots out there, all of a sudden a Bones Fatzinger doesn't look too bad. Y'know, he went to bat for you?"

"He what?"

"Yeah. When the word came down that that sleazy lawyer Peteroff had a witness against you, he didn't pay much attention at first. Bones can only think of one thing at a time, and he was preoccupied with that shoeshine boy suspect. When it all sank in, though, he buttonholed every man in the precinct and told them to say there wasn't one sign of damage to either Whitey or Al. Not that it was necessary, but he did it just the same. Furthermore, he dug up that Portuguese grocer—"

"Soares-DaSilva."

"—who will be happy to testify that the witness, Professor Watkins, is a wino and a shoplifter, should it ever come to that."

Nathan thought about it and smiled appreciatively.

While they were speaking the leadoff batter grounded out on the first pitch. Now Nap Lajoie was at bat. The Baltimore pitcher was being careful with him, keeping the ball low and outside, trying to make him hit it on the ground. The soggy grass has slowed down almost everything hit in the infield.

"I guess I owe him a beer or something," Nathan said, "but my mind is made up. Suspension or no suspension, I'm joining the army."

Hudson shrugged.

"You and Jeremy West," Ralphie joked. Since the episode on Lightcarn Lane, the hapless Jeremy was the butt of much humor, and the newspapers had just had a grand time with his so-called military career. The man who would be governor now took refuge in his bed.

"It can't be much worse than your army days, Beef."

"Say what you want about my army days, but if ever you get to Tampa, all you have to do is mention my name and—"

"And they'll have me cleaning every latrine in the camp."

Lajoie swung on a three-and-one pitch and hit a sharp ground ball that skipped off the dirt between third and short. On the first pitch to Ed Delehanty, Lajoie stole second. The crowd noise grew louder. It roared when Big Ed hit a towering fly ball down the left field line then groaned when the ball tailed off and went foul. On the next pitch it roared again, but this time the noise ended abruptly.

Delehanty found a pitch in his power zone and hit a sizzler toward third, but John McGraw, arguably the best damn third baseman in the league, speared it and caught Lajoie with a long lead off second base. In a wink the game was over. They thought they heard the inebriate who had been seated behind them now cursing Delehanty and hoped that Delehanty would find him. "Use his head for batting practice, Ed," Ralphie shouted as they drifted out with the crowd.

Pasquale O'Dowd was one of the smartest businessmen in the Eleventh Precinct. Every Sunday, while all the other taverns were observing the blue laws, his was quietly open to a special few, the men of the precinct station. As a result, no one ever burglarized, defaced or in any way threatened the peace of Patsy O'Dowd's tavern the rest of the week. It was a perfectly symbiotic relationship. He was also a very thorough man. Noting the ethnic origins of the men of the Eleventh, his free lunch always included bratwurst, rigatoni, blinis and soda bread.

All of these were represented in heaps on the plate of Wilmer P. Fatzinger who, as the current man in charge, sat at a special table near a window where the breezes off the street kept the cigar smoke from lingering.

As promised, Nathan bought him a mug of beer and put it on the table.

"Vott iss?"

"Thanks."

"For vott da thanks?"

"For you know."

"I don't know. None of us knows nothin'."

"I'm going into the army anyway."

Fatzinger nodded resigned approval. Nathan looked at him and chuckled to himself, suddenly remembering something that had passed unnoticed that evening on Lightcarn Lane.

The body had been draped and the conspirators trussed up for the trip to jail, and when Blakeley was explaining to some of the men that the Latin prayers were offered to the devil, that the black candles and strange smelling incense and the stony altar were all part of an intended human sacrifice, Fatzinger had interrupted to ask in the most earnest of tones:

"Oh! Iss *dott* vhy she vass showin' us her tiddies?"

Nathan brought it up again, and Fatzinger laughed.

"Dey vass strange vuns, did you see? Leedle blue circles vass painted around dem."

Nathan thought of explaining Druid tradition but decided it was better to let Fatzinger go on thinking it was just a new fashion favored by the rich. He was trying to picture Strawberry Knockelknorr in blue rings and black cape, and they laughed some more. They had a second beer when Fatzinger noticed Hudson who was standing at the bar arguing with Ralphie, who was shaking his head and guffawing at the same time.

"Hudson don't look too good dese days. Like

a beagle dog mit da worms he iss around da eyes."

"His ulcer is probably acting up. Shouldn't be drinking."

Hudson was on his fourth beer and third glass of rye.

"It ain't hiss ulcer. It's dott goddamn cannonball."

"Cannonball?"

"Yeah."

It was easy to miss anything else that had transpired at the station that afternoon when Peteroff, Whitey, Al, Professor Watkins and the dull man from downtown had teamed up to threaten his badge. As Fatzinger explained it, Hudson had opened a letter as he was cleaning his desk, muttering to himself about the witnesses who had not stepped forward in his case against Jennie Zebers and Little Wally Dorman and about all the time he had wasted when suddenly he had become silent and his face had turned ashen.

It had been there for a few days. Had he not opened it just then, Fatzinger was going to tell him to; the curiosity about a letter sent to the precinct from someone in the office of the San Francisco Chief of Police was reaching the dangerous point. He had even considered steaming it open himself. So as soon as Hudson had put it down and walked away, Fatzinger had debated with himself for less than a half-minute before reading it.

"Dear Lieutenant Hudson:
Your suspect, the one calling himself Jack

Brown is, we are quite certain after studying the fingerprints you wired us, the same man we charged in the case of three missing children. Unfortunately, we were unable to hold him because the bodies of the girls, one age five and the other two age six, were never found. At the risk of turning your stomach, though we were never able to prove it, it was widely speculated here that he destroyed the evidence by carving it up and, we presume, ingesting it. Only a few bones were found in the vicinity of where he had lived at the time of the disappearances and our coroner was unable to present them as conclusive evidence. Needless to say, we wish you better luck with him than we had. Call on us if we can help.

> *Yours,*
> *J.L. Kearney, Captain: SFPD"*

My God, no wonder Hudson's ulcer was acting up. No wonder he was so strange lately. Goddamn Jack Brown had eaten the goddamn evidence.

And then city hall had ordered him to stay away from the suspect and stop harassing the man. Stay away or be demoted to a beat patrolman, ulcer and all.

"Hey, it's only a prank, Beef," he was explaining as Nathan approached. "Good clean fun."

"Doesn't sound too clean to me, Lieutenant."

"Only if we're not careful, Beef, my boy."

Nathan knew what they were discussing. Hudson had mentioned it on the way to the baseball park, which was why he was sure Hudson had already paid a visit to Patsy Dowd's Sunday speakeasy.

"What do you think of his idea, Nate?"

"Aw, he was chicken, too," Hudson complained. "You're both a couple of old ladies. Probably sit down to pee."

Nathan gulped down his beer and smiled, looking Hudson directly in the bloodshot eyes.

"Let's have one more and talk about it."

"I know he'll be along in about five minutes. No more. It takes him awhile to get here with the leg in a cast and he always has to stop in the jake before he goes inside."

Hudson knew all about him. Jack Brown had been his sole concern for weeks. He could lecture on him at a university, he had said, if there was a school with a course in human shitpots. He knew when Jack Brown got up, when he went to the outhouse, the rare times when he bathed, what he ate and drank, and the scum he called friends. Hudson was particularly aware of when and how often he was in the proximity of children, especially little girls. And he knew how long it took Jack Brown to make his way from the Sunday speakeasy he frequented to his room on Railroad Street.

"I see him," Hudson said. "He just crossed the street a block up. See him? He'll be here in exactly four and a half minutes."

They watched Brown making his way toward them, moving slowly on crutches, dragging the leg that Hudson had so proudly put in a cast. He was munching on something he carried in a small bag. Hudson identified it as jellybeans from a booth at a church bazaar on Sixtieth and Atwater.

Nathan knew the section well. Railroad Street was a glorified alley which ran parallel to the railroad for a short time. He and Blakeley had taken it on their way to the morgue when they were following Grover a few weeks ago.

Today he was the driver, and he had eased the horse and borrowed flatbed wagon into a nearby vacant lot gingerly. They found some sooty shrubbery across the tracks where they could lie in wait.

It was a quiet evening. The heat from the bright afternoon sun still radiated from the broken pavement and occasional brick walls. The bells of one of the neighborhood churches tolled lazily, calling someone to vesper services. They could hear a locomotive in the distance and feel the tracks rumbling its warning. Here and there an urchin or a group of urchins could be heard playing and a mother carping that one of them should come home to supper. A woman standing close to an open window was nagging her husband mercilessly, her words entertaining Ralphie who giggled and kept trying to draw her to their attention.

His companions had not smiled for some time. Long before leaving Patsy O'Dowd's their whole attitude had turned grim. More than once he had thought that it would have been infinitely more intelligent of him to go home instead, but a deal's a deal.

"Here he is," Hudson whispered. "Give him a few more minutes, and be quiet."

Jack Brown stopped, turned before entering his building, then changed his mind.

"I told you," Hudson whispered smugly. "Gotta go."

They watched Brown crossing the muddy street and climbing some wooden steps that the neighborhood landlord had dug into the railroad bank. He followed a path which led across the tracks, stopping to look once as the locomotive whistled a mile away. Its black smoke could be seen on the horizon.

"Just a few more minutes."

He propped his crutches against the outhouse and when he was inside they crept up to the little wooden structure and listened, just to be sure he was seated.

"Now!"

"Wh-what the hell . . . ?"

They had rehearsed it on the way from the speakeasy and had it down to clockwork. Nathan and Hudson quickly looped the heavy ropes around the outhouse and pulled them tight enough to keep anyone from getting through the door. Ralphie charged into it like the footballer he was, grunting as he hit and tilted it over. Brown cursed, screamed and pleaded.

"What's goin' on? Who the fuck are you? Please, what's goin' on?"

The locomotive whistled again. The tracks rumbled.

"Hurry up," Hudson ordered.

"My knee is slowing me down," Nathan explained.

"C'mon, Beef, get your ass into it. Pull."

"Who's out there? What're you doin' to me?"

They pulled and shoved until the outhouse was lying across the tracks. Soot from the belching locomotive rained down on them, its black smoke blinding them.

Jack Brown screamed for mercy.

The church bell tolled again. Nathan McBride had been in a poetic mood all day.

"It tolls for thee, you sonofabitch."

"No! Oh God, no!"

The gas lamps of Society Hill were on by the time they got there. It had been a slow journey, understandably, because they had had to move through the back alleys and cross the busier arteries without attracting much attention.

The flatbed wagon, borrowed from a junk dealer, rode clumsily, and the horse seemed much more interested in stepping into ruts than avoiding them. Though the stench of their load sickened them and soot from the train had blackened their faces, Hudson smiled all the way.

Halfway up a hill was the police commissioner's Tudor-style home with its sprawling lawn and little duck pond in the back. They entered the driveway like a large tortoise.

The house was quiet. Nathan remembered hearing somewhere that the commissioner and his family were early-to-bed types. He put his finger to his lips and called for silence as he tiptoed across the lawn and up the flower-lined walk toward the front door. In another minute he was back.

They climbed down.

The outhouse reeked. Ralphie had said he regretted having eaten and drunk so much because he was going to vomit at any moment. His stomach had been bubbling for the past hour.

They tugged at the ropes and lowered the outhouse gently to the ground. As silently as their task would permit, they dragged it across the lawn.

Inside the little house Jack Brown sat frozen. He had done little more than whimper and keen ever since they had pulled the outhouse off the tracks just a blink of the eye before the locomotive roared past.

"Easy does it."

They made sure it was upright.

"There you are, Brown. Maybe they'll have you in for breakfast in the morning."

They left the outhouse there under the gaslight, surrounded by beautifully manicured shrubs. Tomorrow, when the police commissioner opened the door to pick up his milk and morning paper, it would be there to greet him in all its malodorous magnificence.

"You'll like him, Brown. He has two small granddaughters."

They rode off on their rickety flatbed wagon, off toward the Eleventh, far away from Society Hill.

Francis John Thornton

Ducks were frolicking on the pond near the archway.

The trees were alive with night sounds.

Somewhere across the city Hudson knew of another speakeasy.